STRIPPED DOWN

EVA MOORE

For A~
May you always find wonder in your world and humor in your heart.

CHAPTER 1

THREE HUNDRED VIEWS SINCE LAST NIGHT.

Not great, but not awful. It wasn't going to make her money any time soon.

Natalie Carras scrolled through the comments on her last YouTube video as she sipped the steaming hot coffee from craft services far too early on a Friday morning in August. She leaned against her portable makeup table in another chilly garage, waiting for the on-screen talent to show up so she could get started on her assignments for the day. By noon it would feel like a furnace in front of her bright bulbs, but for now she was happy to grab a few cool, quiet moments.

It would be a busy day on Million-Dollar Starter Home as they shot the "Oh no! What will we do?" scenes, but at least she didn't have to shift to a new location. And what this garage lacked in insulation, it made up for in cleanliness, unlike the last project house that still made her shudder. Despite being tucked away in the random garage space at each new renovation, this job was an amazing opportunity to advance in her field. She could put up with a few mice and mystery smells if it put her closer to her dream of doing makeup in the movies.

Once she got started, it would be nonstop blending and

brushing until noon, so she deliberately took these five minutes to caffeinate and check on her side project. She hummed as another sip of rich, black and sweet energy teased her tongue. One benefit of having a caffeine addict for a boss was the ready access to high-quality coffee.

"Natalie! I need you! Now!" *Speak of the devil...*

The imperious commands and frantic pace were the downsides. When the showrunner said jump, one didn't ask how high. One simply leapt into the void and hoped it was fast enough.

Natalie tucked her phone in her pocket and dashed out of the garage, grabbing her portable kit on the fly.

"What's up, boss?" She followed his voice toward the front yard. Jake Ryland and Enzo Valenti stood facing each other, arms crossed, like an Old West standoff. The only difference between the two stony-faced men was that Enzo was currently shirtless. Well that, and only one of them made her want to lick his neck. And it wasn't her boss.

"We're shooting a new feature. Enzo needs to look like he spends his days in the sun."

"I do spend my days in the sun."

Natalie took in the blatant farmer's tan and understood immediately. His pale chest next to those tanned and toned forearms would look ridiculous. While some guys could play the tan lines off as awkward dad-bod humor, Enzo had a decidedly un-dad-bod. The twisting vine of his tattoo would be that much sexier against an even background. He had a great frame that tended toward long, lean muscles and solid shoulders, and his mismatched skin wasn't going to relay that strength on camera. His beautiful olive complexion needed a little help so the cameras could appreciate his hard-earned physique.

She nodded her understanding of the situation to her boss, ignoring the irritated landscaper next to him.

"This is stupid. I don't know why I need to take my shirt off in the first place."

Jake ignored Enzo's protest and rolled his eyes at Natalie.

"We're filming out here, natural lighting, one-hour window. Dirty him up. I need him in fifteen."

"Aye-aye, cap'n."

She gauged the light and turned back toward the garage, confident that Enzo would follow whether he liked it or not. She'd need to pull out all her tricks to get this done in the time allotted. Natalie gritted her teeth as she ran through options. She was going to spend the next quarter of an hour with her hands all over the last man she wanted to be touching. His time in her chair was always the most challenging of the day.

For months she'd had to battle her ridiculous attraction to Enzo Valenti. Something about him just flipped her switches. His steady strength, his ready grin, his work-roughened hands... Goodness, the amount of time she'd spent fantasizing about his hands while she was working on him made her want to blush, and then grab them and put them all over her body. Which she absolutely couldn't do. She had to remember her boundaries. She couldn't have him, and yet she had to run her hands over his abs and make him look sexier. Life could be a real bitch sometimes.

But she was a professional, and her bills weren't going to pay themselves. She'd done just fine without a steady man in her life for the last seven years, and she could keep on doing the same. Her life was her responsibility, and she'd do well to remember that.

ENZO DROPPED HEAVILY into the padded chair that faced her brightly lit mirrors. When the petite makeup artist had showed up with the film crew, his dating radar had pinged immediately. Petite, brunette, and spunky, she was just his type. Unfortunately, no matter how he'd approached flirting with her, the result had always been the same. She seemed determined to keep him in the friend zone. Talk about torture.

He sat as still as stone, and as hard as it too, as she began to pull small vials and what looked like a tattoo gun out of her kit. *What the hell?* He braced himself to let her touch him and not react, letting out a long, low breath as he gripped the arms of the chair to keep his hands occupied. She stood in front of him, an evil grin on her face and her hands on her hips.

"Uh-uh, big guy. I need you to stand for this. Arms up, please."

"This isn't permanent, is it?" He didn't mind a tattoo. In fact he'd gotten one shortly after Gabriel's death, a stylized tree branch and autumn leaves falling across his chest and right shoulder. He still felt like his family tree was missing a limb, but it comforted him to carry his brother's memory on his skin. He didn't think that a stupid television show was a good reason for more ink though. Was she even a tattoo artist? He hadn't noticed any tats on her, and he'd been pretty focused on any square inch of bare skin she chose to show.

"No, it's just airbrushing. It'll come off over the next few showers. Let me test this shade on your wrist."

Taking his large hand in her tiny one, she sent a shiver racing up his arm. He wanted to believe it was from the chilly air blast across his inner wrist, but he knew better. He'd wanted the right to hold her hand for months, and here she was holding his. True, it wasn't quite how he'd imagined it, but he'd take it.

"Perfect. Just close your eyes and hold still. This won't hurt. Much."

He heard the laughter under her words and grimaced. "Go ahead. Laugh it up. You're not the one standing here half naked waiting for the torture to begin." *Great.* Now he had a helpful image of her with their roles reversed tucked into his mind. Her shirt off, arms spread wide, eyes closed, waiting for him to touch her. He shook his head, pushing the image aside.

"Sorry." Her laugh broke free. "You looked like I just told you we needed to do a full-body wax."

"Is that a thing?" He was helpless to control the squeak of fear in his voice as his eyes flew open. No man of Italian descent felt comfortable thinking about depilation.

"It is, but thankfully not called for today. Just close your eyes and think of cannoli."

He obeyed and raised his arms in the sign of the cross. In a way, he did feel crucified, his desire for this woman's affection turning into a cruel torture. Cold bites of compressed air traced over his skin, making his abs jump and clench with surprise until his skin got used to the temperature.

As her spray wandered down his front and up his back, his thoughts took the opportunity to do the same. Filming the show on top of running his arm of the business exhausted him. He couldn't remember the last time he'd stood silent and still for five minutes, let alone fifteen.

When his father had decided to do this damn TV show, Enzo had gone along. If this was the thing his dad needed to do to move past Gabe's death and into retirement, then Enzo would buckle down and do his part, even though he hated being in the spotlight. He'd always been happier in the quiet and solitude of nature. Putting that love on screen was a double-edged sword. He enjoyed sharing his passion for landscaping with others, but he hated feeling like a million eyes were staring at him every time Trina lifted her damn camera. Gabe would have eaten up the attention with a spoon.

They had always been opposites. Gabe had been the bright light at the center of his family's circle. Enzo had been content to flutter around the edges of Gabe's radiance, the only moth drawn by the glare smart enough to heed the heat. Gabe had been full of life, always taking risks, chasing the next high at full speed. Enzo moved at a slower pace, picking up the pieces Gabe left behind, content to be the quiet one and wishing everyone else was content with that too.

When they were kids, Gabe had built a tree house in the backyard. Or he'd started to, before jumping into the pinewood derby, and his dad and Frankie had finished it up. Sofia had decorated the inside for hours, making it cozy, and Enzo had planted himself firmly on the ground, digging in the dirt and finding all

Dad's tools Gabe had dropped, scrubbing off the rust before anyone got in trouble. Trailing his big brother, keeping him out of trouble without him knowing, had been a constant of Enzo's childhood. Now, Enzo's life had lost that constant, and it felt more than a little empty. He needed someone new to tend, to shelter, to love.

Enzo jolted, pulled from his memories by Natalie's warm fingers tracing over his collarbone. The sudden change from cold to heat sent a full-body shiver racing down from the tips of her fingers to his toes. Sure, that was it. The temperature change. His reaction had nothing to do with the fact that this pint-sized beauty was inches from his body with her hands all over him. Her chocolate brown eyes mesmerized him, her irises dilating and the golden flecks around them putting him in a trance as she swayed closer. Maybe he wasn't completely doomed to stay in the friend zone forever.

He hauled in a deep breath, hoping to catch her scent, but all he got was the overwhelming mixture of powder, wax, and aerosol that hovered around her workspace. A missed opportunity.

She smoothed something sticky up his neck and rubbed it over tendons tight with restraint. He fought back the purr that wanted to escape. This was business. She was just doing her job. He shifted his stance, widening his legs slightly to brace for her assault on his senses. Creating a little more space between his legs made a certain reaction to her touch not quite so obvious or distracting.

"What is that?"

"Vaseline."

What the hell? She was rubbing lube on his neck?

"Why the hell are you putting lube on my neck?"

Apparently, he was too far gone to filter the thoughts that were allowed out of his mouth.

"Don't be a prude. It looks like sweat on camera, and it stays shiny for at least an hour. Since it's a sixty-degree morning, I don't think you want to be working up the sweat Jake will demand the old-fashioned way."

He could think of several old-fashioned ways he'd like to work up a sweat with her, but he bit his tongue to make sure those thoughts stayed safely up in his head. She'd shown zero interest, and he was not going to be that asshole at work who couldn't read the signs.

When she turned to her meticulously organized kit, his gaze dropped to her hips, and his fingers twitched with the desire to touch. When she turned back around with a small brown pot, he flushed and raised his gaze to her face.

Jeez. It had been too long since he'd had a girlfriend, but the last three years had been so crazy that he hadn't had the energy to put into growing a relationship. He should definitely make time to cultivate something if he couldn't stop daydreaming about a woman who was patently uninterested.

"What's that?"

"Don't trust me at all, do you?"

"Just making conversation. Making sure I know what's going on."

"It's loose powdered charcoal liner. Now hold still."

She took a large fluffy brush and dipped it into the pot. Holding it a few inches from his skin, she tapped it with her index finger. A fine powder fell against his now sticky skin, and he missed the touch of her hands. On her next pass, she blew through the dusting powder to spread it farther, and that damn shiver came back, rattling his composure. His nipples hardened to tight points as she blew her soft, minty breath across his chest. If she noticed, she didn't seem flustered by it, since she repeated the move on his other pec. Jesus, she was killing him and she didn't even know.

"Now run your hand down your neck, like you're wiping away sweat."

He did, gripping the back of his neck firmly, before running his hand down to his chest. Her eyes tracked his movement, lingering on his flexing chest. She stepped closer still, and he held his breath, waiting to see what she would do next.

She traced the Vaseline along his scalp line and lightly brushed her fingers over his cheekbones. He wanted to cup his hand over hers, pressing it firmly against his cheek. Maybe he'd telegraphed his desire, because he thought he detected a faint blush on her cheeks. He could feel the warmth pouring off her body as she stepped in close to reach him.

Of course, she could just be warmer than he was, standing half naked in an unheated garage on a cold morning on the last day of August in Silicon Valley. By the afternoon, it would reach into the nineties and the Vaseline would be superfluous, but she'd be long gone by then.

"Close your eyes."

He was surely imagining the slight huskiness in her voice. He held her gaze an extra beat, searching for some sign that she felt the attraction pinging between them too. No dice. He closed his eyes, and she blew into his face. The sweet and bitter scent of coffee on her breath shouldn't have been arousing, but God help him, it was. He could visualize her lips pursing, and it almost undid him. *Please be done.* He couldn't take much more of this.

When she turned on the blow-dryer, his eyes snapped back open. "What's that for?"

"To set the airbrush." The warm air danced over his sensitized skin, and he bit down hard on a moan as goose bumps prickled down his arms. "There. All done. Take a look."

Her no-nonsense tone reminded Enzo that she was simply doing her job, and he needed to get his shit together. While she busied herself cleaning her tools and putting each back in its particular spot, he walked over to the full-length mirror to view her handiwork and put a little distance between them.

One glance and he was transported back to the summers of his youth before thoughts of skin cancer and modesty had altered his habits. To the days when he'd run wild through the neighborhood, chasing after the fun that seemed to follow Gabe until the streetlights came on. His chest was a sun-kissed bronze that matched his arms perfectly, and damn if he didn't have an eight-pack he hadn't seen in the shower that morning.

Sexy, dirty landscaper. She'd nailed exactly what Jake had pitched him that morning for the new spot. The commercial teaser shorts would supposedly share quick gardening tips before other shows and would be pushed on social media as well to drive interest to the show. Given the shirtless aspect of the proposal, he could well imagine the kind of interest Jake was hoping to attract. Since Enzo's sister Sofia and their head contractor Adrian had paired off, Adrian had been less willing to play up his buff arms. Instead he and Frankie had taken to trading practical jokes on set, going for the laughter-punch instead. It seemed that Jake had shifted his gaze to Enzo for the sex appeal role. If this worked, it was going to be a very chilly autumn.

But if it leveled out his family's business and kept Natalie's sweet hands on his chest, he'd help out. It was what he did best.

"That's amazing."

"That's my job." Natalie had picked up her phone and was scrolling with her thumb intently. He took the moment to watch her, lips quirked, sneaky dimple puckering her cheek.

"You should smile more." The words were out before his filter could test their wisdom. Said smile disappeared, and her eyes glittered through her half-lowered lids.

"Excuse me?"

Enzo raised his hands as if he could surrender before she even began her assault. "That came out wrong. I meant to say that you have a beautiful smile. Thank you for sharing it with me."

"My smile has nothing to do with you."

Damn. His backpedal wasn't working.

"No, of course not, but I'd like it to." Where the hell had that thought come from? He needed to seriously tighten up that filter. Or maybe not. Maybe he just needed to ask her out and get it over with. No more hinting, no more vague flirting. Just ask her, so she could say no and he could get on with his life.

She snorted her dismissal and turned back to her phone.

In for a penny, in for a pound. He took a deep breath and let his next question fly. "What are you doing Monday? A bunch of people from the crew get together for karaoke. You should come."

"Is this like a date?" Suspicion tightened her features, and she crossed her arms as she waited for his answer.

"More of a fun group outing, with a potential for more smiling and a discussion about the date status." She shared her smile regularly with Sofia and Trina. Hell, even Frankie, who hated the makeup chair quite vocally, could pull a laugh out of her. But for him? Never. He wanted one smile just for himself, and he'd be satisfied. Even as he thought this, his better self called him a liar. He'd only want more from her if he ever broke through the ice surrounding her.

"Enzo Valenti, are you flirting with me?"

"Not yet, but if you come out on Monday, I'll give it my best shot. Think about it." He turned on his heel and left before any more stupid, uncensored truths escaped his lips. He shoved his hands in his pockets to hide his jitters. He needed to focus on business, even if that meant mowing a lawn bare-chested to appease Jake Ryland's creative marketing muse. He always felt more grounded with his hands in the dirt. Natalie's fake grime beneath his fingernails didn't have the same effect.

NATALIE KEPT HER EYES firmly focused on her phone for a good minute after he'd gone, just to be sure it was safe to look up. After spending the last eighteen minutes running her hands over the man's body, her defenses were weak. She needed to put herself back together before she ran into him again. Why did he have to be such a nice guy? If he were a hot jerk, it would be so much easier to shut down his advances. But no, he was a hot guy-next-door type who turned her knees to jello. *Damn it.*

She desperately scrolled through the notifications on her phone. Lord knew, there was plenty on there to draw her attention away from the man she absolutely did not need in her life. Needing men had never really worked out for her. Hell, relying on anyone hadn't gone so well for that matter. She had herself to depend on, and that would have to be enough.

FINAL NOTICE

Natalie flagged the reminder on her phone. She knew to the cent exactly which bills needed paying when. It would all get paid when her check cleared this afternoon, provided nothing came along to shake her house of cards. She could push the cell phone bill out two weeks, and after rent and this overdue medical bill, she'd just break even.

The rent in Silicon Valley was no joke. High demand and low inventory meant landlords could charge whatever they liked. And boy did they like. In LA, things hadn't been this tight, but she also hadn't seen much of her child because of her crazy work hours. Coming up north to work on Million-Dollar Starter Home had been the right move, even if it was costing her an arm and a leg. Hell, there wouldn't be a show concept if the market wasn't crazy.

Working steadily on one show with union/construction hours and picking up the odd weekend wedding hair and makeup gig meant that her afternoons and evenings were her own. She couldn't regret anything that let her spend more time with her favorite person on earth, her six-year-old, Daisy. And the last thing Daisy needed was her mother distracted by a handsome landscaper. Ever since Daisy had been two pink lines on a test stick, it had just been the two of them, and that suited Natalie just fine. She'd learned her lesson about self-reliance from her mother early.

Growing up, she'd never understood why she didn't have a daddy like everyone else. But she knew not to ask her mom about it. Depending on her mood, she'd get a flaming tirade about it being all her fault or a week of icy silence. So when she'd confirmed with the at-home test that she was pregnant, her mother had slapped her and told her she deserved everything she got for being careless. When her boyfriend dropped her, her mother had laughed in her face.

"Good. Maybe now you'll appreciate what I went through raising you. Stupid girl. If you think I'm going to play grandma and help look after the brat, you are dreaming. Oh, and rent is due on the first if you're gonna stay here. If you're old enough to make a baby, you're old enough to raise one. The free ride ends today."

So she'd left and raised Daisy on her own, and had never once regretted her choice. A text chimed to give her the all clear from Mrs. Félice that Daisy had been dropped off at school. She smiled at the photo the older woman had sent of her baby waving in front of her first grade classroom. Finding the retired school-teacher living next door to her rental who was willing to feed her baby breakfast and get her to school on time for a reasonable fee had been a godsend. It allowed Natalie to get in to work for the early call, and then leave in time to pick Daisy up from school herself.

She didn't have family to rely on, so it was on her to figure out all the logistics. Reliable childcare could make or break her, so she was careful not to abuse it once she found it. She was always on time to drop-off or pick-up, and she only used her sitters when she had to work. The idea of paying someone to watch her kid just so she could have some time off was a luxury she couldn't afford. Besides, she worked hard so that she could spend time with Daisy. Why on earth would she pay someone else to take that from her?

She'd made a good life for them both, and she had been blessed to find temporary help after every relocation. This time it had been fate. The room to rent in a condo close to work with a roommate who didn't have a problem living with a kid, *and* Mrs. Félice had all landed in her lap during her first week in the Bay Area. She had taken it as a sign that this was a good move, but at the end of the day it was Nat and Daisy against the world, and that was how it would stay.

Worry about moving her child right before first grade woke her up nights, but so far it was turning out to be great for both of them. Professionally, Natalie was making connections and proving her skills. Personally, Daisy was adapting well to her new school and making friends. Financially, they were scraping by, but the positives outweighed that. As long as she didn't topple for the wrong man again, this TV gig might give them the boost they needed. That meant ignoring the on-screen talent, no matter how handsome, because she'd vowed to never let another man get close enough to hurt them. And Enzo was certainly tempting her to take the risk.

∽

"Roses love to open up under the hot California sun. They thrive in the long, warm season from spring through fall, but they need a firm hand to keep them under control. Enjoy the lush blooms, but when they start to fade, clip that dead wood back hard. It will come back again and again for you in its season." He reached in to snip a full stalk past its prime. "Then in January, we cut this bush back hard to here."

Once again he demonstrated the cuts to the camera, making sure he was looking directly into the small circular lens Trina was holding a foot from his face.

"Next time, I'll show you how to install drip watering systems. There's nothing better than keeping your little rosebuds nice and moist all day long."

"And cut!"

At Trina's thumbs-up, he grinned and relaxed a little.

"I know some rosebuds that are going to be real moist after that segment," Trina teased.

Enzo hated the blush that crawled up his neck, and willed it away. He hated doing the close-up spots for the show. Usually Million-Dollar Starter Home focused on the interiors his sister, Sofia, and her fiancé Adrian Villanueva transformed together. But since he was a Valenti, and Valenti Brothers Construction was the featured talent on the show, he'd gotten roped in. Even Frankie was working on crews and providing comic relief. A real family affair.

"Enzo! A word, please." Jake Ryland rose from his perch on the front stoop of the house.

The guy always looked too clean to be working on a construction site. His button-down oxford shirts and pressed slacks certainly made him stand out from the jeans and sweats crew. Then again, it was the showrunner's job to have their shit together, and Enzo grudgingly admitted that the clothes certainly helped convey that image. Enough that "a word" with him made Enzo feel like he was walking into the principal's office. He'd made sure he'd only had to do that once in school, and he resented being made to feel it again as an adult.

"Sure, Jake. What's up?"

"That spot was great, really. Our test audiences love you. You play really well to the female, 34 to 65 demographic."

"Uh, okay." What was he supposed to say to that?

"It's more than okay. The ladies are going to love it."

Oh shit, here it comes.

"We're going to keep the shirtless aspect of it going."

Yep, "a word" was never a good thing.

Jake continued, unfazed by the sudden tension that gripped Enzo's body or his deliberate silence. "You look much better in the playback after Natalie's efforts. So keep up the good work, and add half an hour to your prep time for her to airbrush you."

Once. One time. He'd stripped off his shirt to wipe the sweat from his brow, and he would never live it down. It was going to be a very chilly autumn. On the other hand, it meant more time with Natalie's hands on him. Damn. It just might be worth it.

Natalie cleaned her brushes and restored her kit to pristine order before grabbing it and her purse. It was two o'clock on Friday afternoon, and she was ready for the weekend to begin. Her early start time meant that she was now free to pick up her little sprite from school. The next half hour was the best part of her day: seeing her baby's face as Daisy ran across the playground to her, and listening as she filled Natalie's heart with hugs and ramblings about the school day. It made every sacrifice worthwhile. She hid her cell phone in her purse along with her worries about bills and ridiculously attractive men, and drove across town in her beat-up Honda Civic to the school where Daisy was starting first grade. She parked two blocks from the school and walked to her habitual spot on the blacktop. When the bell rang, her child sprinted to her, all cheeky grin with missing teeth and bouncing brown pigtails. Natalie caught her up in a tight, twirling hug.

"Hi, Mommy!"

"Hi, Sprite! How was school today?"

"It was so cool. Mommy, did you know that Monarch butterflies migrate all the way from Mexico to spend winters up here? It's in Mon…Men…I forget, but it's close. Can we go see them, Mommy? Can we?"

Daisy's enthusiasm tugged at Natalie's grip and her heart as they walked toward the car. She loved her kid's excitement, but because of their budget she always ended up being the bad guy. Looked like she'd be researching butterflies tonight. "We'll see." Natalie had learned early on not to promise things she couldn't deliver.

"That means no." Daisy's shoulders drooped and pulled Natalie's guilt from its shallow hiding place.

"No, that means let me find out more about it, and we'll see."

"Okay… How was your day, Mommy?"

Visions of her hands tracing Enzo's very tempting torso flashed before her eyes. "My day was a-okay, Didi. Let's go home and surprise Marion with dinner. Will you be my sous-chef?"

"Can I use the knife this time?"

"We'll see."

"Mommy! That means no again." The rise and fall of the predictable whine made Natalie grin as she kissed the little head tucked against her chest. Was it higher today than it had been yesterday? Her baby was growing so quickly.

She missed the days when she could curl up completely around Daisy and snuggle on a rug for hours, finding joy in baby giggles and the occasional hiccup. Natalie swore that was just yesterday. Who was this bright, curious little girl who wanted to push boundaries and explore her world? Where had she come from? And what on earth was Natalie going to do to slow things down?

"It means let's go see what's in the fridge."

~

Natalie was stirring macaroni elbows on the stove as they boiled for her homemade mac-n-cheese casserole, while Daisy practiced her knife skills under her eagle-eyed supervision. That cucumber never knew what hit it.

"Why don't you go watch your show, baby? Mommy needs to film a tutorial while this bakes, and then we'll do your spelling words."

Natalie strained the noodles over the sink, poured them into a baking pan, and then coated them in a luscious cheese sauce. Learning how to cook real food had been one of the first things she'd tackled once she'd moved out on her own. It was something her mother had never taught her. Sharing it with Daisy was such a joy.

A quick layer of melting cheese on top and into the oven for half an hour. If her timing was right, she could just squeeze in her video. She flipped on Netflix For Kids and handed Didi the remote before closing the bedroom door behind her.

God Bless *Octonauts*.

Since they shared a room, Natalie needed to keep Daisy occupied while she was recording. Her job doing makeup for the show filled her bank account, but her online tutorials filled her soul.

Since she'd begun three years ago, she'd built a small but loyal audience. She loved helping people solve beauty problems and showing off her skills for more complicated looks. The community she'd grown sustained her. But she also knew that she was a public figure on the internet, and there were a lot of whackadoos lurking who didn't need to know what her daughter looked like or where she lived. She was vigilant about keeping Didi off camera. Netflix babysitter for the win.

Natalie flipped on her lighting rig, set her phone to record and pulled out her new Sephora splurges and the grocery store brands she was going to compare. She was educating people to be savvy consumers while making the world more beautiful, one face at a time. And she loved every minute of it.

CHAPTER 3

"And that, my friends, is why this grocery store find is my new go-to red lippy! I hope you'll try it and tell me how it works for you. As always, I'll check comments later tonight if you've got any questions for me. Until next time, stay curious, my lovelies, and remember: Makeup doesn't make you beautiful. It lets the beauty inside shine!"

Just as Natalie signed off she heard the front door open and close. Hopefully that was just her roommate Marion getting home, but it wasn't unheard of for her little sprite to get curious and wander outside to explore. She left her chair to investigate.

She respected her roommate's space and didn't want her to feel like she needed to supervise Didi. That was Natalie's responsibility unless she had paid someone else for the job. And Marion had already done so much for them. She refused to impose.

Marion had dropped her computer bag by the door and sat slumped on one of the bar stools on the living room side of the island.

"Hi, Auntie M! I'm watching *Octonauts*. Did you know that a narwhal doesn't have a horn? It's actually a tooth!"

"I had no idea, Didi. That's amazing." Marion's usual enthusiasm for Daisy's details was missing, and as soon as Daisy returned her attention to the television Marion dropped her head on her clasped hands on the counter.

Natalie put on her best French accent to try and tease a smile out of the other woman. Working in the high-stress tech industry in Silicon Valley often left Marion frazzled, and Natalie liked to think that having them to come home to helped her relax. She never wanted to feel like a burden to anyone ever again.

"*Bon soir, Mademoiselle Walker.* This evening we have an artisanal mac-n-cheese paired with a mutilated cucumber *amuse-bouche.* Can I interest you in a glass of wine?"

"What are you pouring this evening?" Marion made the attempt to play along but still hadn't lifted her head from her hands.

"Only the very best, Trader Joe's Goat Wine."

"I thought rosés were for summer."

"I believe in rosé every day if it makes you happy. Besides, summer technically isn't over yet."

"Then make mine a big one, and pour yourself one too. I have a feeling we're going to need a little happy helper."

"What happened?" Nat poured two glasses from her favorite four-dollar bottle and passed one over the island to the woman who'd taken a chance on her as a roommate and had quickly become a trusted friend.

Marion worked in sales in a large tech firm and had bought her two-bedroom condo so she could split the mortgage. When Natalie had applied, she'd been worried about finding someone willing to live with a six-year-old, but she couldn't afford a place on her own. Marion had been enthusiastic, and over the last six months Daisy had bonded with the other woman, calling her Auntie M after her "Friday Night Pizza and A Movie" favorite, *The Wizard of Oz.*

"You look nice. Is that a new lipstick?"

"I just did a short comp video. You can watch it later. Don't change the subject. What's wrong?"

Marion drank half the wine in her glass in one gulp before

she answered. "I got offered a promotion today to a regional management position."

"But that's fantastic news!" Natalie topped off Marion's glass and clinked her own to it. "Congratulations!"

"Yeah, it's great…"

"I hear a but coming."

"Why? Is it farting?" Daisy piped up from her spot on the couch before dissolving into a fit of giggles. Her daughter had big ears and a sassy sense of humor that belied her six years.

"Why don't you go wash up? Dinner's ready."

"But I'm not hungry."

"Wash up anyway. You're covered in school germs."

Once her baby and her big ears were ensconced in a bathroom with running water, Natalie turned back to Marion.

"But…"

"But the job is in Austin." Marion stared into her glass of wine. "I'd start in two weeks."

"Whoa. That's fast."

"Yeah. And…I think I have to sell the condo."

The words hit Natalie like a punch to the chest. It took her a solid minute to get her breath back.

"But…damn, can you rent it?" Natalie quickly calculated what the going rate would be for their square footage. She might even come out ahead if Marion could hold her portion steady and up the rent for the newcomer.

Marion shook her head. "The capital from the sale will go a lot farther in Texas, and I don't want to try and manage tenants from that far away." Marion's words slapped Natalie across the face.

"Ouch. Okay."

"I didn't mean you guys. You know I love you and Didi. But I need to cover the mortgage with rent, and I know you can't swing that. Plus, if you guys stayed and ended up with a shit roommate, I would never forgive myself."

"You have to do what's best for you. I get it."

Natalie's mind spun as she calculated the expense of moving again and began to panic. It had been sheer luck to find this place the first time around. She couldn't take advantage of crew housing because she had Didi with her. And now that Daisy was settled at school, Natalie really didn't want to move her, which narrowed her search parameters even further.

Was she going to have to leave this job before she'd gotten the foot in the movie door she was after? Was she going to have to go back to LA, tail between her legs, and beg for her old jobs back? What would this do to Daisy? And Natalie's professional reputation? And her own well-being? Damn it. They had been doing so well.

Marion grabbed her wrist and pulled Natalie from her spiraling thoughts.

"Listen, nothing is urgent. Take your time looking for a new place. I'm going to take some vacation days to get things in order, so I can help watch Daisy while you look."

"You don't have to do that." This was just another timely reminder that she was the only one responsible for putting Daisy first, and she automatically pushed away any offer to help. She could do it all herself. She'd been doing just fine for the last seven years. They'd get through this challenge together too.

"But I want to. I'm gonna miss that kid. She makes me wish I'd made time to make my own."

"She's going to miss you too." Natalie could feel the repressed tears threatening to make her nose run. She took a strong gulp of pink wine to wash the lump down her throat. She'd gotten too complacent, too comfortable here. She'd even started to think about taking Enzo up on his date.

Bad things happened when she stopped guarding against them. She'd let her radar down and had stopped scanning the horizon for incoming bogeys, so this news took her completely by surprise. She'd begun to trust Marion with Daisy's well-being. She couldn't afford to make that mistake again.

As if Natalie's thoughts had drawn her presence, Daisy

wandered toward the kitchen. Natalie murmured, "Let me tell her."

~

LATER THAT NIGHT, Daisy curled up in the circle of Natalie's arms after they read their stories and sang their songs. As they had so many nights before, her arms felt inadequate to the task of carrying her daughter's fears. And yet they were all she had, so they'd have to do.

"Mommy?" Daisy whispered, her eyes already closed.

"Yes, baby?" Natalie whispered back, pressing a kiss to Daisy's temple, letting her nose nuzzle in the soft, baby-fine hair, inhaling her daughter's sweetness.

"Why does Auntie M have to go?"

"Because she's getting a new job." They'd already had this conversation twice, but Daisy needed to walk through it again.

"What's wrong with her old job?"

"Nothing is wrong with it. This one is just better."

"Then why does she have to leave?"

"Because it's the best decision for her right now."

Daisy thought about that for a second and suddenly opened her eyes wide. "What if we moved to Texas *with* her?" Her excitement vibrated through her body and she sat upright, ready to roll out of bed and share the new plan.

"Baby, we can't do that."

"But we always move around. Why can't we just move with her?"

Natalie sucked in a deep breath. This was the reality of living paycheck to paycheck. Yes, they moved a lot, chasing new jobs or cheaper rent. The people who came into their lives moved around a lot too. Some were attached to movie projects that wrapped after three months, and then they were off to the next big thing. Others were like her, only staying in one place as long as she could afford to. Each new gig or apartment brought new adults into Daisy's life. It wasn't any surprise that Daisy wanted at least one of them to stay.

"My job is here in California, Daisy. If we went to Texas, I would have to start all over, and there aren't a lot of shows out there who need people like me."

"Maybe you could find a better new job there, like Auntie M did."

It broke her heart to tell Daisy no, but she couldn't walk away from the opportunity this show was giving her. With the experience she earned on the set, she might be ready to make the jump to movies in a year or two. Plus with the season renewal that just came through, this was a chance to give Daisy a different kind of stability, one that came from attending the same school for more than a year.

All the same, that didn't fix her baby's broken heart. When was Natalie going to learn to keep people at a distance? If they didn't get close enough to touch your heart, they couldn't tear it out when they left.

"I'm sorry we can't go with her, Sprite. But we'll keep in touch on Facebook. You can do videos with the silly filters."

"Oh yeah? Show me!"

Natalie opened up the app and loaded the filters so her daughter could give herself bunny ears and exploding heart eyes until the hurt faded from her own.

"Get some rest now. We can talk about this more in the morning," Natalie said as she pulled her phone from Didi's sleepy grip.

"Good night, Mommy. Love you."

"I love you too, Sprite."

Natalie held her precious baby in the cradle of her arms, trying to erase the fears with hugs so they couldn't hurt Daisy anymore. They would get through this together. Natalie would make sure of it. She'd do anything for her daughter.

~

Enzo shucked his boots and socks at his parents' door and stepped into his own family circus. Every Friday his parents hosted a big family dinner. It had a rotating cast of attendees, but tonight it was just his immediate family: his mom and dad, Josephine and Domenico Valenti, and his siblings, Sofia and Frankie. It still felt strange not to include Gabe in that list anymore.

Judging by the number of chairs at the table, Seth and Brandy and his aunt and uncle wouldn't be joining them. And he knew Sofia's fiancé, Adrian, needed to be home for his mother tonight.

There was only one extra chair at the table, the one that had been Gabe's for twenty-six years. No one had the heart to move it.

"Hey, Enzo. Want a beer? Ma's still working on dinner." Frankie had anticipated his answer, holding out an open long-neck dripping with condensation.

Enzo took a long pull from the offered bottle. "Thanks, kid." He walked through the kitchen and kissed his mother and Sofia on their cheeks before reaching to snag a parmesan curl from the platter on the counter.

"Here, take this tray into the family room. Dinner will be ready in half an hour." His mom patted his cheek before he turned for the family room where his dad was watching the football game. Frankie pushed past him and dropped next to Dom on the couch.

"Come watch the game, son. The Niners have a real shot this year."

"In a bit."

"Jojo? Where are the pickled pepperoncini? You know they're my favorite."

"Hmm, are they? I imagine that is something I would know, being your wife, and yet you still didn't get what you wanted."

His mother's dry tone scorched a line of fire all the way from the kitchen. Enzo tamped down the urge to open the fridge and find his dad's pickled peppers. *Nope, not getting in the middle of that.*

Enzo wasn't ready to be cooped up in the house with all of his family's bickering and expectations. He would probably do something stupid like try to referee.

He walked out the door into his childhood refuge, the backyard. He scanned for weeds in his mother's burgeoning herb garden. Old habits were hard to break, and tending the garden had been one of his daily chores. Mom had the brilliant strategy of assigning the chores her children actually enjoyed doing to balance out the crappy jobs that had to get done.

Finding none, he settled on the stairs of the deck to enjoy the quiet deepening of the evening. Bare feet in the grass, the evening marine layer rolling over the mountains, Enzo hauled in a deep breath. He needed the time alone. With a finite amount of energy for people-ing each day, the three-ring circus that came with the TV show drained him. Puttering around in rinky-dink backyards wasn't exactly fulfilling him either.

When he'd gotten his degree in landscape architecture, he'd dreamed of creating sweeping spaces for people to interact with nature. He'd certainly never dreamed that after fifteen years he'd still be mowing lawns for his dad's clients. He wanted to chase that dream, but because of his margins working for his dad, there was no chance he'd ever be able to afford to.

On top of all that, he'd had to resist his reaction to Natalie while she ran her hands all over his body. He was operating at a deficit. He needed some peace and quiet to clear out his head.

"How's it going, old man?" Frankie, younger by one year, dropped onto the stair next to him.

So much for quiet time.

"It goes."

"I saw you getting all sexy for the cameras."

"Jealous?"

"Yeah, right." Despite the words, Enzo could tell he'd hit a nerve.

"Ugh. Be grateful you got tapped to be the class clown. It's too cold for early morning nudity. You really want the shirtless job?"

At least that earned a laugh.

"No, I'd rather be respected as a head contractor."

A familiar refrain. The baby of the family, Frankie was always chasing respect. Like the pugnacious runt of the litter, determined to lead the pack despite being the smallest, Frankie was always fighting for position.

But Jake had a leader on the show, Adrian. He'd needed some comic relief, and seeing a natural aptitude, he filled the spot with Frankie, the goofball. It was hard to be taken seriously when a daily shoot involved rafter pull-up competitions and hammer-tosses through windows. This show sparked headaches for everyone.

"You'll get there, Pip."

"Don't call me that."

"What? Pipsqueak?" And just like that Enzo was nine to Frankie's eight again.

"Knock it off, or I'll tell Mom you've got the hots for the makeup girl."

Danger! Don't react. He tried to sound as nonchalant as his nerves would let him. "And why would you do a fool thing like that?"

"Torture. And anything that gets her off my case and onto yours is a win. Plus, I see the way you look at her."

Deflect, deflect! "At Mom?"

"Nice try, idiot, but no, how you look at Natalie."

He shouldn't ask. It would only fan the flame of interest, but he was mortified that someone might have noticed the attraction he'd tried to keep hidden. "Oh, and how's that?"

"Like she's the first pizzelle on Christmas."

Shit. He loved pizzelles. This was bad. "Keep dreaming."

"Uh-huh, okay, sure. But just so you know, I know. And I'm not afraid to use it."

"Hmph." Grunting—he had nothing better to go with than a

grunt. More words would only dig the hole deeper. With an evil cackle, Frankie went back inside, probably to raid the antipasti plates and spill his secrets.

Enzo stayed where he was, willing to sacrifice Ma's marinated olives for a little peace of mind. He'd thought he'd hidden his crush better than that. Maybe he wouldn't have to hide it much longer. He'd see what happened Monday.

Cautious optimism carried him into dinner.

CHAPTER 4

AFTER AN ENTIRE WEEKEND of searching for apartments and trying to convince her daughter that moving again would be an adventure, while trying to hide her panic, Natalie was exhausted. How was it already Monday? She hadn't moved anything else off her to-do list, and now after a busy day she was scrambling to catch up.

Thankfully, Daisy had gone back to school. But working a full-cast morning shoot didn't help Natalie get back on track at all. She'd spent eight hours on her feet with her arms raised, and after walking Sprite home at a glacial pace, stopping to examine every rock and leaf and determine if it made the cut for her collection, all Natalie wanted was a hot shower and a cold glass of wine. Maybe at the same time. The idea of karaoke was low on her list, even though Trina had invited her too.

She unlocked the front door and was stunned to find Marion already puttering in the kitchen, two glasses of wine poured and waiting on the counter. Tears welled in Natalie's eyes. Damn it, why did she have to leave?

"Auntie M!" Daisy sprinted into a waist-high hug before excitedly showing off the heart-shaped rock she'd chosen as her one piece of flair for the day. Early on, Nat had learned to limit the amount of nature that followed her little sprite into their home. "Look, I chose it just for you! So you can always remember me."

The underlying request that Marion love her enough to not forget her pinched at Natalie's heart. She rubbed a hand absently over the ache and pretended it didn't hurt. "Hey, you're home early."

"I took a half day. Listen, I know I blindsided you with all this, and I feel awful that you spent your whole weekend on Craigslist and Nextdoor. So I'm watching Sprite tonight. I've got dinner on the stove and *Octonauts* ready to play. I've got this. Take the night off and do something fun." Natalie opened her mouth to protest, but Marion cut her off. "When's the last time you did?"

Natalie couldn't recall. She didn't hire sitters unless she was working. Daisy was her responsibility.

"When's the next time you will?"

Still, no reassuring answer formed in Nat's swirling head.

"Exactly. Here's your glass of wine. Go take a shower and decide where you want to go. You're welcome."

Natalie pulled Marion into a bone-crushing hug, hoping the older woman knew just how much she was loved and appreciated.

Twin giggles from her friend and her daughter followed her into her bathroom. The wine and water worked their magic, and she warmed up to the idea of a night out. Daisy's questions the other night had sparked the idea of moving, although not to Texas. If she couldn't find a place up here, she might be looking for a job to take them back down to LA where the cost of living wasn't quite so brutal.

Staring down at least one move, another change in routine, maybe another school for Didi, Natalie finished her wine and closed her eyes. Hauling in a deep, steam-filled breath, she pushed away her worries and embraced the gift she'd been given. Her troubles would still be there come morning. Tonight might be her last chance to have some grown-up fun for a long while.

As she scrubbed herself rosy and dry with an ancient towel,

she imagined what to do with her surprise night off. A solo movie that did not have a single cartoon character? A fancy dinner with actual courses that she could eat while they were still hot? Or… An image of a shirtless Enzo danced through her mind. Or she could go to karaoke and see what happened.

She dried her hair into cute tousled waves and took the time to put a little product in. Instead of reaching for her uniform of jeans and a black T-shirt, she chose an outfit. Actually, she chose three before deciding that flirty was the tone for the evening. The clingy wrap dress in poppy red made her feel alive, and the strappy heels put a kick in her step.

Why don't I do this more often? Right—the cost and reliability of childcare. Every time she left Daisy with someone else, worry and guilt fought for top billing in her brain. *Not tonight!* Tonight, her kid was with a friend who loved her. And Natalie was not going to worry. Sometimes she could coach her emotions into behaving.

Sitting down at her mirror, she set up for a date night special, even though this wouldn't technically be a date. Would it? True, Enzo had invited her, but so had Trina. It was more of a group outing. A friendly drink. Practically a work function, with a promise of flirting if she showed up.

God, she missed flirting. It had been the only part of dating she'd enjoyed, since the few men who'd passed through her life in the last seven years had done so quickly. No one had lasted longer than three dates. Tonight she could flirt with abandon, since it was looking increasingly likely that she'd have to move back to LA. One last fling to tide her over during the next dry spell while she rebuilt their lives somewhere else. Again.

Not. Going. To. Think. About. It.

She was excited to head out, even if it ended up just being a friendly hangout. She loved the ritual of primping. Her viewers loved new date night looks, even if she had to invent the dates. She pulled fun shades from her samples box and got ready to create. No matter how many times she did her face, it never failed to please her. Like a kid with crayons and a blank roll of paper, she never ran out of ideas or enthusiasm for her craft.

When she'd found out she was pregnant with Daisy, beauty school had been a cheaper and faster alternative to college that could set her up with a career. The program she'd gotten into was competitive and about four hundred miles from her mom and her ex. So she'd moved from Lincoln, California, a small, sleepy suburb near Sacramento, down to big, bustling LA with a girlfriend who wanted to be an actress. The friend had lasted all of three weeks, but Natalie had thrived out from under her mother's neglect. About month two of classes, she'd realized she had a true talent and interest for makeup arts. Now, she loved continuing to refine her skills and challenging herself with new looks. Working in the movies was her goal. Getting this gig on MDSH was a big leap forward. She would hate to have to leave it.

Enough! No more worrying tonight!

She turned on the lights and camera and settled in to play.

"Hello, friends! I have stunning news for you. I. AM. GOING. OUT! God bless the babysitters, for they shall save a mother's mind! There may or may not be male company involved, so I've put together a look to knock him on his ass."

She shot a cheeky grin at herself on the screen of her phone, and waggled her products in front of her face as she laid out her plan.

"Here's the rundown: primer, foundation, concealer, a little highlight and contour, smokey eye with this new palette that Glitter Monkey sent me, and a bright poppy lip. 1940s Hollywood starlet, all the way. Let's go!"

She kept up the friendly patter as she blended away the worry creases on her forehead and concealed the dark circles and sleepless nights beneath her eyes. With each stroke she created the mask she wanted to show the world tonight, the person she'd pretend to be, just for tonight.

Half an hour later, she spritzed her face with setting spray and signed off.

"Until next time, stay adventurous, my lovelies, and remember: Makeup doesn't make you beautiful. It lets the beauty inside shine!"

Natalie saved the video so she could edit it later tonight and post it tomorrow. She tweeted a quick teaser for it and took one last look in the mirror. She hardly recognized herself. Perfect. Grinning as she imagined everyone's faces when she walked in, the person in the mirror went from wearing a pretty mask to being a beautiful person. The smile, the sparkle—she recognized her playful nature in those gestures, even if she hadn't seen that side of herself in awhile. This bombshell look, so at odds with her usual low-key appearance, would cause a commotion. This was going to be fun!

A drink, a song or two, a little flirtatious banter wouldn't hurt a bit. She might even have fun, a concept that had taken on a different meaning in the last seven years. Marion was right. She had a rough road ahead. Seizing tonight was a gift to herself.

ENZO SIPPED THE TEPID BEER he'd poured from the pitcher half an hour ago and grimaced. He blamed it on the warm beer, but the cold shoulder was equally responsible. She wasn't coming.

He scanned the dark wood-paneled dive bar for the forty-second time, but still no short brunette in jeans and a black T-shirt. A few people from the crew were sitting at the scarred and sticky table with him. Trina and Winston were browsing through the song binder. Frankie and Sofia were joking, while Adrian rubbed between Sofia's shoulder blades. Rico was belting out his eponymous song on stage, complete with the requisite hip thrusts, and Enzo couldn't even summon a smile. Despite sitting at the same table, he was so far from their happy moods that he might as well have been in a different room.

He'd been a fool to think she'd show. He'd let the tendrils of hope grow through his chest, hoping they'd produce sweet-scented jasmine. Instead, the kudzu of broken dreams was spreading like the parasite it was. He'd start pruning back his expectations. Tomorrow.

Get your head out of the weeds, Enzo. You're off the clock and possibly off your rocker... Did I really just compare her to kudzu?

He needed something stronger than this crappy beer, so he could wallow in his disappointment and move on. Turning his back on the two large tables full of jovial crew members and several relatives, he strode to the bar and ordered a single malt whiskey, neat. He stared into the mirror behind the colorful bottles stacked behind the bar, hoping to be less obvious about watching the door while he waited for his drink.

He'd taken his first deep draw when she walked in. Half the fire water spewed from his mouth in his surprise. The other half chose the burning route through his nose.

Coughing and crying, he snagged bar napkins and attempted to pull himself together. Mopping his face and blowing his nose, he prayed that Natalie walked to the tables first so he could control this absurd reaction.

The bartender who was wiping down the counter in front of him went from openly laughing at his folly to staring open-mouthed over his shoulder. Damn.

"Hey there. What did I miss?"

She hopped up on the dry barstool to his left and expected him to speak. Not fair.

Her face had already rendered him speechless. The flash of thigh against the bright red split of her skirt sent his blood racing from one head to the other, leaving him woozy.

"Hello? Earth to Enzo?" She grinned, clearly enjoying his reaction. Of course she knew exactly how gorgeous she was. It was her job, wasn't it?

"Uh, hi." He cleared his throat. He thought he'd left the squeaks behind in middle school. *Damn whiskey.* "You look...different."

"Jeez, Enzo. You've got to stop it with these compliments. You're making me blush."

"Can I get you a drink?" the bartender asked, and though Enzo resented his attempt to grab some of Natalie's attention, he used the interruption to haul in a deep breath and try to find some of the flirtation he'd promised her.

"I'd love a dry rosé."

"On the house, with my compliments." The smarmy bastard smiled.

"No, her drinks are my treat tonight." Enzo glared at the man until he conceded and fetched her pink drink, before he turned back to Natalie. "I'd almost given up on you." He mentally smacked his forehead. Way to sound like a needy creep.

"So you're drowning your disappointment in, what is that, whiskey?"

"Something like that, hence the sputtering and gasping for air."

"And here I thought I just stole your breath."

"You did. You do," he sputtered again, and she grinned, patting her hair. Her sexy chuckle wormed its way into his brain, joining the memories of her smiles he was collecting. "I'm glad you made it."

"I almost didn't, but my roommate volunteered to take care of Daisy, so here I am."

"Well, cheers to your roommate, then!" He clinked what was left of his whiskey against her wine glass and sipped carefully.

When he was sure the liquor had passed his windpipe, he attempted speech again. He could do this. It didn't have to be witty or deep. *Just ask a question and let her do the talking.*

"Who's Daisy?"

There. She'd mentioned the name. Simple follow-up. Was she a cat or dog person? This small-talk shit was easy.

"My daughter."

The patron saint of first dates, San Raphael, must've taken pity on him, because he hadn't yet taken another sip, so his surprise merely set off his coughing again and didn't ruin her lovely dress. He'd be sure to light a candle on Sunday.

"And here's the part where we join everyone else at the table and pretend that you only invited me as part of the crew." She sighed and drank down half of her wine in one gulp before sliding down off her stool, the red hem clinging even higher.

Enzo panicked and gripped her bare arm. The electricity zinging down his arm burned but he couldn't let go. "Wait. Stay."

She froze as if caught in the current too. "I'm not a dog, Enzo."

Okay, so maybe she wasn't as caught up as he was. "Neither is Daisy. Give me a minute to catch up. How old is she?"

"Six."

"Got any pictures?"

With a small smile, Natalie scooted back on her chair and crossed her legs while she pulled her phone from her purse. Enzo couldn't help but stare at the new swath of honey-gold skin she revealed.

"Here she is on the first day of school."

She pushed the phone into his hands, breaking his stare. He didn't think he'd have managed it on his own. Where the hell was his legendary self-control?

A cute little kid with her mother's brown locks and dark eyes grinned at him with a smile missing a few teeth. Her nose and her chin came from someone else. Her father? Who might or might not still be in the picture, despite being physically absent from this picture?

But would she have looked so disappointed a minute ago if she was with someone? And the roommate thing… He wrestled with his desire to know everything about her right away. If he asked wrong, he'd push her away.

"She's beautiful, just like her mama."

He couldn't tell if she was blushing through her makeup, but she lowered her gaze and quirked her lips, as if hiding from the compliment.

"Don't do that."

"Do what?"

"Hide your smiles. If I earn one, I want to see it. They are too precious to waste on the floor."

She just stared at him as if he'd dropped down from outer space. He quickly cast around for another conversation topic.

"So, how was the rest of your day?"

"Busy. I was hopping. My feet are killing me. How about you?"

"Well, after you greased me up, I had to talk about fertilizer strategies shirtless for an hour and a half. This show is killing me. It's taking me ten times longer to finish leveling a freaking yard because I have to keep talking about it. I mean, I want to help my family. My parents really need this show to work out. But I had hoped to have my own landscaping firm up and running by now. I'm getting tired of mowing lawns, but *Valenti Brothers' Construction is solid design for good value,*" he said in his best impression of his dad. "I want to take bigger clients, do more design, but I guess it'll just have to wait. Every time I try to take a step in that direction, this show sucks me back in and steals an item of clothing. What's next, my pants?"

"I wouldn't complain."

He'd gotten caught up in his thoughts. When she smiled, full teeth, he grinned back and his mind went blessedly blank. She reached for her phone and the brush of her fingers against his startled him into dropping it on the floor.

"Shit, I'm sorry."

He bent down to pick it up at the same time she swiveled in her chair to do the same. From his crouch, her wrap dress was barely covering her charms. She uncrossed her legs to step down and Enzo froze, the phone in his hand in danger of being crushed, Hulk-style. She shifted again, and he grabbed her knee to stop her from exposing herself. He looked up to explain and was drawn in by the surprised pleasure on her face.

"If you want me to be able to stand up, please stop right there." A wicked gleam entered her eyes, and he knew. He was a goner. He was in her thrall, and she knew it. He could almost hear the little devil on her shoulder win the argument.

"What if I don't want you to stand up yet?"

She was playing with fire, and he discovered he liked the burn. He slid his hand from her knee down to her ankle, moving her foot to his crouched thigh, never breaking eye contact. "Then by all means, keep moving. But be prepared to handle the consequences."

He knew he was pushing it, but she seemed as turned on as he was. He'd promised her flirting. Did this still qualify? Or had they just blown past all the boundaries? Would she take him up on his dare? All she had to do was swing her knee wider, and he'd be able to see everything. Would she let him in?

Her knee began to move, and Enzo realized four things in rapid succession.

One: this woman was fearless.

Two: he was smitten.

Three: he was inches from heaven, kneeling on the floor of a very public bar, and that was not where he wanted to taste her for the first time.

Four: his control was shredded, and that was exactly what would happen if he didn't stand right the fuck up, erection be damned.

He bolted to his feet before she could finish teasing him and kill his willpower dead.

She laughed again and drank the last of her wine, signaling for another. Sliding off her chair for real this time, her body brushed against his, and he couldn't suppress the shudder of desire that raced through him.

He leaned in closer, still hoping to catch her elusive scent, but all he caught was the smell of spilled whiskey and wine.

She pried her phone from his hand and dropped it in her purse before picking up her newly refilled wine glass.

"Come on, Enzo. Let's go join the others before we do something we'll regret."

Enzo took his heart in his hands and touched her one more time, running his hand down her arm to catch her hand. "Natalie, when we do something, I guarantee you won't regret it."

"Promises, promises."

She danced out of his grasp, and all he could do was follow empty-handed, his whiskey long forgotten.

～

Natalie smiled into her wine. She hadn't felt this loose in ages. She laughed with the crew, joined in their silly games, and even got up for their group rendition of "The Gambler." She hadn't been able to hang out after work before, and she realized how much she'd missed having adult friends.

It also felt good to flirt with a handsome man. The look on his face when she'd walked in and his coughing fit had made the extra effort in front of the mirror worth every second. She toyed with filming a post-date update to share his reaction. But maybe she'd just keep that to herself. She didn't need to share everything with her viewers. She kept Daisy private. She could do the same with her tender emotions.

Natalie shied away from the idea that she'd have any reason to keep things with him private in the future or, heaven forbid, that emotions were involved. In reality, she didn't have much more than tonight with him before her life imploded. *Better make it count.*

Every time their eyes met across the table, her belly tightened in anticipation. She deliberately let her eyes linger on a different feature each time, cataloging every beautiful inch of him in this relaxed setting, until he blushed. She should probably feel ashamed of herself for eye-fucking him in front of their colleagues. No doubt she would in the morning. But he kept staring back at her, and it was just too much fun to get a rise out of him.

She'd gotten a feel of his impressive "rise" over at the bar, and judging by the way he kept fidgeting in his chair, it hadn't gone away. She would much rather play with his reaction to her than think about the disaster her life had become.

It was amazing what a difference a little crisis could make. A week ago, she'd have followed through on her plan to stay self-sufficient. She'd have deflected his invitation and stayed home to focus on her priorities: her baby and her job. She didn't need a man around mucking things up. She'd heard enough horror stories in her chair and had enough crappy dating experiences herself to know how anything long-term would end. Eventually he would get tired of all of her responsibilities and find someone younger, cuter, and happier to fawn over him.

She had little hope of finding a place to live that would be safe and comfortable for Daisy. Her search this weekend hadn't turned up a single listing in her price range. She was wrapping her head around the reality of quitting and moving Daisy back to LA. She had a few friends down there she could crash with until she found a new gig, maybe. But she hated bailing on the show. She'd been able to stay in one place for nearly six months, and the show had gotten renewed. Jake had asked her to stay on, and she'd verbally agreed. Tonight proved that she worked with some pretty great people, and the schedule was perfect for Didi.

She caught her thoughts spiraling back to her troubles and forcibly shut them down, shaking her head. Tonight was different. Tonight was just for fun. Hell, she'd probably be half a state away next week. She didn't want to worry anymore. She wanted to feel carefree, just for one night, and her defenses were weak. What was the harm in a little flirting? A little daydreaming?

Because if she constructed a daydream, it would look a lot like this. A handsome man, making her laugh and keeping her glass full, while she didn't have a care in the world beyond the next moment. If she pretended hard enough, she could almost make herself believe she was worthy of it.

Drawn from her whirling thoughts by a stampede for the stage as the DJ cued up "YMCA," she realized she was well on her way to drunk, and alone at the table with Enzo. He moved to the chair next to her, and it took every ounce of her energy not to put her head on his shoulder. His strong, steady shoulder, that made her mouth water as she stroked it with oil and got him nice and dirty… She snapped her eyes shut, the better to savor the mental image.

"Hey, you okay?"

His innocent question pulled a harsh laugh from her chest. The concern in his tone snuck past her guard, and she was drunk enough to give him a raw answer. Her filters had washed away in the river of rose-colored wine. "I am definitely not okay."

His steady hand on her back and the worry in his eyes weakened her resolve, and her head was suddenly too heavy to hold on her own. It felt as nice as she'd imagined to nestle into his warm, solid shoulder, and tears rose to her eyes as reality flowed past her lips.

"My roommate is moving out and selling her condo. I can't find a new place I can afford that will work for Daisy, so I'm gonna have to quit this job and leave all of this." She waved her hands at the stage where her new friends made silly letters with their arms. "I'll have to ask friends for help, which I hate, until I can find a new place, which means at least two more moves. And on top of that, it would pull Daisy from school again, and she just made a new friend, and she loves her teacher, and I promised her that we could stay awhile at this one, which makes me feel like a shit mom."

She ended her rant on a ragged breath and a hiccup. She closed her eyes to keep the tears from falling along with her fears and worries onto the bar floor, and drew in a deep shaky breath, fighting for control. That was a mistake. Enzo's scent—wood and sunshine and warm man—flooded her senses, and she burrowed her nose deeper into his chest like a bloodhound on a trail.

He pulled her into a one-armed hug, and she was oh so tempted to stay. Just for tonight. She could lean on him just for tonight.

"Hey, don't panic. If you find an apartment, the problems go away and you get to stay, right?"

"In theory, yes, but I've looked, and my budget—" He put a finger to her lip, and the tingling sensation stunned her into silence.

"I know every realtor in the Valley. Let me try and help you before you pack it in for LA."

"Why?"

"Why should you let me help you?" His voice sharpened with offense.

"No, why would you want to?"

He traced that magic finger along the edge of her jaw and drew her gaze back to his. "Because now that I've got your attention, I'd like to keep it awhile. Let me help you stay."

It sounded so good, and unfortunately familiar. Her exes had fallen all over themselves trying to keep her attention. And once Daisy needed more of her energy, they got angry, like she owed them something. Nasty words were hurled, and then they left. It was a familiar pattern. Enzo would get frustrated and drop her the minute Daisy drew more of her focus than he did. But what could it hurt, besides her pride, to let him try to help? She would keep her other plans moving forward just in case, but if he could find something she couldn't? If she could keep her promise to Daisy? "If you pull this off, I could kiss you."

That last bit had been out loud. She closed her eyes.

"I wish you would." His whispered response detonated like a grenade in her mind, shocking her eyes back open, leaving her unable to conceal the depth of her attraction. Kissing Enzo suddenly seemed like the only possible choice.

She tilted her head up, just inches from the curve where his jaw met his neck. What would he taste like right there? She leaned closer, feeling that wall of muscled torso pressing into her from her shoulder down to her hips, unyielding. Would his lips be the same?

Only one way to find out.

Natalie pressed her lips to his, deliberately testing him, and found them to be firm but giving, matching her glide for glide without pushing her for more than she was willing to give. The contrast was delicious, and her tongue darted out to capture more of his flavor for herself. Rich whiskey, redolent with wood smoke, and his own tang of sweat and desire—it was one hundred percent man, and she reveled in it. Each new scent, taste, texture of him flooded her senses. Like an addict taking her first hit of a new drug, she was hooked. How was she supposed to walk away from temptation like this?

Her head was pounding in time with her heart, and her breasts were achingly tender, demanding his touch. True, it had been years since she'd been with a man, but she couldn't remember ever having this kind of reaction to a first kiss. She turned to drape her body more fully against his, wanting the pleasure of his pressure as she deepened the kiss. All of her restraint was gone.

Between her crossed legs, she throbbed insistently. Her battery-operated boyfriends had taken care of her for years, but no B.O.B. was going to help her tonight.

She wanted more.

She nipped at his ear.

More of this man who turned her inside out. Who made her feel protected and wanted. She slid her hand across his pecs and down to the waistband of his jeans.

More of this man…who was peeling out of her embrace and striding for the bathroom.

What the hell had just happened? Had she read him completely wrong? The door swung shut behind him, and she was still sitting, stunned, at the table.

Her head was spinning, and it wasn't just from the wine. She headed for the ladies' room herself, unsteady on her heels and her ideals. She'd thought the loving and leaving would take a little longer. Damn it—no, damn him, for leaving first.

She swayed through the door and managed to get herself in

and out of the stall without falling in. She giggled at a memory of potty training Daisy that hadn't ended so well and congratulated herself on peeing better than a three-year-old. Ah, the joys of parenting. That's what she was, a parent. Didi, Daisy, her little sprite, came first. She stared herself down in the mirror as she wiped the mascara smudges from beneath her eyes.

"Get what you need for Daisy. You can take care of the rest yourself."

She refused to be hurt by his sudden withdrawal. Emboldened by her pep talk, she marched out of the restroom and straight into his solid chest.

Not fair. Damn it, he felt good. She squeezed the hands she'd used to brace herself and moaned at the feel of his pecs under her hands.

No. Nope. Where the hell had the strong girl in the mirror gone? She stepped back, ashamed of her own weakness. She could stand on her own.

"Are you ready to go home?"

"Maybe. What's it to you? Do you want to take me halfway there, and then push me out of the moving car?"

She clapped her hands over her mouth. *Rosé filters. Right.*

Enzo chuckled and leaned into her space. "No, I'm gonna take you all the way there."

He let that innuendo hang while her disobedient but creative imagination filled in all the delicious blanks. *Gah!*

"And then…"

Natalie hung on that pause, eyes locked on his lovely, lush lower lip.

"And then, I'm going to get you inside and into bed."

She nodded and leaned back in, liking all of those words, even more so when her tipsy brain scrambled the order a bit. *Traitor!* Her good little angel screamed as her little devil shoved her from her high perch.

"And once I have you in bed…"

Enzo's voice dropped to a husky whisper, and she leaned in

even closer to catch his words. Yeah, that was why. She needed more of his…words.

"I'm going to take those fuck-me heels off and rub your feet."

She groaned out loud at that image. *How did he know?* She didn't have time to figure it out, because more words were washing over her.

"And then I'm going to tuck you in and make myself leave. Because the first time I get you naked in bed, I want to know that you want it as much as I do."

Wait. What? She couldn't have heard that right. "I want you pretty bad right now."

Maybe her lack of filters would help a sister out right now.

"Is that you or the rosé talking?"

Her lip, which felt a little numb at this point, pushed out into a pout. "Why can't my wine and your whiskey talk this out like adults?" Natalie was perilously close to whining as she struggled to make sense of the fact that she would not likely be doing more than kissing tonight. "Isn't there a song? I'll be your glass of wine, you'll be my shot of whiskey…" She began to hum the melody.

"Natalie. My last whiskey was the one at the bar when you walked in. I don't need anything but you to make my head spin. Now, let me get you home safe."

Shame and disappointment battled it out in her gut, leaving her nauseous and sad. She'd lean on him just this one last time and then Zero Enzo. No more. Cold turkey. She was an independent woman.

"Okay."

CHAPTER 5

ENZO WOKE UP with a frown on his face and an angry hard-on under his sheets. He was tempted, so tempted, to take himself in hand and get some relief. But the thought of beating off to some fantasy of Natalie paled against reality. It felt wrong, disrespectful somehow. He didn't know if it was the added knowledge that she was a mother, or if it was the way she'd responded to him last night, but he knew this wouldn't satisfy him. He wanted his first time with her to be *with her*.

He covered his eyes with his forearm and replayed the evening prior, looking for evidence that he'd done the right thing.

He'd managed to get her address from her before she'd fallen asleep in her car. Digging through her purse yielded her keys, and he'd carried her in, settling her in her bed next to her sleeping child. He'd removed her shoes as promised, and tucked her in. He had contemplated removing her makeup, but he hadn't a clue where to start. She had rolled over and immediately pulled her daughter into the curve of her body, one arm holding Daisy in a hug. Seeing them curled up in each other, two dark-haired angels in repose, had moved something in his chest. Kind of like a car moves a brick wall when it hits it going sixty.

He'd laid her keys gently on her bedside table and let himself out, turning the handle lock on the door before closing it between them. The amount of effort that small move had taken was ridiculous. He'd been proud of his restraint last night, but this morning, with a pounding head and throbbing cock, he was feeling less content with his choices.

She wasn't built for a flirtation. She wasn't quick fling material. This was a woman who needed flowers and rings. That was a problem, since she didn't seem to think she would be staying. Frustrated, he grabbed his phone and shot off three texts to local realtors asking for help finding a listing. If he could fix the first part of the problem, maybe the second part would sort itself out. Until then, the lawns weren't going to mow themselves.

A cold shower and two cups of coffee went a long way toward smoothing his rough edges. He threw on his work grubbies, which consisted of a variety of gray T-shirts, all older than dirt, and ratty blue jeans, and headed out for work. Frankie and Buster were just getting home from their morning run. Buster greeted him with his trademark paws to the chest and exuberant barks.

Frankie's welcome was more reserved, with a smirk and a wave. "So you left with Natalie last night, huh?"

"Yeah, I drove her home."

"Well, that's one way to get in the door." Frankie punched him in the shoulder with a grin, but Enzo didn't feel like laughing along.

"I tucked her into bed. With her kid. Get your mind out of the gutter."

"She's got a kid?"

At least I'm not the only one who didn't know.

"Yeah, cute little girl. She's six."

"Enzo."

The warning note made Enzo's neck hair bristle. "What?"

"Don't be you."

"What the hell is that supposed to mean?"

Frankie's crossed arms and deadpan stare made him squirm. "It means I know you. You take every struggling flower home from the nursery and baby it back to health. Whenever anybody got into a jam in high school, you were the one covering and bailing us out. Remember when Gabe broke Mom's glass vase from Venice, and you spent three hours supergluing it back together?"

"Yeah, and we both got grounded for it. What's your point?" Enzo crossed his arms in a mirror image and frowned.

"You're tenderhearted, Enzo. You look at Natalie and see somebody who needs your help." Enzo bit his tongue against sharing Natalie's current housing struggles. "E, look at me. She's only here for the show. She's not going to stay. Don't get in too deep."

The concern in Frankie's eyes touched him, but he knew what he was doing. He'd been attracted to Natalie even before he found out she had a kid and problems to solve. True, his plan to just enjoy her company was now complicated by her status as a single mom, but did he really mind? Getting involved with a mother was serious, but after that kiss last night he was seriously interested.

"Gotta go, Pip. I'm running late."

CLUTCHING THE SCALDING HOT COFFEE in a paper cup close to her chest was the only thing tethering Natalie to reality Tuesday morning as she wandered into the garage to get set up for a full day. Who the hell went out on a Monday night? Not anyone who had a kid that needed to get up and ready before the break of dawn. And of course, Daisy had stayed up late with Marion, so her child had woken up as a sleep-deprived dragon instead of her sweet fairy sprite.

Her head had already split open, her Excedrin Migraine not touching the headache at all. She leaned closer to the mirror in the dark garage, trying to see if her hasty makeup job had hidden the worst of her hangover. She couldn't turn on her bright lights yet. Hell, she was risking certain death just taking her sunglasses off inside.

The rapid, guttural roar of a lawnmower coming to life cut through the quiet of the morning. Natalie almost dropped her coffee setting it down, and clutched her head, palms over ears.

"Dear God, make it stop."

She stumbled out the door, fighting every instinct and moving closer to the sound, hoping she could get there before her ears started to bleed.

"Hey! HEY!"

Enzo released the handle on the mower and the noise dropped down to an idling buzz.

"Good morning, gorgeous!" He leaned in to kiss her, and she blocked him instinctively with her palm to his chest.

Oh dear. This was going to get awkward. "Tricks of the trade. Don't be fooled. Can you turn that thing off for a minute?" She gestured toward the instrument of torture still running behind him.

"Huh? Oh, sure. Hang on."

He reached over and flicked a switch, giving her just a flash of his beautifully round backside and a thin swath of bare skin at the base of his back. Why was slightly revealed so much sexier than fully bare?

No. Nope. Those were exactly the types of questions she shouldn't be pondering here at work. This was why she didn't date men she worked with! Well, to be fair, the pool of men she worked with had been quite small before this current project, so that sweeping statement wasn't as impressive as it sounded. Maybe she could make an exception since it had never been enforced?

NO! She struggled to get all of her impulses firing in unison. She really needed her brain to wake up and function right now before she did something stupid. Like lean in and let him finish that good morning kiss.

Damn him for making her want. Her life was so much easier when she knew she couldn't have what she wanted. It was so easy to want him.

"I'm glad you came out. I was going to come talk to you in a bit. I wanted to see how you were feeling."

"Yeah, about that. Thank you for getting me home last night. I hope I didn't say anything embarrassing."

"Nothing that embarrassed me. I'm sorry I didn't think to make you take some ibuprofen before you fell asleep. You just looked so cozy curled up with your daughter, I didn't have the heart to wake you. But I can tell by your scowl you'd have been happier if I had."

"You literally put me in bed?"

"I told you I would, and I'm a man of my word, Natalie. I also left and locked the door behind me shortly after I got your shoes off."

Natalie covered her eyes against the brightening morning sun and the liquid shame threatening to spill over.

His hand came to rest on her shoulder and he pulled her in for a hug. "Hey, hey now, it's okay. I didn't mind taking care of you. In fact, I kind of liked it."

Oh. Oh no. She stepped back swiftly out of his hug, despite the fact that it was the most comfort she'd received from another human in years and she longed to stay wrapped up, warm and safe. She couldn't do that here.

She needed to be professional at work. It was one thing she'd worked so hard at for so long. If she lost that accomplishment now, what else would she lose? Her good reputation? Her self-respect? Yes, she needed a good recommendation from Jake, but she also needed to hold to her own moral code because it gave her the strength to make good decisions.

"I...I can't do that. You can't touch me like that at work."

"I wasn't thinking. You're right." Enzo tucked his hands in his pockets, and that absolutely did not help her resolve as his shoulders strained against the well-worn gray cotton of his T-shirt. "Can I maybe touch you like that after work? I would love to take you out for dinner? Or a movie?"

God that sounded so nice and…normal. She didn't do normal. Why did he think she could do normal?

"Listen, Enzo, last night was fun, but I don't really date. I have so little time with Daisy as it is, that I don't like leaving her with sitters. I'm sorry, but—"

He cut her off before she could shut him down. "We could bring her with. Are there any good kid movies showing?"

"No. My kid is not available for dates. I'm not going to break her heart when you leave, just because you want to hold my hand in a dark theater."

"Ouch!" He rubbed a dirty hand over his chest, leaving a streak of soil on his shirt. "Fatalistic much? When I leave? We haven't even gotten started."

"And we're not going to. Everyone leaves, Enzo, and it'll probably be me in the next week or so, so I think it's better if we just keep our distance."

"Not if I can help it."

"Excuse me?" She'd never had someone blatantly ignore one of her brush-offs.

"I've got texts out to a few realtor buddies already. I'm not going to let you leave if I can help it. And if you stay, Natalie, I'm going to want that movie date with your kid." He turned back to his lawn mower and started it up again, effectively ending the conversation.

She'd held her ground, but she still felt like she'd lost that battle. *At least I'm awake now.*

〜

"Hi, Jim. I've got a question for you. Do you have a line on any rental properties coming available here in town? Yes, I know the fall is a slow rental market, but I've got a friend… Yes, I understand. Can you send me anything you come across? I appreciate it. Yes, I'll pass that on to Dad. Thanks."

Damn it. Four days and not one of his realtor buddies had come through for him. He'd moved on to his dad's contacts. That was the third callback he'd gotten, and they had all been less than helpful. Their skeptical responses were killing his optimism that he'd be able to help Natalie find somewhere to stay. He really wanted to have good news before he tried to ask her out again, which unfortunately meant he'd had to avoid her all week.

He tucked his phone back into his pocket as his father crossed the parking lot toward him. Dom was never at work this early, a fact Enzo depended on to avoid uncomfortable confrontations. Like the one he sensed was headed his way.

Dom's face split into a grin, and he waved. "Lorenzo, wait up!"

Damn. His full name. He was screwed. With no choice, Enzo leaned back against his truck to wait. Five minutes. He could talk to his dad for five minutes.

When had talking to his father become a chore? Rhetorical question. He knew the date. Two days after Gabe's military funeral, when his dad had approached him about taking over Valenti Brothers.

"Hi, Dad. Jim Hamilton sends his best."

"What are you talking to him for? Looking at buying something?"

"Nope, just helping a friend. What's up?"

"I need to talk to you about a project."

Here we go…

"Is it for the show?"

"No, it's—"

Enzo cut his father off before he could get caught up in whatever great project he wanted Enzo to drop everything for and work on. It was easier to say no if they skipped the excitement. "Then I don't have time, Dad. I'm slammed with my regular clients on top of the show. That's why I'm already here and getting down to business at seven a.m."

"Just hear me out. I'm tackling some new construction in south Santa Clara county."

Enzo tried for a deep breath, but his voice snapped out through it. "Dad, we've been over this. I'm not interested in building. I wasn't when you asked me last month. I wasn't when you asked me last year. I'm not Gabe. Stop trying to make me take his place."

Maybe he *couldn't* handle talking to his dad for five minutes. Enzo glanced at his watch. Under a minute thirty. That had to be a record for losing his temper.

Dom's face froze in a stiff, blank mask. Enzo's arrow had hit its target, and now he regretted his outburst. He'd spoken to his father the same way Gabe would have, but what worked for Gabe never seemed to work for him. Gabe had never minded pissing people off. They always forgave him. Enzo couldn't brush off the guilt so easily. His stomach churned as he waited for his father's response. He almost backed down just to get that look off his dad's face.

"Listen, Dad, I—"

Dom raised his hand, blocking Enzo's words and apologies. "No. You're busy. I get it. Don't let me keep you."

With a heavy heart, Enzo rounded his truck. Why did it hurt so much to stand up for himself? He paused, trying to think of something to say, some way to fix this, but there was nothing. No way to bridge the ever-growing gap between them. Enzo couldn't be anyone but himself, not even to please his father. He wished that just being himself was enough.

By Friday night Enzo was no closer to solving Natalie's housing woes and was still simmering over his argument with his dad. Bone tired from a packed schedule and filming deadlines, he sat in his truck, staring out the windshield, unseeing. He uncurled his fingers from the steering wheel before gripping it again, his knuckles turning white.

Nope. Not ready to face the family dinner yet.

God, he wished he knew how to fix things with his family.

A sharp rap on his window made him jump. Sofia and Adrian stood next to his truck, identical grins splitting their faces.

His solitude broken, Enzo turned off his truck and climbed out. "I was just catching the end of a podcast."

"Uh-huh. Sure you were. Come on inside. I'm not saving antipasti for anyone tonight." Sofia wrapped his arm in hers so that she was flanked by male escorts on both sides. Could she sense that he wanted to run? That he needed an anchor tonight?

They walked into the dining room and halted abruptly. Dom and Frankie were already seated at the table, which was currently covered in cardboard pizza boxes and bottles of beer.

"Come on in, kids. Grab a slice," Dom boomed before taking another piece of pizza for his own plate.

No antipasti, no wine, no Ma.

They'd never had take-out for Family Friday before. Something was wrong.

"Where's Ma?" Sofia asked the question burning his tongue. He certainly didn't want to be the one to draw Dom's attention to Jo's absence.

"She had some thing tonight. I don't know, some dance for her group. So we're having pizza. Live it up, kids. It's a special occasion."

"Why didn't she mention it? We could have rescheduled."

"She might have told me, but I forgot. I didn't see her reminder note until I got home. Don't worry about it. It's one missed dinner. Anyhow, I'm glad she's not here. I have something I want to talk to you all about. Privately."

Enzo sat back in his chair, ignoring the pizza and beer, focusing instead on his father who was practically bouncing in his chair. The strain between them had seemingly evaporated in the glow of his good news.

"Tell us," prompted Sofia as Adrian sat in the chair next to hers and draped an arm over the back. They weren't married yet, but Adrian already felt like part of the family. It was nice to see Sofia finally relaxed and content.

"I bought some land."

"Where at?" Frankie asked.

"South county, out near Morgan Hill. I tried to get Enzo to come look at it before I bought it, but he was busy so I went with my gut."

Enzo winced at the dig. Great, so if this plan flopped it would be all his fault.

"Why would you buy all the way out there? The return on flip properties is much higher up here," Sofia pointed out.

"I'm not flipping it. I bought fifty acres of old-growth vines. I'm building a winery."

Stunned silence blanketed the table, each young mind trying to connect the dots in their father's mystery plan and failing miserably.

"What?" Sofia was clearly the bravest soul among them.

"The show is doing well. They are already talking spin-offs. I promised your mother that once things were stable, I'd retire. I've been trying it out, this retirement shit. Sitting around each morning reading the paper, drinking coffee… Hell, I can't make it more than two hours without wanting to pull my hair out or bickering with Jo now that she's talking to me again. I hate it. I need something to do. She's been after me to find a hobby, so I bought a vineyard."

Enzo's mind was spinning. He was bored so he bought a vineyard? Must be nice to just be able to follow a dream on a whim. *What the fuck?*

"What?" Enzo wisely bit off the last part of his thought, but it was implied. Dom got his dander up anyhow.

"It makes perfect sense. Your mother keeps talking about

going to Italy like Tony and Elena. She wants Italian villas? I'll give her an Italian villa, complete with a functional winery, tasting room, and B&B. But I need you kids' help to pull it off and keep it a surprise."

"Why a surprise?" Enzo was just digging his own pit deeper. He was going to get sucked into helping with this for sure.

"Because a big mistake needs a big apology, and building her a retirement house is a hell of a grand gesture."

Frankie was watching Dom, eyes squinted with suspicion. Enzo was missing something. What did Frankie know that he didn't?

"Is this why you have been hanging around Jake so much? You were hovering all week." Frankie's arms crossed firmly, daring him to answer.

"We might have discussed filming the construction as one of the spin-offs."

Before Frankie could follow up, Enzo had jumped up out of his chair. "Jesus, Dad! Like one TV show's not enough?" Enzo could already see where this was going. He was going to get roped into another fucking family project. He'd lose even more of his time, and his dreams would get pushed completely off the back burner and onto the shelf. And the really shitty thing? He'd probably let it happen. Frustrated with his own lack of spine, he snagged a longneck from the table and headed for his spot in the backyard.

He sat on the bottom step, dropped his beer at his feet, and inhaled the familiar pine sap and woodchip scents of his childhood. The old swing set and tree house were still standing. Valenti Brothers built to last. He imagined Adrian and Sofia's kids playing back here someday soon. He'd double-check the structures to make sure they were safe. Ideas for a play garden snaked through his head. Someday. When he had time...

So much joy and laughter had lived here. Where had it gone? He buried his face in his hands and cursed every which way he knew how.

This time it was Sofia who came out to find him.

"Tell me how you really *feel*," she quipped, putting an arm around his shoulder.

"I'm stretched thin, Fi. Really fucking thin," he said through his hands.

"I know. We all are."

"Yeah, but you're stretched thin because you're doing what you love. You're getting your design firm up and running. You're designing for the show. You're marrying a great guy." He ticked off her recent life changes on his fingers. "What have I got? A half-baked idea to spin off my company, and zero dollars to do it. A job on camera that I really dislike but am contractually obligated to complete. Oh, and a woman I like who is planning to move away because she can't find a place she can afford to rent and suddenly won't give me the time of day. There's an awful lot going out, and a whole lot of nothing coming in."

Sofia rubbed between his shoulder blades, and he felt about five years old again. She'd done the same thing when he'd fallen off Gabe's bike and skinned his knee. It had helped then too, despite making him feel like a baby.

"Let's take that list one thing at a time. Have you mapped out what you'd need to make to start your own business?"

"No. Not really." She stared him down. "When would I have had the time?"

"That's step one. Make time. You can't know if you're making progress without clear benchmarks and goals."

Enzo nodded, but in his head those hurdles seemed as high as ever.

"As for the show, talk to Dad. Tell him you want out after this season. I'm sure he could be persuaded."

He snorted at that one. *When pigs fly.*

"Yeah, you're right, but it's the best I've got. Now, tell me about this girl. Who is she, and why can't she stay?"

A blush climbed like a trellis rose up his neck before

blooming on his cheeks. He felt every thorny prickle on its way. He cleared his throat. "You know Natalie? In makeup?"

"Yes! Oh my God, Enzo! How did I not see this coming? She's great. But what's this about her leaving?"

"Her current roommate is selling the condo and moving to Texas. Next week. She's trying to find a new room to rent for her and her daughter."

"She's got a kid?"

Wow, she really hadn't confided in anyone. Enzo had been sure Sofia would have already known. "Yeah, a sweet little six-year-old, but I don't think she wants that spread around the set, so let's keep it quiet, okay? You know what the housing market is like around here, so I said I would help. I've been tapping our contacts all week, and so far I've come up empty."

"She's got a kid." Sofia's glowing excitement dimmed a little bit. "You really like her, don't you?"

"Why do you say that like it's a bad thing? Jesus, you and Frankie are way off. We've gone on one semi-date. I'm not shopping for rings. But there's something special about her, and I'd like to help her stay."

Sofia stared at him, almost through him. Her silence unnerved him.

"What? What are you thinking?"

"I'm thinking about my place."

"What about your place?"

"I'm basically living with Adrian, so he can stay close to his mom. I'm still paying subsidized rent to Dad. I've got nowhere to move the furniture, but I could get my personal stuff out and into storage in a few days. If she can cover the rent, I don't see why I can't do a month-to-month sublet for her. She can opt out whenever she needs to. In fact, it would help us save for the wedding."

Enzo let the idea roll around in his mind. Natalie. Living in the apartment next door. All three Valenti kids had apartments in a six-flat building their parents owned. It had been the only way they'd been able to move back home after college. Their parents charged them ridiculously low rent, just enough to keep them honest. It was within her budget.

"That just might work. Are you sure?"

"She's special, huh?"

Enzo stared at the ground but couldn't find the right words to explain there either, so he just nodded.

"I like her too. She strikes me as good people, and she makes me look gorgeous on camera. Plus it makes financial sense for everyone involved. You'll pitch it to her? You've still got my spare, right, Keeper of the Keys?"

Another nod, this one full of unspeakable love for his big sister.

"Walk her through, and see what she thinks."

Enzo leaned over and kissed her cheek. "You know, for a bossy big sister, you're pretty great."

"I love you too, you big lug."

If Natalie stayed… Maybe his outlook wasn't quite as bleak as he'd thought.

"Now, come in and talk to Dad. He's using words like viticulture, and Adrian's eyes are glazing over."

Then again, maybe not. He sighed and followed her into the house, but there was a new bounce to his step as he climbed the old stairs.

CHAPTER 6

"One last touch…"

Natalie spritzed Josephine Valenti's face with setting spray and stepped back.

"*Voilà!*" Though Enzo's mother had already retired, her skin looked twenty years younger. Doing her makeup was a treat, made more so by the fact that she was rarely on set. "What do you think?"

"I think you're a genius, and that your talents are wasted on a ridiculous home improvement show." Jo preened in the mirror, tucking her hair behind an ear to admire her now defined cheekbones. "Honestly, this is the only part of show business I like. The rest can go f— Hi, honey!"

Enzo leaned in to kiss his mother on the cheek, careful not to undo her hard work, and Natalie turned away from the casual affection to straighten her pots and brushes. Was that envy pricking her tear ducts? Surely it was the fumes from the rubbing alcohol she sterilized her tools with as she tucked away the comb she'd just used. Just because her relationship with her own mother sucked didn't mean she was jealous of the clear bond between Enzo and Jo.

She couldn't ogle the man in front of his mother, and she

didn't want to intrude on a tender moment. Her time was running out, and her week of restraint hadn't made any of these yearnings less urgent. If she wanted a taste of this man candy she had to act quickly.

She still hadn't found a place so she was reaching out to old friends in LA. Honestly, this desire for Enzo was the only thing that was keeping her tethered to the Bay Area. Everything else had fallen apart.

But after that kiss and the week of wondering in between, she really wanted to give herself the farewell present of an evening in Enzo's arms. After seven long years of drought, she was flooded with the feelings he'd set free. It seemed only right that she jump the dam with him before she had to go.

How could she let him know she was interested if he was interested? His eyes flashed to meet hers in the mirror as if she'd spoken out loud. She hadn't, had she? *Oh shit!* She glanced at his mother, who was still sitting in her freaking makeup chair, and blushed. No outward reaction from Jo, thank God, but Nat had to get her head in the game. So she was turned on and desperate. She was also a grown-up who could control herself and wait for the right moment.

Why were there so many freaking people on set when she was feeling fifty shades of horny? If they were alone, she'd hop right up on her mirrored table and demand that he not leave her hanging this time. Damn inconvenient, these people. She giggled at her inner monologue, and he smiled back at her before giving his attention to his mom. God help her, that smirk was cute.

"Hi, Ma. You look gorgeous. Hot date tonight?"

"I wish. If your father took me out on a date, I might pass out from shock. I've got a cameo on the show today, and Jake wants me to look my best."

"Well maybe I'll take you out on the town. A little dinner, a little dancing? What do you say?"

"I'd say I raised a sweet boy who needs to take out a woman his own age and get to work on grandbabies for me to spoil."

Jo sent a significant glance toward Natalie behind her back that she caught in the mirror anyway. Was Jo throwing Enzo at her?

Enzo turned to meet Natalie's gaze in the mirror before he replied. "I'm working on it, Ma."

The desire in his eyes was too much to handle in front of his mother. She looked back down at her own hands, hands that she had clenched together because they desperately wanted back in his hair. She had to keep it together and stay professional on set. She was going to need a good recommendation. She didn't think anyone would judge her for her Monday night meltdown at the bar, but that didn't mean she could take the risk of touching him in a personal way at work where Jake might see them.

"Anyway, Jake sent me to find you. He's ready for your one-on-one, and I need to get my spray tan on."

"Ugh. Okay, I'm going, but only because Sofia conned me into signing that contract."

Jo ruffled his hair as she left, and he turned his full un-reflected attention to Natalie. The excitement in his eyes fueled Natalie's own, caution forgotten. She let her hands smooth through his dark chocolate brown hair. He closed his eyes and leaned into her touch. If he'd been a cat, she'd have called the sound coming from his chest a purr. But he wasn't a harmless house cat. He was a big, strong, handsome man about to strip down to his bare skin in front of her.

God, she wanted to taste him again, before she sprayed him down and before she had to up and leave.

He took half a step back and pulled his shirt off over his head. The scent of freshly mowed grass washed over her, and her breath stuttered in her chest with wanting. She would never be able to walk by a well-tended yard without getting turned on. How inconvenient.

"I've got some good news."

His words didn't register as anything more than strings of sound. Natalie was transfixed by the nearness of his bare chest and her mounting desire. Literally. She was contemplating pushing him back and mounting him right there in her makeup chair. It would hold their combined weight for at least one orgasm, surely.

He snapped his fingers in front of her face with a laugh.

"Huh?"

"I'm up here," he teased.

"You can't just go around whipping your shirt off and expect a girl to be coherent."

"As gratifying as it is to know that my chest renders you senseless, I've got news. I think I found a solution to our problem."

"You found a place for us to get busy? I promise I haven't had any wine today." She trailed her fingers down his chest to hook into the waistband of his jeans.

He choked on his next words, breathing them out on a heavy exhale. "No. I mean, yes. Maybe. I found you an apartment."

Her stomach bottomed out in a mixture of hope and regret. *What?*

"Sofia is willing to sublet you hers at the same rate she pays my parents. Isn't that great?"

He kept talking, going through the details, while Natalie's brain swam through a flood of emotions, trying to keep her head above the surface. Her lust left her shaky as it retreated in the face of reality.

Relief over being able to keep her job and hold Daisy and her meager savings stable hit her hard. But beneath the happy there were some vague niggling doubts. She would be reliant on the kindness of Sofia, just like she had been with Marion. She hated moving into another tenuous position, but it might be her only option. Still, if Sofia and Adrian broke up or needed money, would she find herself back on the street? It didn't seem like something they would do, but as she'd learned the hard way, life didn't always turn out how you planned. Someday she'd buy a place for her and Daisy, somewhere they could put down roots.

Somewhere she could stop worrying for a minute. Just as soon as their ship came in.

"So we can move you in this week if that works for you. We'll keep the utilities…"

He was still talking when another thought hit her. She wasn't leaving. He wasn't going to be a farewell fling. She couldn't have him. Screwing a coworker who was practically her landlord was a horrible idea. They weren't even sleeping together yet, and she was having trouble keeping her hands to herself. She couldn't breathe. There was no way she'd be able to hide her reaction to him once she knew how good he felt pressed naked against her.

She'd had her one night of freedom, and now she was going to pay for it. She'd spent seven years being strictly professional, just to throw it away on one rosé-drenched evening she hadn't even gotten off on. If she gave in to her desires now, everyone would find out. On a set this small, there were no secrets.

The memories of everyone staring at her, knowing her business and judging her harshly, came flooding back. Just like that, she was nineteen again and knocked up, trapped in a crappy situation.

She had taken Kyle out for dinner to tell him about Daisy. She'd thought he'd be as excited and nervous as she was. She'd thought they could celebrate together. She'd thought wrong.

He'd gone stone-still when she'd slid the precious pregnancy test across the table.

"What the hell kind of practical joke is this?"

"We're going to have a baby."

"Correction: you're going to have a baby."

"I thought you'd be happy." She wrapped her arms around her still-flat belly, as if she could protect her baby from his anger.

"Happy that you're going to get super fat and unfuckable? You're going to get all stretched out down there, and you're going to have a crying brat hanging around. You stupid bitch. How could you be so careless?" His voice rose along with his body, until he was standing, leaning over her, nearly shouting in the middle of the casual family diner.

"Kyle, sit down. Let's talk about this."

"Talk about the fact that you were dumb enough to get pregnant? If you expect me to pay for that mistake, you're dreaming."

He'd walked out on her then, and left the rest of the restaurant studiously looking at their plates while sneaking glances at the girl crying alone at her table.

She'd thought Kyle wanted her. They had even talked about moving in together. But then he'd called their baby a mistake. She'd tried to talk to him several more times, and each time his questions and reactions had gotten more vicious. It was all her fault. She'd ruined everything. No one would want her once she had the kid and stretched out her tight little body. Why didn't she just get rid of it? She had taken every verbal hit and absorbed it deep to her core. After trying to work things out for nearly two months, he'd disappeared. He'd left her without a word or a penny of support. It hadn't taken her long to get the hell out of the town where everyone she met stared at her belly, wondering and whispering.

She would not go through that again, especially not with these people she liked. She'd heard enough gossip in her chair to know exactly what people would say when their subject was out of earshot. Who she slept with was no one's business but hers. She couldn't put her reputation and Daisy's happiness on the line for a fling. Not if she was going to stay.

She hauled in a deep breath and held up her hands to stop Enzo's ramble and her panic.

She didn't even know if this apartment idea was going to work. *One step at a time. Don't borrow trouble.*

The platitudes weren't helping, and her words came out rushed. "Whoa, slow down, Enzo. I don't even know where she lives, or if the house will be okay for Daisy. Oh God! Does she know about Daisy?"

And so it began. She had tried so hard to keep her private life private. People made snap judgments about her when they found out she was a single parent, and none of them were flattering. She hated thinking that Sofia would look at her differently now.

"I told her, but I asked her to keep it to herself. And yes, she's fine with Daisy living there. She even offered to leave it furnished or take out stuff that isn't kid friendly. I can take you over there today at lunch. We'll walk through, and you can decide if it will work."

She could tell she'd taken some of the shine off his happy, but she had to be realistic, rational, grounded. She was the responsible adult in her life. She had to think about what was best for her and Daisy. She refused to simply take what she wanted, like her mother always had. Sometimes adulting was a real bitch.

And damn it, if his hard work on her behalf meant she couldn't have his hard body, she be very cranky about it, but she'd give him up anyway. It had been stupid to dream. She did better with her feet firmly grounded in reality. Daisy needed her to remember that.

"Okay, we'll go over at lunch. Now, let's get you sprayed down."

If her hands lingered and stroked more than absolutely necessary, well, there was only so much temptation a girl could resist.

ON THE DRIVE over to Sofia's place, Natalie held her tongue. Now that the potential of staying had taken root in her mind, she didn't know what to say to Enzo. She'd opened a big can of worms at karaoke. She wondered how big his "worm" really was…and shut that thought down fast. See? This was why she didn't go out. She didn't need any extra drama in her life. She was forever picking the wrong guy at the wrong time. This was supposed to be a quick fling on her way out of town, and now it was just going to be a long awkward. How did she tell him that even though she'd given him all the signals, and he'd even found her a place to live, she had to back away from the attraction that was clearly driving them both crazy?

"Here we are." Enzo's announcement pulled her from her thoughts.

She checked the street signs and realized she knew exactly where they were. The school was less than half a mile away. They had parked in front of a cream-colored, stuccoed, two-story apartment block on a quiet street. The front yard sloped down to the street with beautifully symmetrical flowering garden beds and trimmed hedges flanking a central walkway. Daisy would love exploring all those flowers. And it looked like there were some raised beds for herbs and tomatoes tucked around the side. Maybe Daisy would finally get to plant something and stay to see it grow.

There weren't any bikes or toys out on the balconies though. Would Daisy be welcome in a building full of older residents? Did Natalie have room to be picky? Yes. She would always be picky when it came to Daisy's well-being.

"My parents own the entire building. It's an investment property we help them manage. I've known all the other tenants in the building for over ten years, and they are great people. I wouldn't suggest it for Daisy if there were any doubt in my mind."

He was vetting the apartment building tenants for her baby's safety? When was the last time someone had helped share the load of ever-present worries about her child? He opened a door in her heart and allowed a dangerous fantasy inside. She slammed that door shut, trying to assess the building, but not fast enough. A wisp of the fantasy remained, tempting her.

The location worked. It wasn't too far from her current place, so she already knew the neighborhood. Daisy could stay at her current school, and she could still go to Mrs. Félice. Lots of plusses.

Enzo unlocked the front door and swung it open, allowing her to enter first. "Welcome home!"

Natalie gasped when she looked inside, and not in a good way. *Oh dear God.*

Sofia clearly had never been around children if she thought this apartment was even remotely kid friendly. Beautiful white leather sofas, pale carpets on dark hardwood floors, and bright pink and green woven accent pillows and throws pulled together a gorgeously designed room. Natalie had appreciated Sofia's genius with textures and color at work on their various job sites. She often strolled through the rooms near the end of renovation, just soaking in the beauty. She had no doubt the rest of the apartment would be just as stunning…and stainable. All she could see when she looked at the living room was spilled grape juice on the carpets, sneaker streaks on the hardwood, and marker stains on those couches. Daisy was not a neat and clean kind of kid. Nat pictured her sprite sitting on those white sofas, spreading out her daily haul of nature's treasures, and cringed.

"I don't know if this is going to work."

Enzo stepped in behind her and placed his large, warm hands on her shoulders. Momentarily distracted by the novelty of the comfort they conveyed, she allowed herself to be propelled farther into the apartment.

"Wait, you haven't even seen the rest of the place. So, you've got the main living space here. The counter separates the kitchen, but gives you a breakfast bar on this side. You'll be able to see your daughter while you cook."

He led her down the short hallway, barely letting her glance at the stainless steel and marble finishes in the cute little kitchen.

"And here are the two bedrooms."

Natalie's eyes popped wide. "Two? Enzo, I can't afford—"

"Yes, you can. How much were you paying at your other place?"

"Eighteen hundred dollars a month, including utilities, for one bedroom and shared common space."

"Sofia is going to charge you what she pays for this place."

"I know, Enzo. I know exactly what this square footage goes for. I've been staring at the market for weeks!"

"Natalie. My parents have owned this building for twenty years, and have charged us the same rent since we moved back in after college. It's just enough to cover one-sixth of the mortgage. Eight hundred dollars."

"No. This can't be real." Natalie's mind was spinning with possibilities. Less than half her rent? She might actually have something to save at the end of the month. The lure of a little financial stability was ridiculously tempting.

"I know it's crazy, but it makes my parents happy to have us close, and it was what we could afford."

Something tickled Natalie's brain. "Wait. We? Us?"

Enzo raised his hand sheepishly and waved. "Hi, neighbor! Frankie is upstairs on the end, and I'm next door."

Neighbors. Her biggest temptation would no longer be just an off-limits work crush, but would literally be the boy next door. She bit her lip to control the tingling there as she remembered their kiss. Her eyes traveled over his long, lean frame hungrily. She blushed when she met his eyes and realized she'd been caught.

"That's right. I'll be just the other side of that wall, if you need anything. Come see the bedrooms."

She wasn't sure if she'd read his tone right beneath the words, but the heat of his body pressed up behind her as he followed her into the first bedroom was unmistakable. How was she ever going to handle this?

She stepped into a little girl's pink dream and forgot all about him for a moment. White walls set the backdrop for pretty pictures framed in pale pink, light pink-and-green checked curtains, and brighter pink reading poufs on the hardwood floor. A sweet little desk was tucked into the corner, with a little pile of books on top. The bed had a pretty white wooden headboard and was piled high with pillows of all shapes and sizes and shades of pink. Her baby could have a bed of her own. That alone made it nearly impossible to refuse.

Natalie would have to be very sure before she showed this place to Daisy. She was going to fall in love.

"Sofia had a little fun in here this weekend after we talked about offering it to you."

"Wait. She did this for Daisy? This isn't how her guest room usually looks?"

"Well, it's always had white walls and the desk, but it was her office. I think she moved her computer stuff over to Adrian's, and we pulled out her childhood bed from our storage unit. She got such a kick out of shopping for the bedding."

Natalie was dumbfounded that Sofia had taken the knowledge that she had a little girl, and had used it not to judge her, but to give her the gift of her talent specifically for her baby.

Do. Not. Cry.

She blinked rapidly and wondered how on earth she could thank Sofia for this. It was beyond special. Maybe she could offer to do her hair and makeup for the wedding…

"Are you ready to see your room?"

Her room. She hadn't had a room of her own in a very long time.

Enzo turned her down the hallway and swung the door open as if he was filming a reveal on the show.

She stepped into a bedroom worthy of a boutique hotel. The calm gray-green walls, the acre of white bedspread, the artfully arranged succulents and accessories with little pops of pale pink. Natalie had the ridiculous urge to flop down on that bed and see if she could make snow angels. Could this really be her room? Her retreat? A place to call her own, however temporarily? It would be an amazing backdrop for her videos too!

Enzo soothed his hands down her arms, but only succeeded in raising her goose bumps.

"So, what do you think?" His deep voice reverberated next to the sensitive shell of her ear, and she gasped. "Can we make this work?"

That was a loaded question. Could she answer the layers separately? Her resolve was shaking. With his hot body pressed against her back, overwhelming her good sense, she looked back over her shoulder and lost. She nodded her head, and when his lips brushed against her ear she couldn't contain the moan that escaped from her lips.

Enzo's lips came alive at that encouragement, tracing down the tendons of her neck and leaving little love bites on her shoulders. She reached over her shoulder and wove her fingers through his hair without conscious thought, holding him in place. All of her reticence faded under the bright light of pleasure he turned on in her body. It had been so long since she'd allowed herself to bask in the warmth of affection. Reason blinded, body aflame, Natalie turned into his embrace and let herself burn.

Years of repressed desire broke free, and she scaled his body, searching for purchase. His helpful hands gripped her ass and boosted her as he turned to the wall. Pinned between a wall of plaster at her back and one of muscle down her front, she felt deliciously secure and set her mouth and hands free to explore. Their lips slid and pressed, frantically finding the ways to make each other gasp and shudder. This was no easy, gentle kiss of exploration. This was a claiming.

Sliding under his shirt, she ran her hands over his chest and his shudder reverberated through her body as well. She tweaked his nipple gently and swallowed his groan with her kiss. He was so sensitive, and damn if that didn't turn her on even more. When he squeezed her ass, pulling her closer, her whimper was muffled by his lips. It felt oddly intimate, absorbing the sounds of pleasure from each other. Would he hold on to hers as tightly as she would his? Would he hold on to her? Could she risk finding out?

It was as if the days since karaoke had never happened, and they were picking up right where they left off.

When he palmed her breast through her shirt and bra, her hips rocked hard against him. With her legs wrapped around his waist, she relished how hard he felt pressed between her legs. She was so far gone, she was ready to take him right now, and he hadn't even gotten her shirt off. When she rocked a second time, chasing that pleasure, she felt his body go still and stiff beneath her. His kiss lightened, and he smoothed a hand down her side. Gentling her, soothing her.

Damn. Something had pulled him back to reality, and she kind of hated that he'd been he one to step away from the edge of madness. She should have been the one to keep her head. She had more to risk, more to lose. She also resented that she'd have to start thinking again. Life was so much more fun when she just reacted.

But she was an adult and a parent. She didn't have that luxury anymore, so she didn't complain out loud when her feet hit the floor. Inside, she might have cursed a blue streak, but he'd never know it.

"I'm s—"

Natalie covered his mouth with her hand. "Don't apologize." She'd be damned if she let him add guilt to her disappointment. "I enjoyed that just as much as you clearly did."

"Okay, then I'm not sorry I pinned you against your new bedroom wall and kissed you like a madman. I didn't mean to jump you while I was showing you the apartment."

"So you meant to wait until I'd moved in?"

Natalie laughed as his cheeks pinked beneath his tan, and he grinned. Being able to take a joke was a great quality in a man, if she were looking for a long-term man, which she was not at all, not even a little bit, not even for those hands… But if she were, Enzo would tick all of her boxes.

"Something like that. I *meant* to ask you out again after you got settled in." His smile was easy, and Natalie found herself returning it.

Could it really be this simple? The apartment was an opportunity she couldn't bring herself to refuse. A chance to stay, in a place she could afford, no job hunt, no new school, and a smoking-hot neighbor who was good with his hands? She'd be a fool to turn that all down, and she'd lost the luxury of foolishness long ago.

Which left this situation with Enzo. He would be right next door. There was no way she'd manage to avoid him now. And to be honest, after sampling his wares, she really didn't want to leave him alone. Maybe this could be easy too. He'd seemed to respond well when she asked him to back off at work. Now that she was doubling down on staying, she really couldn't afford to trash her reputation. But if they could keep the happy times away from work… God, her mind was spinning with the possibilities. She'd just have to figure out a way to protect her heart from his charm, because she needed to be able to walk away whole when the happy times inevitably ended.

Mind made up, she stuck out her hand, eager to seal all the deals. "Good. Let's go with that. You can ask me out after I move in. Tell your sister I'll take it."

CHAPTER 7

FIVE DAYS. It had been five whole days since he'd shown Natalie the apartment. Since he'd lost control and convinced temptation to move in next door. He was trying to respect her space at work, and he hadn't had a moment alone with her since that electric kiss against the wall. So if he was sitting by his front window on a Saturday morning, kidding himself that he was comprehending any of the seed catalog in his hands, while anxiously watching for a moving van, it was only to be expected.

Natalie and her little mini-me pulled into Sofia's parking spot, and before she'd even gotten the kid unbuckled, Enzo was out his door and waiting on his stoop. He tucked his hands in his pockets to keep from touching her in front of her child. *God, I've got it bad.*

"Hi there! Welcome home."

As they approached hand in hand, Daisy peeked up at him and asked in a loud whisper, "Who is that giant, Mommy?"

"That's Mr. Valenti. He's our new neighbor, and he works with me on the show. You can say hi if you want."

She peeked out at him from the safety of her hiding place behind her mother's leg. Enzo deliberately knelt down and handed her the keys he'd gotten cut for their apartment. He didn't know much about kids, but he didn't think that being a giant was a good thing.

"Hi. Your mommy is right. I'm Mr. Valenti, but my friends call me Enzo. I hope that we'll be friends."

The six-year-old took the keys and shook his hand like an adult. She held his eye and stepped out from behind Natalie, judging him to be safe. He'd never felt such an instant flood of relief.

"I'm not supposed to talk to strangers, but since Mommy introduced you, I guess it's okay. I'm Daisy. We don't have a cat because Mommy says the apartment says no cats. I found a rock today, and it's my one piece of flair, so I get to keep it. See? It's shiny!"

The odd juxtaposition of the grown-up mannerisms and the little girl voice shook him. He managed to follow most of that, and when she showed him her rock, he grinned. "That's mica."

"No, mister. That's a rock. Micah is a boy in my class."

Enzo shook his head at her quick-witted candor. She was a pistol. "That kind of shiny rock is also called mica. Native Americans used to build it into their pueblo houses which made them glitter in the sun, so the Spaniards thought they had cities of gold. But it was just lots of mica. It makes a good window."

"That's a good trick."

Not really. It had brought about the downfall of many tribes in the southwest, but he didn't think she was ready for that conversation. "It's a soft rock."

"You mean like the station Auntie M liked to listen to? Gag!"

Enzo chuckled along with her. "No, it means if you scratch it with a harder rock, it will leave a mark pretty easily. It likes to flake. You take good care of that."

"Yes, I will." She tucked the shimmering rock carefully into her pocket and gave it a little pat.

"Didi, go get your bag out of the car, and I'll show you your new room."

Just that quickly Daisy's attention was diverted and she was gone, leaving Enzo and Natalie alone on the sidewalk. Standing slowly, and with more snap, crackle, and pop from his joints than a twenty-six-year-old man should have, he smiled, hoping for some sign that she'd missed him too, but her face stayed carefully blank. Was that because her kid was running back already, or had she had second thoughts this week?

"I cleared today, so when the moving van comes, I'm ready and willing to be your cheap labor."

"How cheap?"

Enzo looked around her, noting that Daisy had gotten distracted by his herb garden on her way back, before he answered honestly. "I've been known to move entire houses for a beer and a pizza, but in your case, I'd accept payment in the form of kisses."

Just the thought of more kisses with her was turning him on. He didn't dare let himself think of more than that with her right now or he'd be of little use moving anything heavy.

"So my kisses are the equivalent of pizza and beer? Or maybe you think because I'm a single mom, I'm used to paying my way with physical favors?"

His pleasant thoughts evaporated in his shock. "No! That's not…I don't… Damn it, I didn't mean it that way. I just…crap."

He'd really put his foot in it this time. Luckily, her hard glare only held a moment longer, and then her laughter broke through. Each pulse of amusement vibrated through his chest, and he couldn't feel bad for his poor choice of words. They had given him the gift of her unfettered laughter, and he couldn't regret that.

"You…should see…your face!" she choked out between giggles and gasps for air. She gripped his arm for balance and he had to fight not to pull her in close. She got herself under control more quickly than he liked. "I'll pay you in wine. There's not enough work to warrant splurging on a pizza. You might as well get started. It's all in the car."

She called for Daisy and danced up to the door with her, hand in hand, taking the keys from her daughter and unlocking the next chapter of their lives.

This is it? Her entire apartment, all of her possessions, fit into a tiny Honda Civic? He opened the back door of the car and pulled the first cardboard box out, carrying it into the apartment. He'd always thought kids meant a lot of stuff, but they hadn't seemed to accumulate very much at all.

She joined him once she'd gotten Daisy settled on the couch with a show. Between the two of them, all of her boxes and suitcases were piled inside the door of the apartment in under twenty minutes.

"Here, let me just unpack the kitchen box. There's a bottle of wine in there somewhere."

"Don't bother. I don't even feel like I've earned it."

She bit her tongue, likely trapping whatever smart-assed remark had flown to its tip. He glanced over at Daisy, making sure she was engrossed in…some show with a bear underwater? Whatever. She was zoned out, so he felt safe adding his real thoughts.

"Besides, I'd rather you keep your wine here…for later."

"Don't count on the wine smoothing your way, mister. I've got a few ideas for how you can *earn it*." She kept her voice low, but he loved the way her tone teased him. The rareness made it even more precious. He was so used to her professional mask that every time she stripped it off and let him in, he was surprised by some new quirk of hers. She turned him inside out when she was relaxed and playful like this.

He couldn't resist playing along. "Oh yeah? How's that?"

"Find the box of linens and make the beds." Her deadpan delivery cracked him up. He sorted boxes into rooms while she unpacked and organized her kitchen gear. It didn't take long, so he did unpack the linens and make the beds. So what if he'd spent extra time smoothing the sheets over her bed, wondering if her skin would feel as smooth stretched out across them. For his own sanity, he left her bedroom after tucking in the top sheet tight.

Natalie was still busy in the kitchen, so he sat on the couch to watch the cartoon with Daisy.

She pointed to the screen without looking at him. "That's a narwhal. Did you know his horn is actually a tooth?"

"It must be hard to find a dentist under the sea," Enzo joked, but Daisy didn't respond. She laid her head down on the armrest away from him. Okay, so his kid humor needed some work. Noted.

"Hey Sprite, why don't you go set up your treasures in your room?"

With a sigh the little girl rose and walked to her mother in the kitchen, resting her head against Natalie's belly. "Mommy, I don't feel so good."

Before Enzo even processed what she'd said, Natalie was pulling Daisy farther into the kitchen. Within seconds, the poor girl was retching and coughing.

Enzo bolted for the door.

~

Damn it.

Things had been going so well. They'd had flirty banter, some much appreciated manual labor, and he'd even made an effort to talk to Daisy. Oh well.

Better to know sooner than later that he wasn't dating material. She'd gotten good at discerning a man's parental potential in three dates or less, which is why none of the men she'd tried to date had gotten to meet Daisy. It was also why none of them had ended up in her bed. No one had made the cut. She refused to put Daisy's hopes and dreams on the line for a good-time guy.

Natalie grabbed a towel from the half-unpacked kitchen box. Add a load of laundry to the never-ending to-do list. At least Didi had made it to the tile. Small favors would save her sanity.

"I'm sorry, Mommy." When her little sprite looked up at her

with tears in her eyes, all of the details faded away. Her baby was sick and needed her mama. Everything else could wait.

Natalie scooped up her fifty-pound first-grader in the same move she'd used as an infant, cradling Daisy's head against her chest and her knees over her other arm. Ignoring the mess on her jeans and the floor, she lifted her onto the counter next to the sink for a rinse. With calm fingers, she wiped away Didi's tears and kissed her forehead in the universal mom move that provided comfort and checked for fever in one economical gesture. A little warm, and God only knew where the thermometer was packed. Hopefully it was just a tummy bug and not the flu.

"It's okay, baby. Mommy's got you."

She was the only one who could say that, and she'd keep working like hell to make sure she made good on the promise behind those words.

The front door slammed, and Natalie felt the jolt through her chest. *What the hell?*

Enzo was back.

His arms laden with paper towels, cleaning spray, and a can of Sprite, and his eyes full of sympathy, he'd come back.

Oh. Oh shit.

Natalie's heart flip-flopped in her chest before falling on the floor at his feet.

While she tried to catch her breath, he dropped his offerings on the counter and knelt to wipe off Daisy's feet.

"I unpacked the towels in the bathroom already if you want to put her in the tub."

Natalie boosted Daisy back into her arms, her tongue frozen in her mouth. What could she say to the man who'd so effortlessly scaled her carefully constructed walls? When was the last time a man had offered to help with Daisy? When was the last time she'd let someone close enough to try?

"Go ahead. I've got this." He unraveled more paper towels and began to wipe up the mess on the floor. Tears pricked Natalie's eyes, and she hustled to the bathroom. She couldn't let either of them see her cry.

She rubbed Daisy's back as she threw up again, in the toilet this time, before settling her into a tepid bath. A few sea creatures bobbed happily in the water, and she poured the yellow liquid soap under the running water to make a few bubbles. The comforting scent of baby bathtime filled the room, cutting through the bitter bile. Daisy sat uncharacteristically still while she poured cupfuls of water down her back.

Soothed by the ritual of bathing her child, Natalie tried to reassemble her defenses. Though she wanted to go back out there and take care of everything herself, she talked herself into letting him finish the floors. It would be stupid to turn down help cleaning up. But it would be just as stupid to tumble head over heels just because the man knew his way around a bottle of disinfectant. He could just as easily be a serial killer, adept at hiding his messes. She chuckled at the image of Enzo in Dexter's coat. Okay, maybe not "just" as easily, but a girl couldn't be too careful. *God, I'm really grasping at straws here.*

He was probably just concerned for his sister's stuff, or his parents' investment. He was responsible for bringing her into their space, and if she left the place trashed it would reflect badly on him. Maybe they'd have second thoughts about renting to her with a kid in tow. Maybe this wasn't the reprieve she'd thought it was and she'd still end up leaving for LA. It would put a no-strings fling with Enzo back on the table, or the door, or the floor—

No. Stop it.

She had to stop imagining that anything real with Enzo was possible. A few nights of pleasure, maybe, but long-term? Out of the question. It would hurt too much when it failed. She might not be able to control her body's reactions to the man, but she would damn well control her heart and her mind.

So much was resting on her shoulders, so much riding on her not making any mistakes. She didn't want Enzo to be a mistake, but she would have to play this very carefully to make sure he didn't become one.

Natalie pulled her anxieties and her baby close, both her constant companions. She lifted Daisy from the tub and enfolded her in a big mama bear hug under the guise of drying her off. This. This was what she could count on.

She found Daisy's bright yellow and white suitcase and pulled out her favorite pair of pajamas. Leaving her to get dressed, Natalie went back to the kitchen to find an emergency puke bowl and some Sprite.

A sparkling clean floor greeted her.

"Is she okay?" Enzo was pouring the Sprite into a small plastic cup he'd unearthed.

Her knees trembled again but her feet braced firmly on the floor against his onslaught of kindness, her earlier heart gymnastics an anomaly.

"She'll be fine. Just a tummy bug, I hope. Thanks for this." She took the glass and the bowl back to Daisy's bedroom. After settling her down in the bed Enzo had made for her, with the bowl, and the Sprite, and her green minky blanket, and her Elephant and Piggie books, and kisses for her eyes and her forehead, Natalie could no longer avoid the inevitable.

She had to talk to him.

She rounded the corner to the living room and pulled up short. Enzo was sitting on the couch with a glass of her wine in a plastic cup with a fairy on it. He was watching Daisy's cartoon.

"I hope you don't mind." He raised his glass in a mock toast as she approached. "I think I earned it now."

The man had just cleaned her kitchen and was joking about it. Sitting on her couch like he took care of sick kids and then watched cartoons every day. Looking like he belonged here in her life. Natalie's heart stuttered again. *Traitor.* She was going to have to be careful with this one. He was dangerous.

He raised a second cup in her direction. "I saved the pink one for you. Come sit down a minute. You've earned this too."

Natalie took a sip to conceal her confusion and perched on the far armrest of the beautiful white couch that had narrowly escaped ruin. She'd have nightmares about that for sure. She still needed to buy a slipcover… And some cleaning supplies…

"How can I help?" Enzo's quiet question pulled her from the mental to-do lists that gave her the illusion of control in her chaotic life.

She didn't even know how to respond to that. So she went with blunt honesty and let the question on the tip of her tongue fly. "Why are you still here, Enzo?"

"You don't have a very high opinion of men, do you?" When she declined to answer his question, he continued. "I'm still here because as I told your daughter, my friends call me Enzo. I'm your friend, Natalie, and friends help each other."

"Is that what we are, Enzo? Friends?"

"I'd like to think so." He reached over to take her small hand in his strong one.

She let it linger, and he tugged her down onto the couch next to him. "Do you kiss all of your friends up against a wall?" She tried to pull her hand back from him as she pushed him away with more words. His thumb traced over her knuckles and dissolved her hand into jelly.

"I didn't say that we were just friends. Can't we be friends and more?"

"I don't know. I've never had that happen before."

"Me either, but I've heard it exists."

She succeeded in getting her hand back, shaking it a little to get rid of the feel of his fingers, and shifted her wine glass into it so he couldn't pull her back in.

"So, what, now we're the unicorns of the dating scene?" She took a deep sip of her wine.

"Better than being the Chupacabra…"

She spit her wine back into her glass to avoid shooting it out her nose. Damn, he made her laugh. Why was that so damn sexy? Maybe it was the way he grinned at her every time she let loose a chuckle that turned her insides to mush. Maybe it was the novelty of having a man take the time to chat with her and figure out what tickled her. It had been a very long time since she'd been able to claim a male friend.

"True. Okay, so we'll be unicorns." Mythical creatures. Together until we aren't, she reminded herself. *Gotta keep it real.*

CHAPTER 8

"Take these broken wings and learn to fly."

It was eight o'clock Sunday night, and Enzo sat at his computer, reluctantly searching for information on how to write a business plan. His large drafting desk was pressed right up against their shared wall though, so what he was actually doing was inadvertently listening in to bedtime.

Daisy's bedroom was just the other side of the wall of his office. He'd never noticed how thin the walls were when Sofia had lived next door. Then again, that room had been her office, not the bedroom of a bright, mischievous six-year-old.

Their murmured conversation of seemingly endless questions had caught his attention nearly an hour ago. He figured it was bedtime next door, and he'd been happy to be distracted from his internet research. He couldn't make out the words, but the cadence of their voices was a familiar pattern. One higher voice pitching up, the lower voice ending on a down note, with a sprinkle of giggles.

Memories of his own childhood flooded him with a bittersweet pleasure. His mother had always handled their barrage of questions at bedtime. He could picture the old bedroom he'd shared with Gabe so clearly.

"But Mom, did you know that the Venus flytrap eats bugs?" Enzo had been fascinated with the carnivorous plants in first grade.

"I'm sure it does, but just like little boys who are supposed to eat their broccoli, I'll believe it when I see it."

"But Mom, why?"

"Well, flies are good for the plants, and veggies are good for growing boys." Jo Valenti had always replied with the calm logic of a parent refusing to be deterred from their point.

"I'd rather eat the bugs," Gabriel had muttered.

"I heard that. Maybe I'll cook you some crickets for dinner." His mother's face had twisted in a particularly maniacal grin. "No, I know! Brussels sprouts!" She had always loved to threaten them with their most reviled foods, but she never made good on the threats.

There weren't many things he wouldn't eat if they were cooked the way his mom made them.

He missed those days. Arguing with Gabe over anything and nothing, getting a few snippets of his mom's attention, cuddles and songs at bedtime until he got too old for that... When had he gotten too old for that? He'd been such an idiot as a kid. He thought sharing those moments with his own kids someday might be a close substitute.

Until Natalie had started singing, he'd been able to confine himself to nostalgia, but her low and soothing rendition of the Beatles' classic was pulling him into the present.

He pictured the two of them, cuddled up in bed, freshly bathed and sleepy. The sweetness of the image warmed his chest with longing. Could there be room for one more?

That thought shook him out of his meandering daydreams. Where the hell had it come from? Had he seriously just gone moony over the idea of a family? He was twenty-six, single and unattached, contemplating throwing away a good job and stepping into the unknown. This was the worst time to think about adding responsibilities and expectations to his plate. He had plenty of those he was disappointing already.

His habit of stretching himself thin to help everyone was already coming back to bite him. Years of trying to keep people happy by making things easier for them had left him with empty pockets and an empty heart. He still didn't know how to say no. He'd have to figure that out quick once he was out on his own. And he really needed to be out on his own.

Living in the apartment his parents gave him, working for the family company, sticking with little projects that made him next to no money—it all made him feel like college had been a waste. Why had he busted his butt at school to just come home and do the same old shit?

That's why he was researching business plans. He wanted to work on larger spaces, private commissions, and special event properties. He dreamed of large-scale parks and museum installations. He could design a small yard in his sleep. He was bored, and that was all he was going to be doing for the next forever if he stayed with Valenti Brothers.

He needed to focus his energy on himself and his ambitions if he was going to succeed.

Adding Natalie and Daisy to his list would set him even farther back. But hell, three days into his new neighbors' lease, and he was pretty sure he'd do anything Daisy asked. He refused to let that little girl down. He would just have to figure out how to keep his distance.

Sure. Easy.

He had a great track record with boundaries.

Friends? Sure, he could handle that. A few benefits with Natalie thrown in? Even better. But daddy try-outs? Nope. Not a good idea.

"All your life, you were only waiting for this moment to arise."

No matter that he tried to refocus on his research, he hummed along under his breath.

EXHALING DEEPLY, Natalie washed her brushes and laid them out to dry. Her head pounded against the confines of her skull and all she wanted to do was go home and sleep for two weeks. Sprite had been sick all weekend, but the fever had broken Sunday morning, and she'd woken this morning right as rain and ready for school.

True to form, Natalie was now fighting the same virus, delayed a few days to make sure she was extra tired and run down from fighting it in her kid. Thanks, Mother Nature. Thankfully, she'd made it through most of her work day before the sledgehammers had set in. She'd managed to finish a bit early, and she was going to ask Jake if she could leave. Once she got Sprite home, she could just curl up and try not to die for fifteen whole hours.

Please, God, let that be enough for me to feel human again.

She closed her eyes and leaned her head against the mirror, as if not seeing her pale and sweaty reflection would make her feel less like a sick six-year-old herself.

This happened at the beginning of every new school or daycare. The kids all traded the germs they'd collected over the summer during the first week of school, and it would be nearly Christmas before they'd made all the rounds. Luckily, Daisy was a pretty resilient kid. It never took her more than a few days to recover.

The downside was that each illness threw their lives into turmoil. If Daisy couldn't go to school, Nat had to find a friend or a sitter willing to watch a sick kid. Mrs. Félice was marvelous, and she had been so understanding about Natalie still dropping Daisy off in the mornings. But she was an older woman and Natalie hated the thought of putting her at risk of getting sick.

At least this time Daisy had gotten sick on a weekend, so Natalie hadn't had to scramble or miss work. Lost hours meant late bills and stress headaches.

So she slogged through her own day, cranky and chilled to the bone, just trying to make it to three o'clock.

"Whoa! You look like hell."

Her eyes snapped open to glare at Enzo. "Just what every girl wants to hear."

Unfazed, he leaned in and put a hand on her forehead. "You're hot. How's that?"

A reluctant chuckle escaped between her frown.

"You caught Daisy's bug didn't you?"

Natalie nodded weakly and instantly regretted it when her head swam and she swooned. Enzo caught her against his side before she could fall. Or had she already fallen and not hit the bottom yet? His arms around her felt so sturdy and stable, she thought she wouldn't mind falling if he would be there to catch her.

"How's she feeling today?"

"All better. She went back to school this morning."

"Then why the hell didn't you stay home?"

The judgment in his voice pricked her pride, and with the last ounce of her energy, she straightened her spine and pulled her head off his shoulder. She should have been ready for that. She didn't have the luxury of trusting that she could lean on someone for support. "That is none of your business. I have a job and responsibilities, and I don't need you or anyone else judging me. I can take care of myself."

"I never said you couldn't. But as your friend, I'm telling you, you look awful, and you should go home."

Natalie wanted to put her foot down and stay to the end of her day, just on principle, but she was afraid she'd actually pass out.

Enzo turned and bellowed out of the garage. "Jake? Yeah, come here a second."

Natalie gripped Enzo's arm, digging in with her nails to get his attention. "What the hell do you think you're doing?" she hissed through gritted teeth.

"Getting Jake in here to tell you to go home, since you won't listen to me."

"Out of fucking bounds, Valenti. I'm handling it."

The stubborn glint in his eyes shot steel through her veins. She hadn't backed down when her mother had called her a slut and stupid for keeping the baby. She hadn't bent when Daisy's kindergarten teacher had given her a nasty look when she'd explained why they didn't need to wait for Daisy's dad. If he thought he could just step in and take control of her life because they'd smooched a few times and he'd been nice to her kid, he had another think coming. No one told Natalie what to do. She wasn't going to let him make Jake think she couldn't handle her job.

When Jake rounded the door of the garage, Natalie cut Enzo off.

"Hi, Jake. I finished up for the day. Do you mind if I head out a little early?"

"Sure, go ahead. We'll need you on the Giles' project tomorrow morning. You have the address?"

Natalie patted her phone. "Sure do. See you tomorrow, and thanks."

Gathering up her last reserves of energy, she picked up her kits and headed for her car.

"What did you need?" Natalie overheard Jake ask Enzo.

"Never mind. It can wait." His voice was already traveling in her direction. Before she made it halfway down the driveway, his long strides had caught him up. "Here, let me carry these."

He tried to take one of her cases, and she instinctively tightened her grip. "I've got it. I'm fine."

"No, really, let me help."

"Oh, like you were going to help with Jake when I told you I had the situation under control? Don't you have a ditch to dig or something?"

"No, I have a friend I'm trying to help right now. The ditches can wait." He tried again to take a carrying case from her, and she tugged hard in the opposite direction, popping the clasp. The case flipped open, showering the driveway with the top layer of the kit. Small pots of eye shadow and various liner pencils scattered onto the concrete, leaving a glittery trail as they rolled into the mulch.

"Damn it, Enzo. I was balanced. And those are expensive!" She dropped to her knees, harder than she meant to as a wave of dizziness hit her. His hand on the small of her back as he crouched next to her snapped her back straight again and she glared. No wonder she was dizzy. The whiplash of attraction and annoyance whipped her back and forth, frothing her nausea to its breaking point.

At her glare, he raised his hands and backed away. "I was just trying to help. I'm sorry."

Natalie threw her precious jars into the case haphazardly, desperate to leave. Her throat clenched and her stomach pitched. *Not here. Oh, God, no!*

Abandoning her kits in the middle of the driveway, she sprinted to the sewer at the curb, barely making it in time to send her lunch down the drain. Yep, she had definitely caught whatever Daisy had.

And now she'd thrown up at work. She couldn't hide her illness from her boss anymore. If Enzo had just let her handle it—but no, he'd had to push and now not only had he seen her daughter at her worst, he was witness to her embarrassment too.

She had some baby wipes still stashed in her trunk, despite the fact that Daisy was well out of diapers, for just such an emergency. Her mascara was likely halfway down her face at this point, and she just needed the cool cloth on her face for a minute before she drove home.

Turning to find her car, she was stunned to see Enzo holding her kits properly closed and the door to her car open. Ignoring him, she popped the hatch and cleaned up with the wipe that always brought back Daisy's baby smell and a smile. Even now, that scent took her back to those early heady but terrifying days of parenthood, when she'd suddenly realized that another human was entirely dependent on her for survival and happiness. The memory of long days and longer nights and sacrifices and Daisy's first steps rushed her. She'd already sent part of her heart out into the world to wander around vulnerably. She simply didn't have enough left over to give into the keeping of this man.

Priorities.

"Can I drive you home?"

Why were they so hard to remember around this man? She was mad at him, wasn't she? And here he was with that relentless friendliness. How was she supposed to fight kindness? Cynical logic? She'd give it a shot.

"What about your truck?"

"I can have Frankie give me a ride back over here tomorrow."

"That's okay. I don't want to make more work for anyone. I'm fi—"

"I know you're fine." He cut her off, shoving her kits in the trunk in a rare show of temper, before slamming it closed. "But I'm worried about you. Let me help."

She had such a hard time accepting help, mostly because she never felt like she could return the favor and hated feeling indebted to someone. She'd never be able to pay him back. She had just enough time and energy to get herself and Daisy through the day. And here this man had already done more for her in the last month than anyone else had in years. The favors were racking up on his side, and she couldn't even conceive of how to balance the scale.

Only the fact that he didn't see it as a debt made accepting his help at all tolerable. Then again, maybe he was just waiting to collect.

Another wave of dizziness hit and she swayed against the bumper. Honestly, the idea of curling up in the passenger seat and letting someone else be responsible for ten minutes was so tempting, she'd have let a mouthy Uber driver take her home.

"Fine. You win. You can drive me home, but for the record I can take care of myself."

"You shouldn't always have to."

His careless words split open a hole in her heart. She fought back tears. *Not an option, dude, but thanks for rubbing it in.*

"Whatever." She tucked what was left of her raggedy shields around her in the passenger seat and closed her eyes. "We have to swing by the school for Daisy."

"No problem."

Damn him. Why did he sound like he believed that? Why did she want to believe it too?

CHAPTER 9

ENZO PULLED UP at the school. What the hell had come over him? Hadn't he decided he was going to stay out of her life? And here he was, sucked right back in. He just couldn't stand to see her struggle under her burdens when he could help her carry them. And yes, he knew that was his problem, but he'd tear that apart another day. Today, she needed him, whether she wanted to or not. He was just trying to do the right thing.

Since Natalie was looking green again, he left her dozing in the car and strolled toward the playground where the kids had all dropped their backpacks to play after school. Daisy saw him and stopped midstride, her eyebrows furrowed and her ponytail askew. She was suspicious. *Good girl.*

"Why are you here?"

"Your mom is sick, so I'm driving her home. She asked me to pick you up."

"What's the password?"

"The password?"

"I don't leave with anyone but Mommy or Mrs. Félice without a password."

Shit. Natalie hadn't mentioned a password before she'd fallen asleep against the window. And now he looked like a creeper on the playground. But he couldn't fault the little girl for double-checking. He was glad she had a safeguard in place, even if it was inconvenient right now. "Is your teacher still here?"

"Yes." Daisy folded her arms across her chest, clearly trying to figure out his scheme.

"Would you ask her to walk with you over to your mom's car?"

"Is my mom in the car?"

"Yes, but she's sleeping. Go wake her up. I'll wait here until you talk to her, and then you can wave and let me know I can join you. Does that work?"

"I guess that would be okay." She shrugged but ran to grab her bag and her teacher's hand. He was too far away to hear the explanation she offered her teacher, but when the older woman made eye contact, he sent her his least-threatening, most-angelic smile. The one that had always convinced his mom it was Gabe's fault. It must have worked, because the pair walked hand in hand toward the idling Civic. A knock on the window and Daisy climbing into the back seat meant Natalie had woken up. Her teacher waved, and he jogged over to the car. He would have loved to let her rest, but his sleeping beauty didn't have that luxury. He'd just have to pamper her a little when he got her home.

~

When they got to the apartment, Natalie had fallen back asleep despite Daisy's chatter about her day. Enzo turned off the car and handed the keys to the little girl. "Remember how yucky you felt this weekend?"

She nodded.

"Well, I think your mom caught it too, so she's going to feel yucky for a few days. But don't worry. I'll help out until she feels better."

There was that suspicious, silent stare again. So much

distrust. It was jarring to feel it from Natalie, but even more so to get it from her child. How many times had she been let down that she immediately defaulted to disbelief in the face of an offer of help?

He let her out the back door and walked around to the passenger side. Daisy raced ahead to unlock the apartment, so he was alone when Natalie all but tumbled into his arms as he opened the door.

"Wha? Huh? Where?"

"Shhh, we're home. I'm going to get you inside and settled."

"I can walk." She struggled to lift her head from his shoulder.

"Sure you can, champ, but why don't you let me carry you anyway? It's good for the ego." Ridiculous pride swelled in his chest when she chuckled and tucked her head against it.

"Okay, you win. Just this once." Closing her eyes, she relaxed in his arms, and he felt ten feet tall. Carrying her over the threshold felt oddly intimate, and he gave in to the urge to press his lips to her forehead.

"Does she have the fever?"

"Huh?"

He'd forgotten for a moment that he had a pint-sized audience who wouldn't understand him kissing her mother.

"Mommy kisses me like that to see if I have the fever. If I'm hot, I gotta have the grape medicine. Maybe Mommy should have some." The waver in her voice broke his heart.

He wanted to pull her up into a hug and tell her everything was going to be all right. But that would probably freak her out even more. He could give her the truth though. Her trust he'd have to earn. "She's just a little warm. I'll give her some of the grown-up fever medicine before I go get dinner started."

Enzo settled Natalie in bed and resisted the urge to tuck her in. She wouldn't appreciate it. He grabbed the garbage can from her bathroom and left it by the head of the bed along with a box of tissues.

Back in the living room, Daisy sat alone on the big white sofa, carefully still, holding her hands clasped tight in her lap. "I can make peanut butter and jelly. Mommy lets me use the knife."

She was just as determined to go it alone as her mother was. Time to earn some of that trust. "No knives while I'm gone. I'll get the fixings for chicken soup, and you can help me chop the carrots. Deal?"

"Deal."

He knelt down in front of her and held out his hand. "We've got to shake on it, so you know you can trust me, and I know I can trust you."

Daisy stared at his hand for several long moments, before she unclasped her hands and tentatively placed her tiny hand in his. He'd never felt so large and awkward as he did holding her fragile belief in his hands, terrified he'd drop it.

"You're not handling this alone, Daisy. I'm going to help, like I promised. I just need to grab some stuff from my apartment. Do you want to make another password so you'll know it's me when I knock?"

A glimmer of a smile tweaked her lips. Enzo counted it a win.

"The password is…narwhal."

He matched her grin, and flipped on the TV to her favorite show. "You've got it, kid. I'll be back in under ten minutes. When I get back I want to know a new Octo-fact, okay?"

"Okay, Mr. Valenti."

"Remember, my friends call me Enzo."

"Okay, Enzo."

Natalie woke to dusky sun coming in through the windows. Her head throbbed and her stomach pitched. Rolling, she found the trash can that had been moved closer by some kind soul. *Enzo.* Vague memories tried to surface before she got distracted again by the demands of the stomach virus.

She owed him for the ride home. Though she could have

managed on her own, it had been nice to have a little help. She'd call him right after she checked in on Daisy. How long had she been alone in the apartment while Natalie had slept? Guilt pinched at her, but she shoved it away. She was doing the best she could.

Slowly, she pushed herself to sitting, as if by moving in slow motion she could somehow not piss off her gut again, and listened for the telltale sounds of her daughter in the apartment. The reassuring strains of the *Octonauts* theme song greeted her. Her baby needed dinner. Confident that if she moved at a turtle's pace she'd make it to the kitchen without falling over, Natalie pulled herself out of bed and leaned heavily against the wall as she made her way to Daisy.

A peek into the living room pushed her to standing way too quickly, shock and panic sending her reeling into the opposite wall, and then to her knees as the room spun.

The couch was empty.

From her position on the floor, Natalie could see that Daisy wasn't in the kitchen either. There was a pot of something bubbling on the stove, and a new panic rose in her chest. Had Daisy been messing with the stove while she'd been out cold? Oh my God, she could've blown the place up! It was too quiet in here. Despite the bubbling pot and the TV show nattering away, there was no other sound to indicate that her child was anywhere in the apartment. Daisy was never silent.

Fighting to draw air past the tight grip panic had on her throat, she whispered, "Daisy?" She forced her voice louder as she crawled to the front door. *"Daisy?"*

By sheer force of will she pulled herself up the door frame and opened the front door, which was unlocked. Daisy knew better than to leave a door unlocked. *Something must've happened!*

"DAISY!" she screamed, her voice hoarse from fear and bile.

"Over here, Mommy!" Daisy popped up from behind the hedge in the front yard and ran to her. Relief dropped Natalie to her knees on the porch as the adrenaline holding her up dissipated. Tears leaked from her eyes as she pulled her baby into a too-tight hug. "Are you okay, Mommy? Does it hurt?"

"No, baby. I'm fine. I just got a little worried when I couldn't find you. You know you're not supposed to go outside alone."

"But I didn't, Mommy. Enzo and I are making a fairy garden. Come see!"

Just then Enzo rounded the corner, calling out to Daisy with a child-sized shovel in his large dirt-stained hands.

"I found the shovel, but I…oh! You're up! Should you be out of bed?" He dropped the small trowel and hurried up the porch. His strong hand at her elbow gave her the strength to stand.

"A fairy garden?"

"Daisy mentioned that you sometimes go on fairy walks after dinner, so we thought we could make them a nice place to come and play closer to the house so you don't have to walk so far while you're sick."

She peered over the hedge where they had cleared a small patch of mulch beneath a gap in the junipers. She recognized Daisy's collection of rocks and leaves from their rambles piled neatly beside it. Her daughter had a smudge of dirt on her cheek that did nothing to hide her dimple as she grinned her jack-o-lantern smile.

"See, Mommy? It's gonna have a house and a yard and a playground and everything!"

"I do see, but we should see about getting you fed. Say thank you to Mr. Valenti."

"But I already ate, Mommy. And we're friends now so I get to call him Enzo. Aren't you guys friends too?"

She wasn't ready to navigate that minefield of a conversation in this state.

"Of course we are," she reassured her too-perceptive daughter. "What did you eat?"

"Enzo made us grilled cheese, and we got to make chicken soup from itch for you! You gotta try to eat some. It's good for you when you're sick."

"From scratch. It's simmering on the stove, or I can stash it in the fridge for later if you don't feel up to eating." Enzo tucked his hands into the pockets of his jeans.

Was it possible for her body to feel attraction even as sick as she was? Surely it was just vertigo. "Why don't you go in and clean up, Sprite? We'll do your reading homework."

"Enzo helped me do that too. He signed the log and everything. I want to keep building." The whine creeping into Daisy's voice and the setting sun behind her meant it was past time to get her in the tub.

"Well, I want to hear the story. In you go, young lady."

"But, Mommy…"

"Hey, Daisy-D. It's getting too dark to dig safely. Why don't I come by after school tomorrow, and we can keep working on it then."

"And you'll bring the sand for the playground?"

"You bet."

"Okay." The drooping shoulders and shuffling feet as Daisy brushed past her tugged at Natalie's guilt string again. But she only had a little energy to spare right now, and she couldn't afford to indulge her daughter tonight. Hell, she understood the desire well. She wanted to curl up with Enzo and not leave either, but she had to get Daisy in bed before she crashed again herself. Still, a head start into the tub wasn't such a bad idea, so she lingered a moment in the glow of sunset alone with Enzo, tempted but wary.

"Driving me home, cooking dinner from itch, playing with my kid? What's your game, Mr. Valenti? You got some kind of hero complex?"

Natalie had been teasing, but Enzo's eyes shuttered. He stepped off her porch and tucked his hands in those damn pockets again as he walked to his own.

"Just trying to help a friend. You've got a great kid there. Feel better soon."

He was tucked behind his own door before she could figure out how her foot had ended up in her mouth. Damn it.

～

NATALIE SHOVED HER HAIR back from her face and huffed out a breath at her just-rolled-out-of-a-sickbed-look in the mirror. Her pale face and tired eyes weren't going to be easy to conceal, but she had skills. She was a professional. Angela, the woman they hired for evening coverage, had filled in for her Tuesday, but Natalie couldn't afford to miss another day of work. Wednesday was office day, so they'd be filming inside and nearby. And she hadn't thrown up since yesterday morning. She might not feel one hundred percent yet, but the worst had passed and she was ready to get back to work.

She began to fix her face in the early dawn hours, scrubbing and exfoliating until a hint of pink returned. She'd just patted her face dry when her cell phone rang. Mrs. Félice's name flashed at her. *Oh no.* An early morning call was never a good sign.

Two minutes later, her fears were confirmed. The older woman had caught the bug too, and it was hitting her hard. Natalie felt awful, but forced herself to click into triage mode instead of wallowing in her guilt. She ran through her list of kid-inappropriate curses in her head. When that failed to make her feel better, she leaned her head against the mocking mirror and let the tears come. When it rained, it poured.

When her tears ran dry, she washed her face and started over. What else could she do?

Enzo drove into the Valenti Brothers Construction office parking lot at six thirty and was surprised to see the little white Civic out front. Surely Natalie needed more than one day off to recuperate. How was she going to recover if she refused to rest? His temper rose to a simmer beneath his calm surface.

She'd accused him of trying to be a hero. She had it all wrong. Gabe had been the hero. Enzo was just trying to be a decent human being. And if she would slow down and take care of herself, he wouldn't have to keep coming to her rescue.

Striding in to confront her, he pulled up short at the sight of Daisy curled up asleep in her school uniform in one chair, and his mother sitting in the other.

"What is she doing here?"

The welcoming smile dropped from Natalie's face at his tone, and she turned her attention back to his mother's cheeks, though Josephine Valenti didn't need makeup to make her beautiful. His mom was perfect just as she was.

"My sitter is sick, and I had an early call time this morning. So she had to tag along."

"You should have called me."

Her eyebrows disappeared beneath her bangs at that. And damn it so did his mother's.

"Why on earth would I call you at the butt-crack of dawn and ask you to make my kid breakfast and take her to school?"

"Because I told you I'm here to help. I'm trying to be your friend, Natalie."

"I wouldn't call a friend and put them out for this. Daisy is my responsibility. I'm her parent, and I've got it under control."

He had no comeback to that, but he was determined to get it through her thick head that she could lean on him. If she weren't so stubborn, she could have taken another day off work, and then Daisy wouldn't have to be out of bed this early. The kid looked exhausted. She might be Daisy's parent, but he was seriously questioning her priorities.

"She can't stay here all day. How are you getting her to school today?"

She put her hands on her hips and her eyebrows lowered ominously. He was just digging the hole deeper.

"Not that it's any of your business, but I'm going to finish up with your mom and Sofia and then duck out to take her."

"She's going to fall asleep at her desk."

At least Natalie had the sense to flush at that, but she bit her lip, silently applying his mother's lipstick.

"Has she had breakfast yet?"

A fierce glare was her only response. Silence stretched, and he realized that was all the answer he was going to get. His temper rose another degree.

It hadn't taken long for Daisy to hook him. She was a sweet kid, with her mother's eyes and an old lady's sarcasm. The fact that she loved anything nature related had broken the ice between them, and three hours of fairy house building had solidified his admiration. For the first time, he hadn't felt awkward while talking to a kid. Cooking dinner together had felt homey, something he hadn't realized he'd been missing. She was an easy kid to like, and the fact that Natalie was being cavalier with her well-being pissed him the rest of the way off.

His mother stepped into the silence, no doubt recognizing the look on his face. "Why don't you let me take her in?"

"I couldn't ask you to do that. You've got scenes today."

"I don't film until nine."

"Seriously, it's fine. This isn't any earlier than she gets up to go to Mrs. Félice's. I can do it."

"It would be a treat for me. None of my lazy children have deigned to give me grandchildren." Enzo blushed at that dig. "So I have to take my kid time where I can get it. She's at Oak Hill right?"

"That's right…"

"All my kids went there. I miss those days." Was his mom getting misty over school drop-offs? "I wonder if Mrs. Cantu is still teaching there. Anyhow, have you got a booster seat for her that I can pop in my car?"

"I do, but…" Natalie had clearly never gone toe-to-toe with Josephine Valenti on a mission. Enzo smiled smugly as his mom steamrolled his…friend.

"Listen, parenting is hard on the best days. On the worst, it's hell. I kind of miss it." His mom laughed, and Natalie joined her. Some silent communication passed between them, and Enzo wished he could tune in to whatever Mom-frequency they were on.

"Okay. That would be a huge help. Thank you. She did have breakfast and has her morning snack in her bag. I'll just go get her seat from my car."

Natalie snatched up her keys and walked past him without so much as a glance.

"You catch more flies with honey, son." His mother met his eyes in the mirror.

"I'm not trying to catch anything."

The denial burned his tongue as he realized he might have just lied to his mom.

"Could have fooled me. Just watch your step. I like Natalie. She's got a lot on her plate."

"That's exactly why I want to help her."

"Is that what you were just doing? Trying to help?"

"She's been sick. She needs to rest."

"She's been a single mom for nearly seven years. I'm pretty sure she knows exactly what she needs to do for herself and her kid. How long have you been a parent, Enzo? When's the last time you had to make a decision that factored in anyone's needs but your own?"

He dropped his gaze and fumed as his mother left to go put the booster seat in her car. He was always putting everyone else's needs before his own. Couldn't she see that? And so what if he wasn't a parent? He could see when a kid was exhausted. If she couldn't, well... He glanced into the mirrors and saw the raw anger on his face. It shook him.

He wasn't this guy. He didn't charge in looking for a fight. He didn't always assume he knew best. That had been Gabe's role, and he'd filled it well. Was Enzo destined to fill the hole left by Gabe's death? Was everyone right in just expecting him to pick up Gabe's mantle?

No.

He hadn't spent his entire childhood fighting not to be painted in the same brushstroke as his brother just to fall into that can of paint now.

He needed to calm down and figure it out before he snapped at Natalie again. He brushed the hair back from Daisy's forehead as she slept on. Whether or not he was pursuing her, Natalie deserved better. Hell, this whole thing had blown up because he thought she deserved better than she was giving herself!

When Natalie reentered the front office, he strode out the back door into the misty morning. He needed some air and some perspective. Hauling peat would help.

~

He was just going to walk away? What the hell? Natalie had been crafting responses to his asshat behavior on her walk out to the car. Now he was leaving before she got a chance to use any of them? Damn it, and damn him too for making her feel like her best wasn't good enough.

She hauled in a deep breath and turned her attention back to his mother as she sat back down in the makeup chair. The woman really was helping her out. The least Nat could do was smile while she finished the woman's makeup.

"You don't have to fake a smile for me, honey. My son doesn't know what he's talking about, and probably deserves every rant you've got running through your head."

Natalie grinned a genuine smile at Jo's uncanny ability to read her mind.

"I wish I could have stayed home today, but I can't afford to lose the hours. And the school frowns on truant days when you're a single mom who moves a lot."

"You don't have to defend a single thing to me. I raised my four while my husband was off building this company into what it is today. I know sometimes the best choice is just the least terrible one." Jo paused and waited until Natalie met her eye in the mirror. "Anyone can see that Daisy is a healthy, happy, precocious child who is well-loved by her mother. Don't let anyone, not even my son, make you doubt that."

Natalie could only nod as tears, threatening to spill over, clogged her nose and tightened her throat. She could withstand all the slings and arrows. Her armor was built for that. It was the kindness of being seen that snuck around the edges to her soft spots. Having another mother validate her struggle and recognize that she was doing the best she could was such a novel experience, she didn't know what to say.

She'd gotten pregnant with Daisy so young, she hadn't really found mom friends. Leaving her hometown for LA hadn't helped. She'd cut ties with her mother and her ex on purpose, but in the process she'd lost most of her high school friendships too.

She'd made a few friends in her cosmetology program, but when they'd headed off for school or work, she'd been headed to the hospital. True, she'd met a few moms through the salons she'd briefly worked at, but changing jobs and then moving up north for the show had taken even those tenuous connections away. She hadn't even realized she missed the support, because she'd never really felt she had it.

"Now, Enzo said you'd been sick?"

"Twenty-four-hour tummy bug that Daisy brought home. I'm fine now, really. You know how the beginning of the school year is."

"Yes, but I'm sure you got behind while you were recovering. Why don't I pick up Daisy from school too? I don't have any plans this afternoon, and you could have a few hours to catch up. I'd love a chance to play Nana. What do you think?"

Natalie's jaw dropped and she hugged Jo hard. "I think I need to make you look as gorgeous on the outside as you are on the inside. Besides, fairy godmothers should always slay. Dom won't know what hit him."

"Dom wouldn't notice unless I hit him with a two-by-four, and even then he'd probably wonder what job site it was missing from. But go ahead. I'll appreciate it just for me."

When Daisy woke and agreed to a cookie-making playdate with Jo, Natalie kissed her on the forehead and sent her off to school. She primed and primped her way through the morning, and when Jake told her that due to a permitting delay he had to cancel all of the on-site shots that afternoon, Natalie had skipped into her happy dance and packed up her kits. If she hustled, she could get a whole week's worth of tutorials filmed AND tackle the laundry. She made a mental list of the Halloween looks she had planned.

1. *Jessica Rabbit*
2. *Venom poster*
3. *Bride of Frankenstein*

One sexy, one scary, one classic with a twist. It was a good start, and she could intersperse them over the next two months. Her favorite holiday would be here before she knew it.

Didi had already settled on being Fawn, the animal fairy, and costume construction was underway. She'd been begging for Natalie to do a video of her Halloween fairy makeup, but Nat was adamant about keeping her daughter's face off the internet for as long as possible. She might put herself out there for the world to see, but that was business. She took reasonable care not to divulge details of her location or personal life. There were some wackos out there.

Once home, she got the first load into the wash, hoping the hot water and detergent would kill any lingering germs, so they didn't get a surprise reappearance of that bug in a few weeks. Then she changed out of her flannel shirt and cami, and into a red bandeau top. She only needed to look like Jessica from the waist up.

She got herself set up and filmed herself silently applying her makeup. She would do voiceovers and play with the speed later. For now, she was free to lose herself in the magic and fun. While she enjoyed working on other people, she was limited to simply boosting their natural gifts. Here she could play with whatever she wanted. It was the one creative outlet she had where she was completely in charge.

She painted her face with movie-grade foundation and contoured in Jessica's high cheekbones. Thankfully the foundation covered any lingering paleness from exhaustion and illness. Layers of primer and purple eye shadow built up the color on her lids. She opted to keep the look an homage, not a cosplay copy or an attempt to animate the cartoon, so she didn't hide her eyebrows or pencil in exaggerated arches. But fake eyelashes were a must.

Her lips were coated in a lush, wet red, but Nat kept it on the natural contours of her lips instead of using a liner to create cartoon-like proportions. This was Jessica Rabbit channeled into real life, over-the-top sex appeal and confidence. She felt Jessica's spirit infuse her with a sensual power, and she rolled and pursed her lips for the camera.

Once her face was set, she combed bold red hair wax into the wisps near her face and shaped the iconic wave despite her shorter tresses. Damn, she looked good, if she did say so herself. A few sultry eye-bats at the camera and a blown kiss goodbye finished the video.

She checked her watch. It had taken her just under an hour. Perfect. With the intro, she could shorten that to ten minutes tops. A quick laundry swap and shower and she could start the next look.

Swapping clothes into the dryer, she moved to strip the linens off the beds. A knock at the door caught her in the hallway, arms full of pink Tinkerbell sheets. *Who the hell could that be?*

She dumped the sheets into the washer and went to peek through the peephole. Her stomach flip-flopped, and not from a stupid virus. *Enzo.*

She was mad at him. He'd made some pretty awful assumptions about her, and she wanted to hear him grovel. She didn't deserve that kind of treatment.

This definitely wasn't the time to resume the incredible kisses they'd been sharing, she reminded her inner vixen. But after channeling a sex goddess for the better part of an hour, her vixen was having trouble listening.

She opened the door, hand on her hip. Stern, mad, NOT horny. "What are you doing here?"

Enzo just stared at her, eyes wide and jaw slack, as if she'd just punched him in the gut. His reaction reminded her of a cartoon, and she stifled a laugh. She'd be lying if she didn't get a secret thrill out of throwing him off his stride. She bit her lip and then rolled them together, waiting for an answer. The way his eyes widened and his pupils dilated made her day.

As long as she was wearing her sex kitten mask, she might as well own it.

"Hello?" She waved her hand in front of his face before deliberately crossing her arms beneath her breasts. True, hers were small compared to Mrs. Rabbit, but from the way Enzo's eyes dropped and lingered, he didn't seem to mind.

"I, uh, I'm… Why do you look like that?"

"Like what?"

He shook his head and didn't answer. Fixing his eyes firmly on the floor, he gathered himself. "Can I come in?"

Natalie stepped back and he followed. She was feeling generous with her time windfall. She could spare him five minutes and maybe work in a few of those epic rants that had been simmering all morning. Except he was smelling like a warm summer afternoon again, and triggering all of her lazy day wants and needs. She fought hard not to notice.

"I wanted to apologize for this morning. I'm sorry."

That took the wind right out of her ranty sails. When was the last time a man had apologized to her without coercion, and meant it? And he did mean it. She could see the sincerity in his eyes. Just like that, her resentments began to float away. She grabbed at them fruitlessly, trying to clutch them inside her chest for cover. Damn it, this sincerity was like kryptonite. She felt her will to resist drifting away.

"I shouldn't have jumped to conclusions. I'm not Daisy's parent, as you said, and I'm sure you were making the best of a crappy situation. I don't know why I got so pissed."

Her resentments were firmly out of reach now, but Natalie sensed a setup and reached for her skepticism defense. "Did your mom make you come over here and apologize?"

"No, but she did call me out on my bullshit. She's remarkably good at that." He leaned against the couch and met her eyes with adorable chagrin.

"It's in the Mom Handbook. Did she tell you I was home?"

"No, after Jake's cancellation, I finished up my paperwork on another job and came home. I saw your car, and thought I'd get this off my chest. I can go get Daisy from school, so you can get back to whatever it is you're getting ready for…"

His eyes took another unsteady trip up and down her body. He was too easy to tease. She believed that Jo hadn't prompted him, but she was pretty sure the older woman had still seen this setup coming. And she'd lost her grip on her mad, which left only her simmering arousal. Those kisses swam back into her mind. It would be a shame to let a free afternoon go to waste. She didn't imagine he would waste her time.

"What do you think I'm getting ready for?"

She stepped closer and then leaned against the back of the couch next to him. Their arms were inches from touching, and she wanted him to close the final distance.

"You don't want to hear that answer," he replied under his breath, eyes still firmly on the floor.

"Oh, I really think I do." She added a breathy whisper to her voice, channeling her cartoon inspiration, inviting him to say what they were both thinking.

"You look like you're going out."

"Coward."

His head snapped up at her disdain, and so apparently did his restraint. "You want to know what I think you're doing?"

"That's what I asked for, Enzo. Tell me what you're thinking."

Her teasing snapped the tether and he turned, pinning her between the couch and his pelvis. His arms trapped her in front of him, and his eyes burned as he stared her down.

She boldly held his gaze and provoked him by licking her lip again. Her inner sex kitten was playing with his desire like it was a ball of yarn, and loving it. It had been a long time since she'd felt this powerful.

"I think you're looking for someone to take to his knees, and I've stumbled across your path."

The image of him on his knees in front of her sent a shudder of desire racing through her body. She borrowed Jessica's words for inspiration. "You don't know how hard it is being a woman, looking the way I do."

"I know exactly how hard it is for me." He stepped in even

closer, and Natalie could feel how hard he was too. *Damn.* And just like that, she was in over her head.

She'd been dancing around this attraction for months already. Now here he was, in her home, clearly turned on. And here she was, child-free, sex kitten awake and ready to play.

There were only so many times she could contour a man's chest without wanting more. Actually that wasn't true. It was his chest specifically she wanted pressed against hers. He was the only one she hadn't been able to keep neatly contained in his "professional" box.

Frankly, she was so tired of all the no's in her life. Today, she was going to embrace "yes." Oh yeah, she was going to embrace the hell out of him.

"Yes."

"Excuse me?" He grinned at her non sequitur, and she matched him tooth for tooth and rocked her hips forward.

"Yes, it is hard." She ran her hand down his impressive length and almost swallowed her tongue. *Good Lord, yes.* "What are we going to do about that?"

He groaned low and thick in his throat, and she wanted to lick that vibration. Goose bumps chased down her spine, and she decided then and there to make that groan her goal for the rest of the afternoon.

More.

"We? Are we a we?"

"Today, we're gonna be." She tugged at his ridiculous belt buckle. Decision made, full steam ahead was her only option. It had been so long. She dropped to her knees to inspect…things.

"Wait, slow down!"

She looked up at him, eyes wide. Was he serious? A woman at his feet, trying to get in his pants, and he wanted her to slow down? She peeked her tongue out of her perfectly glossed mouth and licked her upper lip as slowly as she could manage. His focus snapped back where she wanted it.

"I thought I was supposed to be the one on my knees."

He tugged her up from her knees and bent to take those lips for himself. The moment his mouth met hers, her mind shut off, all her impatience forgotten, her body in full control.

Her senses narrowed to the slide of his tongue against hers as he explored her mouth, slowly now, taking his time. Every lick, every tug, every moan pulled her further under his spell. For so long she had kept everything bottled up. He was uncorking each repressed desire, sipping and sampling his way down her body until she was fizzing over.

He leaned back, breaking their contact, and she instinctively leaned in, chasing that intoxicating feeling. Seeing her lipstick smeared on his face, marking him as hers, lit a fire deep in her belly. This need was primal. Why was he backing away?

"I'm not ready for this."

His words pulled her out of her delightful haze and made her think again. She dropped her gaze to the bulge making itself visible against the front of his jeans, calling him a liar. "All signs point to yes."

"Natalie, I came over here to apologize and pick up your kid from school, not fuck you senseless."

She groaned as that image overtook her imagination and dropped her head to his chest. "Not even if I beg?"

"This isn't how I planned this."

"So? Plans change."

"But the lack of condoms in my pocket does not. I wasn't expecting this, and it's been a long time since I've had a girl-friend. I don't keep my wallet stocked."

"So you're clean?"

"Yes, but also out of condoms." He spoke slowly like she was clearly not grasping that he was trying to protect her.

She grinned. His earnest goodness was so damn cute. "I'm clean too. The boyfriends who make it into my bed have been of the battery-operated variety since Daisy came along."

His jaw dropped. "Six years?"

"Technically closer to seven. My ex bailed pretty early on in my pregnancy, and no other guys seemed worth the trouble after a few dates. And I really don't want to talk about other guys right now. I'm clean and on the pill, and I can't remember the last time I had a sexy man in my apartment *and* reliable child care, so please don't ask me to slow down."

She leaned in and kissed his neck right where it met his shoulder, glorying in the way it pulled her body flush with his again. She loved that *his* scent was strongest at the crook of his neck, like he'd tucked it away there just for her.

"You're sure?" He gasped as her tongue traced his collarbone.

He needed proof? Reassurance that he wasn't taking advantage? She stepped back and whipped the red bandeau top over her head, setting the hook.

"Yes, I'm sure I want you to…what was it you said? Oh yes, fuck me senseless. I'd like that very much."

With her best Jessica Rabbit saunter she walked to her bedroom and reeled him in.

ENZO STOOD FROZEN for a split second, his eyes glued to her swaying ass, wishing she'd dropped her jeans as well. Realizing that she would probably do exactly that when she hit the bedroom got his feet moving in a hurry.

He felt like a car that had only been driven in first gear, once a week to the grocery store, suddenly being sold to a race car driver. His gears were stripped, but damn if he didn't like the speed. He just hoped he could keep up with her.

Seven years of no sex? How was that even possible for a beautiful, vibrant woman like Natalie? Pressure weighed down on his shoulders. He had to make this good. Better than good. Amazing. Epic. She should lose count. He'd better get started. There would be time to talk later, when the requisite blood had returned to his brain.

He made it to the door of her bedroom just in time to catch the way her thumbs hooked into the waistband of her jeans, the way she shimmied her hips to loosen the denim, the way the curve of her ass, covered by a scrap of lace, emerged from the top. The red thong did little to conceal those perfect golden globes. As he watched, she slid that down too, and then there was nothing left between them except his ridiculous clothes.

He had to keep them on just a little longer if he were to have any chance of lasting long enough for his plan. He stalked closer, holding that flirtatious gaze of hers while he placed a hand to her sternum and pushed. She toppled back onto the bed, her breasts bouncing as she landed on her back. Wasting no more time, he pulled her hips to the edge of the bed and gazed at her most private parts. So pretty, so wet already, so trustingly open to him.

He vowed to be worthy of that trust. Her pleasure had become his driving need, not his own.

He dropped to his knees, her mission successful. She slayed him, and he knelt before her, surrendering. He had an absurd vision of swearing fealty to his queen. Then he bent his head and stopped thinking of anything but her. He lowered his lips to her pussy and tasted her. Salty, sweet, uniquely intoxicating. He was drunk on her taste, her textures, her sighs, and he'd only just begun.

She wiped his senses clean and filled them back up with her. Her soft skin, sweet flavors, spicy floral scent, earthy moans. Everything else he experienced in his life would be seen and felt through this new filter and be found wanting. Nothing would ever compare to the beauty of her.

He played, meticulously experimenting with speed and pressure, testing every fold and rise for maximum reaction. He could happily spend hours learning what made this woman tick, and did. Every time her breath started picking up or her hips began to twitch, he shifted his attention, holding back her orgasm until he was content he'd tasted every inch of her. His brain kept a careful tally of her every response.

She liked it hard and fast, just above her clit. With this intimate knowledge, he pushed her over her first quick climax. His cock throbbed painfully against his zipper, and he nearly passed out when she clenched her thighs around his head, riding out her pleasure.

He climbed up the bed, needing to see her face, slack and sated. Moving his lips to her mouth, he gasped, "Again," and kissed her deeply. Starting over, building on the foundation of pleasure he'd laid, he ran his hands over her body. He wanted to keep her in a sensual haze of reaction. He loved being able to make her stop thinking for a while.

She carried so much worry on her shoulders. He ran his hands over the delicate curves that hid her strength, marveling that she'd set those worries down to be with him. Her trust humbled him. She'd said none of the other guys she'd dated had measured up.

He was going to make damn sure he did.

She tried to bring her arms around him, pulling him closer, but he wouldn't be distracted. He wouldn't lose sight of his goal. Today was all about her. He slid lower, and her arms dropped limply on his shoulders. Eyes closed, mouth open, she was completely caught up, and he aimed to keep her there.

Savoring her sensitive breasts this time, he licked and laved her pebbled nipples, one and then the other, alternating his attention and drawing them deep into his mouth. His fingertips traced her velvety curves, marveling at how she felt succulent, soft and dewy like a rose petal. When her hips began to buck off the bed, he listened, sliding one finger, then two into her tight sheath. He matched the rhythm of her hips, and watched as her spectacular ass lifted off the bed, following his hand on each withdrawal.

Was there anything sexier than this woman chasing her pleasure? He'd never experienced anything that came close, and he wanted her to catch it. He kept his pressure firm and steadily increasing, the heel of his hand massaging her clit. She tightened on his fingers, clenching his hand between her legs, her mouth open on a silent scream.

"Go ahead and be loud, baby. The neighbor's not home."

"Gotta...save something...for later," she panted and reached for him again. He swelled with pride.

"Don't you save a thing, Natalie. I want it all."

"Make me." The taunt in her demand pushed him past his last restraint.

He levered off the bed and stripped down in record time. Before she'd even stopped vibrating from her last orgasm, he was sliding inside her. The sensation of her tight sheath pulling him deeper snapped his control. He drove her faster, harder, deeper, loving the feel and sound of his flesh slapping against hers, reveling in the firm grip of her fingers on his ass, refusing to let him pull too far away.

Each mewl and moan was music to his ears, and when he pressed his fingers to her sensitive clit, he was rewarded with her scream as she flew. He chased her over the peak, leaping into the unknown after this woman who held his heart in her hands. He emptied his soul into her, thrusting until every last shudder calmed. He could stay here forever.

He collapsed, half on, half off her, unable to do more while his bones were liquefied. Her small fingers brushed through his hair and sent shivers down his spine. He wanted to purr and snuggle into her touch. Knowing he'd been the first man to please her in years lit him right up.

Her fingers tracing his chest and tapping his shoulder pulled him from his sated haze. "What's this?" Her voice was groggy with satisfaction.

"Sexual bliss?"

She slapped his shoulder lightly and laughed. "No, the tattoo. I've been painting over it for weeks and never asked. What does it mean?"

"The branch is for my big brother, Gabe. He died three years ago. I needed to keep him close."

"How did he die?"

"He deployed in the army with Seth, and didn't make it home. He was the real hero."

"I'm so sorry."

"No, it's okay. It's good to talk about him. Keeps his memory alive."

"Is that why you got mad when I called you a hero the other day?"

"That's part of it. He gave his life serving our country. I could never measure up to that, so no, I'm no hero." Unable to keep his eyes open any longer, he dropped his head back onto the pillow. The last thing he wanted to think about was his failure to live up to his brother's sacrifice.

He was slipping toward sleep when she tapped his shoulder again. "Hey there."

He grunted. Words had not yet returned to him.

"Hey, wake up."

"I need to sleep if you want another round…"

"Listen, I hate to burst your post-coital bubble, but your mom and my daughter are going to be here soon. You need to get dressed and go." She pushed at his shoulder, sliding out from under him.

He sucked in a breath as he slid out of her tight sheath and dropped to the bed. *Damn it.* He wasn't ready for reality to intrude. He wanted more. More of her body, her thoughts, her heart.

"Unless you want Daisy to get a good look at your ass, you'd better move, Enzo. Frankly, I'm not ready to have *that* conversation with her yet." She snapped said ass with a towel before she hustled into the connected bathroom.

How the hell was she full of energy after three orgasms? He was ready for a nap after just one. He creaked and groaned, bending for his discarded clothing. Reluctantly he covered up while he watched her shower.

He wished he'd been invited, but he could wait. He knew he'd hit a lot of milestones today. He'd save this one for another day.

All of her makeup rinsed down the drain and her hair returned to its usual dark sable. In minutes, she was scrubbed all pink and clean.

The bombshell look had been sexy, but her face and body glowing fresh from the shower turned his heart over in his chest.

This was the real Natalie. Her beauty shone through every pore, and he wanted to wallow in it. He wanted to be allowed to stay, to be part of what made her life happy. His desire to stay near her, to touch her again spiked and the impulse became words before he could consider the complications.

He handed her a towel and held tight, using it to pull her closer. "Come over tonight."

"Enzo…I can't."

"I'm right next door."

"I won't leave my daughter alone just so we can hook up."

He took exception to the idea that they were merely "hooking up," but he bit his tongue. That was a battle for another day.

"Okay, I'll come over here."

"Absolutely not. I'm not going to confuse her, and she still comes into my bed when she has a bad dream. This is the first time she's had a room to herself."

"Get a sitter."

"Sure, because those just grow on trees." She tugged on the towel, and he tugged back, pulling her into a kiss, reminding her that there was ungrounded electricity still arcing between them.

He fought to keep annoyance from his voice. Why was she shooting down every idea? Didn't she want more of what they'd just shared too? He knew taking care of Daisy was a priority, but why did doing the right thing always come at his expense? Why couldn't the right thing be right for him too?

"I don't care how you figure it out. Come over tonight. And bring those battery-operated boyfriends you mentioned. I'm not nearly done with you."

He turned and walked out before he gave in to the overwhelming urge to see how she looked perched naked on her vanity. That image followed him home. God, he hoped she would figure something out, or it was going to be a long night.

~

Natalie locked the door behind him, and leaned her head against it. What had she done?

She'd ended a long overdue drought in a most satisfying manner. If it had only been that, a quickie to cheer her up, she wouldn't be feeling this panic. If it had just been the best sex of her life, which it had been, she would be reaching out for more, please and thank you. But it *had* been more than that. It had been Enzo.

For just a moment, she let herself remember the look in his eyes as he'd gazed down at her. His desire, his passion, had burned, and she'd willingly leapt into the flames. But beneath it, there had been a lingering warmth. Affection? Friendship? She couldn't place it, because her physical encounters had never included that elusive emotion before. She could begin to crave the potent combination if she wasn't careful.

He hadn't just taken her to bed and shown her a great time. He'd taken the time to learn what she liked before giving it to her with his mouth, his hands, and his cock. He hadn't just gotten his own jollies and left. He'd gifted her with three orgasms first, taking his time as if he truly cared about her and her pleasure, and then asked to give her more. Damn him. Why did he have to be an attentive lover on top of being a nice guy and sweet with her kid? And yes, she heard how ridiculous her complaint sounded even in her own head.

In a different world, in a different life, Enzo would have been perfect. They could have met and dated, gotten to know each other over time and built a solid relationship. Natalie imagined movie nights at the theater and intimate dinners for two with candles and white tablecloths. They could have hit all the traditional milestones. They would have met each other's families and moved in together. Maybe after a year or two, she'd have hinted at a ring. All of the stability and love she craved wrapped up in one heart-stopping package.

But this was her life. She had a child to raise, uncertain finances to worry about, and a family she hoped to God he'd never meet. She didn't have time for dating or courtship. And thinking about what might have been tempted her to resent the choices she'd made in her youth. Which made her feel resentful of the most beautiful thing she had ever created, Daisy. She refused to let anything make her wish away her daughter. Not even for a second. So she pushed away the thoughts of Enzo and his glorious hands, because she couldn't wish for that fantasy and be present in her real life too. She couldn't have the fairy tale.

By the time Jo Valenti showed up with Daisy and a tray full of peanut butter cookies in tow, Natalie had scrubbed away all traces of her sex kitten and the fun she'd had. Clad in clean sweats and a hair wrap, she'd moisturized to tend to the faint stubble burn Enzo had left behind and kept her face bare. Hopefully the older woman's mom-eyes would see the splotchy texture as proof she was still recovering.

"Really, I can't thank you enough for picking her up from school."

"It was my pleasure!" Jo ran a hand over Daisy's mop of dark hair. "I've always wanted to be an active grandma, but my children are proving to be remarkably slow in that department. If they don't get a move on, I'll miss my window."

"You strike me as a woman with a lot of life and love ahead of her." Surely she wasn't thinking she'd die before her grandchildren arrived, was she? Jo's kids were still fairly young to be thinking about children of their own. She didn't want to mention that she'd gotten pregnant with Daisy really young. She liked having the good opinion of the older woman and didn't want to lose it.

"Plans change, dreams fade."

Natalie heard the pain and dejection behind those words, and her inner therapist clicked on. Her years behind the chair had made her a keeper of secrets and a giver of advice. She recognized the need to talk about a tough subject.

"Come on in. Stay awhile."

She plated the cookies, smiling at Didi when she silently

begged for one.

"Why don't you grab a snack and read in your room, Daisy? Jo, can I offer you some tea or coffee? Water? Wine?"

"I'm tempted by the wine, but I'll stick with tea. Story of my life."

Natalie puttered with mugs and the kettle while Jo sat at her own daughter's beautiful kitchen table.

"I wanted to thank you for letting Sofia rent me her apartment at your subsidized rate. I know how much this property is worth."

"Nonsense. You're doing us all a favor keeping it occupied and paid for, while she saves for the wedding. Plus, the only reason you're in this mess is because of my husband's crazy scheme. It's our pleasure."

Pouring the hot water over the tea bags, Natalie felt self-conscious over her lack of a proper teapot. Jo seemed like the kind of lady who would appreciate the finer details. "I'm sorry I don't have china."

"It's just how I make mine at home."

"Do you take cream, sugar, lemon?" *Shit, do I have a lemon?*

"Just a little sugar, sweetheart. Relax." Jo's hand covered hers and gave it a reassuring squeeze before she tipped a scant half teaspoon of sugar into her mug and neatly strained her teabag, before lifting her mug in a toast. "To mothers helping mothers."

The simple sentiment made Natalie's eyes water, tingling the inside of her nose. Why did even the smallest hint of commiseration turn her into a watering pot? She'd been doing just fine on her own, but she had to admit she was doing better with help. Witness her afternoon of fun… On second thought, she pushed all memory of that afternoon aside. His mother was the last person who needed to witness her reaction to that particular event. Her blush would give her away for sure.

"I know that parenting solo is hard. Hell, joint parenting is no picnic. It was the hardest thing I've ever done, and my kids are grown. Now that they are, I envy your freedom."

"Freedom?" She had never seen her seven-year drought as freedom.

"I just think about how things might have been different if I had been the one to make all the decisions, to be the one in charge. I compromised on so many things that now I'm left wondering what I believe in anymore."

Having to make all the decisions, handle all the questions, solve all the problems was exhausting. She'd give an awful lot to have a pair of strong shoulders to help carry the load. Her mind's eye flashed to the very nice pair of shoulders she'd left a bite mark on not an hour ago. "This isn't the ideal."

"I don't know. I wonder if we had done something different would Gabe still be here? I don't regret raising my kids with Dom, but now that we don't have them holding us together, I think about freedom a lot." Jo's hands gripped her mug tightly, as if that could hold her life together too.

Natalie covered one hand with hers, offering connection and understanding. "You two have raised some pretty amazing kids who are smart and independent. I'm sure Gabe was too." She paused, before asking the question hanging in the air between them. "Are you really thinking about leaving Dom? You've invested a lot of years together. Would you really just walk away?"

"If he won't work with me, why would I stay?"

Natalie thought of the years of shared history and family, but kept her mouth shut. She knew when to listen and when to speak.

"When I met Dom in high school, I fell hard. So tall and strong. So handsome. I was putty in his hands." Jo looked up at the ceiling, lost in memories. "When the kids came along, I molded myself into the mother they needed me to be, and then the office manager Dom needed to succeed. That man is allergic to paperwork." She let out a watery chuckle and took a sip of her tea, fighting for control. "After all that bending to fit the needs of others, I'm ready to find my own shape again. I want to enjoy this next phase of our lives, but he won't let go of the past so we can reach for our future. I'm thinking I might have to reach for it by myself."

Jo exhaled a shaky breath. Natalie understood how scary it could be to say things out loud for the first time. She doubted Jo had talked about this with anyone else. Her words were too raw to have been shared before. "What would your next phase be? What's that new dream?"

Natalie was knee-deep in the kid phase. She hadn't even considered what her retirement would look like.

"We were supposed to pick up new hobbies, spend time together, play with our grandchildren and just relax. I've been waiting for years, letting Dom set the pace, but when we lost Gabe something changed. I'm not willing to sit back and let life pass me by. I don't know if I can make myself follow his lead anymore." Jo gripped her mug so tightly her knuckles turned white.

"There's nothing wrong with wanting something more or different for yourself. That's why I do my makeup tutorials. But think about what you'd be giving up."

"Some days it just feels like it would be easier to walk away and start fresh, than keep digging at the same pile of shit between us."

"I thought digging in shit was Enzo's job."

The laughter broke the tension, as Natalie had hoped. Jo's shoulders shook with laughter before dropping back down from her ears.

"Just don't do anything rash."

"That's my line." Jo laughed, but her voice held no humor. "I've spent my whole life playing by the rules, and what did it get me? An empty home, a son in the ground, and a husband who dismisses my needs out of hand. Maybe rash is exactly what I need."

The idea of willingly stepping away from stability made Natalie cringe. Jo had a husband who stood by her, even if he did work too much. They had a family, property, history, all those hallmarks of a settled life that Natalie craved. If she was considering walking away from all that, maybe the ideal of a long-term marriage wasn't the answer. It was something for Natalie to consider.

After all, she didn't need a man to get those things for Daisy. She was doing just fine on her own. Her child was well cared for and loved. Finances were tight, yes, but money wasn't a good reason to marry someone. This wasn't Regency England, and she wasn't a wallflower widow. For all the times she wished she wasn't alone, there were other times that she was grateful for her ability to be flexible and take an interesting job or pursue a great opportunity. She wasn't tied down to one spot or another adult's life, and she and Daisy had gotten to explore a lot of unique things together.

Her free time was hers alone, and she spent it with her vlogs that filled her well quite ably. A man in her life would mean sacrificing some of that time to his needs. They always wanted more of her time than she had to give. That's how it had been with her ex before he left, and every other ex after him. Jo had lost herself, giving so much to everyone else. Natalie couldn't do that. She'd already given so much to Daisy that there was very little time left for her own pursuits. The minute a man protested that his needs were third on the list, he was gone, either by his decision or hers. She didn't have time to mess with men who didn't understand.

Hell, if Jo had been sacrificing herself for forty years and getting nothing but promises and excuses in return, who was Nat to judge her for wanting better? Natalie's mind swirled with this new perspective, until Jo gripped her wrist fiercely.

"Please don't say anything about this to my kids. I know you're friendly with them. I just needed to blow off steam and talk to someone who might get it. You're a very good listener."

"They teach us that in beauty school. And don't worry, beautician's code." She held up two fingers and snapped them like scissors. "Your secrets are safe with me."

LATER THAT NIGHT, tucked into her bed all alone, Natalie tortured herself with the thought of Enzo lying just next door, waiting for her. Their encounter had awakened all kinds of sensory memories she'd kept dormant. Now she was struggling to put them back into hibernation. Her system was vibrating at a frequency that made her skin pebble and shiver.

Although her body was determined to convince her otherwise, her mind was made up. She was happy as she was. She didn't need to bring a man into her life and complicate everything. She would learn from Jo's experience and keep her freedom. Even if her body was screaming with need for this man. Even if her heart needed him too. Her mind was terrified.

She'd thought she'd learned her lesson about needing people years ago. She'd needed her father when she was a child, but he'd left her and her mother when she was a baby. She never even knew who he was. She'd needed her mother, but Portia Carras had a difficult time finding enough energy to take care of herself, so she only really cared about Natalie when it impacted her own well-being. She'd kept Natalie alive because she didn't want to go to jail, but love and concern was more than Portia could muster.

When her mother had responded to news of Daisy by asking for rent and shaming Natalie for getting herself into the same situation she had, Natalie had not been surprised. Disappointed, but not surprised. Natalie had discovered dating early, and she had needed a lot from her boyfriends. That scared most good boys off pretty quickly. Which left the bad boys, like Kyle Amblin. Kyle had seen her need as a turn-on. He liked that she had needed him and tested her to see how far she'd go to please him. Until even that hadn't been enough.

He'd tried for nearly two months after she'd found out she

was pregnant, although most of his "trying" revolved around convincing her to get an abortion. Whenever her attention started to shift to the baby, he'd accused her of neglecting him. Her nonstop morning sickness really put a damper on how much energy she had for taking care of his needs. And sex with him had been the last thing she wanted to do, even though she'd been hormonally horny as hell. Every time she tried to talk about the baby, he shut down. One day he'd just ghosted, and they hadn't spoken again. He'd never even contacted her to see the baby. His loss.

Alone, she'd set out for LA and rebuilt her life. School and salon jobs had filled her time before Daisy came, but the friends she'd made had been fleeting. They'd thrown her a shower and come to meet the baby, but they were still just young adults. After the fun parts were done, they'd gone back home to their lives filled with boyfriends, classes and new jobs. No one had been there to help with changing diapers or folding laundry or rocking the baby so she could get some sleep.

She'd signed up for one of those mommy websites to track the baby's growth and development. When it sent her an article about how to accept help with the baby, she'd broken down in tears. She would have gladly accepted help if anyone had offered. But they hadn't, so she'd learned to manage everything by herself. It hadn't been easy, but now it was her reality. She was the only one she could count on to keep herself and Daisy happy. She didn't need anyone.

She continued poking all of her soft spots, trying to toughen up her armor against the overwhelming temptation of Enzo. She couldn't afford the risk, so she stayed tucked firmly into her own bed, alone, caught between her responsibilities sleeping in the bedroom next to hers and her temptation next door. It was going to be a long night.

But when Daisy climbed into her bed just after midnight, tears still wet from her nightmare, Natalie knew she'd made the right decision.

CHAPTER 12

"Hɪ, Eɴᴢᴏ. Wʜᴇʀᴇ's ᴍʏ ᴍᴏᴍᴍʏ?" Enzo's heart blipped in his chest when Daisy ran over to his car parked at the school, all smiles.

"Things ran late at work. I'm going to bring you home while she finishes up." When he heard Jake asking Natalie to stay a little later, he'd offered to help out. He couldn't resist a chance to try and get back in her good graces. He was hurt that Natalie hadn't come by. Not that first night, or any night in the last two weeks. He saw her every day, but when he tried to bring it up, she always evaded. Maybe he'd pin her down today and find out what he'd done wrong.

"Okay." Daisy reached for the door handle.

Enzo pushed the lock button. "Wait a second. Aren't you going to ask me the password?"

"But I know you now."

"You should still ask, especially since your mom made sure to tell me there was a new one."

Daisy grinned, her tongue peeking through the gaps left by lost teeth, knowing what he was going to have to say. "Okay, what's the password?"

"Let me see. I had to write it down." He playfully patted his pockets before turning over his hand where he'd written it down in Sharpie. He'd never thought about having kids outside of an abstract *someday* kind of thing. But spending time with Daisy was making those nebulous goals pull into sharper focus. He wasn't going to lie and say he wasn't trying to cultivate a relationship with her mom, but hanging out with Daisy wasn't a hardship. She was a great kid.

"Beeeeeeeeeeeeeeep Badoongy Face?"

Daisy burst out laughing, and he unlocked the door so she could climb in. "That's it."

"What does that even mean? Your mom wouldn't tell me."

"You don't know *The Book With No Pictures?*" Her eyes widened before narrowing deviously. "Oh, I'm gonna make you read it when we get home. Can we work on the fairy houses some more too?"

Daisy chattered on about her day, but Enzo's brain snagged on that word. *Home.* In his mind, home was still his parents' house. His apartment was just a place he slept. It held none of the warmth or connection that he associated with the word. Natalie must be a pretty special mother to have her daughter calling yet another rental apartment "home" after a few short weeks. Was he jealous? No. Wistful, maybe.

He looked around his apartment critically. The loden and sage green walls with dark brown accents had been one of Sofia's projects. He'd let her decorate his place for her portfolio years ago. As a result, almost none of the furniture in his place was his. The brown leather couch was just a place to drop his weary bones after a hard day. His bedroom was a place to sleep, but he hadn't chosen any of the pieces to fill it. He was rarely awake there long enough to care.

The only things he'd added to the space were his books and his plants. He had a spider plant and a pothos from college competing for longest tendrils on top of the custom chestnut bookcase his cousin Seth had gifted him last Christmas, and an aloe plant in the bathroom for tending his various cuts and scrapes.

He kept his babies in the kitchen window. The stragglers from the nursery had a tendency to find their way into his truck and his heart, joining the collection on his sill until they were strong enough to be transplanted outside. He was such a softie. Sofia teased him every year about his Charlie Brown Christmas trees, but he couldn't bear to leave them behind. He grinned at the thought of having Daisy help him decorate his tree this year.

But if he removed the books and the plants, there was nothing that made his space a home, nothing holding him in place. He had never really considered this a permanent living situation, just a stopping-over point after college. Somehow that had turned into six years of stasis.

He should start actively putting down his own roots, make some changes, look for his own place. But where to even begin?

Before he could sort any of that out, he was pulled into the snack and homework whirl at his kitchen table. He listened to Daisy read for twenty minutes and signed her log while she ate toast and orange juice. He made a mental note to stock some kid-friendly snacks in his cabinets.

When she was done, he followed her outside to the fairy garden with the tiny chairs he'd fashioned out of tree trimmings and morning glory vines. While she gathered leaves and flowers to decorate the magical bower, Enzo was pulled from the project by his insistent cell phone.

"Dude, where are you?" Frankie sounded annoyed. "I just drove by the Mariano job looking for you."

"I'm at the Block." The nickname for the condo his siblings all lived in had come from his parents' teasing that they needed a cell block so they could lock up their kids and keep them out of trouble, but still get them out of the house. Mission accomplished.

"It's three thirty."

"So?" Enzo strolled away from Daisy toward his porch. "Last

time I checked, I wasn't on anyone's clock." He'd been aiming for assertive, but the defensiveness crept into his voice. The grown-up version of *You're not the boss of me!* was sure to set Frankie off.

"Well, that works out anyway. I'm heading down to south county for Dad, and I need you to feed Buster and take him for a walk. I'm going to hit traffic coming home, I think."

Buster, Frankie's rescue mutt, was a good dog with a lot of energy that could turn destructive if he was left alone too long. He needed his routine of food and a long walk to burn off that energy. Frankie'd had to replace two armchairs and a table leg, because he'd shredded the cushions and chewed down the wood.

"Sure, I've got him. No problem." He was that guy, the one with everyone's key on his key chain, everyone's "in case of emergency." But he didn't want to take Daisy along for a walk when Buster had been cooped up all day. He had big paws and a bad habit of jumping to say hello to new friends. He didn't want to scare her.

"Thanks, bro! See you later."

Enzo turned back and saw two dark heads bobbing over the top of the low hedge where he'd left just one. "Hey, you're back."

Natalie stood and smiled carefully. It wasn't the smile she gave him when they were alone that melted him inside. This was a fake pleasant smile, like the one she gave him on set. Something was going on in that head of hers, and he was pretty sure he wasn't going to like it.

"Thanks for picking her up. I reminded Jake that extra hours don't really work for me, but Angela was out sick, and since she covered for me…"

"I get it. It's no problem really."

"It is a problem for me. I don't want to take advantage of our friendship. Come on, Sprite. Let's go inside. Time for homework."

Crouched in the grass, dirt smudged on her cheek, a geranium tucked behind her ear, she did look like a woodland sprite, and a disgruntled one at that. "But Mom, I already did my homework with Enzo and had a snack. We just started working on another fairy house. Please can I stay? Please?" Daisy's voice was perilously close to a whine, and Enzo could see Natalie was battling for patience.

"Totally your call, Mom, but I've got about an hour free if you're okay letting her play. Her book log is signed and in her bag, but she was going to read me *The Picture Book*."

"No, silly." Daisy laughed, and it broke the tension. *"The Book With NO Pictures."*

Natalie looked back and forth between them, like they'd gone and turned green while she was away and she was nervous about what color would come next. It took her a solid swallow and a deep breath to manage words. "Okay, then. I'll go inside and work for a bit. Just send her in when you have to leave."

She slowly turned and walked into the house, shooting worried looks back over her shoulder. Enzo kind of liked surprising her, keeping her off-balance. He couldn't deny that a certain warmth and fullness entered his chest every time she trusted him with her kid. Those looks were laced with confusion, not concern. But he liked spending time with Daisy, and he was glad Natalie could see it.

He wove thyme sprigs into a fragrant little welcome mat for the fairy door. Daisy leaned up against his side, a warm weight, while she tried to rig large basil leaves into a hammock.

"Enzo, can I ask you a question?" Daisy kept her eyes on the hammock in her hands.

"Sure. What's up?"

"Do you like me?"

She still wouldn't look at him, and he caught the slight tremor in her voice. This was a serious question and deserved a serious answer. "Daisy, I think you are an awesome kid, and I like you very much."

"Then could you try and be friends with my mom? Maybe if you liked her and she liked you, we could all play more."

"Daisy, look at me."

The little girl met his eyes, her own full of nerves and caution.

"I like you, and I like your mom. There's nothing I'd like more than to spend time together with you both."

She held on to her wariness an extra-long beat. "Do you mean it?"

"If we shake on it, will you believe me?"

She considered that carefully and held out her hand. He shook it firmly, sealing his sincerity. This kid had him hooked.

"I'm gonna grab the book now. Can you hang the hammock over there?"

He knelt down and tinkered with the leaves she'd tried to tie around two twigs stuck in the ground, pleased he'd passed her test. This was fun, and that was something he'd had precious little of lately. He missed the simple summer days spent playing in the backyard, the four of them exploring, chasing, laughing, crying. Over it all, his mother's mock threat not to end up in the emergency room because she was not going to pay for it. He grinned at the memory.

"Here you go." Daisy set the book in his hands and climbed into his lap with a sneaky grin. "You read it." She could barely contain her giggles, and he was charmed.

What had he gotten himself into? He hoped the answer was his future.

Natalie closed her eyes as the quiet of the apartment settled around her. Daisy had grabbed her book and run back outside after a quick kiss to read with Enzo.

Despite her self-inflicted torture every evening and her deep conviction that she needed to keep control over the situation, she'd failed. When he'd advanced, she retreated. When he asked for more of her time, she'd claimed that Daisy needed her. When he'd asked her out on a date, she'd asked him to be her friend first. And damn him, he had. He should have started running far and fast by now.

She had made it two whole weeks, but nothing had gotten easier. No matter how hard she tried to stay self-sufficient, life kept throwing her curveballs that brought Enzo back into her space. Today, he'd just happened to be there when Jake had asked her to stay late. His ready offer of help meant she didn't have a good excuse to brush off Jake's request, and she'd ended up having to stay.

And now her baby was falling in love. She could see it all over Daisy's face. She was getting attached to this guy who was by no means permanent, and she was going to get her heart broken when he left. Seven years of celibacy and careful dating had been worthless, only postponing the inevitable.

Daisy had never had a father figure, and so she had no defense against the first man to ever show interest. Natalie didn't have the heart to take away that joy just to protect her. All she could do was be there for Daisy when she needed her. Hopefully Enzo would let her down easy. Maybe she could talk to him about that...

While she pondered, she stirred the chicken enchilada melt she'd left in the crock pot that morning, filling the kitchen with the scent of warm, spicy comfort, and flipped through the mail, pouncing on a padded envelope.

She'd been waiting for this new palette to arrive, and she danced into her room, worries tabled for later. Flicking on her mirror lights and setting up her phone, she pushed her plans to do a longer Halloween look to another day. The time she had left today was perfect for an informal live new product show-and-squee instead.

Laying out her tools and the new eye makeup, she prepped her space and then her face, meticulously cleaning off her makeup from the day. It was hard to put herself out there on the internet without her mask, but it was the only way to show people the whole process from the beginning. She opened her YouTube account and began a live video post.

She buffed foundation on her face as she waited for fans to show up, the familiar scents of her liquids and powders providing a different kind of comfort. This was her realm, and she was in control.

"Hello, everyone! I just got home and look what came!" She waggled the shiny new palette in front of the camera. "I know you've been waiting for the Rosé All Day eye shadows to release, and I got one early! Official launch is in two weeks, but I couldn't wait to try it out here with you. So while I finish blending my foundation, comment below if you want soft and sparkly or a bold matte look today! Here's what we're working with." She opened the compact so her viewers could see the fifteen shades of rosé pinks it contained.

As the comments started to trickle in, she was gratified to see the "viewing" number ticking higher into the low hundreds. *Solid.* She chattered as she concealed below and primed above her lashes before scrolling through the suggestions.

"Sounds like you want soft and romantic today, so I think I'll go with Fizz on my lids, Pop Pop as a highlight, and Corked for the shadows." As she swept the glittering shadow across her eyelids, she grinned at the camera. Like a three-year-old getting into her mom's purse, Natalie just loved to play with pretty. When Daisy had done that exact thing, Natalie hadn't even been able to get mad despite losing close to a hundred dollars worth of product. She'd just wanted to be like Mommy, and the colors were so tempting.

When she worked on other people's faces she approached it as an artist might approach a color-by-numbers canvas: she was limited to what that face could carry and what the look was for. It was still challenging and she enjoyed it, but sometimes she craved a little variety.

When she worked on her own face, she could try anything she

liked. She could follow her fancy and become anyone she wanted to.

So today she'd be soft and romantic, something she rarely allowed herself to be in real life.

"You guys, this shadow is so smooth. It's sliding on like silk. Even though it's a sparkle shade, it's not flaking when I blend it. So pretty to work with. It's really letting me build up the color. Now I'm going to highlight along my brow line and inner eye, to brighten the areas where the light will already catch. It will make you look like you're standing in perfect lighting even when you're not."

She held up an angled brush and the palette again.

"Now I'll take the darker color for the crease and corners. I'm going to blend this into a light smokey eye. Take that sparkle into sultry territory, but not so far that we end up a vamp. Before you @ me, there's nothing wrong with vamp, just not the look we're going for today. While I blend, comment below and tell me who you want to sparkle for. I've got an extra palette and a new brush for one lucky winner!"

She looked forward to reading the comments most of all. Obviously she couldn't read very well with one eye closed, but she always went back and replied to as many as she could.

Some of her fans had been following her for three years. She knew where they lived, the people they loved, and what made them laugh. They were her community no matter where she landed, and she loved them for it.

As she finished blending her other eye, the door behind her opened and she froze.

Daisy knew better than to come in while Mommy was working. And she always, always knocked.

"Hey, I just wanted to let you know—" Enzo broke off, taking in her half-done makeup and the bright lights. Did he realize he was streaming live to hundreds of viewers right now? No. Of course he didn't. Why would he know anything about her vlog? "Wow. You look amazing. Softer somehow." He shook his head and started again. "I've got to go, but the kiddo is watching TV."

"Okay. Thanks." She didn't know what else to say. At least it hadn't been Daisy at the door. As much as she shared with her community, there were some awful people on the World Wide Web, and no one needed to see her baby. At least Enzo was old enough to fend for himself. Maybe, if she was lucky, he wouldn't even show that much on screen.

"Yeah, no problem."

He lingered a minute, and she couldn't tell if he was hoping she'd say something or if he was just intrigued by her half-done face. Before she could rally her wits, he turned and closed the door behind him. She closed her eyes for a moment, giving herself time to calm. When she opened them for the camera, calm, cool vlogger Nat was back.

"So what do you think of the shading here? I'm going to do a simple highlighting on my cheeks and a pretty pink nude lip and you can tell me what you think."

Wait, hold up. Who was that?

Who's the hottie?

Is that the babysitter? Guuuuuurrrrrrllllll!

Did you see the way he looked at her? You better finish that makeup quick and go after him!

Damn. So much for getting lucky. They'd all seen him.

Is that who you're sparkling for?

That last one brought a blush to her cheeks. Thank God for foundation. The last thing she wanted was to add fuel to the fire. At least they hadn't recognized him. She could still downplay—

Wait. That guy looks familiar. Is he on TV?

Fuck.

～

How did she keep getting more beautiful?

Enzo unlocked his own condo and went through his routine.

Keys on the hook, mail in the bin, boots on the rack, work clothes off, comfy clothes on. But his mind was still in the bedroom next door.

Every time he saw her it was like meeting her for the first time all over again. When he'd seen *50 First Dates* as a teen, he'd thought the amnesia plot was a little hokey but the walrus jokes saved it. Now he could see the appeal of sticking around to see who this amazing woman would be from day to day.

Enzo's mind whirled with the many faces of Natalie before coming to rest on the way she looked after he'd made her come. He'd changed into mesh shorts, an old gray T-shirt and gym shoes for his run with Buster. He couldn't think about that mental image before heading back out in public. Trying to calm back down, he pictured her in her partially done makeup from earlier.

He'd clearly interrupted her work on a new look, but even halfway primped, she captivated him. He'd debated going to her for a kiss, but decided against it, given the proximity of Daisy and the likelihood he wouldn't be able to stop there. He wished he could stay, but he was already pushing his luck with Buster.

He grabbed his keys and unlocked Frankie's door, bracing for impact. Strong paws landed on his stomach in a familiar greeting, and Enzo rubbed the broad head trying to nuzzle his chest. Buster was supposed to be a guard dog for the construction sites, but this was his signature greeting. He'd never met a stranger, only a friend not yet made. The only way he was taking someone down was if he caught him unawares with his gut punch.

"Hey there, Buster. Ready for your dinner?" The black and white Staffordshire bulldog/Lab/mutt mix ran in frantic circles around him as he tried to get the door closed and into the kitchen without tripping. Frankie was late often enough that Enzo arriving for dinner and a walk wasn't a surprise for the active pup.

Enzo poured kibble into the stainless steel bowl on the floor and got out of the way before Buster muscled him aside. He'd landed on his ass a time or two before he'd learned to be quick about it.

While Buster inhaled his chow, Enzo conducted a quick survey of the apartment, looking for damage. Chew toys and rawhide bones littered the living room, but no missing table legs or shredded couch pillows, so that was good. He peeked into the bedroom, where it looked like a bomb went off.

The quilt hung drunkenly off the bed, clothes strewn everywhere, a pile of knocked-over books next to the bed. In other words, completely normal. Frankie had always been a slob, one of the side effects of being the baby. There had always been someone bigger to help clean up, usually Enzo. He'd noticed Natalie's bedroom had been spotless.

Shaking his head, he closed the door and headed for the last room where Buster tended to cause trouble. The bathroom.

"Buster! Did you do this?" There had to be at least two rolls worth of toilet paper shredded on the floor. How in the hell had he gotten two?

In the grand scheme of things two rolls of toilet paper wasn't that bad. The feather pillow had been more expensive and a pain in the ass to clean up. The plastic bottle of vitamins had required an emergency vet visit. But still, a point needed to be made.

"Buster. Buster, come here."

The sixty-pound dog slunk closer with his head down and knees bent as if he could army-crawl himself into looking smaller. He watched Enzo with a mournful side-eye and whimpered. Clearly, he'd learned the best way to own up to his mistakes was with carefully cultivated regret.

Enzo did his best not to laugh when Buster lay down on top of the mess and rolled over, exposing his white starburst chest for a belly rub.

"Buster! No more toilet paper. Okay, dude?" It was irresistible. Enzo knelt down and scratched the miscreant's cute belly. "Now I have to clean all this up before our walk."

At the W-word, Buster sprang into action, remorse forgotten

as he tried to push Enzo into motion while chasing his own tail. The toilet paper went flying. And they said it didn't snow in the Bay.

"Okay, cleanup can wait. Let's go, boy."

With Buster in his harness and the heavy-gauge leash in hand, Enzo led the dog outside. Correction: Buster pulled Enzo's shoulder out of its socket in his excitement to get the hell out of the apartment.

Frankie used to bring Buster along to job sites, but with all the filming equipment and cords and extra people, it just wasn't feasible anymore. Enzo felt bad that this bundle of energy was cooped up all day, so he didn't mind helping with the jailbreak.

They walked side by side away from the condo so Buster could do his business, before loping into a steady run around the three-mile loop he'd mapped out. On weekends, he preferred to run the trails, but this close to dusk, and with a dog, the threat of mountain lions kept him on the pavement with his headphones in and his phone strapped to his arm.

Usually running was just another chore to be checked off the list, but today he had energy to burn. Filming had slowed every-thing down to a crawl at work, and he missed the good, honest sweat and tired muscles at the end of a solid day's work. His body was still crackling with energy he needed to burn off before bed.

He knew how he'd like to burn off that energy, but she hadn't come over since the night he'd issued his invitation. It was prob-ably more about not leaving Daisy alone. At least, he hoped that's what it was and not a reaction to his performance. In his defense, he'd been overwhelmed and had probably rushed, but she hadn't been faking the pleasure he'd seen in her eyes. Still, a man deserved more than one chance to get it right, didn't he? There was so much left to explore. Practice made perfect.

He could make all the assumptions in the world, but if she didn't come back and talk to him, he was still going to be wrecked. He couldn't stop thinking about her. And worse, he didn't want to.

So how could he make it okay for her to step away from her baby for a bit? Working on a hunch, he detoured their run toward the historic downtown area, and a small parenting boutique he remembered that had moved into the old barbershop. He walked in and was immediately overwhelmed by the tiny frilly dresses and elaborate silicone contraptions. He and Buster were as out of place as they would have been on the moon. The woman behind the counter just stared at him for the longest time. But when he found his voice and asked his question, she had the answer for him.

With his little brown bag on his arm and a grin on his face, he jogged back toward his place. Nothing like the pleasure of a problem solved.

LADY LUCK WAS ON HIS SIDE. When he rounded the last corner, Natalie and Daisy were sitting on their stoop, hip to hip, enjoying popsicles at sunset. The unseasonably warm autumn night called for one last gasp of summer joy. Natalie licked her pop from the bottom to the top, and he almost tripped. His mind shot straight to filthy. God, that was hot. She jolted when she saw him and bit off the tip of her tasty treat.

Note to self: don't surprise her. Enzo grinned and crouched down in front of them before his mesh shorts could embarrass him.

"Enzo! You have a dog?"

"Nope, Buster here belongs to Frankie. I just get to take him for walks sometimes. How's that popsicle?"

"Cold. Do you want one? Can I take Buster for a walk?"

"No, thanks. I haven't had my dinner yet. And as for the walk, Buster doesn't have the best manners, and would probably drag you behind him before he jumped all over you."

"Can I pet him?"

"Sure." He got a good grip on Buster's harness as Daisy and

her popsicle came closer. "You might want to let your mom hold that, unless you want to share it with Buster."

Daisy passed off her treat to Natalie and approached Buster on her knees. "Hi, buddy. Are you a good boy?"

Buster's tail was whipping a mile a minute, and he vibrated as he tried to keep his butt on the ground while Daisy scratched under his ear. Losing control, the pup jumped his feet on her thighs and licked her face. Her precious laugh pealed out loud and long. He turned to share a smile with Natalie, but her face remained stoic.

"Mommy made enchilada bowls. You and Buster should try some."

He waited a heavy second for Natalie to extend the invitation, but she just took another firm bite of her popsicle.

"I've got food next door, but thanks for the offer. I just wanted to drop this off for your mom in case she changes her mind."

Natalie still hadn't said a word.

He handed her the brown paper bag, placing all of his longing into her keeping. "See you later?"

He wished he could turn that last question into a statement, but that was up to her and she wasn't giving him any clues. Without waiting for an answer, he ruffled Daisy's hair and walked away.

Back in his own apartment, he stared at the leftover beef and broccoli he usually loved, and grimaced because it wasn't chicken enchiladas.

CHAPTER 13

WHEN NATALIE WOKE the next morning at four thirty, she reached for her phone. She usually spent ten minutes checking on her posts and email before grabbing a quick shower and getting dressed. The notifications on her YouTube app made her blink and look again.

She clicked on her live video, and then closed her eyes, for longer than a blink this time.

She'd always wanted one of her videos to go viral. Why did it have to be this one?

Her fears yesterday had been well-founded. Enzo had been correctly identified around two in the morning. The video had been shared over a thousand times. Hashtags had been added.

#NattieLandsAHottie

#GoodWithHisHands

#MDSH

#MillionDollarStarterHome

#BabysitterBootyCall

Her gut clenched. Now she was going to have to tell him about this thing. The one thing that was truly hers, she now had to expose and defend. How would he react? Would he freak out? Would he care at all? Was he immune to publicity because of the show? Given the glimpses of shyness and modesty she'd seen in him, she didn't think so. He was not going to be happy about this.

He also wasn't likely to be happy with her, because she hadn't gone knocking on his door last night.

A baby monitor. He'd given her a baby monitor. Which she'd opened in front of Daisy. Who promptly asked if she was going to have a baby with Enzo, because she was okay with it, because she really wanted a baby sister, but not a baby brother, because now that they had two bedrooms, she could share her room with the baby, but only if it was a girl.

Navigating the baby talk with a sugar-hyped six-year-old up past her bedtime had sapped what little energy she'd had left, and she'd fallen asleep getting Daisy down.

And now here it was, four forty-five a.m., and she'd already ruined his day too. Well, screw him anyway. A kernel of anger burned in her chest. She hadn't asked for his help yesterday in the first place. She hadn't asked him to come waltzing into her room. In fact, she'd told him to just drop Daisy off. This was his own fault. And now her best-performing video wasn't the one she'd worked really hard on producing—with half of her face done with drugstore finds and the other half designer. No, it was this stupid video because a hot guy had walked on screen. The pleasure she usually felt over a well-performing post was filtered through all of her worry and frustration. She could barely summon the energy to be excited about the ticking numbers beneath it.

The buzz of a text shook her from her stupor.

See me when you get in.

Jake. Great. Today was going to be just great.

SHE DROPPED DAISY with a much-recovered Mrs. Félice and hustled in to work. She'd hoped she'd see Enzo before Jake, but when she checked the call sheet that hope evaporated. He wasn't due in until seven. No chance she could avoid Jake for another hour. Especially not when he rounded the corner into the garage with two cups of coffee in his hand.

"Good morning, Natalie!" His chipper tone put her on guard.

"Hi. Thanks." She took the coffee from his outstretched hand and sipped. It was just the way she liked it, black and sweet. Did the man keep a spreadsheet of employee minutiae in his head? She wouldn't put it past him. He was one of those showrunners who had his hand in everything. Jake Ryland ran a tight ship. Almost too tight.

"I caught your video last night. It was very interesting."

Jake Ryland followed her? No way. He must have notifications for the Million-Dollar Starter Home hashtag. Did the man sleep? More importantly, was he angry? He didn't seem angry.

"Enzo was helping me get my daughter from school, since I had to cover for Angela yesterday."

"No excuses needed. I think it's great. I just wanted to align strategy. I noticed you only have it up as a YouTube Live video. You need to share it to Facebook, Twitter, and Instagram as well, and include #MDSH and #MillionDollarStarterHome. I'll get everyone on the show to share it and post it to the network's official page as well."

Oh no. She had to stop him before he completely took over. He was a god in this realm, in control of all he surveyed. The way he got the film to tell the story he wanted was miraculous. It was what made him a rising star in the world of reality television. But she didn't particularly want to bow down and hand over her precious show as a sacrifice to appease him.

"Whoa, whoa, whoa. Slow down! I don't think Enzo even knows he's in it."

"I'll fill him in later. Natalie, you get how rare it is for something like this to hit. You've got to move quickly for your own sake as well as for the show. Get that video spread as widely as you can. I'll talk to Enzo about doing an actual scheduled guest spot on your next video. You can do that, right? Man Makeover Monday? Hey, that's catchy."

"Jake, I…" Her words shriveled in her mouth.

"Listen, this isn't just about your little beauty blog. We need the show to do well and keep gaining viewers. Every little bit helps keep you and your friends employed. When the show does well, so does everyone else. When the show falters, we have to make cutbacks. Understand?"

Natalie nodded. She really had no choice here, did she? How did he always talk her into seeing things his way? "Let me tell him, okay? I'll post the stuff now, but when he comes in, let me explain."

"Sure. Just get him on board. This is too good an opportunity to miss."

She could do this. Natalie smoothed down her hair and squeezed her hands on the back of her neck to stop the tears. *Sure. Just get him on board. Just take this beautiful thing you've created and nourished with all of your time and energy, and turn it into a viral joke. Bring in a man who doesn't give two shits about makeup and entertain the people who want to look at hot guys so another man's show can reap the benefits.*

It was painful, this anger, this betrayal she felt. All Enzo had done was open a damn door and be himself, and he'd taken years of hard work and self-confidence away from her. And she was supposed to ask him to do it again. Deep in her belly, she ached. Losing control of this dream she'd built was literally gut-wrenching.

She stepped outside, away from Jake and his demands, to welcome the pink dawn just breaking over the horizon. It was a new day. Breath by breath, she rebuilt her walls, tucking away all of her fears and frustrations behind her smooth façade. Confident that she could handle her mission, she stepped back into her domain.

She would mourn later in private. Right now, she had a job to do and a man to persuade. And she would do it. Because a rising tide lifts all boats, and, damn it, she needed her boat to rise up for Daisy's sake.

She used all of her talents and tools to craft just the right mask for today. She blended foundation over her mottled complexion, hiding the red splotches anger had left behind. With her highlighting palette, she contoured the soft curves of her face into sharp planes of light and shadow. Softening her cheeks slightly with blush and blending, she covered her lids in war paint, battle colors, bold and bright, before slashing beneath them with a hard black cat's eye liner.

She carefully lined her lips, as if that could keep her words in line as well, before she coated them in glossy red lipstick. She was no green recruit when it came to the battlefield between men and women. If she could get a man thinking about sex, he was ten times more likely to be agreeable in hopes that she'd be agreeable too. She also hoped Enzo was at least as desperate as she was. Her resistance could work in her favor.

She carefully glued on her fake lashes, the better to shield her true emotions, and gave them a thick coat of black mascara. It was her man-eater look. *I should probably do a tutorial on it.*

That last thought arrived unbidden, and it almost ruined her hard work with tears. She was no longer in control of the content she created for her vlog. She couldn't just choose to do what she felt like. Now, she had to jump through hoops set up by men for their own gain. *Damn them all.*

She pushed hard on her philtrum, praying that the pressure point held off the tears so she could face Enzo, calm, composed and convincing. Man-eater. Slayer of Dreams.

Was this going to hurt like hell?

Yes.

Was she going to do it anyway?

Yes, damn it, because as much as it hurt her soul, her pragmatic mind and loving heart had to put Daisy first. If she lost this job, or if Jake decided to blackball her, Daisy was the one who would suffer the most. Moving (again), changing schools, leaving friends, *and* losing her time with her mother because Natalie would have to go back to booking any job that came her way...

No, that was too much to ask of her six-year-old just to salvage Natalie's pride. She'd already moved her once to forestall this catastrophe. Yes, that was now causing problems, but at least they were problems she'd made for herself. She'd learned about the sacrifices a mother would make for her child a long time ago. She could certainly do it again now.

So when Sofia showed up for her makeup, Natalie was able to keep her anger and grief firmly behind her mask. She joked and teased and made her beautiful for the camera.

And when Enzo sat in her chair and put his face in her hands, the smile held. She stood behind him and spoke to his reflection in her brightly lit mirror. "Good morning."

"Hi."

What did he have to be so surly about? *Oh. Right. The monitor.* She had to find the right tone even though she was annoyed at him for that too. She opted for sarcastic amusement.

"Thanks for the, uh, gift last night. Daisy wanted to know if you were going to give her a sister or a brother. For the record, she likes pink over blue."

His face blanked as he met her eyes in the mirror.

"Don't worry. I told her that wasn't going to happen, but the whole conversation wiped me out and I fell asleep. You're not mad, are you?" She ran her hands over his bunched shoulders and squeezed. Hopefully, he'd take it as a massage and not her way of letting out her rage over having to pacify the man who'd ruined everything.

When she squeezed again, she felt the tension begin to recede. She needed him putty before she broached the next topic, so she put a more force into the impromptu back rub, which also helped her work down more of her anger. His deep groan of relief shook her fortitude. She knew that moan intimately, and she fought hard to keep up her defenses, locking her own arousal down hard inside her walls.

She dug her elbow into the crease between his neck and shoulder, where she'd last pressed kisses that had filled her head with wood and man. He let out another moan, this one tinged with pain, and he dropped his head in defeat. She had him. *Putty.*

"I'm sorry. I didn't think of that when I dropped it off."

"It's okay. You made me a viral sensation. You're forgiven."

"I did what now? I gave you a virus? Are you sick again?"

His head snapped back up, and she laughed, a deep throaty laugh that encompassed amusement, desire, and indulgence all at once. She saved it for special occasions to maintain its efficacy. Today called for the big guns. She ran her hand down the back of his head to his neck and smiled when she saw the shiver chase the rest of the way down his spine.

"When you came in yesterday to say you were leaving? I was filming a live makeup tutorial."

"And I walked right into the middle of it. Shit, Natalie, I'm sorry. I should have knocked."

Okay, he got points that his first reaction was comprehension and apology. If he was feeling guilty, maybe she could use that to persuade him on the rest. And God, that made her sound mercenary. But she would do what she had to do. Maybe that did make her a little mercenary. For all the best reasons, of course.

"Well, my ladies sure loved it. They want more #Babysitter-BootyCall. My phone was blowing up this morning."

"Oh really?" He grinned that bashful grin of his that made her want to hug him even when she was pissed with him.

But there was no hugging on the battlefield. She stepped up her assault, running her fingernails up his scalp and leaning over the side of her chair to whisper in his ear. She made sure she jutted her hip back and pressed her chest against his arm before she spoke. "Yeah. They can't get enough."

When she glanced sideways to judge his reaction she knew she had him. His eyes were darting from the curve of her ass to the profile of her breasts to her slick red lips and back again. Just to punish him a little more, push him a little farther, see how far he'd stretch before he snapped, she licked her lips and caught the shell of his ear in the same motion. His eyes fluttered closed and a tremor shook him as he clutched the arms of the chair. *Surrender.*

She'd won. Now to negotiate concessions. She knew she was taking advantage of his good nature, and she hated herself a little for it. And then she did it anyway. She had no choice.

"Would you help me?" she whispered in his sensitized ear, and he drew in a sharp breath for his quick reply.

"Of course. What do you need?"

"Would you come on my videos?"

His eyes snapped wide open and searched hers. She stood upright. Had she lost her advantage by being too direct?

"What kind of videos are you making?"

"I told you, makeup videos."

He started laughing and trying to keep it in. "Is that some kind of new skin regimen?"

"What?" Natalie couldn't follow the thread of the conversation. As much as she had tried to keep her own desires carefully concealed behind the castle walls, his laughter was a carefully aimed catapult. She wanted to laugh with him, but she couldn't afford to. Every concession tore down a bit more of her defense, and she was scrambling to patch the holes, but she couldn't figure out where she'd gone wrong. She backed up. "Look, I don't want to fight with you."

"Were we fighting? You just asked me to *come* on your show." His emphasis clicked in the double meaning, and his open grin invited her to join him in the humor of it all.

But as much as she wanted to relax her guard she couldn't. She hadn't achieved her goal yet. So she pulled out her man-eater smile instead and charged back into offense. "That's a different kind of video. I'm not against making one of those for a private audience, but I was talking about doing your makeup."

With two sentences she body-slammed him back into lust. His laughter choked off, and his eyes glazed over. She could just imagine what he was picturing, and damn if it didn't get her hot and bothered too.

He was just so freaking open. He let her see too much. How had he made it through life with all of his emotions just out there for everyone to see and exploit? She'd teach him how to protect himself. Just as soon as she finished exploiting him.

The thought sickened her. *Finish this.* She wasn't equipped for a prolonged siege, and the end was in sight.

"I was thinking of showing a few men's looks, say for portraits and Halloween. Maybe an airbrush demo. Can I count on you?"

He nodded, still glassy eyed, and she immediately turned away to the safety of her kit.

"Great. Thanks! Let's get you set for today." She wondered if he'd picked up on her fake enthusiasm, because inside her chest something tender had just died and she didn't feel very cheerful.

Enzo stood slowly and stepped toward her, backing her into the mirrored counter behind her. When he whipped off his T-shirt, she quit thinking about anything but him. His skin pebbled in the unheated garage, and she wanted to rub her body against his to warm him up. She barely caught herself before she did just that. She was at work! Her reserves were drained. How on earth was she going to get through the next half hour with his abs in her face?

His hands rose to cup her face, and she knew she'd been outgunned. When he paired sweetness with strength, she surrendered. This sneak attack took her out at the knees, and when she faltered, he simply used his strength to boost her hips up onto the counter and stepped between her limp legs. Pinned between his body and the cold glass, she couldn't hide her desire anymore. She didn't want to be angry at him and had lost her steam for it. She ran her hands up his back, pulling him even closer.

"You know I will help you any way I can. You only have to ask."

Natalie leaned into his words and his strength, wishing they were hers to keep for real. His kiss on her forehead pricked her eyes with repressed need and regret.

He stepped back abruptly and pulled her down to her feet. She was still finding her balance when Jake cleared the end of the counter.

"So, full airbrush today?" Enzo asked, stepping back even farther so he could grip the chair in front of him. Natalie knew exactly what he was hiding, and she shivered at the delicious memory.

"Yep, we're going to do a few more teasers. Natalie, did you…"

"Yes, all good."

"Great. I knew I could count on you. I need him in thirty."

"You got it."

Alone again, Enzo stepped up behind her, wrapping his arms around her in a hug that drew her back against his full length. He pressed his temple to the top of her head and rocked his hips forward. Her hips instinctively rocked back into him, cradling his hard length.

"For the love of God, Natalie, set up the damn monitor tonight," he growled.

She nodded, not meeting his gaze.

Outgunned, outmanned.

Damn it.

CHAPTER 14

ENZO PACED THE CONFINES of his apartment. It hadn't felt confining before, but his anticipation filled the space to the brim, leaving no room for second thoughts or patience. It had been hell just getting through the day. After having to be touched and not touch in return for half an hour, and then spend a full day on camera, he was ready to unwind. He knew exactly how he wanted to do that, if she would just show up. As it was, he'd had to cancel on family dinner tonight, because he wasn't fit for company.

He'd vowed not to push or pressure her. He needed her to choose him. But he was getting desperate.

When the doorbell finally rang at seven, he pounced on the door handle and yanked it wide. There she stood on his threshold, biting her lip and shifting from foot to foot. Where was the femme fatale from earlier? She looked the same, but her bravado was gone. Then she spoke, and all questions flew from his mind.

"Hi. Are you ready?

"Oh, God, yes!"

Grabbing her free hand, he tugged her into his place and into his arms. His hunger snapped its tether, and he held her close, absorbing every little curve of her body with his. He took her mouth as well, spilling his frustrated desire into every kiss. God, she was sweet, and so small he just wanted to pick her up and carry her so he wouldn't have to stop kissing her on the way to the bedroom. The now fully stocked bedroom.

Pleased with that image, he lifted her, grabbing her ass and wrapping her legs around his waist while he closed the door behind her. But when he turned, she pushed him back, hands on his shoulders, eyes wide.

"Wait."

One of three words he wouldn't ignore. The others were *stop* and *no*, and he tried to take comfort that she was giving him the most optimistic of the trio. He dropped his head to her shoulder and hauled in a deep breath, flooding his head with her scent and doing nothing to calm the beast inside.

"I ca-came to see if you were ready to film the first makeup video."

His mind blanked.

She hadn't… She wasn't… Damn, he'd screwed this up royally. "I thought…"

She put a hand over his mouth, easily cutting him off, and he realized he was still holding her suspended. If they were naked, he could just… *No.* He tried to make his thoughts behave, but her soft hand over his mouth made him wonder where else she was soft, and if she liked that he was hard and rough the same way he liked that she was his opposite.

"Don't apologize. I've got the monitor charging for later, but the video rig and lights are at my place, and Daisy is still awake."

That did it. The reminder that her sweet kid was awake and waiting for Mom made him loosen his grip and let her slide to the floor. Every torturous inch of the slide burned. "Right. Okay. What were you thinking?"

"That I really want you to pick me up again later."

Good Lord. "Not. Helping."

"Sorry."

"No, you're not."

"No, I'm not."

She swayed toward him, and he was seconds away from combusting when he heard a faint, "Mommy? Where'd you go?"

He stepped around Natalie to open the door again. "She's right here, Daisy. She just came to get me for a video."

"How come you get to do a video, and I don't?"

Natalie stepped into the doorway and the conversation. "Because you are just a kid, and you're too cute for Man Makeover Monday. Sorry, kid. I need the big, scary-looking guy for this one."

"Me big and scary." Enzo raised his arms like a monster and grunted a few times as he lumbered after Daisy, chasing her back into her house.

"You're funny. Come play with me." Daisy tugged on his arm and pulled him into their apartment.

"He's here to help Mommy work, and remember you're going to sleep after the episode of *Octonauts*."

A mulish pout replaced the child's grin, and even Enzo could tell that a bedtime meltdown was on the horizon. He was only a year older, but he could still remember Frankie's epic tantrums before bed. They were still mentioned around the table at family dinners.

"Natalie, why don't you go get us set up?" He reached for Daisy's hand and walked her to the couch. Her hair was wet and combed, and she wore a nightgown covered in whales. "What's this episode about?"

"Spinner dolphins. Did you know they swim in their sleep?"

"I had no idea. Let's finish watching it."

Spending twenty minutes on the couch with her kid wasn't the quality time he'd dreamed of spending with Natalie, but he had to admit he enjoyed it. The kid was so interested in everything and had a memory like a steel trap. She'd clearly seen this one before, because she was able to tell him all the science facts before they came up in the story. Her memory was incredible.

Natalie came back at the end of the show to call time. Enzo did his best to help with the transition.

"Goodnight, bellis."

"Bellis? That's not my name."

"Yes, it is. *Bellis Perennis*, from the Latin name for the flower commonly known as a daisy. Also the root word for *bellisima*, which means beautiful in Italian."

"Oh." She blushed bright pink and ducked her head. "What's Latin for Enzo?"

"I don't know, but Enzo is short for Lorenzo. Only very special people call me that."

"Am I special?"

"Very."

When the little girl pecked a goodnight kiss on his cheek, his heart just melted.

"Good night, Lorenzo."

"Sleep tight, *bellisima*."

Natalie trailed her into her bedroom, and he waited for her to come back out. He listened to her read that book without pictures and sing "You Are My Sunshine" through the closed door and wished she'd left it open, or better yet, invited him in. He was contemplating starting another *Octonauts* when she came back out with her hands on her hips.

"Mr. Valenti, are you flirting with my little girl? Just what are your intentions?"

"What can I say? I'm smitten," he teased, before he caught the real concern in her eyes at odds with her casual tone. "Are you seriously asking me that?"

"She's just a little girl, Enzo. A little girl without a dad."

"No, she's just a great girl, active and curious and smart and funny. I've got no ulterior motives here. I like spending time with her."

"And you're not charming her just to win points with me?"

The quiet question snuck under his guard and punched him in the gut like Gabe had that one time he'd wanted to learn to box. How could a few words hurt him so much? He rose stiffly and headed for the door. He wouldn't even dignify that with a response. If she thought he was the kind of man who played games with a kid's heart to get to her mother… Fuck that. He had better ways to torture himself.

"Wait." There was that word again. The one he couldn't ignore. "I'm sorry. I haven't dated anyone seriously since Daisy was born. Mostly because guys seemed to tolerate her as a package deal or tried to fawn over the idea of her to impress me. Needless to say, none of them actually met her."

"Then those assholes were missing out." Enzo rubbed a hand over his chest, willing the pinching pain to subside. Was this where Daisy had learned her distrust? What more could he do to prove himself?

"I can see you really mean that. Again, I'm sorry." She rubbed a hand up and down his arm, as if he needed soothing. Hell, maybe he did, because it was working. "I'm figuring this all out as I go along. Dating while parenting. Asking the right questions. Protecting my kid. I'm not sorry I asked because your reaction was exactly what I needed to see."

"Trusting me isn't a mistake. You might not believe that yet, but you will. And I really do like spending time with Daisy."

"Okay."

And just like that the pressure in his chest eased.

"Will you come into my room?"

Laughter danced under her question, and he wanted to return it, to be inside the joke with her, but the memory of him hovering over her in her bed, feeling her contract around him, setting off his own release, blazed through his mind and rendered him mute.

Part fantasy, part recollection, the inferno he'd manage to subdue came roaring back to life.

"Too soon?" she asked softly, as if she was melting from the heat he was putting out.

"Not soon enough." His voice was hoarse with need.

"Go sit in the chair. I'll get you some cold water."

He nodded and did as he was bid. Cold water would be good. Maybe he could knock it in his lap since he couldn't consume it in shower form. When she placed it in his hand, he gulped it instead, hoping it would douse the flames. He judged his internal wildfire to be fifty-two percent contained, but one good gust of hot wind and he could flare back up.

"So, tonight I'm going to do a simple Halloween look. All you have to do is sit still and smile. I'll take care of the rest."

"Okay, and after?"

"And after, I'll turn on the monitor."

He sucked in a quick breath, trying to temper his excitement. "Okay."

He steeled himself to withstand her touching for an hour. He could handle it as long as he knew he'd get to touch her back before the night was through.

"Put this on." She tossed him a khaki-colored button-down.

He stripped off his T-shirt and caught the stutter in her breath. *Good.* He didn't want to be the only one struggling here.

She flicked on all of her bright lights and set up the phone. "We're going to do this live, because I don't want to spend time editing tonight." She blushed all the way down to her chest so he could see it. He had much better plans for their evening than video editing. Good to hear she did too. "So watch what you say and do because I can't cut it out."

He nodded. "Understood."

"Then let's go."

≈

"Hello, everyone! Natalie here, and I've got a surprise for you. Yesterday, you guys correctly noticed that Enzo Valenti from Million-Dollar Starter Home made a brief cameo. You got so excited, I asked him to come on for real this time, and he said, 'Yes!'" She stepped back from her phone so her viewers could see the full frame and Enzo gave them a cheeky wave. "So tonight we're going to do a quick, easy Halloween look for your guys: Indiana Jones."

She turned to Enzo, her buzzing nerves hiding beneath her best on-camera smile.

"You ready?"

"As I'll ever be."

"We'll be starting with a gel bronzer. I like this one because it's an olive-y brown, not orange at all. But it dries super fast so work it in quickly in sections and don't overlap or it'll get splotchy. Now I know Enzo works in the sun and has a pretty good base tan, but it's not Indy-in-the-desert tan."

Good Lord, she was babbling to avoid touching him. This was terrible. That kiss had turned her inside out and she felt exposed, like her heart was outside her body, where anyone could see. Perfect time to go live on the internet in front of... She checked the screen. *Holy shit!* Five thousand people. And climbing. She was rubbing the gel into his face and neck but not really seeing him until he winced and pulled back.

"Are you okay?"

"Yes, why?"

"You're blending pretty aggressively. I wondered if I pissed you off."

She had to laugh. She was being ridiculous. "No, it's just the gel. I promise to be more gentle with the next product."

"It's okay. I like it a little rough sometimes."

That thought zinged straight to her happy place. *Damn him.*

"I'll just bet you do. Now, make sure you get the bronzer all the way up to the hairline and down his neck." She reached a hand down into the open V of his button-down, smoothing the gel over his chest before tweaking his skin and making him jump in the chair. "I thought you said you like it rough."

"Sometimes, but tonight I feel like making it easy on you." He reached up and flicked open two more buttons, exposing more of his beautiful chest for her to touch. He was pushing her on purpose, and she was falling right into his trap full of vipers.

At the last second, she grabbed hold of the vine at the edge of the pit and clung to sanity. "See ladies? He's so helpful." She pulled the gaping shirt wider to expose his still-pale chest. "On another show, I'll walk you through the steps I take to turn this into the beefcake you see on TV. But today let's move on to a little contouring. Not Kardashian-level, but enough to make him look a little weathered, like he's been out under the hot desert sun and maybe got a little burned."

As she spoke she worked the darker highlighting powder into the shadow areas on his face: under his cheekbones, his hairline, under his nose and lower lip. Dragging her brush along his lower jawline tempted her to taste that spot where she could see his pulse beating.

"See how when I shade beneath his cheekbones, they instantly pop? Not that his cheekbones need any help, amiright, ladies? But his stubble does. Next, I'm going to take this peachy blush and just hit the high points. A little kiss of sunshine, if you will."

She took her big blush brush and flooded him on the nose with it, making him sneeze. That was the key. She had to keep this funny, or she'd melt down right here on camera.

"Now, for Indy's five o'clock shadow." She ran a hand over the bristles on Enzo's face. "As you can hear, Enzo's got a pretty good start on that, but no one wants to kiss real stubble. Ouch! As he's quick to say, 'It's not the years, honey, it's the mileage.' We need a few more miles on these cheeks to make them match Mr. Jones. Ready for more aggressive blending?"

"Hit me with your best shot."

She pulled out a kabuki brush and a medium taupe eye shadow, and vigorously stippled his beard zone, creating the illusion of shade.

"Ow! I was kidding." He winked at the camera, and she watched the comments spike. Her viewers were eating this up. It was hard to be bitter about it when so many people were clearly enjoying it. She just hoped they continued to watch her once he was gone. "So, Indiana Jones, huh? He a favorite of yours?"

"Oh yeah. I used to watch him all the time when I was a kid. Totally wanted to be his archaeologist girlfriend. I even did the 'love you' eyes for a boy at school once. They smudged, and he couldn't read them, of course, so I just looked like a nut with bad eyeliner."

"What happened to the archeology dream?"

Life had happened. She had literally created life, and lost her chance to study it. She shrugged it off. "Next we're going to use a small eyeliner brush, the darkest eye shadow you've got, and a little water. If your man has any growth, you're going to try and match the length and direction to thicken it up. If not, pick a short length and have at it, aiming for natural growth patterns and not a haphazard polka dot effect. Go slow and be deliberate. It will make all the difference."

She leaned in to make sure she was getting her thin lines the right length, and Enzo's body went rigid. She glanced up and realized he could see straight down the front of her shirt. Deliberately, she tucked her arm closest to the camera firmly against her body as she cupped his chin to hold him steady. The motion had the added benefit of plumping her small breasts closer together. She felt his jerky swallow under her fingertips and grinned.

"One more finishing touch." She selected her largest brush and her translucent setting powder and brushed it liberally and flamboyantly over his face, making him laugh. "If you guys have any other suggestions for creating fake stubble that don't involve glue and hairpieces, comment below. I'd love to try them out."

She tucked a battered brown hat down on his head and turned his face back and forth for the camera.

"And there you have it. Give him a golden idol and a leather whip, and he's ready to party. Let me know what you think. We'll be back in a few days with some other fun man makeovers. Be sure to follow my page here and my channel on YouTube, so you don't miss a thing! What do you think, Enzo?"

"I think it's brilliant."

"Can you do an Indy impression?"

He scrunched up his face, and in a voice that sounded more like Sean Connery said, "Snakes. Why'd it have to be snakes?"

She laughed at his terrible impression, but had to give him points for knowing the quote. "There you go, everyone. As always, I'll check comments tomorrow if you've got any questions for me. Until next time, stay adventurous, my lovelies, and remember: Makeup doesn't make you beautiful. It lets the beauty inside shine!"

"Bye!" Enzo waved and grinned for the camera, and Natalie cut the broadcast.

"Whew! We made it through our first one!" Natalie slumped back against her counter, drained. She closed her eyes and rolled her neck. Trying to be funny and entertaining, while keeping a firm grip on her attraction to him, was harder than she'd thought it would be.

Enzo rose and brushed a lock of hair back from her forehead and tucked it behind her ear, leaving a trail of awareness in its wake. "You tired?"

"Exhausted."

"Okay." He kissed her forehead and left the room. She didn't realize he was leaving until she heard the front door close behind him.

Even though she was tired, she was also horny as hell, and she knew for a fact that he was even worse off than she was. What had it cost him to walk out that door?

But he'd given her back the control over the situation again. All of the pleasurable ways she could take control raced through her mind as she cleaned her brushes, organized her powders, and turned off all the lights. Opening the door with the caution of a seasoned parent, she peeked in on Daisy, fast asleep in her bed. The red light on the monitor showed it was on. Time to test its range. She kissed her little angel on the forehead before slipping back out.

Tucking a pack of makeup-removing wipes into her back pocket and clipping the monitor handset to the other, she headed for the door. There was no need for fussing with her hair or changing into fancy undies. Given the way he'd been looking at her all evening, she doubted he'd even notice her underwear before they hit the floor. And if there was any tearing to be done, she'd gladly sacrifice an old pair.

Fixating on the image of him tearing off her clothes, Natalie wandered next door and knocked.

And waited.

And waited.

She knocked again, and finally gave in and rang the bell. *What the hell?*

At last, Enzo came to the door, dripping wet.

He'd thrown on a pair of gray sweatpants, but his chest was bare and covered in goose bumps. Natalie swallowed convulsively, trying to control her sudden salivary reaction. He literally made her mouth water. The man should come with a warning label. *CAUTION: May cause severe thirst when operated bare and wet.*

"Hey." That was all she could manage and not openly drool.

"Hey!" Silence stretched. Was he surprised?

"Can I come in?"

She glanced around him and saw that his apartment was the mirror image of hers, but it had been decorated in shades of brown and dark green. Despite the different color palette, she recognized Sofia's hand here too, in the artfully arranged glass vases and textured throw pillows. But it wasn't a sterile show-room any more than her place was after a few hours with Daisy. His muddy work boots sat by the door, and he had plants sitting in a tray of water on his countertop. She hadn't noticed much when she'd come in earlier since she'd been overwhelmed by his kisses, but now she marveled over how neat and tidy it was.

"Yeah, what's up?" He stepped back from the door to let her

pass, and she couldn't resist running a hand down his chest. He was freezing.

"What's up? Aren't we… Didn't we…It's later. Enzo, help me out here. You told me to bring the monitor. I told you to bring the condoms. I thought we had a plan."

He trapped her hand against his chest, cutting off her supply of words. "We did. I thought… You said you were tired."

"Yeah, I am, so you might have to do a little more of the heavy lifting, but I'm also horny as hell. Is that going to be a problem?"

Before she could finish her sentence, she was in his arms, legs wrapped around his waist, pressed up against his ice-cold chest. Her nipples pebbled to match his. He caught her mouth with a quick, brutal kiss of relief.

"Nope. No problem at all."

His cold hands skated over the sliver of bare skin at the base of her spine at the same time as his hot mouth clamped onto her throat, sending a shudder of competing senses racing through her. He pulled back with a grimace.

"What's wrong? And why are you freezing?"

"You taste like makeup, and I was in the middle of a cold shower when you knocked."

"Well, I can fix both of those things." She pulled the packet of makeup wipes from her jeans. "Let's get us both cleaned up, and then we can see about getting you warmed up."

"You don't want me to keep the Indy look for you? I don't mind a little role play." He wiggled his eyebrows, and she had to laugh. His ability to make her laugh was quickly becoming one of her favorite things.

"Not tonight. Tonight, I need Enzo."

The laughter faded, and he reached for the makeup remover. Taking a wipe in his hand, he traced from her hairline, down her cheeks, caressing her neck. He dragged it over her lips, erasing the last of her vixen red. He cupped her chin, holding her still while he gently removed her lashes and wiped away the smudged mascara and liner.

"There you are." With three words, she felt completely seen.

Natalie had never felt so cared for or so naked in her entire adult life. He stripped down every last barrier she had with a soft caress. Her defenses fell like dominos. Who knew she'd have to resist the temptation of the sweet harder than the stings of the sour?

By the time her face was clean, Natalie was undone, her control dissolved, bare to his gaze. Gone were the layers of protection she'd built in her years of facing the world alone. She thought of the decorator crab Daisy had told her about, who added camouflage to its shell trying to hide from its predators. She felt like she'd spent almost a decade working on her shell, just to have it gently lifted off her back. He'd stripped her naked without removing a single item of clothing. And it was a relief to have that weight gone, but also terrifying because the weight had held down all the insecurities now rushing into the gap.

What did he see? Did he like it? Would he stay? She couldn't stay here in this vulnerability alone.

He sat down hard on a chair and just stared at her.

"What? Say something."

"Ever since that first night, you've been knocking me on my ass. But tonight, I have to disagree with you. You keep saying that makeup lets your inner beauty shine through, but I think you've been hiding behind it. You've never looked more beautiful to me than you do right now."

"You…watched my shows?" she whispered, her voice choked up with tears.

"It's been weeks since you let me be with you. It was the only way I could spend time with you."

Moved beyond words, she took a fresh wipe and returned the favor. Taking time, taking care, she cleaned off all of the make-believe until all that was left was Enzo.

"I thought for sure you'd want to keep Indy around for a while."

"Why would I waste time on a fictional character when I've got a real hero waiting for me?"

He shook his head at that. He didn't believe her still. She'd fight that battle another day, not wanting to spoil the mood.

"Did you really think a cold shower was going to help after all that foreplay?"

He shivered when she teased a hand over his still impressive erection. "It did yesterday. And the day before that. And all the days since the last time you let me in."

"I'm sorry you thought you had to try it tonight."

He shrugged as if torturing his body into submission was no big deal. "You said you were tired."

"I am. Take me to bed, Enzo."

And thank God, he did.

CHAPTER 15

THE FIRST TIME they'd been together, Enzo had been surprised and had tried to give her all he could before she changed her mind or her child got home, whichever came first. He'd rushed and had regretted it at the end of the day.

This time he was prepared. He'd spent too long alone in this bed these past weeks, picturing her in her bed, just the other side of his wall. So close, but so far. He'd imagined all the ways he'd like to touch her, to please her. He'd always had a very active imagination, a blessing and a curse. Now that she was here, he wasn't going to waste his chance to explore.

Every face, every facet of this woman intrigued him. Each new look she presented to the world highlighted a different part of her personality. Who would she be now that he'd removed every trace of artifice? Who was the real Natalie?

He picked her up again, more romantically this time. One arm beneath her knees and another around her back, he lifted her and held her close. The way her head nestled into his chest made the heart inside it beat slow and thick, and he struggled to draw in a full breath. She had complete control over him, right down to his autonomic responses.

Carrying her over the threshold to his bedroom clarified the appeal of the old tradition. Bringing her into his space with his own power made it feel more like a home than it ever had before, and awakened a possessive impulse deep inside him.

Now that he had her, he didn't want to let her go. He didn't care if that made him sound like a caveman. Only an idiot would loosen his grip on paradise.

No other woman had ever felt right. Now he just had to convince her to give "right" a chance. He laid her gently on the bed and took a moment to imprint the image of her stretching out across his sheets. He pulled the monitor from her pocket and set it up on his nightstand after he checked that Daisy was safe and in bed. Then he opened the drawer and pulled out a string of condoms, tossing them onto the bed with a swagger.

"I'm prepared this time, if you want them."

She laughed that rare laugh and lifted his soul. "Feeling cocky, are we?"

His cock twitched and tented his gray sweatpants. He watched her watch him, naked hunger surpassing humor. He took her hand in his and cupped his hard length.

"I'm feeling confident. You're feeling cocky." He dropped his hand, but she kept hers there, exploring and playing with him through the gray cotton. He enjoyed this playful side of her. Really, really enjoyed it, as his eyes rolled back in his head and he hissed out a breath. So often, she had to be serious and in charge. Watching her relax and play turned him on just as much as her admittedly sensational touch.

Tonight was about cherishing her. Thanking her for bringing herself to him and trusting him to take care of her. He took his mission seriously. And after his reluctant celibacy, he was seriously going to lose it if she kept rubbing him that way.

He stepped back, freeing himself from her grip, and she pouted prettily. Giving in to impulse he leaned over her and sucked that pouty lower lip into his mouth. Gone was the waxy film. All he could taste was her, sweet and soft. She gasped, and he grinned.

"Patience is a virtue."

"So is generosity, and I wasn't finished giving."

"I've got other ideas on how to be generous." Too many clothes stood between him and his plans, but he was determined not to rush this. Every patch of skin his fingers touched as he removed her shirt he covered in kisses. He traced her curves with his lips from her hips up to her rib cage, down her arms to her sensitive wrists, absorbing every gasp and moan. He wanted to know her, every flavor, every sound, every scent, each texture on her body. Removing her bra gave him the opportunity to do the same to her breasts.

Those beautiful, small breasts plumped beneath his touch, like they'd been crafted for his hands. Like she was so in sync with him that they'd swelled to fit his hands perfectly. He molded her breasts to a peak and lightly pinched her nipple, and her hips bucked off the bed. And so sensitive! He replaced his fingers with his lips, laving her with the rough flat of his tongue, and she squirmed beneath him, latching her legs around his hips and gripping his hair in her fingers, desperately holding him in place. She was so hot, so open in her responses, and he wanted more.

Sucking one nipple hard into his mouth, he tweaked the other one in time, loving the way she rocked beneath him. He gave her more, asked for more, until she was writhing. Her hips spasmed against his and she let out a keening wail. A flash of pride and wonder lit him up as he held her vibrating body close. Had he just made her come with his mouth on her tits? Was that a thing? Because it was seriously the best thing. "Did you just…"

She nodded, her eyes dazed and glassy. "I've never…"

"Me either."

They stared at each other for a long moment heavy with awe. He wasn't sure who moved first, but they surged back together, riding out the wave with one pulsing refrain. *More.*

Natalie was in over her head, drowning in her desire. She watched the surface of sanity glittering above her and had zero impulse to reach for it. Shouldn't she? Shouldn't she be trying to save herself? These thoughts floated away on the current he was stirring up before she could grab on to them. She kept getting distracted by Enzo's hands. His beautiful, scarred, work-rough hands, that lifted heavy things and moved mountains every day, were touching her so gently, so intently, that it felt wrong to pay attention to anything else.

Scuffed and scarred and dark against the pale honey of the skin she kept hidden from the sun, his hands were beautiful in the way a cliff face or a pine forest was breathtaking.

Those hands were taking her breath away again, sliding fingers in and out of her still-quaking body, unleashing new tremors when his palm brushed hard against her sensitive clit.

He breached all of her boundaries, and she was letting him. The first glimmer of panic surfaced at that thought. Hell, she'd come knocking on his door. She couldn't very well run away now. Even if a small part of her wanted to retreat to the safety of her own space.

So this was what it felt like to be completely open to someone. Feeling him beside her, over her, and inside her all at once overwhelmed her. Her heart raced faster even as her limbs filled with molasses, heavy and sweet and just a touch bitter.

Another orgasm rolled through her, pulling her deeper into the quietest part of herself. The place where she couldn't hear or see or think. She could only feel and react. She drifted, aware that his touch had changed, receded. She had been alone for so long. Alone was safer. Now that she knew the power of his presence, she didn't want to be alone here, but she was helpless to reach for him. Completely limp, she could only pray he came back. Open and vulnerable, she needed him close to help her regain that sense of security. How far she'd fallen…

When she felt the heavy pressure of his cock at her entrance, sliding over her, readying himself and her with her wet response, she relaxed.

He was back. She wasn't alone. The first glide inside went so deep that she felt joined with him, connected. Even when he withdrew, he pulled part of her with him. But it was okay. He was coming back. Again and again, he came back, pushing her fears back into the dark with long, slow strokes of reassurance. As he increased his speed, arousal took panic's place, and she came back into her body. Every thrust pushed her higher, closer to the sun, nearly to the surface.

"Natalie." Her name on his lips was a plea for more, and she could deny him nothing.

His hands were everywhere, holding her to him, pulling her in for each frantic thrust. She gasped for air as one long wave of orgasm pulled her back under the surface. It rose and fell and rose again, tied to his insistent rhythm, breaking only on her last shudder as he chased her over the crest. His beat became shaky as he lost his control as well, jerking the last of his pleasure inside her.

And then the stillness. The quiet. Too much room for her thoughts to expand. Not even his soft kiss on her forehead could soothe the worry.

"Hmm, you good?" She nodded, unable to speak or meet his gaze. Thankfully he took her speechlessness in stride, and ran a hand down her spine, pulling her more firmly against him. "Good. You, here, it's good."

His cock was still thick inside her, tethering her to him as surely as his arms, and he closed his eyes. The weight of his body at rest was a tempting lure, and Natalie reveled in it for just a moment. She bet that if she had his bulk by her side, her own walls wouldn't have to be so thick. But the thought of losing him and his support, leaving her weak and defenseless, pulled her back into panic, which had no competition for her attention now that he'd passed out next to her.

She been naked with men before, obviously, but she'd never

felt so exposed. She didn't like it. Scared and pushed beyond her limits, she needed to regroup. She slipped from his grasp as carefully as she could.

Clothes.

Clothes would be a good initial barrier until she could pull her internal shields back together. She'd thought she could handle this. Handle him. She still couldn't believe how easily she'd dropped her hard-won defenses against the onslaught of his seduction. What had possessed her?

He had. He'd possessed every corner of her body and mind, tempting her to let go. And when she had, she'd found out that she couldn't swim very well and was out of her depth. Echoes of that possession skittered through her system as the cotton floated over her hyper-aware skin, and she wondered if she'd ever not remember that feeling of his hands caressing her body.

She was tugging her jeans up her legs when he stirred.

"Where you going?" *Damn him.* Even his sleepy voice was sexy and tried to pull her back in.

Be strong. You can do this. Now she was talking to herself. *Great.*

"I have to get back." It was a weak excuse, since they hadn't heard a peep from the monitor, but it gave her the few seconds she needed to fasten the button on her jeans. Another tangible barrier in place. True, she hadn't gotten her underwear on yet, so the inside seam of her jeans was torturing her sensitive folds and reminding her how much nicer his fingers had felt there. Part of her wanted to shuck them off again and let him show her just how much nicer. Another part urged her to run the fuck away quickly, because maybe the friction would give her another orgasm and remind her that she could do this on her own.

The one thin slice of her mind still clinging to reality poked her hard because she needed to get herself home before she lost her grip.

"Stay. I didn't mean to rush again. I just need a little nap to recover."

He'd rushed things? Oh dear God, if he ever took his time, she'd…never find out, because him "rushing" had pushed her way outside her comfort zone, and she couldn't come back here again.

"I can't stay."

"Why not? Daisy is fine. Come back to bed." Enzo gestured to the still-silent monitor.

"Enzo, I have to go home. I…I can't… Don't ask me to do this."

"To do what? To stay and let me love you again?"

Her head snapped back at his use of the L-word. This had gone deeper than she'd thought. "To ask me to put you ahead of my child."

It was a low blow, but she was getting desperate.

"I never asked you to do that."

"But you are arguing with me about leaving, while my baby is home alone in the dark."

"And what about you, Natalie? Do you want to be alone in the dark?"

She shook her head and walked away, snagging her underwear from the floor before she turned. "What I want and what I get are two very different things."

"Wait. I'm sorry. Of course Daisy's safety is important to me too. Please, say you'll come back."

Natalie paused. Could she come back? Could she stay away? She was completely overwhelmed right now, but even so she could admit that his lure would be difficult to resist. She would likely end up back here, in his bed, in his arms. But she would make damn sure that didn't happen until she was ready for it. Until she could protect her heart, while still enjoying him with her body and her mind. That pesky heart which she thought she'd toughened up over the years was still just a tender mess beneath all the padding. She had some work to do, but at least she could leave him with hope.

She nodded. "I'll come back when I can."

But it would be on her terms, when she could handle it. She had to be sure he couldn't break her. She couldn't afford to lose herself in him. It had been hard enough to rebuild after Kyle. If Enzo left her, it would be so much worse, so much harder to bounce back from losing his love.

Her brain shied away from the word, but her heart beat a thick, sickening beat in her chest and her belly flopped.

She had to go. Now. She raced to her own unit and made it to her bathroom before literally turning her stomach inside out.

"Mommy? Are you okay?" Daisy rubbed her eyes in the open doorway to the bathroom.

"I'm okay, baby. Did I wake you?"

"I heard the door slam. Did you throw up?"

"I did, but I'm okay. Everything is going to be okay now."

She pulled Daisy in for a hug and prayed that fate didn't make her a liar.

~

"WHAT WAS THAT BUG DAISY had a few weeks ago?" Sofia dropped into Natalie's chair on a huff.

"It was just a twenty-four-hour tummy flu. Why?" Nat smoothed the hair back from Sofia's face, pulling it off her forehead and into a band before she began.

"I feel like crap lately. I'm think I'm just exhausted. I've been juggling too many projects, and we've got the wedding planning rolling along. And for the last three days I can't stop throwing up. I thought maybe I'd caught her virus."

"Nope."

"That sounds definitive. Why not?"

Natalie brushed a hand over her forehead again to confirm. "No fever, and it's already lasted twice as long as hers and mine did."

"Well then, you might want to put on gloves in case whatever this is, is catching. You'll have to do some serious work today to hide this." Sofia gestured to her pale green complexion.

"Trust me. I'm a pro."

While she blended and brightened, Natalie plotted a quick trip to the drugstore.

Jake interrupted her speculations with a joyful slap on the back. "Good morning! Have you seen the numbers yet?"

"No, we were running late. How's Indy doing?"

"It's blowing up. You passed fifty thousand views around six a.m."

"Wait, what?" She'd checked in on Saturday morning, but then she'd tried to put Enzo and work out of her mind and focus on time with Daisy. She'd needed to step back from the scary door she'd found herself staring at Friday night. She'd taken Daisy hiking, and they had collected all sorts of new bits and bobs for what was quickly becoming Fairy Town.

She grabbed her phone and pulled up her account. She'd gone from a few hundred followers on her page to over five thousand, and Jake was right. The Indy video had closer to sixty thousand views now, and her other older videos were climbing too! *Holy crap!*

She posted the video immediately to her Facebook and Instagram pages, kicking herself for waiting so long. This was the kind of thing that could bump her up into the earning bracket.

"Hello?" Sofia waved a hand in front of her face. "You still with us?"

"Huh? Yeah, just a sec. Jake, this is crazy."

"No, this is chemistry. Can I count on you to keep doing these tutorials? Say at least two a week?"

She barely hesitated. She could still do her content around this. Hell, she'd stay up till two filming to make it all work. If she got enough views to start earning, this could be the financial answer for her and Daisy. It might at least give them a cushion. Stability was a powerful lure. Pride didn't stand a chance.

"I'd be an idiot to say no. And I'm not an idiot."

"Great. Don't forget the hashtags. I'll keep sharing them through the network's page and the show pages." Jake was already walking away. Now that he'd gotten what he wanted, he no longer required her presence.

Natalie was still trying to make sense of all of this, when Sofia asked her another question.

"Did you just tell Jake that you would keep filming makeup videos with my brother?"

"Yes. The first real one we did is exploding!"

Sofia blinked and waited a beat. "Don't you think that's something you should talk over with him?"

"Have you met Enzo? The man is a born helper. He can hardly stop himself from helping me, even when I ask him to back off. I'm sure it'll be fine."

Sofia raised a hand when Natalie moved back in with her makeup brush full of blush and her mind a million miles away.

"Do you know how he ended up working for my dad?"

"No, he hasn't told me that story."

"He came back after college to earn money while he got his own business off the ground. He never intended to stay. When Gabe died, our dad told him he wanted Enzo to take over the business. Enzo said no, but he'd stay and help out for a bit until Dad figured it out. And here he is three years later, barely getting paid, because he can't say no to our father."

"What are you trying to say?"

"I'm saying that helping you out once or twice is different from committing to a long-term video project, and I know that I would want the option to choose."

Sofia had a point, but Nat really didn't want to give Enzo the chance to back out. Plus she wasn't quite ready to have a deep conversation with him yet. She was still rebuilding her walls after he'd torn them all down Friday night. She'd let it ride for now and give him the option to back out after it had grown a little bigger, maybe big enough to keep earning without him.

"I hear you. I'll talk to him." *Eventually.*

～

Natalie left work to run through the drugstore on an early lunch break. She picked up a few of her beauty staples that needed updating. She was religious about keeping her makeup fresh. She browsed the new-release endcap and tossed a sparkly green shadow into her basket. Gummy bear vitamins and fruity toothpaste for Daisy joined it, and pads and tampons for herself. At the end of the aisle, she found the item she'd really come for. A pregnancy test. She grabbed the two-pack and tossed it into her cart as well.

After checking out she drove back to work, mentally girding herself to do Enzo's makeup after lunch. He hadn't been on the schedule until one, so she hadn't seen him yet to tell him the good news about the video.

Tucking one of the test sticks into her pocket, she left the rest of her shopping in the car and went to discreetly find Sofia. She walked through the house, and the designer wasn't in any of the rooms. Nor was she in the garage or out by the craft services table. On a hunch, Natalie swung by Sofia's car, and there she was, windows all rolled down despite the chilly breeze, fast asleep.

If she was right, and Sofia had morning sickness and not a virus, she didn't want to steal any of her precious sleep. Tucking the little foil-wrapped test into Sofia's lap, she backed away from the car slowly. Memories of her own experience with that particular test swam back from the depths of her pre-baby brain.

She'd graduated high school, and Kyle had been planning to become a mechanic. She'd gotten accepted to college, but hadn't figured out how to pay for it before she started throwing up violently every morning. After a week of not being able to keep any food down, she had begged her mother to take her to the doctor. She'd been convinced she had some horrible disease or stomach cancer. *Thanks, internet.*

Her mother had taken one hard look at her, as if she couldn't quite figure out how Natalie had turned out so dumb, and gotten in the car. Instead of driving to the doctor, her mom had gone to the convenience store and bought the pregnancy test. So not only had Natalie discovered she was pregnant, half the neighborhood suspected it by the next day.

Staring down at the two pink lines, a new reality had washed over her. She was going to be a mother. All of her plans for happily ever after disintegrated. Her plans for college, her job, her future, all gone. There was no way she could afford to raise a child and pay for school. And she couldn't see her boyfriend supporting them both on his mechanic salary. She needed a job, and she needed one fast. Because she was going to be a mother, and damn it, she was going to do better by her child than her own mother had. She had been young and poor and scared, but she had loved Daisy from the moment she saw those two little pink lines.

And when Kyle had ghosted her, and her mother told her she deserved it, she'd found the strength to chase a dream in LA because of Daisy. Everything good in her life had come from that kid. Seeing someone else starting that amazing journey was making her weepy.

Blinking back tears, she walked back into the garage to find a shirtless Enzo sitting in her chair. Her already turbulent emotions roiled inside her as lust wrestled with sanity and ambition tried to referee.

"I hope you don't mind. I made myself comfortable."

"Not at all. Actually, I wanted to ask if you would let me film your transformation in a time-lapse video today."

"Sure, anything to help."

See? She'd asked, and he'd offered. Sofia was way off base. If anything, he was too helpful. Natalie could admit that the way he jumped in to fix everything sometimes got on her nerves even as she planned to use it to her advantage.

If she asked for help, that was one thing, but other times she was perfectly capable of handling things on her own. She'd spent nearly a decade doing so, and when he stepped in unasked, it pissed her off. Did he think she was incompetent?

As she set up her camera rig, her head began to ache. She needed his help, but she didn't want to. She wanted his body, but she didn't want to bare her soul. Her needs and wants were a messy tangle, and she didn't have the time or patience to tease them apart right now. There was too much going on. So she was stuck in the middle of the tangle, being tugged back and forth, and it was exhausting. She felt as beat up as Sofia did, and she didn't have a baby to blame.

So she tried to blank her mind as she airbrushed Enzo's torso. It was just another bare man-chest. She couldn't think of it as the chest she'd licked or the arms that had carried her to his bedroom, or she'd get pulled too far to the lusty side of her tangle. Enzo must have been fighting it too, because he was holding himself unnaturally still.

When Sofia came running from the house through the garage, it distracted them both.

"Have you seen Adrian?" Before either of them could respond, she was yelling, her voice borderline panicked. "ADRIAN! Where are you?"

Adrian ran in from the outside door, a half-finished cup of coffee splashing over his hand. "What? What is it? What's wrong?"

Sofia threw herself in his arms, and his coffee dropped to the floor forgotten as he caught her mid-leap.

"Jeez, you two. Get a room," Enzo teased.

Natalie watched them, a little misty-eyed, and punched Enzo in the shoulder. "Don't be a jerk. Give them some privacy."

"If they wanted privacy, they shouldn't make out in the middle of their workplace."

"Be quiet, would you? They're having a moment."

Sofia whispered in his ear, and Adrian's face went pale in shock for a split second, and he dropped her feet back to the ground. Sofia handed him the little white plastic stick, and a huge grin split his face before he picked her up and spun her around. She slapped at his shoulder and shoved away from him, lurching for a garbage can. He reached to hold her hair back, his grin never slipping, as she tossed her cookies.

Natalie felt a pang of envy. Kyle's reaction had been anger and accusations. Losing his sexual access to his girlfriend because she had horrible morning sickness carrying his kid had been too much for him to handle. He had never expressed an interest in the baby outside of how it would change his life, so Natalie hadn't been too surprised when he'd bailed.

Bitter resentment she thought she'd buried long ago threatened to rise up and swallow her whole. Seeing how Adrian took care of Sofia made the girl Natalie had once been long for a different path. Back then, she'd been desperate for an ounce of caring from anyone. Now, she and Daisy were a team, and she didn't regret a thing.

She was well shed of Kyle and her mother. She was a strong woman, and she could take care of her kid all by herself. That didn't mean she couldn't still wish that she'd had someone to hold her hair and rub her back in the midst of the scariest time of her life. But she knew that kind of love wasn't for girls like her.

Enzo seemed to have caught on, because he'd quit teasing them and was grinning like a fool. "You knew?"

"I had a hunch. Looks like I was right."

He swept her up in a bare-chested hug and spun her around with a bright, happy grin. "I'm gonna be an uncle! Hot damn."

She grinned back and cupped his face, pulled into his excitement. "You're gonna be a great uncle."

He looked at her with his heart in his eyes, and kissed her tenderly. She pulled back from the intensity of that emotion and tapped his shoulders.

"Now put me down. You're getting me wet!"

His wiggling eyebrows made her laugh, earning her another whirl and kiss before they went to congratulate the happy couple.

～

LATER THAT NIGHT, as she edited the time-lapse video, that twirling kiss threw her for a loop. She watched as he picked her up and spun her around, his lips pressed to hers, and she pined. She wished she could slow down life like she could this video. She wanted him again, but things were moving too fast. She knew it was a bad idea. Her heart was still too tender, but she wanted him anyway. She kept it in the video, because she didn't want to edit him out of her life before she needed to. She wanted to believe in the way he looked at her for just a little while. She published the video before she could second-guess herself and went to bed, holding her dreams tight for company in her empty bed.

CHAPTER 16

Enzo would never understand women. Natalie was driving him nuts. During the day, she kept things completely professional. He could understand that. Her reputation meant a lot to her. She had a lot on her plate, but surely when he was in her chair she could crack a smile? Or give him one of those heavy-lidded looks she used to give him when she was rubbing Vaseline over his chest? But no, he got steel-faced Natalie, while Sofia and Frankie and even Adrian got smiles and conversation. What was up with that?

He jammed his shovel into the ground and wished he was wearing his T-shirt so he could wipe the sweat off his face. That had been another one of her ideas he didn't get. She'd convinced Jake that asking him to work shirtless would let nature even out his tan lines and save money on airbrushing costs.

So here he was, sweating his balls off getting skin cancer to save on a few ounces of makeup. Ridiculous!

He'd have been flattered if she'd wanted him to work shirtless so she could subtly ogle him at work, but not once had she left that damn garage to take a peek. Plus his natural tan shortened the time he got to spend in her chair. He missed her running her hands over his chest for half an hour every morning. If he were less secure, he might think she'd orchestrated this on purpose to avoid having to touch him.

Enzo stalked to the back of the truck for a drink of water, hoping it would cool down the fire in his gut. Something was wrong. Everything had felt just a little bit off for weeks.

Picking up the handles of his wheelbarrow, he pushed it over to the dump pile and filled it with more gravel. As he shoveled the crushed stone from one pile to another, he attempted to do the same with his thoughts. Maybe if he could find the right order, they'd start to make sense.

If he just looked at her behavior on set, he might think she wasn't interested or that he'd done something wrong. All signs pointed to her not wanting to be around him. But if he took the evenings into account, he got a different picture entirely.

Most evenings, after Daisy went to sleep, Enzo heard a light tap at his door. Natalie liked to pounce on him the moment he opened the door. The way they touched, the way they kissed, didn't make him think she wasn't interested. In fact, she barely let him get a word in before she caught him up in her passion. It had been so much easier to step back when he hadn't known exactly what he was risking missing. He was so far gone on this woman. He wanted to keep her in his bed forever, because there they made magic.

Outside his bed, well, that was a different story.

He dumped the gravel out on the path he was constructing and began to level it out with the back of his shovel.

This pattern of work and play might not have bothered him if she'd kept the serious at work and the fun at home. But she didn't.

Enzo wanted her to stay, snuggled up against him, ready to play again later. But the moment he fell asleep, she snuck back to her apartment. She didn't even say goodbye or offer excuses. She just grabbed her clothes and left. He knew she had to get back to

Daisy, but he was starting to feel like a hookup instead of a boyfriend.

Once he'd tried to play the garden boy to the dancing princess, staying awake through his post-sexy times snooze to ask her questions about nothing and everything. Her answers deliberately left him in the dark and pissed him off to no end. They had both spent the next day tired and cranky, and she had still managed to slip out without saying goodbye.

Lately, he'd been closing his eyes right after they'd had sex. He wanted to keep the image of her happy and in his arms, so he held that behind his eyelids, while she and her confusing reactions walked out the door.

He needed an invisibility cloak or some magic flower that would grant him the power to follow her and figure out her secrets. He wanted to know everything about her. He wanted to be welcome in the rest of her life.

Unfortunately, life wasn't a fairy tale, and he didn't care about twelve dancing princesses. He only wanted to build a kingdom with one. Well, two.

He spotted a heart-shaped rock in the gravel he was shoveling, and he tucked it into his pocket. When he saw Daisy after work, he would give it to her for her collection.

Playing with Daisy in the afternoon had become an unexpected bright spot in his day. She was precocious and loved learning about the plants in his garden. And the Fairy House had become Fairy Town, leaning toward Fairyopolis.

Yet, as fun as it was, he wanted more. He wanted to spend time with them both together. He'd suggested movie dates, trips to the park, picnic hikes, anything he could think of that Daisy and Natalie might both enjoy. And every time, he got a different brush-off. Daisy had a school project, a birthday party, a head cold. Natalie was too busy or too tired. He was beginning to think she didn't want him around.

Sometimes he caught her watching them play with a wary look on her face. She'd never said anything, but he got the distinct impression that she didn't completely trust him around her kid, and that if they hadn't already established their afternoon routine, she'd find an excuse to miss that too. In his mind, he was thinking of them becoming a family. In her mind—well, he didn't have a fucking clue what she was thinking because she wouldn't let him close enough to know.

He could see all the puzzle pieces for a happy life. He just couldn't figure out how to fit them all together, and she was keeping one hidden in her hand.

He slammed his shovel into the gravel path and broke through the weed barrier.

Damn.

"Hey, man. You okay?"

Rico walked over from where he was digging holes for the agave that were going in on this project.

"Yeah, I'm fine. I just broke the weed block, so I'll have to dig this back and lay another piece."

"Yeah, I'm not worried about the weed block, dude. I'm worried about the thunderclouds."

Enzo looked up at the clear blue sky, and Rico laughed.

"Not up there." Rico twirled his dirt-stained index finger at Enzo's face. "These right here. What's got you pissed?"

"Nothing."

"Oh, woman trouble, huh?"

"What do you know about it?" Enzo shoved him and went to go get the liner roll from the truck.

Rico blocked him with a forearm to the chest. "I know that things were going great between you and the makeup lady, until they weren't."

Damn, was it obvious to everyone?

"I just don't get it. During the day, it's like I don't exist. After work, she tolerates me. And at night, she's all over me, and then bam, she's gone. What the fuck am I supposed to make of that?"

"Either she's using you for a booty call..."

"Or..."

"Or she can't stay away."

Enzo let the words sink in. He didn't think he was a booty call for her. The second rationale made a sick sort of sense. Why would she want to stay away though? All he could think was that she was afraid of things changing for Daisy. Was she testing him?

Well, he was going to pass this test with flying colors. He'd just step up his game. Show her he was in this for the long haul. He wanted to be part of their lives, so he'd just make a place for himself there and fill it reliably until she could trust that he wasn't going anywhere.

He'd start tonight. He could bring pizza over for dinner so Nat wouldn't have to cook, and then he could play with Daisy so she could get some filming or editing done. Once a week he was still her male model, but he knew she was still keeping up with her regular features too. He didn't like being on display, but it was the only time he got her focused attention out of bed. Some days watching her videos was the only way he got to spend time with her. It made him sad to think about it that way, but it didn't stop him from watching clips while he ate his dinner alone.

The plan was coming together, and Enzo felt more energized and optimistic than he had in weeks.

"How did you get so smart about women?" He clapped Rico on the shoulder and grinned for the first time all morning.

"Well, when you date as many as I do, you pick up a few things."

Enzo didn't intend to earn his dating knowledge the hard way, not when there was only one woman he was interested in figuring out.

~

Enzo spent the rest of the day shoveling, shifting, and otherwise pummeling the bare yard into his vision of a suburban oasis. When they broke off at five, he swung by the pizza place and stared at the menu. What was their favorite pizza? This was something he should know, but he hadn't been trusted with that information. He hadn't been invited far enough into their lives. His resentment rose, and he tried to tamp it back down as he ordered a cheese and a supreme.

They didn't date. They didn't hang out as a family might. He entertained the little girl and slept with her mama. What kind of man did that make him? One who needed to fix the situation he was in fast before it got any worse.

Grinning, he knocked on Natalie's door, imagining how happy and surprised she'd be. Maybe they could even make this a routine. Taco Tuesday. Pizza Wednesday… Weeks of evenings spent together spun out in his mind's eye, until the door opened on World War Three.

The TV was playing *Octonauts* again, Daisy was crying, and Natalie looked frazzled with her hair sticking out sideways from what had been a messy bun to begin with. He looked down at the floor where it appeared some small animal had fought hard in a pillow fight and lost.

She looked tired. He realized how rare it was for her to show her tired to the world.

"Hello, ladies. I come bearing pizza."

He walked into the apartment, pizza boxes balanced dramatically on one hand.

"Oh, I made chicken."

"Ooooh! Pizza! Does it have ham and pineapple?" Daisy, tears forgotten, was jumping on the couch now.

Enzo made a mental note. "No, but it will next time. I've got plain cheese or one with a little of everything."

Turning toward the kitchen counter to put down the boxes, he almost ran into Natalie who had snuck up behind him and was blocking the space between the peninsula and the fridge.

"I made chicken, but thank you."

"I don't like chicken. I want pizza." Daisy's voice inched back toward tears.

"Are you asking me to take the pizza and leave?"

"I'm saying that I've got dinner under control, and Daisy and I are in the middle of something, so…"

Daisy grabbed his leg and tried to pull him into the living room. "Come see, Enzo! Mommy and I are working on my Halloween costume. I'm gonna be Fawn the Animal Fairy."

He resisted. He had to be absolutely clear in this moment with Natalie. It was crucial to his understanding of whatever the hell was going on here. He couldn't let himself be distracted.

"Just a second, *bellisima*. I need to talk to your mom."

Daisy stayed where she was, gripping his jeans in her hand, her eyes wary and fixed on her mother.

"Enzo, you can't just come in here with pizza. We have a routine. Dinner is almost ready, and as you can see we are in the middle of a project. I don't have time to entertain you tonight."

"I don't need to be entertained, Natalie. I came to spend time with you both, and maybe help a little by bringing dinner."

"Mommy, please can he stay? Please?" Daisy turned on the puppy dog eyes and hugged his leg harder.

Natalie looked down at Daisy, and then back at him. She literally bit her tongue until she winced. He hoped that's where the tears in her eyes came from as well. He watched her chin set and her eyes flare with anger. This was not the reception he'd expected at all.

"Fine! Whatever." She took the pizza boxes from him and threw them down on the counter. Turning off the burners on the stove, she moved the simmering pots into the sink where they sizzled and popped, and stormed into her room. The door slammed and locked behind her.

What the hell? Enzo had only been trying to do something nice. Why was she so angry? If she thought—

A tiny hand slipped into his and pulled him from his thoughts and into the living room. "Will you come see my costume?"

As much as he longed to knock on that door and demand answers, he wouldn't, not in front of her little girl. But damn, her reaction pissed him off.

"See? I'm gonna have a tiger lily dress just like Fawn and an acorn hat." She gestured to the orange cotton that looked like it had been attacked by a Sharpie and a circle of brown felt and scraps all jumbled into a pile at her feet.

"What's that for?" He pointed to the pillow leaking feathers and the mass of white and gray fur that looked like a raccoon who'd met an unfortunate end on the highway.

"I gotta have a Gruff to carry with me."

"Who is Gruff?"

This launched into a long discussion of the NeverBeast and required a viewing of the same movie while they munched on pizza. Natalie stayed in her room.

"Will you come back to help me with my costume?"

"You bet, Daisy."

"Promise?" She reached out a tiny hand for his. He was touched to think that she trusted his handshake, and gave it wholeheartedly.

"I promise, but right now it's getting late. You need to get to bed."

When the movie ended, he cleaned up their dishes and asked Daisy to brush her teeth. He tapped on Natalie's door. He hadn't heard a peep from her all night.

"Do you want me to start a bath for Daisy?"

"No. Just…go." Her muffled response filtered through the closed door.

"Jesus, Natalie, will you talk to me? What did I do?"

"Nothing. I've got it from here."

What more could he do?

He gave Daisy a hug and walked home more confused than ever.

NATALIE EMERGED FROM HER BEDROOM, eyes puffy and soul drained. She was an idiot for overreacting like that, but the stress of the day plus a special project with Daisy had already drained her reserves of patience. And damn it, she wasn't ready to be calm and rational about it yet, so she'd hidden in her room and sulked like she was the six-year-old, the worst kind of sulking there was. *Good riddance!*

Clearly, she wasn't done with the sulking portion of the evening.

He just didn't think. One little thing and he'd thrown their carefully orchestrated evening off schedule, not to mention the fallout tomorrow. This was why she was better off without idiot men in her life.

It was a Wednesday night. Daisy had school in the morning. And he'd just shown up, no warning, no plan, and stolen their whole night. And expected to be praised for it?

Daisy still hadn't done her reading homework, and she'd just spent the last two hours in front of a glowing screen, instead of getting her usual half hour of *Octonauts* and then turning it off. Bedtime was going to be so much fun. And who was left to handle the tantrums on the way? Not Enzo. No, just Natalie. Because someone had to be the responsible one who made sure her kid was clean and fed and rested and safe, even when that kid was being a punk. And the only someone who would always be there for Daisy was Natalie. Always. And she refused to let her daughter down.

Who did he think he was, coming in here and throwing her world into chaos? Moving the items from her to-do list to her done list was her proof that she was doing right by Daisy. It was hard enough to accomplish on a good day.

No bath, no progress on that Halloween costume, and now she was going to have to cook again on Friday night at the end of a long week because he'd gone and stolen pizza night out from under her. She'd even cooked tonight and not eaten it! She regretted that her temper had cost her that meal prep but damn it, she'd been too angry to think clearly. She mentally plotted out an early morning grocery run.

On a good night, she had just enough energy to keep up with her carefully ordered life. She didn't have it in her to clean up after Enzo's "surprises." He was like someone walking into a party, tossing handfuls of glitter in the air. Beautiful and fun in the moment, but a real pain in the ass for whoever had to come in behind him and pick up the pieces.

When she heard the front door close, Natalie gathered what was left of her sapped energy and sanity and got to work. No one else would do it for her.

She ran a tub of water for Daisy, pulled costume scraps back out of the bag, organized them and laid them flat, before putting them back in the project bag, and re-loaded the dishwasher so everything would get clean. She reluctantly gave Enzo points for packing up what she'd cooked into Tupperware and attempting to fill the machine, but it didn't balance out the extra work he'd made for her. This was why she never asked for help. It was more trouble than it was worth.

She pulled Daisy's homework log and reading book out of her backpack and tossed it on her bed before ducking back into the bathroom to make sure her daughter got all the shampoo out of her hair because she wanted to do it all by herself.

So much of her life was wash, dry, repeat, she could do it on auto-pilot. So while her hands gathered dirty clothes for the wash, and towel-dried Daisy's hair, her frustration continued to simmer. They finally curled up together on Daisy's bed a full hour after her usual bedtime, and they still had to do reading homework.

Tonight, of all nights, Natalie wished they could just skip it. But she was teaching Daisy responsibility and how to honor her commitments. Modeling that behavior was the best teacher, at least according to all of the parenting books she'd read. Not having a reliable parent to go to for answers, she depended heavily on the knowledge of others. Sometimes the knowledge of others sucked.

She couldn't remember her own mother ever curling up in

bed and reading to her, and she'd turned out fine... *Nope.* She couldn't go down that path for even a night. Clearly she hadn't turned out all right, because her emotions were a hot fucking mess and she kept making bad decisions.

She was just so tired.

Daisy read, and if Natalie nodded off at times, well, there was no one here to notice or judge, was there? Dr. Seuss was brutal any time of day. Log signed and book stacked, she finally kissed her baby goodnight.

But Daisy wasn't ready to let go. Her little arms wrapped around Natalie's neck for a hug that kept her close for her interrogation.

"Mommy, does Enzo make you sad?"

Her quiet voice broke Natalie's heart. How could she explain?

"I'm not sad, baby."

Daisy was close enough to see the tear streaks down her cheeks. "But he made you cry."

"I was frustrated and angry that he didn't ask me before coming over here. You didn't eat a balanced dinner, and now we can't have Pizza Friday like we planned. We didn't make any progress on your costume for Halloween. And you're still up an hour and a half past your bedtime. Tomorrow is going to be hard for you at school. If I had known he was coming, we could have planned things so they didn't get so out of control."

Daisy pondered all of that for a minute. It was a lot to take in, but Natalie had always been honest with her about the limitations and realities of parenting. After all, they were a team of two, depending on each other to survive and thrive.

"Can we invite him over more, then? So it's not a surprise? I like it when he comes to play."

"Oh baby, that's just it. We can't play all the time. We have responsibilities too."

"But if he lived here, he could share those too, right? I like him, Mommy. You like him too. I saw you hugging him in your video."

Daisy's voice was rising in pitch and tempo, prelude to the oversized tantrum warming up in her tiny, tired body.

"You watched my videos?"

"Yes, Enzo lets me borrow his iPad sometimes."

Natalie's own tantrum woke back up. He was giving her six-year-old unsupervised access to YouTube? Did he know what kind of bad things popped up in the recommended videos? Panic and anger fought for top spot as her brain exploded.

"You know I don't like you to watch YouTube."

"But why can't I even watch your show? Why can't I have any fun? Why can't Enzo come live with us?"

Natalie wished she could say she was surprised by this conversation, but she'd seen it coming. Daisy wanted a daddy.

She tried and failed to keep her voice calm. "Because he lets you watch YouTube, but he doesn't make you do homework. He's not your parent! I am. I get that he's fun to hang out with, but he isn't your father. You can't expect him to act like one, just because you wish he was."

"But you—"

"Young lady, this conversation is over. Now go to sleep."

The mutinous glare on her daughter's face suggested there wasn't a snowball's chance in hell of that happening, but Natalie wasn't in the mood to fight her anymore. She'd already broken her heart. She didn't want to break her spirit too.

"This isn't fair," Daisy spat at Natalie's back.

"Baby, no one ever said life was fair."

Next door, Enzo's heart cracked a little in his chest as he shamelessly listened to them on the monitor. He'd resisted the temptation to eavesdrop on bedtime for weeks, but tonight his confusion had pushed away his reluctance. And now he knew the reason for the saying. Eavesdroppers never heard anything good.

He'd been trying to help. So what if he wasn't her father? He could learn, couldn't he? Was that what he wanted? He touched the shiny bubble of the vision in his mind and it didn't pop. It morphed to encompass and include him, a happy family trio. Suddenly, it was exactly what he wanted. How else could he prove that he cared? That he deserved to be welcomed into their lives? Despite tonight's setback, he wasn't giving up.

CHAPTER 17

NATALIE DRAGGED HERSELF into work the next morning. Daisy had been up several times during the night. Finally, Natalie had just pulled her baby into bed with her. Daisy had clearly gotten used to having her own bed, because she promptly turned into a starfish, taking up three-fourths of the bed and hitting Natalie in the head and lower back simultaneously. Daisy had finally fallen asleep, but Nat was wrecked. She'd gotten used to sleeping alone too.

Halloween was less than a week away and costumes weren't done. Halloween was her favorite holiday, and she always made their costumes from scratch. The first year, it had been a necessity, because money had been so tight. She'd taken a little green onesie and pasted on white felt letters to make her little peanut an M&M. This year she was going to be Tinkerbell to Daisy's Fawn, but she wouldn't be anything if she couldn't get the damn costumes made. If she could just get through work, the grocery store, school pickup, snack and homework, maybe she could squeeze in a nap on the couch before she started sewing… God, even making her to-do list was exhausting.

As she walked up the driveway and into the garage, she passed Enzo already hard at work on the yard. Though she ignored him, the scent of mowed grass chased her all the way inside, reawakening her desire and frustration simultaneously.

She methodically applied makeup for everyone with an early morning call, but she couldn't summon her usual bubbly self to chit-chat.

"Are you okay?" Sofia finally asked.

"Just a rough night. But I should be asking you that question. How are you feeling?" Natalie asked as she smoothed Sofia's hair back into a chignon.

"I'm good, but…weird. Everything is just weird. I wake up with weird new aches, weird things smell bad, weird touches will set me off. I guess I'm still adjusting to my body not being my own."

"I remember that. With Daisy it was raw chicken. I couldn't even see it without wanting to vomit." Being around Sofia brought back all the memories of her own pregnancy. Her body had still been developing so puberty weird had merged with pregnancy weird, and she'd never been sure which was which. But weird was definitely the word for it.

Her breasts had ached and burned to be touched at the same time. She'd felt bone tired, but unable to sleep. She'd been starving, but only for the three foods that didn't make her want to throw up. Weird.

"But my doctor says all of it is normal. She must think I'm an idiot."

"All first-time moms are clueless. That doesn't make you an idiot. It makes you a good mom-to-be because you are noticing and asking questions about what you don't know. Number one rule of parenting: you are always in learning mode. They are always changing, and you will have to adapt with them. You're just practicing for the main event."

"Thanks, Natalie. It makes me feel better to hear that from you."

"To hear what?" Adrian stepped up beside her and pressed a kiss to her cheek.

"Hey! Easy on the blush there, big guy!" Natalie swatted him back.

Sofia giggled and added a natural flush beneath the artfully applied blush on her cheekbones. She was radiant with love and hormones.

"To hear that I'm not crazy."

"Verdict is still out on that one. Did you tell her about the butter and pickle sandwiches at two a.m.?" he teased.

"Nope. Not crazy. In fact, that sounds strangely delicious right now."

"You're *loco*! Both of you!" Adrian backed away with his hands raised.

"Hey, what are you doing back in here anyway? I thought you were filming the living room demolition."

"Yeah, we got bumped, so I came to see if you were hungry for an early lunch. Jake says there's some problem with the lighting rigs so we probably won't start until this afternoon."

"One o'clock at the earliest." Jake came in behind them, fresh coffee and an everything bagel in his hands. "I came to warn you. I'll need you to cover touch-ups until Angela can get here this afternoon."

Natalie cringed as his garlicky, onion-y breath wafted to her on his words. *Ugh.* The content of his words was bad enough. He didn't need to add insult to injury. She stepped back toward Sofia's fragrant and fresh shampoo scent before she answered. "No problem, boss."

"What's next for Man Makeover Monday?"

"I've got one more look before Halloween. We're going with Groot. I thought it would be fun to turn the landscaper into a tree. Lots of fun details."

"Outstanding. I was thinking we should start posting them on the MDSH page directly."

It sounded like casual business chat, but he didn't fool her for a second. Jake never made a suggestion that wasn't carefully calculated for his own benefit. She was honestly surprised he hadn't pushed for this earlier, so she already knew what her answer would be. "No."

"Excuse me?"

"I said no. This vlog is mine. My content, my creation. I get that you like the hits and the attention it brings to the show, but it's mine. I worked damn hard to build that audience, and now that it's starting to pay out, I'm not going to let you take it away."

Jake looked stunned that she had dared to talk back to him, but she wasn't going to back down on this. Her show was her passion project, and she wasn't about to let years of hard work get taken from her.

"Good girl," Sofia murmured.

"It was just a thought." Jake backpedaled on his idea, and pride filled Natalie's chest. She'd stood up for herself and the world hadn't ended.

"We can definitely talk about cross-promotion or guest spots, but my content is my content."

"Understood. Drop by after lunch, and we can talk about the Halloween posts across our platforms."

"Sounds good."

He left, and she let out a full exhale she hadn't realized she'd been holding.

"That was impressive, Natalie. Way to stand up to him." Sofia was beaming and Adrian tugged her hair as if she was one of his sisters. She felt the warmth of their friendship surround her in a metaphorical hug.

"We know that wasn't easy, but you handled it well."

"Thanks, guys. I'm just glad you were standing here. But you'd better go grab your lunch while you can. Feed that baby."

Natalie watched the couple leave hand in hand and only felt a little twinge of envy.

HAVING TO REDO EVERYONE'S MAKEUP right before she left meant she was exhausted from a full day on her feet and had to hustle to get Daisy from school on time. So much for the grocery run. As expected, Didi was tired from a full day as well and cranky with it.

"Mommy? I want a snack."

"Is that how you ask for something?"

"Yes. I'm hungry."

Natalie battled the urge to roll her eyes and focused on getting them home without falling asleep at the wheel. "Try again."

"Enzo just gives me a snack."

Oh goody. This again. She was getting mighty tired of hearing how great things were when Enzo watched her. It wasn't fair that he got all the credit for the fun, while she had to be the responsible one. And, she reminded herself, there was that tricky word. Fair. No one said raising a kid would be fair.

Natalie decided to pick her battles. This one wasn't worth the fight today, so she bit her tongue as she parked in front of their apartment and went inside.

"Hey! I got a letter. It's addressed to me!" Daisy's petulant sulk had transformed into delight in a flash. God, wasn't childhood great? She wished she could pull herself out of a bad mood as quickly.

"Well, you'd better open it and see what it says." *Please, let it be a birthday party invite.* Natalie would gladly buy the newest Shopkins set in exchange for a few Daisy-free hours this weekend to catch up.

"It's from Enzo. It says:

Dear Daisy,

I hope you had a good day at school. Would you and your mom like to come to dinner on Friday night with my family? My mom asked if you will help with the cookies since you're an expert. I would also like to come over and help with your costume. I can be there Saturday at eleven if that works for you. Please circle yes or no and send this back.

Mommy, he even drew a narwhal! Can we go? Please, Mommy?"

Damn it. Why hadn't she read the damn card first? She took it and skimmed the contents, his words carefully printed large enough for Daisy to read. She was reluctantly charmed by his reply card with the narwhal horn pointing to the yes box. And how could she refuse or deflect when her baby was bouncing up and down and full of light?

"Okay. We'll go."

～

Friday afternoon, after snack and an early bath, Natalie brushed Daisy's hair methodically, trying to restore order to her own chaotic thoughts as well as her daughter's locks.

She knew all of these people. They were colleagues. Friends, even. She liked them and they liked her, as far as she could tell. So why the hell was she so nervous about having dinner with them?

She knew the answer, but she didn't want to face it head-on, so she was hiding behind obsessively grooming them both. She was on her third dress and second hairstyle.

She was "meeting the parents." She'd never met anyone's parents before, not like this, and she was scared shitless. The pressure building in her chest, urging her to run, was ridiculous. She smoothed down Daisy's dress and her own before forcing herself to walk away from the mirrors and out the front door.

"Do I look okay, Mommy?"

The downfall of making her living in mirrors and hiding behind makeup was that Daisy had internalized a lot of her habits.

"Baby, you know that you are beautiful inside and out, no matter what you wear."

"But what if this is the wrong dress?" Daisy plucked at the hem of her skirt, twisting it between her fingers.

"The wrong dress for what?"

"The wrong dress to make them like me."

She'd known Daisy was excited for this dinner. Nat hadn't realized that she'd picked up on the significance of the occasion as well. How could she put her daughter at ease when she was so conflicted herself? Wasn't that the story of her life?

"It's just dinner." Her own anxiety levels spiked over that falsehood. She clamped down hard on her own worries to project calm confidence and tried again. "Well, that's not exactly true. It's a special dinner because we got invited, but you already know Enzo and his mom. We're going to Jo's house, where you made cookies."

Daisy nodded. "Right, but what about the rest of them?"

"They are going to love you, because you're a pretty cool kid." And if they don't, I've got your back, she vowed silently. No sense in adding worry about the possibility of failure.

Daisy blushed and ducked her head. "I just really want them to like me."

The whispered confession broke Natalie's heart. She heard what Daisy wasn't saying. *I hope they'll like me enough to keep me.* She heard that desire loud and clear, because she'd felt it herself. Surely there was room in the Valenti clan for two more.

This was the longest they'd ever stayed in one place, and Daisy was starting to put down roots. And she wanted those roots to include Enzo. As much as Natalie enjoyed the fantasy that they would eventually belong somewhere, the realization that Daisy felt the lack too pinched at her heart. She wasn't enough family for her baby anymore. She was letting Daisy down. And this was going to hurt like hell for them both when it ended. Add one more check to the #MomFail tally.

"Let's go, Sprite. It's going to be fine. You'll see."

Natalie grabbed the wine and flowers and bundled Daisy out to the car, before she lost her nerve or gave in to despair.

~

Enzo was pacing a track in the floor of his mother's front hall. He should have gone to pick them up. They could have ridden over together, but he'd been late at a new job site, and Natalie had insisted that she was fine driving. So here he was, imagining all sorts of vehicular disasters that could have made them— He checked his phone. Seven minutes late, and no texts or missed calls. Flat tire, fender bender, highway robbery...

"Would you relax?" Frankie shoved his shoulder, pushing him out of his loop, and handed him a slice of prosciutto from his mother's famous antipasti trays. "They'll get here when they get here."

"Okay, Zen Master. I'd like to see how you feel, putting your heart in a car and hoping it arrives safely on the other end."

"Buster can't drive."

"Very funny."

"Oh, I know I'm funny. I don't need you to tell me that. Do you need me to tell you to pull your head out of your ass and tell her how you feel?"

No. He knew. He'd fallen head over heels for two lovely ladies, and he'd been clumsy with it. He couldn't find the words to tell them, and his attempts to show them kept going sideways somehow. But he'd figure it out. The alternative was unthinkable. "No, I've got a handle on that, thank you very much."

"Good, because they just pulled up."

Enzo spun to open the door, and Frankie laughed at him and clapped him on the back. He didn't care. They were here, safe and sound, and he was bringing them to meet his family for the first time. True, they had already met most of them, but the symbolism here was important.

When you loved a woman, you brought her home to meet your family. He'd never actually done it before but he knew the rules. He was entitled to some nerves, he decided as they walked up the path, Daisy gripping Natalie's hand like a lifeline.

"Hi! You found it okay."

Idiot. Of course they had. They were standing right in front of him.

"Yes, just had to stop for gas. I'm sorry we're late."

"Not at all. No worries."

"Sure, no worries at all," Frankie teased over his shoulder.

"Shut up," he muttered. "Come on in." He kissed Natalie hello, his relief flowing from his lips to hers. When she stiffened, he realized his misstep.

He'd never kissed her in front of Daisy before, or in public really at all. Despite his many attempts, they hadn't actually been out together as a couple. He shouldn't have taken no for an answer. He should have hiked with her up the highest mountain so he could shout his love to the world. He should have started every day at work with a kiss to make her and the rest of the crew blush. Plenty of time to change that though. *Let the public courting begin.* He bent down and lifted Daisy's hand to his lips as well, which made her giggle.

"I brought these for Jo." Natalie held up the wine and flowers.

"She's back in the kitchen. Let me show you."

This felt awkward. *Why is this so awkward?*

"Natalie! Daisy! Welcome!" Josephine folded them both into a warm hug, any awkwardness dissolving into the brilliant sunshine of his mother's smile. "I hope you're hungry. I went a little overboard tonight." She gestured to the laden countertops around her and the sink full of dishes. "I made antipasti, salad with goat cheese and pomegranate seeds, pumpkin ravioli from scratch, and there's a roast beast in the oven."

"Roast beast?" Daisy asked, wide-eyed.

"Enzo loves watching *The Grinch* at Christmas, and I used to always make this for Christmas Day dinner, so we fell into calling it roast beast instead of beef. I also wanted to make some more cookies for dessert. Maybe you could help me roll them, Daisy."

She nodded, still intrigued by the beast in the oven, and bent her head to accept the too-large apron Jo slid over her head.

Enzo ran a hand down Natalie's back and felt her pause. "Dad also picked up a few pumpkins for us to carve after dinner if there's time."

"You didn't have to go through all this trouble." Her face looked as composed and beautiful as ever, but her fingers fidgeted with the belt at her waist. She was nervous too.

He smiled. That had to be a good sign. This was important to both of them. Reassured, he ushered her into the dining room to meet his extended family of aunts and uncles and cousins who had all come because he'd asked. She handled the introductions with grace and poise, and he beamed.

Soon everyone was sitting down at the table, talking to, over, and around each other, leaving no room for nerves.

His heart settled as gratitude backfilled into the nervous cracks, grounding him. Natalie and Sofia were swapping pregnancy notes like a veteran counseling a grunt before the big battle, and Dom kept butting into their conversation with his two cents. At least he seemed to be amusing them with his observations.

On the other end of the table, his mom had taken Daisy under her wing and Frankie was cracking knock-knock jokes. Enzo couldn't help the goofy grin that spread across his face. Her little laugh just lit him up. His mom was going to be such a great grandma. He was glad that Sofia and Adrian were getting that ball rolling, but maybe he could add to the grandchildren count a little earlier. Seeing Natalie and Daisy so comfortable, all wrapped up in his family, made him ache to keep them there. This felt right, as if he finally had all those puzzle pieces right where he wanted them.

"Hey Natalie, how are your beauty videos doing?" His mom asked politely.

"They are great. My viewership has grown like crazy in the last month." Natalie lit up. "For the first time, I hit the earning bracket."

This was news to Enzo, and he wasn't quite sure what it meant, but if she was happy, he was happy.

"I'm sure that has nothing to do with Enzo stripping down for the airbrush," Frankie teased. "I still can't believe you convinced him to keep coming back."

"That might have been the episode that pushed us over the top, but the backlog bump has been sizeable."

She was officially speaking a different language.

"So are you going to start getting endorsement deals and free stuff?" Sofia asked.

This sounded more and more serious. Enzo had just thought he was doing her a favor to get Jake off her case. Sure, he'd watched the videos and noticed that they were getting good comments, but he hadn't considered it anything but a fun hobby. Was she making money off of this?

"I haven't been approached yet, but a girl can dream."

"Hey, Enzo," Frankie teased. "Maybe you should keep your shirt off for all of her videos. I bet you'd be rolling in it then, Natalie."

Natalie's grin faded a bit when she saw the confusion on his face. He couldn't help but blurt the first question to surface from the swirl.

"Are you making money off me?"

Natalie's smile froze, and her tone was just as frosty. "I'm making a little money off my videos, yes. Your features brought in a bunch of new viewers, but they are watching all of my content, not just your makeovers."

He didn't know why he was so pissed off, but he was. He didn't begrudge her success, but he wished she'd kept him in the loop. This felt like work, another responsibility on an already overflowing plate. What if he didn't want to do it anymore? Would he be taking away her income? He'd put up with it because he thought he was helping her out for the show. But the little voice inside him, who'd been piping up more and more, told him he was being taken advantage of. Again. He hushed that voice, because this was not the place to hash this out. But the kernel of resentment simmered in his chest.

After the salad and pasta courses, Jo brought out the roast beef, redolent with garlic and rosemary, surrounded by potatoes and carrots roasted in the same pan. Enzo's mouth instantly watered, but Natalie turned decidedly green. She excused herself from the table before Jo even got the thing carved.

Enzo followed her out the back door onto the deck, where she stood braced on the railing taking deep, gulping breaths. "Hey, are you okay?"

"Yeah, I'm fine."

She was clearly not fine, but then she strode down into the grass. His yard. His special spot. Maybe now was the right time and right place for the right question. How to broach it though? "It seems to be going really well."

"What was this, an audition? Were we trying to win a walk-on role?"

Okay, clearly that wasn't the right track.

"What? No, I just meant it seems like you're both enjoying yourselves. At least you were until you bolted from the table."

"Sorry, my stomach is still a little touchy. Maybe that virus is lingering, but something about the beef smelled off, and I needed some air."

"Everything okay?"

"Everything is fine. Why do you keep asking me that?"

Seriously? She was annoyed that he was inquiring after her well-being after she said she felt sick? "Because I'd like to help you if I can."

"Oh, like you helped with pizza night?"

The sarcasm in her voice cut like a razor. Clearly not the right time or place. Maybe not even the right woman, given the anger in her eyes. "I'll admit, I screwed up. I should have called."

"You should have trusted that I've got raising Daisy under control."

"I think you're a great parent—"

She whirled on him, arms crossed. "Well, thank you for your expert opinion. I'm sure I'm gratified to have your approval."

He'd had just about enough of that tone, and felt his own rising to meet hers.

"Hold up. Where is this coming from? All I tried to do was help—"

"We didn't need your help!" She slapped away his words, inflaming his temper even hotter.

"Oh, but you needed my help on your videos? You said it yourself. All of the videos got a bump after I walked in. And this is the thanks I get? You are just like everyone else. Jake. My dad. You all take and take until I've got nothing left."

She blanched and stepped back. "Don't you dare. Don't you dare try and take credit for my success."

"I wouldn't have to if you'd shared it with me. Instead I find out when you crow about it to my family? And now I'm the bad guy?" Enzo raked his fingers through his hair, as if pulling his hair straight would take the rest of the conversation with it. "I fixed everything I messed up, and you're still mad. Unreal!"

"Hold up. What do you mean you 'fixed everything'?"

"When I brought the pizza, you said I screwed up Pizza Friday and your costume time, so I invited you to Friday dinner, so you wouldn't have to cook. And I'm going to help with Daisy's costume tomorrow. What more do you want from me? An apology tattoo?"

"How about a little honesty? I'm damn sure I didn't mention either of those things to you, because once again, in case you didn't catch it the first eighty times, I've got things with Daisy handled!"

"You don't share a goddamn thing with me! I overheard you on the monitor and damn it, Natalie, I was trying to fix things."

She took a step backward, her jaw slack, her voice deadly quiet. "Let me get this straight. You eavesdropped on a private conversation between me and my kid?"

"You wouldn't talk to me. You barricaded yourself in your room."

"So that makes it okay?"

"No, I—"

"And you don't think I can handle feeding my child, so you offered us a pity plate at your mom's table, so I can see how it's done?"

"That's not—"

She cut him off again. "Did you even think about what significance Daisy might put on this meal? Also, what the hell do you mean by letting my kid watch YouTube videos by herself so she can see videos of you hugging me?"

"What? No. She missed you, so we watched it—"

"STOP IT!" The yell, heavy with rage, tore from her chest and made him obey. He froze. "Just…stop. I can't do this, Enzo. I can't let you tear me down. I can't let Daisy fall in love with you and your family too. Because they're great, wonderful, really. And very tempting for a girl with no family."

Was she talking about Daisy or herself? And what did that "too" mean?

"Letting you in makes me weak. And Daisy needs me to be strong, invincible. I'm all she's got." Her voice had gone scary quiet, and she wouldn't look up from her locked hands. He could feel her pulling those tentative tendrils she'd put out back inside. She was convincing herself to run away again.

It doesn't have to be that way. You can have me too. He wanted to shout it from the rooftops. Well, he'd wanted to ten minutes ago. Now, he didn't know what the hell to say. Apparently she didn't need his response.

"I get that you think you are helping, but you're not. I need…" She drew in a deep breath, and he waited, breathless, for her next words.

Whatever she needed, he would be the one to give it to her.

"I need you to back off."

She walked calmly into the house, not waiting for him to find the words to make things right, not even looking back to see his heart fall from his chest like an autumn leaf caught up on the wind of her departure, chasing her, always two steps behind.

Enzo sat heavily onto the bottom step and rested his forehead on his knees. *What the hell just happened?*

He'd been minutes from offering his family, his life, and his heart to this woman for a lifetime, and it had all fallen apart. How had he misread her so badly?

Every accusation that had come flying steadily out of her mouth had been such a shock, he hadn't known how to respond. He'd frozen like the Tin Man without his oil. He felt like his chest was empty too. His heart had deserted him, leaving him bereft.

He didn't know how long he'd sat there in the cool darkening of the evening, before a sound startled him from his thoughts.

The creaking of the back door whipped his head around, but it wasn't her…coming back to, what? Apologize? Explain? Kick him in the balls for good measure? Nothing else she could do would even touch this hurt.

Instead, his father came through the door and sat down beside him on the stairs. "It's a shame Natalie isn't feeling well."

"It sure is." Enzo would leave her whatever excuses she'd offered, because he could do without the third degree from his family.

"Daisy had to leave before we even got to the pumpkins. You'll take one over there for her tomorrow."

"Sure." He'd ask Frankie to do it. He'd earned a few favors in return for handling Buster.

"At least Jo was able to send them home with some of the cookies they baked."

"Nice." Maybe if Enzo kept it to short answers his dad would give up.

"She's a cute kid, that one."

"Yep."

"And smart too. I thought my kids were smart, but I'm beginning to wonder. You stuck on her mom?"

"So what if I am?" Enzo looked out across the backyard toward the setting sun. His chances with Natalie were right on the cusp of disappearing too. He didn't need to hear his father slam her.

"I was just going to say I like her. She humored an old man's memories of his wife's pregnancies."

Great. She'd listen to his father ramble about ancient history, but she wouldn't let him get out a single sentence?

"Listen, I'm glad I got you alone."

Yep, alone and destined to stay that way, since he would truly never understand women. "Sure, Dad. What's up?"

"I need you to go down to the Morgan Hill property this weekend. I need a site assessment for…"

Dom kept rambling about his plans for this crazy vineyard, but Enzo had checked out. He'd promised his girls he'd help with the costumes. But they weren't really his. Had they ever been? His presence was likely no longer welcome. They wouldn't even miss him.

"No problem, Dad. I'll take care of it."

CHAPTER 18

IT WAS SATURDAY. Natalie had held her breath as eleven came and went. He'd listened, and gave them their space, but Nat didn't think Daisy would be thanking her any time soon. She was curled up on the couch watching her second hour of *Octonauts* and ignoring her.

Sitting down at the end of the couch, she rubbed Daisy's ankle. "Do you want to work on your costume?"

Without looking up from the show, Daisy sighed. "He's not coming, is he?"

"No, baby, he's not. I can help…"

Daisy shook her head.

"Do you want to go outside for a bit? We could work on Fairyopolis."

Another silent head shake.

"We could read a book…"

Daisy stood up and walked toward her bedroom.

"Baby?"

Daisy spun, her little face twisted up with the pain of disappointment. "This is all your fault. If you had been nice to him last night, he would be here today, like he promised. I hate you."

Nat didn't have the heart to scold her for slamming the door.

Damn him for going around her and writing directly to Daisy. This was exactly what she'd been trying to avoid. She rubbed her own broken heart as if she could ease her pain long enough to take care of her daughter's. As usual, she was the only one here to pick up the pieces. She had to fix this. She couldn't let her baby down.

She pulled out the project bag for Didi's costume. She finished cutting the little acorn cap and affixed it to a headband so it would stay on Daisy's head. Stitching together the tiger lily panels by hand was oddly soothing. She let the repetitive motion calm her jittery hands, and her scattered thoughts began to settle. They would be okay. They'd gotten through worse together. She was just so tired. That's why this was so hard to handle. Maybe if she closed her eyes and rested for just a minute, she'd feel up to fixing things…

She woke to a doorbell and the thunder of little feet running across the tile. Before she fully came to, Daisy had swung the door wide. If Enzo was there… Natalie pushed herself up from the couch to see who it was before she kicked into fight or flight mode.

Instead of the man both she and her daughter had clearly expected, a delivery man dressed in brown stood holding out a large package addressed to Daisy. Nat signed for the box and closed the door.

Daisy's face was wet with fresh tears. "I thought…"

"I know, baby. I'm sorry." When Daisy turned into Natalie's arms for a hug, she knew everything would be all right. They would find a way through this together. "Do you want to see what's in the box?"

She nodded and swiped her drippy nose with the back of her wrist up to her elbow.

"Tell you what. You go wash your face and hands, and I'll get some scissors. Meet you back here in thirty seconds."

"Don't open it without me!"

"I won't. I promise."

Scissors poised, she waited for Daisy to return to the couch.

"What's all this, Mommy?" Daisy pointed to the froth of orange and brown making an inadvertent blanket for Natalie's nap.

"Well, I didn't want you to not have a costume, so I started working on the tiger lily dress. But I need you to try it on before I close it up so I can make sure it fits."

Daisy hugged her again, and held on long and tight. "I'm sorry, Mommy. I'm sorry I yelled at you. I was just so mad."

"I know, honey. I was mad too. But even when I'm mad or sad or frustrated, you know I always love you."

"I love you too, Mommy."

"Do you want to see what's in the box?"

Daisy nodded. Natalie had no clue what it was, but she hoped it would bring a smile to her daughter's face. She deserved a little happy at the end of the crappy.

She sliced through the tape and let Daisy reach into the box. She pulled out a pair of orange wings first, followed by a burnt orange fairy dress, complete with a Fawn brooch and a tag from the Disney store. Was this how he'd expected to "help" with her costume today? By buying her one? By taking away the fun of designing and creating a costume together? Exhausted, Natalie dropped her sword. If Daisy wanted to wear this one, she wasn't going to fight or fuss. She was going to accept defeat gracefully, and live to fight another day. But his callous disregard for the traditions that she had worked so hard to build for her and her baby, after growing up without any of her own... It just confirmed that she'd been right not to let him get too close. He just didn't understand.

She set aside her own turmoil and searched Daisy's face for a reaction. Natalie was startled by her complete lack of expression.

"Are you okay, Daisy?"

"Why did he send me this? We talked about how much I wanted to make my own. He was supposed to be here, not a stupid box with a baby costume in it."

She threw the dress on the floor, and Natalie's heart swelled. Maybe they would be all right, just the two of them.

"Can I try on my tiger lily dress now, Mommy?" Daisy reached for the orange frock in Natalie's lap and held it up to her front.

Natalie crushed the dress and her daughter in the big mama bear hug she needed and held on tight. "I love you so much, Sprite."

"And I love you, Mommy." She let Natalie hold her for an extra-long hug before she pulled back. "Now, let's make our costumes. We've got to finish the pom-poms for your shoes too."

And just like that, Natalie's world righted. She and Daisy were going to be just fine, and Enzo could go eat rocks for all she cared. Her chest still felt oddly hollow, but that would take care of itself over time. The essentials were right back where they needed to be.

~

ENZO PULLED HIS NOTEBOOK from his pocket and scribbled down ideas and reminders as he walked the vineyards. The property his father had purchased was a gorgeous bit of land. He scanned the horizon of gently rolling hills covered with well-established vines and understood his father's impulse to buy it. The family who had owned it for generations had slowly gotten out of the wine business. For the past two decades, they'd simply sold their harvest to larger vintners, letting their own production go completely and all but abandoning the structures on site. The family had scattered across the country, and no one willing to shoulder the responsibility was left.

Imagine that. Younger generations not wanting to follow in their parents' footsteps. He could understand why the eldest grandson had caved to family pressure from his siblings to sell so they could access their inheritance, trading one liquid asset for another.

Meeting him Saturday had been a treat. He'd learned so much about the history of the land and the family who'd poured their lives into making these vines thrive. He still didn't have a clue about how to care for a vineyard, but he had definite ideas for the rest of the property. He walked down the rows of vines again today without distraction to nail down those details.

He could see this becoming the micro-resort his father envisioned. His list of outdoor venue spaces grew as he added a dining terrace out in the fields, a flexible event space for weddings off the main building, and terraced gardens up the drive to welcome guests.

According to Frankie, the plans for the house were extensive. It was going to take a ton of time and money to turn this into the gem Dom wanted. But he was convinced that this surprise project was going to save his marriage. He'd always been one to get an idea stuck in his head and bull his way through it, but this was ambitious even for him.

Enzo hiked back up to the main house that hadn't seen so much as a paintbrush since 1982, where Frankie was plotting away with the old blueprints for this place. He needed water and some advice.

Despite all the energy and interest he'd put into this vineyard over the last two days, his situation with Natalie and Daisy hadn't been far from his mind. He'd pictured Daisy exploring these fields by his side, collecting twirly dry bits of grape vines to use for her Fairyopolis. He may have even pocketed a few tendrils to bring home, before he realized he might not be welcome to give them to her.

When he'd pictured the event space for weddings, he'd pictured his own large family overflowing the current back patio as he stood hand in hand with Natalie dressed in white lace. It was an image he couldn't shake, and as much as it pained him, he didn't really want to let it go. But he had to face the fact that he might have to.

The costume had arrived. He knew because he'd gotten the

delivery notification. But they hadn't called. He didn't know if it fit or if he'd found the right one. The not knowing was killing him, but he wasn't going to call. Natalie had asked him to back off, and he was going to try and respect that. But how he was going to walk away from his heart he didn't have a clue.

He couldn't stay where he wasn't appreciated, and he wouldn't force himself in where he wasn't welcome. Despite his best efforts, he'd never felt welcomed into their lives. He'd been a cheap babysitter, a bare chest, and an easy lay, nothing more.

He rubbed a hand over that aching chest as he walked into the old family house. He'd been ready to propose, and she'd been ready to drop him cold. He'd gotten so caught up in the fantasy of her, he hadn't accounted for her reality. They hadn't even gone on a real date. Maybe he needed a little space and perspective too.

"Hey."

Frankie didn't look up from the blueprint when he came in.

"Hey!"

"Huh? Oh, hi."

He wasn't more interesting than the blueprints, clearly. "So do you think it's gonna work?"

"I'm gonna make it work. Trying to figure out how many of these walls I can lose right now."

"No, not the building. Dad's plan to win back Mom." Enzo wondered what his mom would think of all this. Would she be pleased, or would she be just as pissed off as Natalie had been when he'd made decisions without her? *Oh. Oh no.* He was turning into his father! No wonder Natalie was angry.

"Oh, that. God, I hope so. I can't imagine her leaving him, but things are getting serious. She didn't speak to him for over six months. She still won't discuss the show without muttering curses."

"Last week, she referred to the set as 'that godforsaken viper's pit.'"

"Sounds about right. Does Jake qualify as head serpent? I

swear he'd tempt his grandmother to the dark side if he thought it would get him ahead."

Enzo raised his eyebrows. "Trouble there?"

"Not today, Satan! Seriously, it's nothing I can't handle. You should know I'm pitching this place as a season-long spin-off with me as the lead contractor and talent. Kind of a 'how to build a specialty property' thing. With Sofia and Adrian all tied up making babies, this is my chance to show Dad what I can do."

Enzo heard the words, but all he could picture were his dreams slipping farther out of his reach. Frankie would need him to work on the landscaping for this place to make it the family showpiece. Which meant another contract and another show. Another year farther from moving out from under the family umbrella. Another complication keeping his dream of building his own company just out of reach. He'd almost worked out how to get off Million-Dollar Starter Home, and now he'd have to juggle two shows? Maybe his dream just wasn't meant to be, and this was fate's way of opening his eyes to that.

"Sounds like just the boost you need," he said.

"Yeah, this place is going to shine. Take a look at these old blueprints. I'm going to nearly double the square footage of this place by the time I'm done. Dad wants an Italian villa, and that's what he's going to get."

"Sure."

As they looked over the schematics and mapped out changes in form and function, Enzo tried to adapt the plans in his head to match. But every time he tried to tweak an image, he found it turning black and rotten in his mind. This place would be a showplace when it was done, but it wouldn't be his.

"You okay?" Frankie's concern broke through his melancholy.

"Yeah, sure."

"Yeah? Because you don't seem okay. It's not like you to brood."

"Well, it's not every weekend a man loses his grip on two life dreams at once, is it? Forgive me for being human."

So much for keeping it bottled up inside.

"No wonder your mind isn't on these plans. What dreams have you lost?"

"I don't want to work for Valenti Brothers anymore." It was the first time he'd mentioned it to Frankie, and he wasn't sure what to expect. "I'm glad the TV thing has worked for you, but I hate it. I want out. That's not going to happen if you and Dad keep extending contracts. All of this show business nonsense is slowing me down. I don't have enough capital yet, and I'm not getting any closer because I have to refer new clients to other firms. I'm too busy getting my makeup done to grow my business!" His frustrations spilled out of his mouth unfettered.

"Enzo. If you don't want to do this, I can hire another landscaper. Dad just thought you'd want to be involved because it's a project for Mom."

"That. That right there! Every time I think about leaving, you guys drop some guilt trip on me, pulling me back in. First, it was 'Gabe's gone,' and now it's 'We don't want Mom to leave.' None of this is my fault! None of it will be fixed because I mow the fucking lawn!"

Frankie took a moment to absorb his anger before replying quietly. "No. Mom's not going to stay, and Gabe can't come back. But I am going to hold together what's left of this family any way I can. You want to go work on your own? Do it. You want me to hire someone else? I will. Just keep showing up on Friday nights, okay? Don't walk away from your family, E."

Enzo slumped back into a rickety chair around what had been someone else's family table. A family that had grown so far apart they'd forgotten how to tend what they'd built.

He wouldn't let that happen, but he had to stretch his own branches toward the sun or he'd starve.

The silence stretched between them while he considered the details. This was exactly the kind of large-scale project he dreamed of tackling, but he wanted them to hire him as his own company instead of just assuming he'd help out. Could he stay that close to his family and not let them overwhelm him? He didn't even know what that would look like. He needed to think.

Frankie broke the silence first. "You said two."

"What?"

"You said you'd lost two dreams. Number one is your own business. What's number two?"

Actually, the job was number two. It was easier to talk about the job than the dream that had snuck its way to number one in his heart. He hauled in a deep breath for courage. If there was anyone he could trust with this, it was Frankie. "Natalie asked for some space."

"Ah, so you don't actually mind the time in the makeup chair?"

"Ha ha." He hesitated, gathering the right words to share. "I love her. I love her and Daisy."

"Does she know?"

Enzo shrugged.

"Dude, that is so not an answer to that question. Either you told her or you didn't."

"Doesn't matter now. She told me to leave them alone."

Funny how quickly he'd grown to dislike that word—alone. Even with the limited time he'd been granted, he'd gotten used to having Natalie and Daisy in his life. He missed the quiet moments with Natalie in his arms before she slipped away. He missed helping Daisy with her homework and listening to her read him stories he remembered from his own childhood. He could be a father. God help him, he still wanted that. He hadn't thought about the reality of it before, and maybe she was right. He had made some mistakes. He would probably make more, but didn't it count for anything that he wanted to keep trying?

"She doesn't think I'm father material, and damn it that hurts. I tried to help her, and I didn't get it right. All she sees is the failure, not the intent. Go figure, I don't know how to be a dad. I've never done it before! She won't let me in, but I was willing to try. Damn it, I wanted to try."

Enzo dropped his head into his hands. That's what hurt the

most. She hadn't been willing to let him catch up. He'd thought he was making progress toward winning their hearts, but she'd always been one step from walking away. Had any of it been real? Or had he been making love to one of her façades while she kept all of the real bits hidden away inside?

Meanwhile, he was feeling like the velveteen rabbit from Daisy's reading homework, bruised and worn down by love. Except he'd been dropped onto the burn pile before he'd been loved enough to be made real.

He ran his hands down his face, wiping away the tears that had escaped.

"You weren't kidding. You really love them, don't you?"

He'd temporarily forgotten that he had an audience. Frankie had just witnessed him splaying his heart open wide. What could he do but nod?

"Okay, you get one more day of hide-out time down here to brood, and then I'm kicking you out to go fight for your family. It's what we Valentis do."

A sense of rightness filled his chest. He'd made so many mistakes, and yet he wasn't ready to give up yet. All he could do was keep trying until he got it right. He might not like her reactions, but he still loved her. While putting his business on the back burner again sucked, he'd cope and come out stronger. If he lost these two people from his life, he didn't think he'd ever recover. There would always be pieces missing from his puzzle. He couldn't give up. Now, if he could just convince her to feel the same way.

"When did you get so smart?"

"About the time I realized my own dreams were worth fighting for." Frankie grinned and shrugged, like life-changing epiphanies came every day.

CHAPTER 19

Something precious had been shaken. Despite their marathon costume session, the bond between Daisy and Natalie felt fragile, in need of tending.

Or maybe she was just fragile and needed more time with Daisy to shore herself up. This was the first bad breakup she'd gone through with Daisy as witness, and she was feeling a little shaky.

Daisy first. Daisy always.

Natalie wasn't going to turn into her mother.

Too many times growing up, Natalie had taken the blame for every ill in her mother's life. Her child would know that no matter what, Natalie loved her first and didn't blame her for any of the struggles they faced. They were a team.

Sitting cross-legged facing each other, Natalie practiced Daisy's full makeup for Halloween. She let every brush stroke, every smoothing blend carry her love for her art and her baby.

It would be enough. It had to be. She was all they had. When she finished, she had a perfectly polished and seriously sad little fairy.

"He didn't even call us."

Sigh. They'd already had many iterations of this conversation yesterday. Daisy was still stuck on it, so they'd have it again.

"Well, we were pretty mad at each other. He might not want to call us. Let me take a few pictures of your face"—*in case you start to cry*—"and then I'll get set up for my Tinkerbell tutorial. Do you want to help me with that? Maybe after, we can go out for ice cream."

"That's okay, Mommy. I think I'll just watch my show."

Daisy smiled and turned her head back and forth while Nat snapped her close-ups, but her spark was dim. Not completely gone, but flickering, fighting for hope. He'd done this with all of his sweet attention and care. He'd drawn them in and dropped them flat. True, she'd pushed him away—protected them—but it had been too late. Her own eyes wanted to water as she scrolled through the flat-eyed fairy photos on her phone. She set the phone on the counter to charge before she filmed and gathered her supplies.

She'd fix this. Of course she would, little by little, until her baby's heart was whole again. She ducked into the bathroom to contain herself and piled products on the counter haphazardly, her motions made careless by nerves. Desperate for any mask to cover up her own raw emotions, she pushed through the piles of makeup to find what she needed for Tink. Highlighting powders, barely there foundation, fake lashes, brown mascara and eyeliner, that emerald green glitter eye shadow… Maybe if she kept her hands busy, she'd keep herself from reaching for the doorknob. Now, where was that green sparkle shadow she'd picked up at the drugstore?

Still in the bag she'd tossed under the sink of course. She snagged the compact, dropped the bag, and moved on. Iridescent glitter for her pixie dust, pale pink lipstick. Did Tinkerbell have freckles? She'd have to check.

Something teased the edge of her mind, and her hands slowed their frenzy. The bag called for her attention, and with shaking hands she opened it again.

Time slowed though her brain was spinning in neutral, gears refusing to engage.

Pads. Tampons. Pregnancy Test.

Pads she should have needed by now. Tampons that were still unopened. The gears began to click as the math in her head provided a scary answer, and it jumped her mind into third gear. The tummy troubles, the weird aversion to garlic, the super tender breasts and overwhelming arousal.

Fuuuuuuuuck.

It had been eight weeks since her last period. Six since she'd slept with Enzo that first glorious time. Right after she'd puked up everything, including her birth control pills. She'd missed several days in a row between Daisy's stomach flu and being exhausted. She'd never had to worry about being one hundred percent accurate with her pills, because celibacy had taken care of the not-getting-pregnant piece. She stayed on the pill more to control her periods. Well, she might not have to worry about that for a while.

Nat flicked the lock on the bathroom door as the tumblers in her mind fell in place as well. She leaned her head against the hard, cool wood of the door and clenched her eyes shut. She didn't even have to take the test. She knew. But she would anyhow just to confirm.

God, how had she ended up here again?

She'd been so careful. Seven years of no sex, and the first time she'd opened up, she gotten screwed, squared. What was she, some kind of Fertile Myrtle?

A knock on the door reverberated through her skull.

"Mommy?"

"I'll be out in a few minutes, baby. Why don't you go get a snack?"

She stared at the foil-wrapped stick. This might change everything. What would she do?

No sense worrying until she knew for sure.

But once she knew, she couldn't unknow. She clung to the last minutes of having her life somewhat under control.

Another knock.

"Mommy? Are you okay?"

"Yes, baby." Her stomach flip-flopped, calling her a liar. "I'm fine. I'm just going potty."

Maybe if she said it often enough, she could make it true. She had to make it true. She wouldn't fail.

Just do it already. She opened her eyes and tore open the silver seal.

Two pink lines.

She was really beginning to hate two pink lines.

No, that wasn't true. Two pink lines had announced Daisy, the best thing in her life. These two pink lines would be just as treasured, just as loved. Eventually. Right now though, Natalie felt them like the painful lines left by the lash of a belt. It hurt, knowing that something so good had gotten her in trouble again. This is what she got for reaching for more. When would she learn?

Natalie carefully hid the stick, the wrapper, and the boxes in the bottom of the garbage, before opening the bathroom door. Who was Daisy talking to?

"Yes." She paused. "It was nice of you to send it, but Mommy and I make our own costumes every year. It's tradition."

Oh no. She'd gotten into Natalie's phone and called Enzo.

"Why didn't you come to help me like you said?" Her voice broke on a suppressed sob at the end, ever her mother's daughter. Too strong. Bearing too much sorrow alone. She wished she could hear what Enzo was telling her. "Well, we are going to borrow the wings from it, so it's not a complete mistake. Neither are you. I know Mommy said some things while she was mad. But you know what she always tells me after she yells?"

Natalie held her breath. What did she say after she yelled? It was always a crapshoot to hear Daisy's interpretation of what she'd said.

"She says, 'I don't like what you did, but I will always love you. Nothing can change that.'"

Daisy paused again, listening. That was what she told Daisy. Did the same apply to Enzo? Did she love him, even though she didn't like his actions? Tears threatened again, and Natalie sniffed them back. She'd have to give that some thought.

"Are you coming for Tricks and Treats downtown? I heard the stores give out good candy, and I really want to show you my costume."

Good, she had some time to decide what to do about all this before she saw him again.

"Okay, good. Bye, then."

Natalie joined Daisy on the couch with a big plate of cookies. She took two cookies from the plate and snuggled up around her baby in a big spoon hug.

Oh God! She was going to have another baby!

Doctor.

Diapers.

Baby clothes.

Labor.

Job? Home?

What was she going to do?

"Love you, Mommy." Daisy laid her head on Natalie's tender chest and centered her.

"I love you too, Didi, forever and ever no matter what." That's exactly what she'd do. She'd give this baby all of her love just like she had with Daisy, and everything would work out fine.

She would pick herself up and do what was best for her kids.

Jesus, plural. Kids.

Another baby.

All the sleepless nights.

All the worry and panic.

All the giggles and little toes.

All the love and joy.

Maybe that meant moving back to LA where she had job contacts and a doctor. She even had one or two friendships she could try and revive, even though almost everyone who'd been around when Daisy was born had since scattered.

Or even moving back to Lincoln with her mother. No, that was a horrible idea. She was never putting herself back into her mother's circle ever again, certainly not with her children.

But LA might work. Now that her YouTube following had spiked, she could maybe afford to drop her evening gigs and still make the rent.

God, she was really doing this again.

Buckle up, Buttercup. Life is about to get interesting.

BUDGETS, start-up costs, equipment catalogs, and tax code swam in his head. It was late Monday night, but Enzo had used his wallowing day to his advantage. His dream was coming together. He had known that he wanted to take on bigger landscaping challenges. He'd factored in how much his fraction of the Valenti Brothers business was worth and was prepared to ask his father to pay for it to stay. Now he knew exactly how much it would cost to go out on his own. He also knew he didn't have anywhere near that amount. He still needed to figure out how to approach the banks for loans, but he could go to them with solid numbers.

He'd made progress thinking about Natalie too. The Dom Valenti approach to love sucked. Yes, he'd grown up seeing it in action, and it had mostly turned out okay. He'd watched his father solve the family's problems growing up. He'd learned that was how a man provided for his family: he worked hard, he made the tough choices, and he solved problems as they cropped up.

But after the blow up with Natalie, he finally understood why his mom was so mad. Jo hadn't gotten to have a say in most of those decisions, and she'd had enough. Natalie had been trying to tell him the same thing. All of his "help" hadn't really helped because they hadn't figured out the problems together. He'd just made things harder for her. All so that he wouldn't feel so out of control around her.

He'd made it all about him, and it needed to be about them.

The phone call from Daisy had given him hope. At least she still wanted him around. So he had another chance to convince Natalie that he could learn.

He'd ask them to his parents' house for Halloween. He wouldn't let Daisy down again. And if he was very lucky, he could convince Natalie that he could learn from his mistakes. He could compromise and work together to solve problems. He could love her the way she needed to be loved.

NATALIE DIDN'T SEE Enzo again until Tuesday morning, which gave her time to lay the groundwork of her plan without distraction. She made a few phone calls, renewed connections in the business that she'd allowed to lapse during her time in the Bay, and felt out a few of her old salon clients. Daisy had been strangely subdued, like a bird during an eclipse, waiting to see if her world was going to end.

She must have overheard one of the phone calls. Nat couldn't bear to have that conversation yet. Not until she had concrete plans that she could share. The worst thing was getting Daisy set on one plan and then having to change it.

Figuring out her plan was the easy bit though. Figuring out what to say to Enzo was tearing her apart. Honestly, the first day, she hadn't even thought about him. Her thoughts had all centered around her and the baby and Daisy. Maybe it was just force of habit, years of handling everything by herself, but she hadn't even realized that she was going to have to figure out how to tell him until Monday night.

But now it was Tuesday morning, and he was back on the shoot list and in her chair. Luckily, his tan had mostly evened out, so he only needed a quick powder for the cameras.

She was so nervous, she bopped him right in the nose with her puff, making him sneeze and choke in a cloud of setting powder.

When he'd recovered he grinned at her like nothing had happened between them, like they were still friendly and not fighting.

"I'm sorry I missed Man Makeover Monday. I had a project out of town, and I didn't think you'd still want me to show."

"It's okay. Jake did it. I made him Dracula. It seemed fitting."

He chuckled. Maybe this would be okay. Her words Friday night had been spoken in a haze of anger and hormones, but she stood by the content if not the tone. She needed him to keep his distance if she had any hope of protecting them.

If he could sit here, laughing and joking with her, maybe he'd come to that realization as well. That they weren't suited. That they should go their separate ways. *God, that would make this so much easier.* She wouldn't have to change. She could leave and keep taking care of everything herself.

She couldn't put her child's—no, her children's—welfare on the line for a maybe.

"He's certainly a blood sucker. I, ah, brought you something."

Startled, she met his eyes in the mirror, wary of grenades masquerading as gifts.

He reached into his back pocket and pulled out her monitor, placing it on the counter in front of him. Surely this had to be a sign that they were over.

"Thank you for understanding, Enzo. I really like you, but I…"

"Oh, I don't like you." He cut her off, that affable fucking grin still on his face. "I don't like you very much right now at all."

He turned in the chair toward her, taking her face between his two hands so she couldn't hide from his words.

"But I still love you. And I love Daisy too. And I'm not going to back away from my heart. I'm just going to have to earn your trust the hard way. By showing up and learning from my mistakes."

He kissed her briefly, just a peck on the lips, nothing compared to the other kisses they'd shared. But this one left her stunned and reeling as he walked out the garage door. Because it had been the casual kiss of a man in love. With her. Damn him. What had just happened?

CHAPTER 20

Natalie clutched the seat of the toilet bowl closer as she tried to regain her balance after losing the piece of toast she'd tried for an afternoon snack. Whoever had named it "morning" sickness was a lying sadist.

Regaining her feet, she splashed cold water on her face and looked at herself critically in the mirror. A hazard of the job—she knew exactly how awful she looked. She was going to end up matching her green dress.

She primed and concealed and blended to the best of her ability, but she still looked tired and wan to her own eyes. She'd just go as Tinkerbell fighting a hangover. God, she wanted a drink to help handle tonight, but that was off-limits now. Hopefully, Enzo wouldn't notice her appearance or her attitude. She still wasn't sure how to handle him and his offhand declaration of love. Who did that?

Hair pinned flat against her head, she tugged on the wig cap and then the little blonde pixie wig, and prayed she wouldn't puke again. Losing the wig in the toilet would suck, especially when she had to explain what happened when she shipped it back to Alexis, the prop manager friend she'd borrowed it from.

Daisy opened the door a crack, and her autumn fairy face peeked in the gap. "You okay, Mommy?"

In what was becoming almost a refrain, Nat reassured her too-perceptive daughter. "I'm fine, baby. How do I look?"

Daisy pulled her into a big side hug and grinned at their joined reflections in the bathroom mirror. "You look like the best Tink ever! Now come on! We gotta hurry!"

"Honey, Tricks and Treats doesn't even start for another hour." The downtown business area opened their doors to the neighborhood kids, and it was all Daisy and her friends could talk about at school.

"I know, but Enzo is going to be here soon to take me to see Jo Nana before that starts. She promised me full-sized candy bars, so we gotta be ready when he comes!"

Oh no. Had he set her up for disappointment again? Was he actually going to show this time? After his declaration on Tuesday, she didn't feel confident predicting his actions.

"Daisy, when did you plan this?"

"I asked him to come for Halloween when we talked on the phone the other day, and then Jo Nana and I talked yesterday when she picked me up."

"Stop calling her that, Daisy."

"Jo Nana? But it's a joke, about a banana at snack—"

"She's not your Nana. Please stop."

Daisy's face set into a mulish pout, and Natalie didn't have the energy to tactfully talk her way around this. She was exhausted, so straightforward commands were about all she could manage. Unfortunately, she knew exactly how well that tended to work with her independent child.

"She could be."

"No, baby, she can't."

"If you quit being mean to Enzo, she could. He could be my daddy, and we could have that whole big family. I checked. He's not married."

"Honey, you don't understand."

"No, I don't." Daisy snatched up her NeverBeast doll and turned her back on Nat.

The doorbell rang before Natalie could correct Daisy's assumptions. Her daughter darted to open it, and there he stood, a man-sized fairy in full leather jerkin.

"Terence! Oh my gosh, Enzo, you're Terence!"

The significance of him dressing up as the only cute boy in Pixie Hollow—and Tinkerbell's boyfriend—was not lost on Natalie. When had he come up with this?

"Yep, I bought my costume to make sure that I had the right one. But maybe next year you can help me make mine."

Oh, not fair. That was a low blow. He shouldn't be giving Daisy something to look forward to a year out. Who even knew where they'd be in a year? But he wasn't thinking about that, because she hadn't found the words to tell him yet. The little secret growing in her belly was her worry alone for the time being because that was all she could handle right now. He couldn't know the minefield he was walking through as he bent down to show Daisy the leather pouch full of golden ultra-fine glitter.

"I even brought pixie dust!"

"Nope. No. Uh-uh! Get out of this house right now. Sofia will never forgive me if I infect her apartment with craft herpes."

He stood and met the challenge head-on. Yes, she'd said it jokingly, but she'd told him to leave once again. He held out a hand to her, daring her to be brave.

"Okay. Come with me, then. Are you ready?"

The way he held her gaze as he said it loaded the question with extra meaning. Which she ignored, letting Daisy sweep ahead of her and snag his hand. She followed them out to his truck.

Was she ready? Ready for what? What was his game? Why wouldn't he just stay gone after she brushed him off? He was like a burr that kept showing up weeks after the hike. She'd never kissed the burr though. Never made a baby with one. Never longed to keep one around. Her ridiculous thoughts spiraled away from her. What was she going to do?

During the short drive to his parents' house, Daisy filled the cab with all of her little girl excitement for her favorite holiday. Her prattle covered Natalie's quiet consternation as she tried to figure out the man behind the wheel.

"Do you think Jo Nana will have Snickers bars? Those are Mommy's favorite."

"She might. Let's go find out."

They pulled up in the drive and let Daisy run ahead of them to ring the doorbell. Natalie reached for her phone and realized she'd left it behind in their confusing exit.

But Enzo already had his raised, filming Daisy's first trick or treat of the year, with his mom answering the door in a goofy bat hat, playing along and not recognizing the little fairy.

It felt…odd. She assumed that this was what "normal" felt like to every other two-parent family. Just for a moment, she allowed that daydream to spin out in her head. The dream where she had a big, strong fairy of her own to lean on, to help share the responsibilities and the joys of parenting, and work, and life. And love, so much love.

Her heart wanted to swell out of her chest, to encompass the other two people standing on the porch, not just the one she'd birthed. And that scared the crap out of her.

How could she trust him with the most important parts of her life? It was so much safer to keep her gates closed to everyone than to take a risk on letting someone breach the perimeter and hope he was trustworthy. No matter how much she longed to let him in. Damn him for making her want more.

"Oh, hello, Tinkerbell. I didn't see you there. Our little Fawn here says you like Snickers."

Jo was pulling her into the warm circle of fun at the door, and it was so tempting to lean in and accept that unconditional welcome. She stepped into the offered hug, but her mind screamed *caution*. Because she knew what happened when she made herself comfortable—she would step funny and get the rug pulled out from under her feet. Fate was a petty bitch, and she couldn't afford to trip right now.

"Thank you, Jo. I do." She took the candy bar, and her stomach pitched and flipped. *Oh God, not now.*

Hopefully it would just stay nausea, since she was completely empty. In more ways than one.

"Why don't you guys take her up and down our street? Our neighbors will get a kick out of seeing you all dressed up, Enzo."

Sure, just show off her baby to the neighbors with their son in matching costumes. That wouldn't set tongues wagging. God, it was already going to hurt Jo when they left. She didn't want to make it any worse.

Nat tried to hide her frustration at having other people make decisions for Daisy. She needed to cover up her tender heart before Enzo and his adorable family slipped in any further. It was already painful enough just pushing him away.

"Is that all right with you, Natalie? What other plans do you have tonight?" Enzo asked.

It set her back enough that she answered without thinking. "We are going to meet school friends at Tricks and Treats, but we've got forty-five minutes before we need to be there. I don't want to be out too late tonight, so maybe just down and back?"

"Great. Let's go!" He reached a hand out for Daisy, and she happily took it and danced down the porch before sprinting ahead of them, chasing the Holy Grail of childhood, a full bag of Halloween candy.

Strolling along behind her, Enzo tried to take Natalie's hand, but she ignored it and crossed her arms, walking a little ahead to keep her full-steam anger building. "I wish you would stop all this."

"All this what?"

Oh so he was going to play dumb? Did he think she'd back down? "All this pretending that Daisy is part of your family. And promising her next Halloween? That was low, Enzo. All of this is confusing for her."

Enzo stopped in his tracks and stared at her until she turned back and met his narrowed glare. "I don't think she's the one who's confused."

"What the hell is that supposed to mean?"

"It means pull your head out of your ass and look around. Does any of this look like I'm joking? Like I'm just stringing her along?"

"Very mature."

"Yeah, falling in love with a woman I find attractive on many levels, and her kid, and finding ways to be part of her life to convince her I'm not going anywhere feels pretty mature to me."

She didn't know what to say to that, but it didn't faze him. Apparently he'd been saving up.

"Has it occurred to you that I want her to be part of this family? That I want *you* to be part of my family? Or that maybe, just maybe, you could let me be part of yours?" He bit off each word, his frustration pushing him hard.

She wasn't in the mood to be pushed. She opened her mouth to reply, but caught a whiff of garlic from someone's dinner as they swung their door closed and her stomach revolted.

She made it to the curb, but couldn't stop retching helplessly, though nothing came out. His hands supported her waist and her shoulder, his torso curled around hers as if he could protect her or take her suffering for her, and she couldn't stop the tears that streamed down her cheeks. She wanted to deserve this, to expect this, to count on this so badly.

This was a horrible time to have lost control of her emotions.

Damn hormones.

She wrapped her arms around her stomach, protecting the baby from her own frustrated thoughts.

Blessed baby.

Daisy came running from the house two doors down. "Mommy, you keep throwing up. Do you have the fever?"

"I'm fine. Go ahead to the next house. We'll catch up."

"You keep throwing up?" Enzo asked. "You and Sofia should start a support group. Pukers Anonymous. She's been miserable—"

She saw the moment suspicion entered his eyes. He was connecting hypothetical dots, and she didn't have the strength to pull on a mask. Her chagrin and guilt were right there on her face for him to read.

"Throwing up, exhausted, look like hell, moody. Don't make me ask this question, Natalie. Don't make me be the asshole who guesses wrong."

She could only stare at her fidgeting hands, lips pressed tightly against the words that wanted to fly out.

"Are you?" The way his voice softened and sweetened almost broke her resolve. But by the time she found the courage to look up, anger and suspicion had hardened his features. "Were you going to tell me?"

She'd been right to keep it to herself. She couldn't answer, couldn't explain why her first impulse had been to run.

"I see. You know, Natalie, all I ever wanted was a chance. I tried to find ways to help you, support you, love you? I tried to lighten your load and give you and Daisy a little fun."

"That's just it, Enzo! Life isn't a game. You don't just get to show up for the fun parts when you're a parent."

"I want to show up for all the parts, but you won't let me get close enough."

"That's not fair. I was just trying to protect my child."

"I'm not the bad guy here. I love you, and I love her like she was my own. I want a chance to love this baby we've made. Look, I know I screwed up, but I'm trying. You need a partner, not a helper. But I can't be a partner by myself. This isn't about Daisy. This is you protecting yourself from having to change and let someone else in."

"No, I..." Had she pushed him away because she was afraid of losing herself, not for Daisy's well-being?

"You know what? That's fine. Your choice. But if you think for a second that you can choose to keep me out of my child's life, you're crazy. You should have told me!"

"You don't understand. I can't—"

"Oh, I think I understand pretty well. I'm good enough to sleep with, but you don't think I'm parenting material, so you'll just push on without me." He was shouting now, and she wanted to curl up in a little ball to hide her fragile heart, but they were in the middle of the sidewalk in his neighborhood. "Excuse me for not knowing when pizza night is, and not being able to sew a freaking costume, and not consulting you before planning a surprise. I've got about six years of catching up to do, and nine months to do it. But make no mistake, Natalie, I will catch up. I will be the best damn father to that baby, and Daisy too if you'd only let me. You will not take that away from me."

The resolve in his gaze sliced at her, making a space for a stubborn tendril of hope to sprout in her chest. Yes, he was angry, but not because of the baby. Because she hadn't trusted him and had kept the news from him.

"We should catch up with Daisy too, but I'm not done talking about this." His eyes narrowed until she nodded.

This wasn't how she'd planned on telling him. To be honest, she hadn't gotten that far yet. She'd wanted to have her plan in place so she could present it as a done deal. Now she was going to have to compromise and coordinate. Not skills she'd perfected in the last decade. He was right though. They weren't done talking about it.

She turned and looked for Daisy, needing to recenter herself after that disorienting conversation. Had she really been protecting her own heart, using Daisy as a shield? She didn't like to think so, but she couldn't deny how it looked from his perspective. Letting him know and watching him leave scared the crap out of her. She'd never even let herself consider that he might stay.

Scanning up and down the street, she saw ghosts and superheroes, baby pumpkins and the cutest little firegirl. But no orange fairies. Her mommy spider-sense was tingling, and Enzo was already striding up the block, his shoulders stiff as he stretched to see farther.

"Daisy?" His voice boomed down the block, turning heads.

"Daisy?" Her own shook with panic. "Daisy, where are you?"

She had one job in life, keeping her kids safe, and she'd failed both of her children miserably tonight.

Enzo ran up to a house with its door open to a trio of ninjas. "Excuse me, have you seen a little orange fairy come through here?"

"Yes, a few minutes ago. Gorgeous face paint, but she was crying. She went that way."

The older woman holding the bowl of candies pointed farther up the block.

"Thanks, Mrs. K. Her name is Daisy. If she comes back, can you bring her inside and call my parents?"

"Sure, Enzo."

Natalie stumbled along behind him as he raced from door to door activating his neighbors to look for her baby. The laughter and shouts of happy children dimmed as they became aware that someone was missing.

What must it be like to be known like that? To have people who'd known you since childhood and people who didn't know you at all but felt connected to the neighborhood enough to help, willing to step up? Several people joined them in calling out her name as she frantically scanned the masses of children.

"Daisy? Daisy! Answer me!"

Flashlights flickered on, and her daughter's name echoed up and down the street.

Enzo doubled back to her, his long strides eating up the distance. "What do you want to do?"

Natalie just shook her head. She couldn't think straight, every terrible thought torturing her at once. "I don't... I can't..."

He gripped her shoulders and looked her straight in the eye.

"Breathe, honey. How does this sound? You keep going house to house to check her path. Stay with the group. I'll go back to the house to get the truck. It'll be faster to search. I'll pick you up wherever you are, and we can keep looking together. Do you feel okay walking a little farther?"

She nodded. "That…that sounds good."

He pulled her in for a quick kiss on her forehead. "We'll find her. I promise."

She watched him charge into action. They would find her. They would. Beneath the terror, a sense of surety and trust pushed for space. Enzo wouldn't give up until he'd found her.

"Daisy?"

She kept calling and walking, knocking on doors until they stopped confirming Daisy's path. The trail ended just around the corner, but she couldn't think about what that might mean. She just had to keep looking or… No, no alternatives. She had to find her baby.

CHAPTER 21

ENZO RACED BACK to his childhood home in a state of panic that was completely unfamiliar and overwhelming. He'd just discovered the depths of his feelings for this little girl by jumping into the deep end of the parenting pool and hitting bottom.

He couldn't lose her now.

Barging in the front door, he scared the crap out of his parents who jumped and spilled candy all over the floor.

"Daisy's gone missing. I don't know if she wandered off or if she was taken. I've told everyone to call you if they see her. I need my keys. Where are my keys?"

Jo put her hand on his chest as if he'd just said he'd lost his shoe. How could she be calm at a time like this? Didn't she understand? He had to hurry. If anything happened—

"Enzo, breathe. I was just going to send Dom to find you two. She's in the backyard. Poor lamb, just ran straight through, crying her eyes out."

"Dad, go find Natalie. She doesn't have her phone."

Enzo choked on his relief and ran out the back door, not waiting for his dad's confirmation. He knew he could trust Dom to get the job done. He scanned the dark yard. A flutter of orange tulle and the rustling of candy wrappers drew him to the old tree house.

He hadn't used it as a hideout when he was a kid. It had always been too full of siblings, and he preferred to build his own forts on the ground. But it would be a perfect retreat for a scared little fairy.

Climbing the rickety ladder, he prayed it would hold his weight. When he poked his head through the hole in the floor, the sight of Daisy tucked into the corner crying set off a complex spiral of emotions: relief, love, anger, frustration, concern, confusion. His first full breath in half an hour left him dizzy.

This parenting business wasn't for sissies. He realized that no matter what Natalie said, Daisy was his. She'd carved out her own space in his heart, and he wasn't going to let her go. He pulled himself the rest of the way into the tree house and ducked into the corner. When he opened his arms, Daisy crawled into his lap and that piece of his puzzle that had been temporarily lost clicked into place. Despite the orange wire wings poking him in the face, he leaned in and hugged her close, letting her little girl scent of strawberries and soap reassure him that she was here and unharmed.

"Thank God, you're safe."

He kissed the top of her glittery head and let that reality sink in. He was still feeling jittery, the adrenaline in his system slow to recede.

"I...I got scared...and sad. I couldn't keep trick-or-treating, so I walked around the block and came home."

He squeezed her a little tighter. She was home now. "What scared you? You know everything out there is just pretend. Everyone is just wearing a costume. None of it's real."

"What about the part where you said you loved me, Lorenzo? Was that real or pretend?"

Her whispered question slayed him. Oh God, how much had she heard? He was getting thrown in the deep end of parenting tonight. Big surprises, dead panic, and emotionally fraught conversations: The Parenting Trifecta. How he handled this would weigh heavy with Natalie.

"That was absolutely true. No matter what, Daisy, I love you."

"Can I come live with you?"

"What? You live with your mom."

Daisy's hiccuping tears began to flow faster. What had he done wrong now?

"I…I think…I think my mom…is dying. And I'm so scared." Once she'd broken the seal, the words came pouring out through her tears. "She keeps throwing up and falling asleep all the time. And…and she was talking on the phone about going away and sending me back to LA." She buried her head against Enzo's chest. "I don't want to go back. I want to stay here with you and Jo Nana and my friends. And I don't want my mom to d-d-die!" The wail at the end of her flurry of words squeezed his chest. He hugged her tight and pressed a kiss to the top of her little head tucked against his chest. This little fairy had big ears.

Natalie hadn't told Daisy about the baby yet either. Somehow that made him feel better, but this LA business needed a conversation. He wasn't going to let her out of his sight.

"Daisy, I want you to take a deep breath and hear me. Your mom isn't dying. She is a little sick right now, because she's…I… we are going to have a baby. It's making her feel not so well right now, but it's all normal, from what I've heard." He rubbed a hand up and down her arm while he found the words he wanted. "What you need to know is that I love you, and I love her, and I love this baby. So no, you can't come live with me, but maybe we could work on becoming a family. Would you like that?"

Daisy relaxed in his lap and nodded. Now that her imminent fear had been removed, she was limp and drained. The wave of relief swamped him. She played with the lacings on the front of his leather jerkin silently.

"So I'm going to be a big sister?"

"Yes."

"Is it a boy or girl?"

"I don't know yet."

"And you're the daddy?"

"I am."

"Do you think…maybe, you'd want to be my daddy too?" Her little voice wavered with nerves. Such a brave little sprite.

"There is nothing I'd like more, Daisy."

"Promise?"

"Shake on it?"

He held out his hand, stretching his heart out as well. When she put her hand in his, he felt that love returned in the firm shake.

"I promise." He vowed silently to do everything in his power to make this promise come true.

He pulled her in for a hug, holding her in a safe space, letting her recover from the rollercoaster emotions of the evening. Going from *My mom is dying* to *I'm getting a daddy and a new baby*, all in one night, was bound to be overwhelming. When her quiet whimpers subsided into deep, even snores, he shifted her sleep-heavy body onto his shoulder and carried her out of the tree house. He was just hitting the bottom of the deck staircase when Natalie came flying out of the house, tears streaming down her face.

"Oh my God! Is she okay? Is she hurt? Where was she?"

Natalie reached for Daisy, trying to pull her out of his arms, but he wasn't having it. He tightened his grip around her.

"She's fine. She's just asleep. Let me carry her." He brushed past her and carried Daisy upstairs to his old bedroom and tucked her in.

Natalie was right on his heels and collapsed onto the bed, curling up behind Daisy in a full-body hug, as if she could protect her child from the rest of the world with the strength of her love. He wanted to have that right too. To protect this little family with his love. His voice softened to a whisper, even though his heart wanted to scream.

"She got scared when we were fighting and only heard part of it. She put that together with the way you've been feeling lately and a phone call she overheard. She thought you were dying and were going to send her back to LA. Was that your plan, Natalie? Run away to LA and leave me in the dark?"

"All of my friends and my doctor are there."

Natalie spoke through tears and refused to meet his eyes. *Damn.* She rose from the bed and stepped into the hallway. Enzo followed, gently closing the door between that exhausted little girl and their brewing argument.

"All of your friends? I'm sure there are some people downstairs who'd be upset to hear that. I thought I was your friend too, Natalie."

She crossed her arms over her belly. "I can't make a baby and a kid and a job work here in the Bay."

"Certainly not alone, but what about with a partner? What about with me? I love you, Natalie. I want to be your partner for the hard times and the fun."

"Don't you get it? I screwed everything up again. I don't deserve this!" She swung her arm wildly around the room. "I don't deserve you. I don't get to have the happily ever after."

The idea that he'd almost lost them all had shaken him to his core. The idea that she thought she didn't deserve to be loved cracked his chest in half. She hadn't trusted him enough to stay, because she didn't think she deserved to be happy. He couldn't let her go without a fight. He couldn't let his future slip away. He had to prove that she could trust him. That he could make decisions that held all of their best interests at heart.

"You deserve all the happiness in the world and more. Don't run away from this, Natalie, from us. I'll be downstairs."

❧

NATALIE CLIMBED BACK into bed behind Daisy and absorbed the warmth of her child, safe and asleep in her arms. Her own tears began to fall as relief replaced panic. She began to shake as the fear left her system.

All of the horrible thoughts that had raced through her mind when she couldn't find Daisy were harder to dismiss.

She could've been hurt, taken, trafficked, abused, or worse, and Natalie wouldn't have been able to stop it. Not being able to find her had been the scariest moment of her life. She had raced around the rest of the block and the next, screaming until her voice was hoarse. She didn't have her phone, so when Dom had pulled up in Enzo's truck, she'd been confused, but it had quickly turned to relief when he told her Daisy was at the house. Seeing her limp child in Enzo's arms had spiked her terror again and almost taken her out at the knees. She'd lost her, and the love flooding her now that she was safely returned overwhelmed her.

She kept stroking Daisy's arm and smelling her hair and planting kisses against every alive-and-well inch of her little head, reassuring herself that her kid was indeed okay.

And poor baby, Daisy had thought she was dying? Apparently Natalie hadn't hidden her morning sickness as well as she'd thought. She had a lot of apologizing to do. Starting with everyone she'd dragged from their homes on Halloween because of her negligence.

"Mommy? Is that you?"

Daisy rolled to face her and fluttered her red and swollen eyes open.

"Yes, baby, I'm right here. You had me so worried!"

"I'm sorry. I just needed to come home."

"No, I'm sorry I scared you, baby."

"Is it true?"

"Is what true?"

"That I'm going to be a big sister and Enzo is going to be part of our family?"

Oh, wow. "Would you like that, baby?"

She nodded and closed her eyes again, burrowing into Natalie's hug. "And you're not going to die?"

"No, Didi. The baby just makes me feel tired and sick for a few months. It happened with you too."

"He said he wants to keep us no matter what. I like that. We shook on it," Daisy whispered, as if she was afraid Natalie would disagree.

She wondered about how that conversation had gone down, but Daisy was already sinking back into sleep.

He'd told Daisy about the baby. He'd said he wanted to be part of their family. What did that all mean? Half asleep and drunk on relief, she let her mind wander and picture that alternate reality.

A baby asleep on her chest, Daisy curled up next to her on the couch, and Enzo walking in the door at the end of the day. Daisy would run over and give him a hug. He would wash up and give her a quick kiss before taking the baby for a cuddle. They would sit around their little table and share their dinner and their days. In her mind's ear, his laughter blended with her children's to make the most beautiful harmony.

When Daisy and the baby were down for the night, she would settle next to him on the couch. They'd watch about eighteen minutes of Netflix before she'd fall asleep, cradled against his chest. He would take her in his arms in that way that made her feel cherished and wanted, and would carry her into their bed. They would make love until they slept, side by side. When the baby got up, he would take his share of the turns and let her get some sleep. And in the morning, he would still be there, loving her and her babies with that gentle perseverance he had. It was a beautiful dream. She could picture every detail so clearly it hurt. His reaction tonight confirmed that he wanted the role. Was this dream something she could make real? Was she brave enough to reach for it?

He had been right earlier, when he'd accused her of protecting herself. It was true that she'd been trying to save Daisy from the heartache of him leaving, but it had absolutely been her own insecurities convincing her that he was destined to leave. Everyone else in her life had. Why wouldn't he?

But he'd shown her again and again that he was willing to show up for her, if she would only let him in. After tonight, it was going to hurt more to push him and this dream away again than it would if he eventually left.

She loved him. He was worth the risk. Her life would feel half empty without him there. No other man had touched her heart so profoundly, and she'd panicked. The well of the emotion he'd opened had been impossible for her to navigate alone. But buoyed by his love, she could embrace her own feelings and be brave. She wanted whatever time she could have with him.

She wanted that for her children too. She believed that Daisy deserved every good thing in this world. And if her daughter deserved to live happily ever after, didn't she deserve it too? She wasn't going to back away again.

She wanted the dream and the reality. It was up to her to stay and fight for it.

CHAPTER 22

ONCE DAISY'S LIMBS HAD GONE LIMP, Natalie roused herself to go face the crowd downstairs. She could hear the combined chatter of family and neighbors from all the way upstairs. They had all rallied around her and her little girl tonight, and gratitude warmed her heart even as embarrassment heated her cheeks. She wanted to thank them, but she was mortified to have lost Daisy in the first place.

As she tiptoed down the wooden staircase, worn smooth by years of Valenti children, the noise quieted. At first, she thought she'd been spotted, but no—as she reached the hallway she saw that everyone's attention was focused on Dom and Enzo facing off in the middle of the living room. Friends and family alike were riveted to the standoff.

"What kind of idiot plan is this?" Dom roared into the now silent space between them.

"It's not idiotic. I've been thinking about it for a while, and the time is right."

"The time is not right. Why the hell do you need me to buy you out?"

"Because starting up my own landscape design and maintenance firm is going to cost money."

This was the first she'd heard of him wanting to start his own business, but she could see it. She'd seen how much he hated the show business side of things and jumping whenever someone told him to. He'd be much happier as his own boss.

"So stay here, and work for Valenti Brothers."

"I need to build my own, Dad. I need more than backyard gazebos and lawn care."

"This is a big ask, and we've got a lot going on right now. The show, the new project...I don't have the capital right now to indulge your whim."

Enzo's face flushed with anger and his temper lashed out. "Bullshit. You just don't want to slow down on your 'project.' You don't want to step back from the show. You, you, you. This is all about what you want to do. You are choosing those plans over my dreams."

"And why shouldn't I value concrete plans over speculative dreams? It's my business. I built it with my blood, sweat, and tears. Nobody handed me anything."

Enzo's head snapped back as if he'd been slapped. "So the last decade of my blood, sweat, and tears, poured into growing this side branch of the business, doesn't count for shit? How much revenue did I bring in last year, that you are now pouring into this money pit in Morgan Hill?"

"We are a family business. Everyone contributes—"

"But you are the only one who gets to make decisions and plans. I see. Someone just taught me the folly in that. You might want to rethink your strategy. Though this makes it even easier to walk away."

He turned to do just that, walk away from his father who looked ready to explode, and caught sight of her on the stairs. What had she just witnessed? He crossed to her and leaned against the bannister, pitching his voice just to her.

"Hey, how's she doing?"

"She's fine, still sleeping. Are you okay?" She reached out to run a hand down his arm, and he flinched.

"I'll be fine. I had just hoped that my dad would support my dreams and respect what I've brought to Valenti Brothers. It's clear he doesn't, so I'm done."

"Now wait just a damn second!" Dom protested, but Enzo's gaze never wavered from hers.

"Why are you trying to sell out?"

"Because someone I know is dead set on going back to LA. I've been dreaming of going out on my own for years, but now I've got a solid plan and a reason to make it happen. Relocating might actually make it easier to pull off."

"Why are you moving to LA? You'll break your mother's heart." Dom clearly wasn't done with this discussion even though Enzo had turned his back on it.

"More like your wallet," he shot back without turning away from her.

"I can't give you the cash right now. Just stay here, and we'll work something out. Then next year we can talk about this."

Dom laid out his plan like it was a done deal, expecting Enzo to fall in line, just like always. But Enzo never looked away from Natalie. She was mesmerized, hanging on his every word as if her life depended on it.

"I can't do that, Dad. I'm needed in LA right away. Like you said, you started from scratch. So can I. I've only got nine months to get myself established. I can't wait on a maybe. If my company doesn't do well right away, that's okay. I know how to work hard. You," he said, making sure he had her full attention, "this dream we are building, is more important to me than anything or anyone. Love won't wait."

He held out his hand, waiting for her to take it.

She had always felt like his hand was trying to trap her or hold her back. But not now. Now she knew—he was just trying to walk by her side and share his love. Natalie drew in a choked breath, tears cutting off her words before his lips took over the job. Was he really going to leave all of this, his family, his job, his home, to follow her down to LA? LA was just a place she was running to because she didn't think she would get to stay. She couldn't let him make this sacrifice. She pulled back from his kiss and put her hand in his, squeezing tight, willing him to understand her next words.

"Enzo, you don't have to—"

"No, we are in this together. I'm not letting you run away." His other arm pulled her into a hug, and she wrapped hers around him as much as she could with it pinned beneath his. "Wherever you and our kids need to be is where I need to be. What's it going to take for you to believe me?"

Gasps from behind them told her that he hadn't shared their news with anyone until that moment. She closed her eyes, shutting out everyone but him. She pulled back and his arm loosened and dropped. She opened her eyes. The dejected look on his face shamed her. She'd made him doubt so much, and still he was ready to walk away from it all for her, for a chance at "them." God, she wanted that chance too. She couldn't let him think she didn't. Time to be brave. When his hand slackened in hers, she gripped tighter and shook it.

"Is Daisy the only one who can promise on a handshake?" She turned her hand, weaving her fingers between his. She had to fix this. "Enzo, I do believe you. You've proven I can trust you. But this is a decision we should make together."

She felt his hand relax into hers. She'd put this man through the wringer, and he'd still stayed by her side. He rested his forehead against hers, and she sighed in relief.

"I have to admit, I like the sound of us making decisions together. What changed your mind?" His voice growled straight through her.

"Daisy. Even though I might lose her someday, I can't stop loving her now. I couldn't love her any less just to protect myself. She deserves to live happily ever after, and for the first time I realized that I do too. I can't stop myself from loving you, even if someday I might lose you."

She kissed him deeply, needing him to feel the truth in her words, before she continued.

"Do you know what I had today?"

"No, what?"

"A true partner. Someone who cares enough about me to stand by me on my worst day and help me find my child. Someone who cares enough about my needs to turn his own life upside down. Someone who loves me enough to open his heart, even when I was being a jerk. I didn't know how much I needed that until I had almost lost it. I need that with you. I owe you an apology."

His eyes searched hers for the truth in her words.

How did he make it through life with his heart right there in his eyes for anyone to see?

Stripped down, no shields between them, she let him see what he needed to see, even though it made her words stutter in her chest. Her heart, in her eyes and in her hands, his for the keeping.

"How do I explain? No one ever... Everyone leaves. I...I always believed I deserved it. I was convinced it was because I'm not built for happy ever afters. Maybe it's because I never gave anyone a chance to be right. Or maybe it's because I hadn't met you yet."

Natalie glanced over his shoulder to see Jo gently herding half the neighborhood into her kitchen, giving them a small sliver of privacy, before returning her gaze to meet his head-on.

"The first time I got pregnant, I had to handle it all myself. When I found out about this baby, I fell back on old habits. I've been the only one making the decisions for my family for a long time. I made plans, assuming I'd be on my own with this baby too. That I'd need my old circle of support. That was wrong of me. I'm so sorry, Enzo." She rested her forehead against his, and he pressed a soft kiss to her lips, before letting loose all the questions in his head.

"How long have you known?"

"I figured it out while you were on the phone with Daisy."

"So you haven't been plotting to leave me for weeks. That's a relief. How far along are you?"

"Well, I have to assume it happened that first night, but I haven't even been to a doctor yet. My old OB/GYN is down in LA."

"Okay, well, if you want to wait until we get down there—"

"Hold on, Enzo." She gripped the hand she still held tighter. "The only reason I was going to LA was that I couldn't imagine doing this alone. Last time, I'd just lost the support of my boyfriend and my mother in one swoop. I had to build a community quick."

"And if you need to be around those people, I'm willing to move, as you just heard." He gestured toward the living room behind him.

She hadn't gotten a chance to apologize. Though the people had gone into hiding in the kitchen, the living room was still filled with the photos, trophies, and mementos that documented the life of the family in this house. His family. Possibly her family. She'd like to add some memories to this room.

"I did hear that, and I appreciate that you would be willing to upend your entire life to be there for us. But those friends were fleeting, and can't compare to the amazing support we have here. I had to cobble together a family before. I think I'd like to try it with a real family this time around. That is, if you were serious when you asked Daisy about being her daddy."

Enzo pulled her up into his arms and spun around. "Are you kidding? I'd be honored to be her dad. Would you seriously consider staying up here?"

"The only reason I was leaving was that I didn't think you'd want us to stay. I was afraid, Enzo, so afraid because you see, I'd gone and fallen head over heels for you, and if you left us, I didn't think I'd be strong enough to put myself back together again. If I was the one who did the leaving, I might have had a chance. But I've got a great job, amazing new friends, and a loving partner right here. Let's stay."

His kiss tenderly pulled her battered heart out of her chest and tucked it into his for safe-keeping. It was a strange feeling, not altogether comfortable yet, but she liked the idea of getting used to it. She trusted him to take good care of it.

"I can't offer you much. I don't make a whole lot working for my dad, and it looks like my plans to get my own business up and running might take longer than I expected, but—"

She put a hand over his mouth. "Enzo. Stop. You're already my hero, and I don't need a savior. I'm not helpless. I need you to be my partner and build our future, together. Work out solutions with me, not for me."

"I'm just trying to show you that I will do everything I can to take care of our family."

"*We* will take care of our family, together. Now, about this dream of yours, how much capital do you need to get started?"

"I've got this business plan worked out, but it assumed that what I'd built would be worth something to Valenti Brothers."

"Well, redo your calculations. I've got this popular little web show starting to take off. There's a hot model that my fans are going nuts over." She grinned, teasing him into smiling along with her, before she gathered herself for her apology. "I made the mistake of taking him for granted, but I think I can convince him to keep sitting for me if I pay him what he's worth. I'm so sorry I just assumed you would be okay with it. I should have asked."

He pulled her into a hug that muffled her next words, so she had to lean back and try again.

"If my channel keeps growing and going viral, we can earn quite a bit to put toward your seed money. It might mean putting up with the show for a few more months, but we'll get there."

"But that's your show. You've worked so hard to get it going."

"And I'll keep it going, but this is *our* life, right? You were just about to tank your career and uproot yourself to support our family. How about we not do that, and you let someone believe in your dreams for a change?"

The grin on his face teased out one of hers to match. "Our family. God, that sounds good."

"It really does, doesn't it?" She burrowed her head into his chest and breathed deeply, treasuring the right to fill herself up with his comfort and love while she found a little more courage. "When I was a little girl, I used to dream I was part of a big family, with lots of noisy brothers and sisters, and nosy aunts and uncles, and parents who gave a damn. It's one of the few things I've regretted not giving Daisy growing up. Do you think your family will mind growing a little bigger and maybe a little louder?"

The door to the kitchen swung open and banged against the staircase wall as Jo came flying through.

"Mind? You're already part of this family! Get in here and give me a hug! Oh, another baby! It's just so exciting!" She wrapped them up in a big joint hug, kissing both of their cheeks and grinning wildly. "I hope you got all of that straightened out, because I stayed in that kitchen as long as I could. I want credit for my restraint."

"Noted." Enzo grinned at his mother, the love and humor on his face clear, and Natalie knew she'd made the right choice. This was a man who knew how to love, and he loved her.

"Can I have hugs too?" Daisy's voice piped up from the top of the stairs where she had snuck silently and clearly listened in.

"Looks like we have more than one eavesdropper in the family," Natalie teased as Enzo held out his arms toward her little girl.

Daisy threw herself into the hug, and Natalie surrounded them both, pulling them both tight. Daisy tugged away with the enthusiasm endemic in six-year-olds and almost toppled them off the stairs.

Enzo leaned in and whispered in Natalie's ear as he steadied her. "Rule number one in big families: privacy does not exist."

Jo laughed at him, clearly demonstrating his point, before holding her hand out to Daisy.

"Speaking of which, there are a lot of people in the kitchen who were very worried about you, little girl. Let's go tell them the good news." She led them into the kitchen where family and friends lingered around the table.

A cheer went up when Daisy came through the door, and another for Natalie and Enzo. Sofia and Adrian had been on their way over to see Daisy's costume when they'd gotten the call about the excitement. Frankie had a standing Halloween date to mooch chocolate from the trick-or-treat bowl. A few neighbors who'd helped search had stayed for wine and beer once they'd found out Daisy was safe. Exclamations of relief and congratulations mingled as multiple conversations flowed around the room. Jo raised her voice and clinked a fork against her wine glass.

"Attention, please. Since I will soon be an official grandma, I will henceforth be known as JoNana to all of my grandchildren."

"Including me?" asked Daisy, shyly.

JoNana pulled her into a side hug and grinned. "You most of all! You've got the important job of teaching all these babies how to say it, seeing as you're the only one who can speak!"

"Can I be the cool aunt?" Frankie joked. "Sofia's much better at being the bossy one."

"Hey! I resent that!" Sofia slapped her sister on the shoulder and laughed before turning to Natalie. "Also, if you need a recommendation for a doctor up here, I can give you the number of my OB/GYN. I love her." She pulled Natalie into a tight hug. "Our babies are going to be cousins! I'm so excited that they are going to grow up together."

No privacy was right. Natalie had barely had a minute to let her decision settle for herself and here she was playing Twenty Questions, to which the answer was always, "I don't know yet." She'd asked for a big family, and she'd certainly gotten one all at once.

Dom stood off to one side, holding himself removed from the festivities, and Nat escaped her fifth hug to stand beside him. He dropped a heavy arm around her shoulder.

"Thank you," Dom muttered gruffly.

"What for?"

He looked at Enzo and cleared his throat. "For letting him stay." He turned his gaze on his wife. "For giving her a reason to be happy." He swiped a hand across one eye. "For teaching this old fart a thing or two."

She leaned into the hug. "You big softie."

"Welcome to the family." He kissed her on the top of her head and then stepped outside to compose himself.

Enzo slid into the vacant spot next to her, and she leaned into his shoulder. She was exhausted, but she didn't want this moment to end. He took her hand in his and let her lean, wrapping their joined hands around her hip. She wasn't deluding herself that this transition was going to be easy. There were a lot of unknowns and a lot of adjustments to be made.

But Natalie was ready to figure out the answers and make those changes, because she wouldn't be doing it alone. She squeezed Enzo's hand behind her, and he squeezed back, raising their joined hands to his lips for a kiss and a promise.

Together.

CHAPTER 23

THREE WEEKS LATER, Natalie was chewing her nails to the quick in the waiting room of the OB/GYN. Sofia had highly recommended her doctor, so here they were. Daisy bounced next to her on the couch, unable to contain her excitement about getting to hear the baby's heartbeat. Nat handed over her phone to try and calm her down with a game.

When Enzo strode through the door, her nerves eased.

"Yeah, Dad. I told you I'll get back down there to measure it out for the blueprints, but I can't fit you into my schedule until next Tuesday… Yes, I'm aware that you hired me for a job. It's also Thanksgiving tomorrow, and I'm going to spend it with my family… No, I've got other clients booked this weekend." He mockingly covered his eyes with his hand. "Yes, that's what happens when you start your own business. Dad… Dad… Tuesday. Yes. I have to go. I'm at the doctor's office now. Yes, I'll take a video. Okay. Love you too. Bye."

With a smile and an eye roll, he tucked his phone into his pocket and dropped kisses on Daisy's head and Natalie's lips.

"Hi, babe. How are you feeling today?"

"Better now that you're here."

"Do you think you'll be up to Thanksgiving with Adrian's family tomorrow?"

"I hope so. I told Sofia to expect us. I don't want to screw up her first year hosting."

Enzo placed a warm hand between her shoulder blades and rubbed gently. "You won't screw up anything, either way. I don't want you pushing yourself."

She was still getting used to his casual affection after years of not being touched by anyone but her child, but it was a good adjustment. She hoped his kisses never lost their power to flood her with love. Her heart thrilled every time.

She couldn't undo a lifetime of solo programming, nor did she want to. She was proud of the woman she'd become during those years. She was a damn good mother and a successful artist and entrepreneur. But she could acknowledge that this new season of her life and the mother she would become would be made infinitely better by the man leaning on the armrest of the waiting room couch.

"Valenti/Carras family?" A nurse called out as she read from the top of her chart.

"We should fix that soon," Enzo said under his breath.

"Oh yeah?"

"Oh yeah." The look he gave her burned her cheeks as they walked back to the exam room.

"If that's your idea of a proposal, think again."

"No, you're a flowers and ring kind of woman."

She stared him down, but he'd pokered up. She vowed to pin him down about that cryptic comment later.

Natalie hopped up on the exam table and draped the paper blanket over her lap. Time to sort that out later. She needed all of her attention focused on the baby now. She'd worn a flowy dress for ease of access, depending on what the doctor needed to do, and she fidgeted with the hem. She just wanted confirmation that everything was going well with this little life they'd made. Maybe a due date. And if a miraculous cure for morning sickness had been discovered in the last six years, she'd take that too. Then she could relax.

She'd been through this before and remembered vividly the joy and wonder of hearing Daisy's heartbeat for the first time. For Enzo and Daisy, this was a first. They were beyond excited, and Natalie had relented and let Daisy miss school for this appointment. Though she was currently engrossed with her game on the phone, Natalie was glad she'd decided to let her come along. This was a family-building moment. But if she was a little distracted for all of the exam stuff that came before, that would be just fine.

Enzo stood propped against the wall, watching Natalie's every move.

"Calm down, would you? You're making me nervous!" she teased and reached for his hand. He gave it readily. She squeezed, and he squeezed back.

Holding hands had become part of their love language. To the outside world, and Daisy, it was an innocent gesture, but between them, it reaffirmed their commitment to face challenges together, partners in life.

A brief knock at the door heralded the doctor's arrival.

"Hello, I'm Dr. Reimnitz, and I'm so glad to meet you. Sofia has told me all about you. Let me get some medical information before we begin the exam."

While Natalie walked her through her medical history and the initial exam, Enzo did his best to keep Daisy distracted.

"Let's talk about what I was thinking for Halloween next year—"

"That is eleven months away!" Daisy protested.

"It's never too soon to start planning. Next year, we will have the baby to consider for the theme. I was thinking Dr. Seuss. *Cat in the Hat, Horton Hears A Who, One Fish, Two Fish, Red Fish, Blue Fish.*"

"I do not want to be a fish," Daisy asserted firmly.

"Okay, it was just a thought."

"Everything feels good in there. Are you ready to find this heartbeat?" Throughout the visit, the doctor's kind and calm efficiency reassured Natalie that she was in good hands, and Enzo seemed more relaxed too. He got out his phone and set it to record.

Daisy hopped up next to the table too. "Do we get to hear the baby now?"

"We sure do. Are you excited to be a big sister?"

Daisy nodded and bounced on her toes while Dr. Reimnitz readied Natalie's belly for the Doppler. Pressing the device to her lower abdomen produced some gurgles and groans. Daisy's eyes bulged wide, and the good doctor laughed.

"That was just your mommy's lunch, not the baby. Let's try over here." She slid it to the front and they heard a heartbeat, but it didn't sound quite right. Fast and erratic, it didn't sound like any heartbeat Natalie had ever heard.

Dr. Reimnitz frowned and her eyebrows drew together as she tried a different spot. Enzo put down the phone. With one hand, he pulled Daisy in for a hug, and with the other he squeezed Natalie's hand even tighter. She'd never been more grateful for his solid presence and his love. Whatever happened next, they would face it together.

"Doctor? What's…what are you hearing?" Enzo was clearly trying to keep the worry out of his voice, but hadn't succeeded.

Dr. Reimnitz continued moving the device to various spots on Natalie's slightly rounded belly. She tried different angles and listened very carefully, before she looked Natalie straight in the eye with a no-nonsense expression. "With your permission, I'd like to do a quick ultrasound before I answer that."

Natalie nodded, and soon her belly was covered in icy goo, and she was shaking. She tried to contain her panic, but she felt intensely vulnerable, and her thoughts were spiraling through worst-case scenarios.

Enzo kissed her forehead. "I'm right here, babe."

Natalie felt some of the fear recede. No matter what happened, she wouldn't have to face it alone.

"I'm sorry it's so cold. Usually, we do these in the tech's office with the warmer. Okay, let's take a look."

As Dr. Reimnitz moved the paddle back and forth, black and white flecks glowed on the screen. She tapped buttons that zoomed in and out, and Natalie felt her own heartbeat quicken. It hadn't been this complicated to find a heartbeat with Daisy.

Dr. Reimnitz looked over her shoulder at Enzo and smiled.

"You're going to want to film this bit." She put the paddle back on Natalie's belly, and Enzo let go of Daisy to lift the phone and film once more.

"Here we go. See this black space? That is an egg sac, and it's well attached. Inside, see that white curly thing? That is a baby. Now listen, here's the heartbeat." She turned up the volume on the machine.

Natalie smiled and started to cry. There it was. Her baby's heartbeat, strong and steady. Her worry faded as she listened to that heart flutter, holding the hand of the man she loved.

"Is it a boy or girl?" Daisy asked.

"It's too soon to tell. You'll have to come back for the twenty-week visit to see that. Weren't you guys talking about Halloween costumes earlier?"

"Yeah, Enzo wants me to be a fish."

"Well, I think you'd be better off going as the Cat in the Hat. That way you can have Thing One and Thing Two tag along." She slid the ultrasound wand to the far side of Natalie's belly. "The heartbeat sounded muddled before because it was picking up two. Here is the second egg sac with the other baby. Another strong, healthy heartbeat. You're having twins. Fraternal, by the looks of things."

Natalie's jaw dropped along with the tears of shock and joy running down her cheeks. Enzo looked like he was about to pass out, and Daisy was screaming and dancing in circles. All Natalie could hear was the strong second heartbeat, with echoes of the first one filtering beneath it.

Two.

Twins.

Two babies.

Wow!

She wasn't prepared for any of this.

Enzo raised their joined hands to his lips for a steady kiss, and the panic faded away.

"We've got a lot to be thankful for," she murmured.

"I'm thankful that I get to be your partner on this crazy ride," Enzo said. "Let's go tell our family."

That was the best thing she'd heard all day.

THE END

Want a bit more? Read on for an extended epilogue I published in the Worst Holiday Ever Anthology, Decked Out. Please enjoy Natalie and Enzo's first Christmas.

DECKED OUT

ORIGINALLY PUBLISHED IN WORST HOLIDAY EVER ANTHOLOGY

"Are you excited for Christmas this year?"

Natalie heard and felt Enzo's words rumble in her ear pressed against his chest. The lounge chair on his parents' deck was not meant for two. Nor was it generally called into service on December twenty-first, but they were making it work. Natalie snuggled into the warm V of his legs, draping her thighs over the side of his lap and tucking herself more firmly into his embrace. His hands stroked down her arm gently as if she was fragile and precious, even as his work-roughened skin caught at the wool of her poncho.

She knew that she was tougher than he believed, but she appreciated his tendency to pamper her when he pressed a kiss into her hair. It was still such a novel experience. Carrying his twins was exhausting, and they were only just out of the first trimester. She toyed with the button on his flannel shirt while his heart continued to beat steadily beneath her ear, trying to find an answer she could say in the near presence of her six-year-old, Daisy, up in the tree house.

"Excited is one word for it."

"What's another?" He pressed, not letting her evade.

"Nervous. Terrified. Exhausted. Oh God." Natalie pressed her palms to her eyes as if she could block out the swirling images of her own personal Nightmare Before Christmas.

"Babe, what's got you worried?"

"I don't know. Meeting your entire extended family around a holiday packed with sensitive traditions and managing the expectations and sugar intake of an over-stimulated six-year-old while pregnant with twins? You're right. What could I possibly be worried about?"

Enzo's hand slid from her arm to underneath her poncho, coming to rest on her barely bulging belly at the mention of the babies. The warm weight of his fingers cherishing the lives they'd created eased a bit of her nerves. She was still new to this whole trusting-a-man thing, but this was Enzo. The man she'd fallen in love with, the man who had proven himself trustworthy, the man who was still by her side.

"You don't have anything to worry about. I'll be right here to help with Daisy and to keep my rowdy family in line." His hand shifted from her belly higher, cupping her sensitive and swollen breast beneath the cover of her wrap. "I've got a few plans to help you relax, too."

As much as she had longed for his touch throughout the day, she tugged his arm away.

"Stop it. Daisy is right there."

Enzo bent his head and pressed a kiss to the shell of her ear that made her shiver just as much as his words.

"So she'll see that I really love her mama."

"I'm sure she already knows that, but we have to leave for the winter recital soon." She wiggled her hip against his already stiffening cock. "How do you plan to hide that?"

"Worried the other moms will be jealous?" He chuckled.

She turned and pressed a kiss to his lips before levering herself out of the chair.

"They already are, babe, but gloating isn't attractive."

As she turned to get Daisy ready for her big night, Enzo grabbed her hand and pulled her back in for another searing kiss. When she raised her head faster than her eyelids, he grinned.

"You are always attractive to me. Don't worry about Christmas. I have a few surprises lined up. It's going to be a big family holiday to welcome you and Adrian. All you have to do is sit back and enjoy."

"Surprises? Enzo, what surprises?" In her life, they had never been good. Enzo booped her on the nose as he rose to stand beside her.

"It wouldn't be a surprise if I told you, now would it? 'Tis the season for giving, Natalie. Let me give you this." He turned toward the tree house that still stood, sturdy and weathered, in his parents' backyard. "Come on, Daisy. Time to go."

Enzo surveyed the sea of cars in front of his old elementary school. "Why don't you ladies hop out here, and I'll go park the car."

"Sounds good." Natalie hustled Daisy out of the car.

Enzo rolled down the window and called out, "Break a leg, *bellissima*," before slowly pulling away from the curb.

The neighborhood was packed for the winter recital, and he ended up parking four blocks away. The principal was up on stage making announcements by the time he finally squeezed into the packed auditorium. Enzo scanned the assembled parents looking for Natalie. He crept up the aisle, finally spotting her near the middle of a row. Flanked on either side by more parents.

She hadn't saved him a seat. He rubbed away the pinching in his chest. She needed time to adjust, he reasoned. Old habits died hard. He was trying to be patient, but every time she forgot to include him felt like a paper cut. Annoying, impossible to ignore, and painful when things got salty. He had a lot of lingering paper cuts. He'd almost prefer one big slice that he could heal all at once.

He waved to get her attention and gestured to the back. The apologetic shrug she gave him didn't make the ache feel any better. He pushed it aside. They'd get there, once he became a permanent part of their lives...

As the first graders began to sing "Deck The Halls," he took a space standing behind the back row of seats. Daisy sang two more songs, one about eight kandelikas and another about dancing snowflakes he doubted she'd ever seen. Maybe he could take them to Tahoe next year. Family vacations. With *his* family. It was all so new, but he couldn't wait to get started. Christmas Eve. He could be patient a few more days to set his plan into motion.

Daisy followed her classmates off stage and when she waved at her mom her little face fell. Nope. Not happening. Not caring if it was embarrassing, he cupped his hands and yelled, "Didi!" while waving madly. The grin on her face and her little wave made the rest of the stares worthwhile. He would yell across any gym so that little girl would know he was there for her, even if her mother had forgotten.

~

By Christmas Eve, Natalie was a nervous wreck over those stupid surprises. She'd been so distracted at the recital that she hadn't noticed when someone took the seat she'd been saving for Enzo until it was too late.

He hadn't said anything, but she could tell he'd been upset. She was still trying to figure out how to fix that. But tonight, she was simply too overwhelmed to think, let alone tackle heavy emotional conversations. She had to get presents to Jo's house for tomorrow morning, and get everyone dressed and out the door for a late Christmas Eve dinner and Midnight Mass. She wasn't completely happy about keeping Daisy up into the early hours of the morning, but it was an important tradition in Enzo's family. This Feast of the Seven Fishes was another important tradition, one that everyone in Enzo's family cherished, so she was going to try and fit in there as well.

Enzo's entire family. She was going to meet even more of them. Plus surprises. Was it any wonder she was a nervous wreck?

A lifetime of insecurities threatened to rise up and drown her, but she clung to Enzo's love like a buoy. He'd found plenty inside her to love, and she would just borrow his confidence until hers showed the hell up.

They walked up to Jo and Dom's house, arms laden with bags of presents, bottles of wine, and the platter of fish sticks Daisy had baked all by herself. Daisy was so excited for her first real family Christmas, and Natalie wanted it to be perfect.

Thank goodness the show was on break for the holidays. She'd had time to indulge Daisy's enthusiasm.

The door opened, and they were immediately enveloped in hugs and noise, warmth and love. Natalie's nerves eased up a little. This family was amazing.

"Look, JoNana. I made the sticks for the fishy dinner all by myself! Well, Mommy took them out of the oven, but..." Daisy clearly shared none of her mother's nerves, chattering away as she disappeared into the kitchen with Jo and her casserole dish.

Enzo took the presents to put under the tree, before following Daisy back into the kitchen, leaving Natalie alone with her bottles of wine. Stopping for hugs with Zia Elena, Zio Tony, Seth, and Frankie, she made her way over to Brandy who seemed to be managing the makeshift bar next to the fireplace. Brandy's corkscrew curls glistened in the dancing light from the fire, and Natalie admired the young woman's style. The bright red sweater dress suited her to a T. She fit here in Jo's living room, all decked out with draping holly and ivy and gold accents. Brandy was an outside addition to the family, and if she could feel at home here, so could Natalie. Eventually. She was already holding out a wine glass of sparkling water by the time Natalie made it to her.

"I don't know how you're doing this without wine," Brandy

teased, taking the bottles of wine and adding them to the stash, before turning back to the cocktail she was mixing. Natalie nodded dramatically and took a long sip of her club soda, earning a laugh as an older lady toddled up beside them.

"Do you have my Manhattan done yet, girl?"

Brandy's back tensed, but she dropped in the cherry and presented the drink with a smile.

"Here you go, Prozia Dulce. Have you met Natalie yet?"

Dulce turned her attention to Natalie as Brandy had intended, looking her up and down. "You're Enzo's girl."

Natalie nodded.

"Hmm. Got yourself knocked up with twins, I hear."

Natalie's mouth dropped open, words deserting her. How did one respond to that? Apparently, Great-aunt Dulce did not require a response. She patted Natalie on the cheek and sipped her cocktail.

"Good girl. Now get a ring on that finger." Dulce turned her attention to Brandy. "You've been with Seth long enough. Why haven't you made any babies yet? You got something wrong down there?" The woman who had to be pushing ninety circled a finger meaningfully at Brandy's belly. Much to Natalie's surprise, Brandy gave the old biddy a civil answer. Her talent must have come from years of tending bar. Natalie didn't have that level of calm in the face of rudeness anywhere in her arsenal.

"We are waiting until I am out of my nursing program and my career is a bit more stable."

"Bah! Careers. A career is what you do until you catch a man. You two have already done that. Now get on with it. I want babies to cuddle before I die."

With another deep swig of her Manhattan, she toddled off to harass someone else.

"Rude old bat."

Natalie grinned. "How old is she exactly?"

"Don't do the math. It doesn't matter. She's so well pickled she'll never die. That's her second drink in under an hour. I'm mixing a pitcher if she asks for another one." Brandy muttered and picked up her own red wine. "Come on. Let's step away, or I'll never be off the clock."

Natalie knew that Brandy had worked as a bartender during her off hours, but had thankfully been able to cut back significantly now that her nursing program had begun. Nat certainly didn't want the poor woman working through her holiday. They didn't make it far before Jo's voice rang out from the kitchen.

"Domenico Valenti, I swear if you do not get out of my kitchen this second, I will never make your pepperoncini ever again!"

There was no teasing lilt in Jo's voice to soften the threat. Dom must've caught that too, because he hustled out of the kitchen with a frown on his face, just in time to answer the next doorbell. Jake Ryland, show runner for Million-Dollar Starter Home, the Valenti family's reality show, walked in, his arms weighed down with gift bags.

"Hi, Dom! Merry Christmas!" He accepted a clap on the back from the family patriarch as he moved further into the room to set down his gifts.

"What's all this? What are you doing here?" Frankie asked from her perch by the fireplace, her confusion clear.

"Frankie!" Dom chided.

"No, it's okay, Dom. Your father found out I was going to work through the holiday, and he invited me to join you all. *These,*" he arranged the bags at the foot of the tree, "are presents to thank your family for having me."

"All work and no play." Frankie found her trademark sass quickly, pushing past her shock.

"I don't think anyone has ever called me a dull boy." Jake returned without missing a beat.

"There's a first time for everything."

Natalie practically heard the sparks flying as they clashed wits. *How long has that been going on?*

Their banter was interrupted by another peal from the doorbell.

The front door opened and the number of people in the room doubled. The noise level tripled. Adrian and Sofia's arms were full of wrapped boxes, and Adrian's younger sister, Luciana, carried in several aluminum trays.

"Welcome! Welcome!" Dom relieved her of her burden, placing the food on the sideboard. "This smells amazing."

Adrian's mother, Graciela, followed behind Luciana, gripping her older daughter Mahalia's arm tightly. Her husband Rey was right behind them with little Jeremiah tucked in his arms. Adrian's middle sister, Aracely, shut the door behind them with her foot, her hand full of a large stockpot.

"Homemade horchata," she explained as she shimmied past hugs on her way to the kitchen.

"I made shrimp tamales. I hope they turned out. There are chicken ones for your freezer, too." Graciela looked a little spacey as she explained, and Natalie wondered what kind of medication she'd taken to overcome her fear of leaving her house tonight.

"I'm sure they'll be delicious," Dom said, offering his arm. "Come on back and say hi to Jo."

Luciana joined Brandy and Nat near the de facto bar.

"Wine. Any color. Any kind. My God, dealing with my family at Christmas should not be attempted sober." Brandy handed her a glass of red wine and grinned. Luciana drank deep and sighed before holding out her other hand to Natalie. "Hi, I'm Luciana, but everyone calls me Lucy. You must be Natalie."

Natalie nodded, and raised her glass of water in cheers. "Welcome to the mad house."

"At least we're all here now. We can just relax, eat some good food, and drink some good wine. Well, except for you, Preggo." Brandy teased.

"Don't remind me." Natalie sighed. The doorbell rang again, its peal sending a wave of confused silence through the room. Natalie was profoundly grateful that she stood near two strong young women, because when the door opened, she leaned on them, hard. A woman with heavy makeup and a face permanently set into a scowl stepped inside, followed by a tall lanky man with long black hair and a slimy smile.

What the hell?

Enzo came from the kitchen into the nearly silent living room. Seeing the two newcomers hovering near the door, he went to greet them, arms wide open. "Welcome!"

He pulled her mother into a hug. "You must be Portia. I'm so glad you could make it."

Natalie gasped. He knew who she was. He'd been expecting her. Had he invited her? No. No, he wouldn't have done something like that without talking to her first. Would he?

"And you are?" he asked, turning to the man standing next to her mother, the man she never thought she'd see again.

"Kyle, Daisy's dad, and I'm here to get my family back."

With a strangled cry, Natalie dropped her glass and dashed into the kitchen.

MAYBE NATALIE HAD a point about surprises. Enzo certainly hadn't expected this when he'd invited Portia Carras to Christmas. He had wanted to meet her and get her blessing before he took the next step with Natalie. He'd hoped that news of the twins might help Natalie build a bridge with her mother. In his world, babies and growing families were events to celebrate. He certainly hadn't anticipated her bringing Natalie's ex-boyfriend along.

"Well, that's something we should talk about."

"I've got nothing to say to you." Kyle pushed past Enzo, and planted himself on the wall nearest the kitchen door, settling in to wait for Natalie.

Shit. When Enzo and his mom had brainstormed how to make this Christmas special for Daisy, they had both thought that having both sets of grandparents would be a nice surprise. God, how was he going to salvage this?

"Can I get you something to drink, Mrs. Carras?" he asked as he led her across the room to the spot her daughter had left vacant, all the while keeping one eye on the brooding tag-along.

"It's Ms. Carras," she winked at him before turning to Brandy, who had stepped back towards the bar. "And I'll take a vodka martini. Don't even look at the vermouth." Brandy shook, strained, and poured the requested drink, intently focused on the conversation in front of her.

"So how was the drive down from Lincoln?" Enzo asked, determined to be hospitable. Portia took a deep drink with her eyes closed before replying.

"Awful. When I offered a ride to Kyle, I expected him to be grateful. He's been asking questions about Natalie lately, so I thought he'd be excited. But all he did was bitch and moan the whole way." She knocked back the rest of her drink in one swallow. "After all that, he didn't even offer to take a turn driving. Can you imagine? Another." She set her glass back down in front of Brandy and snapped her fingers. Brandy sucked in a breath as her eyebrows drew together. Enzo hadn't seen her angry before, but he had no doubt that when that cool composure blew it would be impressive.

"Why don't you let me make that for you?" Seth stepped in front of Brandy, picking up the glass while simultaneously spinning his fiancé out of range. "Brandy needs to go help Tia Jo with the cioppino."

"Is that that fishy soup? Ugh. I hate fish." Portia wrinkled her nose in disgust.

Enzo's brain stuttered. She'd come to the Feast of the Seven Fishes and didn't like fish? Fucking perfect.

"The only seafood I like is shrimp. Not that there's anything shrimpy here." Portia eyed Seth and Enzo speculatively as she took her glass back, with a sauced wink. Enzo was sure she'd meant it to be saucy, but she'd already crossed into less than sober territory. He had to wonder when she'd started drinking.

"Oh, that's good then," Lucy chimed in, trying to ease the tension. "My mom made shrimp tamales."

"I don't eat Mexican food." Portia sneered, smoothing a hand over her waist to her hip. "So fattening," she added with a significant glance at Lucy's belly. "When are you due?"

Lucy's angry growl faded as Adrian wrapped an arm around her shoulder and pulled her away from the toxic woman. Enzo tried to salvage the situation. God, he hated conflict, and here he'd invited it in on Christmas Eve. He had to get her out of the house, even if it was just for a few minutes.

"I'm sure we'll figure something out. Let's get the rest of your things from the car. We're putting the presents under the tree." He heard Lucy muttering, "That bitch," to her brother as they walked past, and he couldn't help but agree. Natalie came back in from the kitchen then, and Enzo realized the full extent of his fuck-up.

Her face was blank and pale, eyes wide and glassy, as she crossed the room.

"Hello, Mom."

"Hello, Natalie." Portia looped her arm through his, and squeezed his bicep. His stomach churned with disgust. "This is quite the fellow you've caught. So nice of him to invite me for Christmas when my own child couldn't be bothered."

"And Kyle? Was he invited too, Mom?" Natalie asked, still not looking at Enzo. Yep, he'd definitely stepped in it this time.

"He's been asking about you and his kid."

Kyle stepped from the wall, but Natalie held up her hand to stop him.

"You mean, Daisy? Your granddaughter?"

"Really, do you have to rub it in my face that I'm a grandmother? I don't look like I should be a grandma yet, do I?" Good Christ, had she just batted her eyelashes and rubbed her breasts against his arm? Enzo disentangled himself with a shudder and didn't answer.

"So you just decided to invite my ex-boyfriend along for the ride?"

"You know I hate to drive long distances. If you'd sent me a plane ticket, I wouldn't have needed a car buddy." She turned her attention back to Enzo. "I've always relied on the kindness of the men in my life. My daughter has always been so ungrateful."

Natalie flinched at that jab. Enzo reached for her hand, and it lay limp and clammy in his grip. She still wouldn't look him in the eye. How on earth could he apologize for this?

"I'm sorry that raising me was such a burden." Natalie replied with a cold, flat voice. "While we're on the subject of the ways I've ruined your life, congratulations. I'm making you a grandma again. We're having twins." And on that verbal hand grenade, Natalie pulled her hand from his and walked away.

Kyle stepped into her path, putting a hand on her shoulder. Enzo stiffened, but when Natalie nodded, his heart fell to his feet. All he could do was watch her walk away with her ex trailing behind her. She'd given Kyle a nod, but she wouldn't even look at Enzo. He was so screwed.

The rest of the room was unnaturally silent. Even Buster, curled up by Frankie's feet, seemed to be judging him with soulful eyes before looking away from the mangled train wreck he'd caused.

"Let's go get your stuff from the car."

"Oh, all I have is my overnight bag. Which room is going to be mine?"

"She can have mine," Frankie said. "You couldn't pay me to stay here tonight," she added under her breath, but loud enough that they all heard her anyway, to Jake who'd taken the seat next to her on the couch. "Where are you staying tonight?"

"I had planned on crashing here, maybe on the couch, but it seems like the house might be a little more crowded than expected," Jake said.

An awful thought flashed through Enzo's mind. Did Kyle think he was staying here tonight? *Over my dead body.* It may not be a very Christian sentiment, but surely there was room at an inn, somewhere far, far away.

"You can sleep at The Block. I'll give you a ride later." Frankie added. "It'll give me a chance to harass you about the new contracts while you're tipsy."

"That would be a solid plan, but I don't drink."

"Well, damn it. Then you can drive me home later. I have a feeling tonight is going to call for more wine than usual."

"Deal." Jake grinned at Frankie before shaking his head at Enzo.

Yeah, I know, damn it.

He didn't need the know-it-all show runner to point out that he'd messed up royally.

"The antipasti are ready." Jo announced as she and Aracely came into the dining room, bearing heavy platters of delicious snacks. "Who's hungry?"

No one had stopped her or questioned who she was with when she'd walked straight through the kitchen and out onto the back deck followed by Kyle. She hoped that meant she was trusted and not that they didn't care at all that she'd just left with someone other than their son. In her mind's eye, she flashed back to the last time she'd been on this porch and wished she'd pressed Enzo harder about his freaking surprises.

She owed them all a huge apology. She didn't doubt that her mother had been horrible to everyone in that room, well, everyone she didn't have a vested interest in charming. Natalie had spent her childhood apologizing for her mom and isolating so that no one else had to deal with it. All of the old guilt and anxiety came flooding back. She hadn't wanted to bring toxic drama into this house, but it had followed her anyhow.

At least she'd managed to keep Daisy clear of it for now. She hadn't wanted to go upstairs, but Natalie had insisted and Jo had backed her up with promises of extra presents if Daisy would hide out up in Enzo's room until Nat came to get her. If at all possible she was going to protect her baby from the jerk who'd abandoned them both. Arms crossed, she turned to face Kyle, praying for the strength to get through this.

"Well? What do you want?"

"Come on, Nattie. Don't be like that." He tried to brush the hair back from her face, but she jerked her head back out of his reach. He'd lost the privilege of touching her a long time ago. Seven years ago, to be exact.

"Cut the crap, Kyle. Did you forget that I'm well versed in all of your bullshit? Suddenly you want to see me, after walking away from us without a backward glance?"

"How would you know if I looked back? You disappeared."

"Correction: I built a life for myself and my daughter." Had he been looking for her all this time? No. The Kyle she'd known wouldn't have bothered. If he had cared, he'd have found them long before now. No, she wouldn't slip up and fall into giving him the benefit of the doubt.

"Listen, I know I was an ass back then, but I've changed. Don't you think you've kept her from me long enough?"

Natalie's jaw dropped. The nerve of this guy! Her stomach was churning over the fact that she'd ever let him touch her. That she'd ever fallen for his false charm. She had to get to the bottom of this before he undid all of the hard work she'd done to put herself back together.

"What's this really about?"

"I've been thinking..."

"A dangerous pastime." Natalie chuckled at the quote that flew unbidden from her mouth, but Kyle didn't get the joke. Of course he didn't. He hadn't spent the last six years immersed in Disney movies with Daisy.

"...And I want to give us another shot." Kyle finished his

thought with what Natalie was sure he thought was a sexy smolder. All it made her want to do was smack him upside the head with a cast iron skillet. Definitely too much Disney in her life.

"Do you need money? Is that what this is about?"

"No! I miss you. I've seen your videos, and I keep thinking that we should be doing that together. I'm way better looking than that dude in there."

Ah, money AND fame. Well, she had her answer. Her videos had crossed his screen, likely through a mutual friend on social media, and he was here for his cut. Now that she was getting some attention, he was ready to step back in front of her spotlight. He'd always hated being second best. Hell, he had never been any best, not for her.

Kyle stepped closer and put a hand on her shoulder while she was lost in thought. Did he actually think she was wavering?

"I want us to be a family," he murmured.

"What's her name?" Natalie asked.

"Whose name?"

"Our daughter."

He hesitated a moment too long, and Natalie knocked his hand away. He raised it again, catching himself mid-swing, his face crumpled with anger.

"Go ahead. Hit me, you stupid fucker, and see how fast your ass lands in jail."

"Mommy?" Natalie's gaze swung across the yard, searching for the source of her daughter's voice. Her little legs swung down from the tree house. Apparently, Daisy hadn't stayed upstairs. "Are you okay? Who is this? Where's Enzo?" she asked as she clambered down the rope ladder. She sprinted across the yard into Natalie's arms. The shaky panic in her baby's voice shot steel down Natalie's spine. This farce ended now.

"I'm fine, baby." When Daisy reached the top step, Natalie pulled her back against her midsection and wrapped her arms around Daisy's shoulders, as if she could protect all of her babies at once. "This is Kyle."

He got down on one knee, and reached a hand toward Daisy. She kept hers tucked behind her back.

Good girl. Natalie was damn proud that Daisy's bullshit meter was strong and accurate.

"Hi, Dana. I'm your dad." Kyle said, his eyes never leaving Natalie's.

"You might have donated the sperm that made her, but you will never be her dad."

"Think about it, Natalie. We were good once."

"You had it good. *We* were never good. And her name is Daisy. Go away, Kyle. We're done here."

Daisy turned to bury her head in Natalie's torso as Kyle stalked back into the house. She'd never stood up to him like that while they were dating. If she'd known how easily he'd back down, she might have found the strength to leave him sooner. But then she wouldn't have this little angel in her arms. So, no, no second-guessing. And definitely no looking back.

Natalie did just that though, in the next second, peeking over her shoulder towards the kitchen window and saw their future. Enzo stood in the glowing light, his expression unreadable. He'd clearly watched the whole thing and had turned to talk to Kyle. That would be an interesting conversation.

"Was that man telling the truth? Is he my dad? Why did he call me Dana?"

Finding out what was going on in the kitchen would have to wait until she'd navigated the minefield of these revelations with Daisy. Just how she'd imagined spending Christmas Eve.

"He is my ex-boyfriend. You know how we talked about how a boy part and a girl part have to come together to make a baby? He gave me the boy part that made you."

"And Enzo gave you the boy part for the twins."

They'd had several conversations down this path already since they'd told Daisy about the babies. Natalie watched her bright child piece together the data in front of her.

"That's right, but that doesn't make him your dad. That man

will never be the father you might want him to be. That's why he can't remember your name."

"Do you think Enzo will be my daddy, like he will be for the twins? Or will he have to go away, too?"

Her precious child had already lost so much. Natalie hoped she wasn't lying when she answered.

"I hope Enzo will be your dad, and I'm sure he'll be around for a long, long time. Enzo is a good man who loves us very much. Kyle only loved that I loved him, so good riddance."

Daisy squeezed tighter around Natalie's waist.

"I love you, Mommy."

"I love you, too, Daisy. Forever and ever."

BACK INSIDE ENZO had seethed and paced his way through their conversation, trying to calm down enough to ask Kyle a question without punching him in the face. His mother had bustled around behind him, finishing dinner, but he'd barely noticed.

All of his focus was on Kyle. He'd dared to put his hands on Natalie. True, she'd handled it, but when he'd raised his hand in anger, Enzo had almost charged out the door like a mad bull. When he'd dropped to his knee, Enzo had nearly gone through the window. He'd be damned if that asshole swooped in and beat him to the punch.

Only the rage on Kyle's face when he burst in the door and stalked through the kitchen made Enzo feel any better. This was his chance to corner the bastard. *Carpe diem, and all that.* Somehow Daisy had gotten involved and likely had questions, so Natalie was occupied. Enzo followed Kyle into the living room, where he'd just poured a stiff glass of tequila. The jerk knocked it back and poured another before deigning to turn his attention to Enzo, who held his temper in check by a thread.

"Worried?" Kyle asked. Enzo was dying to wipe that smirk off his face, but he refrained. His mission was too important.

"Not in the least. I'm going to marry her."

"Oh yeah? Funny, she didn't say anything about that to me."

Enzo refused to be baited or pulled away from his goal.

"I want you to sign over your rights to Daisy. I'm going to adopt her."

Kyle's eyes burned with hatred and Enzo grinned, aware that he was baiting the beast.

"Fuck you."

"No, thanks. You will never be that little girl's father."

"Oh yeah? Watch me. I'll fight for custody, and then Natalie will come back to me. She'll be so scared of losing her brat that she'll do whatever I say. And you'll be shit out of luck. No more YouTube videos. No more money. No more Natalie." Kyle got right up in Enzo's face, and it took all of his restraint not to head-butt the asshole. How had Natalie ever fallen for this guy? "I can't wait to fuck her again. She always was a hot piece of ass."

"I thought you didn't like fucking her pregnant."

The words left a bad taste in his mouth. Enzo hated talking about Natalie as if she was an object, but it was the only way Kyle would understand he couldn't have her. The simultaneous anger and disappointment on Kyle's face as he shook his head was priceless.

"No. No, she would have said."

"You can congratulate me. We're having twins."

Kyle looked around the room for confirmation, which Frankie gleefully supplied by nodding and asking, "So are you ready to be a daddy times three?"

"You son of a bitch! You ruined everything." Kyle growled and threw his tequila in Enzo's face. Undeterred, Enzo stepped right up to the challenge, and stated his bottom line.

"You are never going to get anywhere near either of them again. They're mine."

Kyle roared and lunged, and Enzo sidestepped so that Kyle glanced off his shoulder. Before Kyle could regain his balance,

Enzo decked him with a right cross that sent him crashing into the Christmas tree.

Enzo leaned over the man and tried not to appear as pleased as he felt about the split lip.

"Now, are you going to sign the papers? Or are we going to do this the hard way?"

From his spot amidst the presents, Kyle spat blood at him and replied. "Fuck no, and I'll press charges for assault."

"You might want to rethink that." Lucy pointed to her cell-phone that she held up in her hand. "I got your punk ass on camera. I think a judge would say this was self-defense."

Enzo stepped between Kyle and Luciana just in case, and crossed his arms. "See you in court. Now get the hell out of my house."

Kyle crawled out of the presents and marched out the door, slamming it behind him.

Enzo was not one to go searching out violence, but he had to admit punching that asshole had felt good. A primitive power flowed through his system, setting his blood aflame. He flexed his fingers, absorbing the pain as his penance. Maybe with that jerk gone for good, he could get his plans back on track.

"Well done, big brother." Frankie clapped him on the back, before pulling him into a fierce hug. "What a jerk! What did Natalie ever see in that guy?"

"I have no idea." Enzo said, sarcasm thick on his tongue, emboldened by the adrenaline pumping through his veins. "He's a real winner."

"Once upon a time, he was a way out." Natalie said softly from the doorway, before she dropped her eyes to the ground and backed into the kitchen she'd just left. A tense silence filled the room. *Damn it, when was he going to catch a break?*

"So are you interested in filmmaking or the law?" Jake asked Lucy, breaking the stillness.

"Both," she replied with a grin.

"Well, I just hope no one got me anything fragile." Great-aunt

Dulce sipped from a full Manhattan. "I'm not doing returns the day after Christmas because of that asshole."

"Dinner's ready," Jo called from the doorway to the kitchen before she saw the scene in the living room. "What the hell happened to my tree?"

~

Natalie wanted to crawl under the table as she helped cover it with platter after platter of food.

Fried salt cod in pasta, calamari, insalata di mare, poached lobster tails, cioppino, Daisy's fish sticks, and Graciela's tamales joined spaghetti, kale cakes, polenta, and a huge green salad on the groaning table. Her mouth should be watering now that she was past the hell that was her first trimester, but instead it was her eyes threatening to spill over.

Thank goodness Kyle had left, but Daisy was shaken by the destruction in the living room, and Natalie still had her mother to contend with. Somehow she would get through the rest of this meal and Midnight Mass. Maybe if she just kept her head down and her mouth shut. It had worked for large portions of her childhood.

"Would you please pass the baccalá pasta?"

"Sure. Does anyone need more wine?"

The conversation stuttered around the table as the Valentis tried to get their holiday back on track. People were trying to ignore what had happened, but their brains were so full of it, no one could manage more than basic requests and pleasantries.

No one except Prozia Dulce.

"Enzo, did I ever tell you that your Prozio Emilio was a boxer? I think you inherited his right hook. He was so sexy when he knocked the shit out of someone. It was usually some upstart who had the nerve to flirt with me, of course."

Prozia Dulce reminisced and didn't touch the food on her plate, but sipped from her full cocktail. How was it full again?

What number was she on? Natalie had no clue how the woman was still awake, let alone remembering her husband from seventy years ago.

"Zia, please," hushed Dom. "There is a child at the table."

"Never too young to learn that a man who will defend you is one worth keeping." Natalie caught the meaningful look Dulce shot her but didn't rise to the bait. Portia did though, because of course she did.

"So you want my granddaughter to learn that violence is an acceptable response?" Portia turned so Natalie could see the disapproval on her face. "Natalie, I don't know what you see in these people."

Well, then it's a good thing I stopped caring about your opinion a long time ago. Natalie bit back her retort, and tried to change the subject.

"How's your dinner, Mom? Did you find enough to eat?"

Portia toyed with the lovely salad on her plate with a moue of distaste, before pushing her plate away and picking up her wine glass. *Great. More alcohol is just what this situation needs.*

"I'm sure it's fine for you, but I've lost my appetite. The smell of all this fish is turning my stomach. And really, who serves frozen fish sticks at a fancy meal? They look disgusting." She poked at one on her plate with her fork as if she was afraid it would wiggle off.

Natalie took an extra serving of the fish sticks, and looked at Daisy as she bit into one.

"These are delicious, baby."

"I agree," Jo chimed in crunching into her own fish sticks with enthusiasm. "I'd forgotten how tasty these are. Thank you for bringing them, Daisy. I think we should make them a permanent addition to the menu."

Daisy just stared at her plate, silent and still.

That did it.

Every nasty comment, every unfounded accusation, every pain-filled holiday memory of her childhood flooded into Natalie's mind. She'd spent large portions of her childhood staring down and wishing she were anywhere else. That desire to leave had driven her to overlook Kyle's behavior because he'd promised to take her away. It had taken her eighteen years to find the strength to cut her mother out of her life.

She would do better than that for her daughter. From the day Daisy had been born, she'd vowed to be a better mother than her own had been. Her bright and bubbly baby shouldn't have to put up with the same bullshit. Natalie had to confront her mother about her behavior. As soon as dinner was done, she'd kick her right back where she belonged. Out.

"Everything was delicious, Jo. Thank you again for having us."

"You are always welcome in my home and at my table, Natalie. You know that."

We'll see how you feel about that tomorrow morning.

Daisy came around the table and leaned into Natalie's side. She didn't have to say a word. Natalie could practically see her mind whirling with all of the questions tonight had churned up. Daisy had barely touched the fish sticks she'd been so proud of. Natalie rubbed her hand up and down her daughters strong little spine, hoping she'd raised her with enough backbone to bear the coming turmoil. Inside, Natalie was seething. How dare her mother come in here and spread her crap all over this family?

"Why don't you let me take her up and put her to bed?" Enzo murmured, placing a hand on Nat's shoulder, jolting her from her thoughts. She hadn't noticed that almost everyone was done eating. She glanced at her watch. It was nearly ten! No wonder Daisy was fading. Better that she not witness the coming ugliness.

Natalie pressed a good night kiss to Daisy's forehead and let the man she loved lead her baby up to bed. If anyone had told her a year ago that she'd find a man like Enzo who she would trust with her whole heart, she'd have called them a liar. But here she was, even now, even after this horrible evening, confident that this man had her and her child's best interests at heart. They were going to have words about his idea of a surprise, but she still felt this welling up of love in her chest when she watched him walk away, hand in hand with Daisy. It was a miracle.

Natalie stood and began clearing the table, needing to order her thoughts before she approached Portia. She would never win if she went into the argument emotional. She had two hours before they had to leave for Midnight Mass. Half an hour washing dishes, probably wasn't a bad idea.

"You don't have to do that, Natalie. I've got it." Jo protested.

"You've spent all day in the kitchen. You go sit and relax with your family for a bit. Besides, I think I've caused all the damage I can for tonight. Let me at your china."

The joke fell flat, and she backed into the kitchen with her arms full just praying for this night to end.

ON THE WAY UPSTAIRS, Enzo stopped Daisy in front of his family's nativity scene. At this point, it had its own table. Each year, new pieces were added, and everyone had their favorites. He pointed to the empty manger.

"Do you know this story?"

"I know baby Jesus was born on Christmas."

"Yes, and after Midnight Mass we'll put him in his cradle, but that's not the important part. God gave Jesus to Mary in a miracle, but he couldn't stay and help raise him on Earth. That's where all of these people come in, to welcome him. But Joseph, he was special." Enzo held out the carved figure of a man for Daisy to take. "Joseph loved Mary, and when Jesus was born, he loved him too. He adopted Jesus and raised him as his own."

"He wasn't mad that he had to raise someone else's kid?"

"No, he wasn't, and neither am I. I'd be so proud... This isn't how I imagined tonight going, but I have something important to ask you before you go to bed."

Daisy looked at him with world-weary eyes, too old for her

little face. His mistake had put that doubt there. He hoped his apology could take it away again.

"Daisy, I want to be your dad. I want to marry your mom, and for us all to be a family. I love you both so much. But you should get to have a say in this too. What do you think?" He watched the words filter through her agile mind, and prayed she'd come to the same conclusion he had.

"Would we all live together?"

"Yes. You, me, your mom, and the babies."

"And that scary man will go away?"

"I promise I'll never let him near you again."

She dropped her eyes and her voice, suddenly shy. "And you'd be my dad for real?"

"With all my heart."

She hugged him fiercely then, tears streaming down her cheeks.

"Is that a yes?" Enzo had to be clear before he could set his next plans into motion.

"Do I get to keep JoNana instead of Portia?"

Though he wished he could agree wholeheartedly, he had to be honest.

"Well, Portia will still be your grandma, but yes, so will my mom. She will be so excited to be your nana for real."

Daisy's tiny face scrunched up with the intensity of her thoughts. Enzo thought that witch might be a deal breaker. His heart leapt in his chest when she stuck her little hand out solemnly.

"It's a deal," she said as she took his hand. He shook it seriously, before picking her up in a bear hug.

"Deal. Can you keep it a secret until tomorrow? I want to surprise your mom."

"Sure...Dad."

His heart grew three sizes, filling his chest to the point of bursting. He carried her upstairs and got her settled on an air mattress before searching out Natalie.

His mother found him first in the hallway.

"Oh, Enzo, what have we done?" Jo moaned.

Enzo just shook his head and chuckled. They'd screwed up Christmas good and proper. Jo continued.

"I feel like I pushed for this big family Christmas. I had this picture in my head of how things would be. Poor Graciela has barely said two words all evening because she had to be sedated to come here. Midnight Mass might push her over the edge. And that woman, Portia, she's a piece of work! Who brings her daughter's ex along for Christmas and then proceeds to hit on every man in the room under forty?"

"I missed that last bit."

"I may have promised Seth extra tiramisu for tolerating her. Enzo, did I ruin Christmas?"

"No, Ma. You can't ruin Christmas. It's still the day God sent his love to the world. All we can do is try our best to do the same. We were trying to bring families together. It just backfired."

Jo pulled Enzo in for the best gift of all, a mom hug. "Those Sunday School lessons really sunk in, huh? You're a good man, Enzo. Okay, let's go fix this. I'm going to thank Graciela for coming and ask if she wants to go home. I think Rey can probably drive her. As for Portia—"

"Leave Portia to me and Nat. I'm learning that when we don't plan together, shit hits the fan."

"An important lesson to learn. Do you know what I've learned tonight? I am pretty damn grateful for our family."

"Me, too, Ma. Can I ask two favors?"

"Anything."

He leaned in and whispered in her ear, earning a smile.

"Of course. They'll be ready and waiting first thing. And the second?"

"Will you kill me if I miss Mass?"

"Go fix things with Natalie. I'll consider that penance."

"I love you, Ma."

"Love you too, baby. Merry Christmas."

~

ENZO FOUND Natalie up to her elbows in soapy water, scrubbing plates and glasses.

"Did she go down okay?"

"Out like a light. How are you holding up?" He rubbed a hand up and down her tense back.

"Honestly? Awful. I hate her. I hate my mom and the way she makes me feel. And I hate that it makes me feel like a terrible daughter."

Tears mixed with the sudsy water as she wrung out her sponge. His chest tightened at the sight. He had to fix this.

"I'm so sorry. I didn't know."

"You could have asked me, Enzo." Her voice broke. "You should have asked."

"You're right. I should have planned with you. I guess I'm still learning to take more than one person into account."

"It's a shift, isn't it?" Natalie turned from the sink, wiping her cheeks with wet hands. "I forgot too. The night of the recital, I should have saved you a seat. It's been eating me all week. I had planned on it, but I got so distracted by your 'surprises' that I didn't notice when that lady sat down. I had picked up my purse to look for my phone—"

He cut her off with a kiss. "I still got to see the performance, and Daisy knew I was there for her. It's okay. Can you forgive me? Can you still trust that I will be there for you?"

"Is it just that easy for you?"

"I've had longer to get over it, and your mistake was minor compared to this fiasco. But the way I see it, we are going to make mistakes over the next fifty years. If we can't talk about them and forgive each other, it's going to be a long haul. I am so sorry, Natalie. I promise I won't make this mistake again."

Natalie smirked and dried her hands on a snowman towel.

"Only fifty years?"

"Well, by the time we're as old as Prozia Dulce we'll have it all figured out, right?"

She smiled her real smile then and Enzo felt a flicker of hope. She tucked her head under his chin and let out a sigh as she leaned into his strength.

"I really am sorry. It wasn't fair for Ma and I to spring Portia on you." Enzo smoothed his hand over her hair.

"Jo was involved?"

"She got it in her head that we should have a big family Christmas, and I got caught up. I thought the babies might bring Portia back into our lives. I never thought that we might not want her to be part of our lives."

"She never wanted to be a mother. Becoming a grandmother again only makes her feel old. It wasn't ever going to go over well." Natalie shook her head under his hand and pulled back. She began stacking wet dishes on the counter. Enzo snatched up a towel instead of the woman he loved, and began drying to keep his hands occupied.

"What was she like growing up?"

"Pretty much the same. When she's around, I go right back to being that quiet insecure kid who has to apologize for existing." Natalie's voice went higher and softened, as if she were that young girl again.

"I still can't believe she brought Kyle, although after tonight I have a better appreciation for just how desperate you must've been to leave."

"Apparently he got wind of the videos blowing up and he thought he could get his slice of fame by playing nice with me and Daisy."

"I'll admit it took all of my self-control to stay in the kitchen when he raised his hand to you." Enzo stacked the last dry plate in the cabinet and turned to face her.

"What stopped you?"

"You were handling it." He shrugged and added. "I'm kind of glad he came though."

"What? Why?" Natalie asked, incredulously.

"I asked him about renouncing his custody rights."

"Custody? Enzo, don't you think this is something we should have talked about first?" Natalie grabbed the large stock pot from the stove and shoved it into the sink, before snatching up the steel wool pad.

"It is. We are right now. Do you trust me to help parent Daisy?" Enzo stilled her frenzied scrubbing with a hand on her wrist, begging her to look up.

Natalie shook her head. "You know I do. That's not the point."

"The point is the opportunity presented itself, and I seized it."

"Is that what happened to the Christmas tree? You seized Kyle and took out Christmas?" Natalie finally looked at him, and there was a hint of hope and humor in her eyes.

"No, other way around, and that happened when I told him we were pregnant. Lucy got it on camera if you want the slow motion replay. But between that and the fact that he didn't pay support or ask for visits for six years, proving his abandonment should be easy in court.

Enzo skimmed the hair back from her cheek, and she leaned into his hand. He pulled her back into his arms for a hug, wet hands be damned.

"You've done your homework," Nat murmured against his chest.

"I'm serious about making a family with you. I want Daisy to be mine as much as those babies in your belly are."

"I want that too."

Enzo pulled back and then held out his hand. When she took it, his heart felt whole again. "Then we can figure out the rest as it comes. It's time for desserts."

SOME MUCH-NEEDED coffee was being passed around the table laden with desserts when Natalie and Enzo came back into the dining room. Natalie felt stronger now, having worked through things with Enzo. All she had to do was make it through this last course.

Mahalia and Rey had taken baby Jeremiah and Graciela back home, and Daisy was still resting, but everyone else was crowded around the amazing spread of sugar and chocolate. Portia sat like a duchess at a peasant table, her trademark sneer on her face.

"Jo, really it's okay." Adrian reassured Jo. "She was excited to try and come. We've been working on expanding her boundaries. Tonight was a good step forward."

"I just feel bad that I pushed so hard. I hope she wasn't scared."

"Nonsense. My mother knows her mind. If she'd wanted to say no, she would have." Adrian patted Jo's hand before Portia cut in.

"Really? I didn't think your mother knew that word. Is it the same in Spanish? After all, she has how many children and no husband?" Portia delivered the barb with the tone of a joke, but everyone saw the ugly for what it was.

Dom half-rose from his chair to defend the now-absent Graciela and Adrian looked ready to explode, but Natalie stayed them with a raised hand before facing down her mother.

"Did you say no, Mom? When you got pregnant? Or to any of the parade of men you traipsed through my childhood?"

The way her mother's face went pale made Natalie wonder if she'd struck the truth. A truth she'd never considered before. It would explain a lot if her mother hadn't consented to the life she'd been thrust into carrying.

"I'm not going to air our dirty laundry here in front of strangers."

"They aren't strangers. They are family. And don't pretend we've ever talked about my conception alone either."

"It's nobody's business."

"I'd say it's my business why my mother has barely tolerated me since birth."

"I did my best."

"Your best was borderline neglect. But you know what?" Natalie moved closer to the table so she could look her mother dead in the eye. "I forgive you. I forgive you for every nasty comment and every forgotten birthday. It's clear you gave all you had to give."

"I don't need your forgiveness." For the first time, the anger on her mother's face didn't hurt.

"No, but I need to give it and move on. I deserve to be loved and happy, no matter what you think. I have found that and more from the people around this table. I don't need it from you anymore. You're free."

"What do you mean I'm free?"

"I won't saddle Daisy with an awful father just because he happened to donate the sperm. I've chosen a better man for that, one who loves her, heart and soul. Why should I settle for anything less? Just because you gave me life doesn't mean you get to make it a living hell anymore. We're done."

"You think you can just toss away all those years, all the sacrifices I made for you?"

"No. I thank you for keeping me alive, but I no longer need your toxic mothering in my life. You can go now."

The shock on Portia's face was oddly satisfying, as if she'd never considered this possibility.

"Are you kicking me out? On Christmas Eve?"

"No, I'm telling you you don't have to stay."

"Daisy will be disappointed if I'm not here in the morning." She was clearly casting around for excuses, but Natalie wasn't having any of it.

"Why? Did you bring her a gift?"

"I didn't know I needed to buy her love."

"That's not what I meant. It's the only reason I could think of that you'd want to say for morning. But the fact that you didn't bring her a present on Christmas is typical. It's just more evidence of your narcissism. She'll see the grandma who loves her in the morning, whether you stay or you go." Natalie looked across the table at Jo, who nodded her support.

Portia took in the stone faces of everyone seated around her, before focusing her rage back on its usual target. Natalie's shield was strong and holding, though.

"You're going to regret this."

"No, I really don't think I am." Natalie turned her attention to Jo, emotionally and physically drained. "The panettone and those honey struffoli look amazing, but I'm exhausted. I think I'll go lay down for a bit."

Jo ran a hand down her back. "Go get some rest, baby. There will be more treats in the morning."

Enzo followed her into the hallway, his warm hand heavy on the base of her spine. As they reached the stairs, Natalie heard the front door slam and Prozia Dulce burst out laughing.

"This is the most entertaining Christmas you've had in years, Jo. Who's ready for Mass?"

Natalie just caught Brandy's muttered, "How the hell is she still awake?" and grinned. She'd found quite the family for herself.

These people had welcomed her and her child in with open arms, and when her crazy past showed up for dinner, they'd simply hugged her in tighter and supported her while she figured out how to handle it. Warmth flooded her chest as the gratitude she felt reached out to touch each member of her new family. She wondered if they realized how special that kind of support and understanding was. Leaning into Enzo's shoulder as they climbed the stairs, she vowed to make sure they knew how amazing they all were. Starting with the man next to her.

"You are incredible." Enzo whispered against her neck as he shut and locked the door of his old bedroom.

"I'm just done. None of us deserve that kind of hate."

"The way you handled her was amazing." He smoothed his hands over her shoulders. "You are so strong." He kissed the top of her spine and felt the shiver beneath his lips. "So smart." He licked a path up to her ear and her head dropped heavily. "So loved." He turned her to face him and kissed her with all of his pent-up admiration and relief. "You know that my family is your family now, right?"

She nodded, her eyes glassy with tears.

"Natalie." He kissed her again, needing to chase away her hurts, but when he tasted her salty sadness on his lips, he pulled back. "What's wrong?"

"Nothing."

"Talk to me about this."

"Really, for the first time in my life, there's nothing wrong. The relief is overwhelming." She leaned back into his kiss, eager and sweet. "I think I've been a pretty good girl tonight. What do you say you give me my Christmas present early?"

Enzo grinned. "When we were kids, we always got to open a present early as a reward for making it through mass. You definitely earned a reward tonight."

"Your flexibility is noted." She kissed the hollow below his Adam's apple, and he groaned.

"Care to start unwrapping?" He held out his arms and she giggled, happy in his arms. Her fingers slowly worked at the long line of buttons down his flannel shirt. The anticipation was going to kill him before she even made it to his belt. Gripping either side, he tore his shirt open, Hulk-style.

"Oh. You're that kind of gift-opener? I don't think this is going to work." He raised an eyebrow as she slid her hands up his torso and over his shoulders, pushing the torn flannel to the floor. "You see, I like to take my time, let the anticipation grow, before I finally open the package."

"If you let this package grow any bigger before you open it, I might not be able to walk tomorrow."

She cupped him through his jeans and his hips thrust against her, instinctively reaching for more of her love. In the end, he gave her just what she wanted, a long torturous build up, tasting and savoring every new gift of pleasure, until they were both beyond frantic. When he finally gave her the gift that keeps on giving, she was out of her mind with pleasure. He kissed her hard to muffle her cries, but he was humbled by the joy she took from him with every stroke. She stroked his cheek as they came back down, and he knew everything was going to be okay. Exhausted and sated, she curled up in his old twin bed, tucking the cover under her chin and nudging his bare ass out onto the floor.

When soft snores emanated from the bed, he quietly dressed in his clothes for morning and headed downstairs. He had a few Christmas miracles left to pull together for the woman and children who deserved all of the love and magic he could muster.

NATALIE WOKE to Daisy's giddy face two inches from her own. Around three, Nat had woken alone in bed. She had tiptoed down the stairs and found Enzo passed out on the couch, fast asleep. After loading the stockings and leaving her own special gifts from Santa, she had pulled a crocheted afghan over him and went back upstairs to steal a few more hours of sleep.

"Wake up, Mommy! It's time!"

Her daughter bolted from the room, job done, leaving Natalie to tug on clothing and follow. She stumbled downstairs and into the softly filtered early morning light that edged the scene in the living room with a golden glow. The tree had been righted and presents had multiplied over night. The mantle was nearly covered by all of the stockings.

Frankie and Jake came in the front door with fresh coffee from Starbucks. Sofia and Adrian were snuggled up on the couch. Brandy and Seth were discussing the nativity scene with Daisy, and Enzo was nowhere to be seen.

"Where's Buster?" Nat asked.

Frankie grinned. "For the safety of the presents, I left him home. He really likes shredded paper."

"Look, Mommy! I got to put baby Jesus in his crib. Now they are a real family." Seeing her daughter grin over the idea of family made Natalie's heart jolt. She was so close to being able to give this family to her baby.

Dom came in from the den with his hands cupped in front of him.

"Here, Daisy-girl. Add these to the scene."

He handed her a delicately carved little girl holding a flower and a figure of a mother cradling her pregnant belly.

"Did you carve these, Dom?" Natalie asked, watching the older man's eyes go shiny as he watched her daughter carefully admiring his work.

"It's just a hobby. Everyone has a special piece in the nativity."

"So these are for me and Mommy?" Daisy asked quietly.

"They sure are. You're part of the family now." Daisy hugged Dom around the waist and his tears ran over. He reached for Natalie, pulling them both into a bone-crushing hug. Swiping his eyes, he released them and coughed.

"Will you make ones for the twins next year?"

"You bet. Now, let's get this show on the road. Jo!" he bellowed towards the kitchen. "Are you ready?"

"Almost!" Came her hollered reply.

Moments later, Enzo appeared bearing a tray of cookies that looked like they'd been cooked in a waffle iron and then coated with powdered sugar.

"What are those?" Natalie asked, her mouth watering at the smell of almonds and caramel.

"The first pizelles of Christmas." He shot a look at his sisters that Nat couldn't begin to fathom. "Don't even think about it, you two." He turned back to Natalie. "Someone once told me that I looked at you like the first pizelle of Christmas, hot off the griddle. That's when I knew this was serious. So it seems only fitting that you get the first this year."

Natalie grinned and took exaggerated care in picking one and biting in. "Mmm. That's delicious." She licked the powdered sugar off her lips slowly, teasing him deliberately, enjoying this relaxed and playful Christmas morning after the evenings turmoil.

"Come here and give me a taste." He leaned in to kiss her in front of God and family, and she happily let him.

Dom took the tray from the distracted Enzo and set it down on the coffee table, laughing as the hordes descended. Jo came in with a tray of sliced panettone and coffee cakes, and set it down on a side table, before sitting down next to her husband on the couch, to the shock and wonder of all. No one was more surprised than Dom, judging by his dropped jaw and bulging eyes.

But when Jo dropped a hand on his knee, he unfroze and wrapped his arm around her shoulder. The tender kiss pressed to her temple drew them together before he sat back, wiping his eyes again.

Christmas miracles were in the air. Daisy was tasked with delivering gifts to everyone. Dom's gift of a starter nativity set for each of his children was topped only by the framed set of three sonograms from Natalie and Sofia.

Jake's gift of a muzzle harness to Frankie prompted much teasing and laughter.

"It's for Buster, so you can bring him on set again."

Natalie never thought she'd see the day her boss turned beet red with embarrassment, but it was clearly a day for firsts.

Daisy was on cloud nine. She'd never seen a pile of presents so high and all of them bore her name. Natalie smiled indulgently as Daisy tore through the paper, uncovering a big sister t-shirt, a pair of binoculars, and a Fairyopolis book.

Natalie handed Enzo a big shipping box with a grin. "Here. This one's from me."

She grinned at the way he tore through the paper, remembering their time alone last night. He opened the huge box to find two smaller boxes wrapped inside.

"Well played, stinker."

He opened the first box inside and stilled.

"What is it?" Frankie asked.

"It's business cards for my new company. These are gorgeous, Nat. Where did you get them?"

"Sofia helped me design them. Open the other one."

He opened up the other small box and laughed.

"Sunscreen."

"Gotta keep my man safe from those UV rays. Airbrushing is so much safer than a real tan." He leaned in for a kiss that did nothing to quiet the butterflies in her belly.

"Keep going," Natalie said.

Enzo looked into the big shipping box again, eyebrows furrowed.

"It's empty."

"Yeah. So are half of the drawers and closets at my place. Maybe you could fill it with some stuff and move in?"

She'd done it. She'd reached for what she wanted, putting her desires out into the world. When he kissed her deeply again and Daisy began making gagging noises, she knew she'd won. Her smile broke their kiss and Enzo leaned away from her.

"Okay, your turn, you two."

He pulled a stack of gifts from beneath a table and Daisy reached for them eagerly.

"Wait! There's an order. Here, open this one first or it'll spoil the surprise."

"More surprises, Enzo?" Natalie teased.

"I've got a good feeling about these. Trust me."

Miracle of miracles, she did.

He handed Daisy a small shoebox wrapped with a candy cane bow.

"It's more fairy furniture!" Daisy crowed. "Two cribs, two stump chairs, and two little mushrooms."

"I made them so we can welcome the twins into our fairy family too."

"I love them. Thank you, Enzo."

"You're welcome. Now this one." He handed Daisy a flat box that looked like it would hold clothes. She opened it and paused, her eyes full of confusion. Natalie leaned over and in the box was a stack of papers and a charm bracelet. Enzo hastened to explain.

"Daisy, that's the paperwork to apply for adoption. I want to be your dad, but I'm giving you that to hold onto until you're sure." He lifted the bracelet out and fastened it around her little wrist. "See here? There's a charm for each of us. A daisy for you, a shovel for me, a lipstick for your mom, and two bottles for the twins. We can keep adding memories to it in the future. It's my promise to you that I'll always love you and take care of our family."

Daisy threw herself into his lap and cuddled hard. Enzo laughed, and Natalie had never seen anything more precious.

"Which leaves this for you." Enzo held a small flat circular present out to Natalie. It looked like a powder compact...and it was. She tossed the wrapping paper onto the pile on the floor and murmured, "Thank you," hoping she'd kept the disappointment out of her voice. She'd given him half of her apartment, and he'd given her makeup?

"Open it."

She looked into Enzo's eyes and saw the laughter and love dancing there. She opened the compact and inside was a sparkling little diamond ring. She was speechless, so Enzo filled the silence.

"It's not a big stone, but it carries a big promise. I will love you, Natalie Carras, for the rest of our lives. I will provide for your comfort and happiness, and I hope you'll do the same for me. I want to parent these beautiful children with you. I want to sit in this living room surrounded by *our* family every Christmas morning. Marry me, Natalie."

Still struck mute by the best surprise, she nodded and threw herself into his lap too, pulling the two most important people in her life close to her heart. The rest of the room erupted into cheers and applause, and Natalie knew she was finally home.

THIS WOULD GO DOWN as the worst and her favorite Christmas ever. She grinned as she turned her hand back and forth, letting her diamond twinkle in the lights from the tree. Everyone had scattered while Jo made brunch. She and Enzo alone remained curled up on the couch. A Christmas Story played muted on repeat on the TV in front of them.

"You know, I always hated the holidays. They never lived up to the ones in the movies."

"I'd say this year was right up there with the Griswolds." Enzo ran a hand down her hair.

"Closer to A Miracle on 34th Street." Natalie grinned and snuggled closer into the security of his arms.

"Our love is a true Christmas miracle." Enzo kissed her forehead. "Natalia. In Italian, your name means born on Christmas," he mused.

"It certainly feels like I'm starting a new life today. I can't wait to get started."

THE END

~

Want to start the Exposed Dreams series from the beginning? Try Christmas Spirits, my cross-over novella featuring Seth Valenti and Brandy Henderson.
Here's a little peek!

~

"I asked for a supra, non-fat, sugar-free, no-whip, eggnog latte."

Brandy Henderson narrowly refrained from answering Ms. Prada-purse-and-yoga-pants in the same bitchy tone. It was three weeks until Christmas, and Brandy was whipping and foaming drinks at Sweet Tea and Joe's as fast as she could while dealing with the customers in line waiting to order. She had to dig deep to find the spirit of the season at six a.m.

"That's what I made you, ma'am." She was proud of her even tone and friendly smile as she pitched her voice over the hissing steam spitting out of the espresso machine, her hands busy assembling the next order on auto-pilot.

"There's no way this is sugar-free. Make it again."

"I assure you, ma'am, I used the sugar-free eggnog syrup right here." Brandy gestured to the bay of syrup pumps next to her station. "Piccolo peppermint latte, for Ted?" She spun the finished drink on to the counter pick-up window.

"And I'm telling you, you screwed it up. Make me another goddamn coffee!" The woman's voice pitched higher and more shrill than the screaming steamer as Brandy foamed more skim milk.

The customer is always right. Brandy silently chanted the mantra as she sent an apologetic glance to the restless customers in line. Many of them were regulars who wouldn't mind, but she hated to keep them waiting.

"Yes, ma'am." She reached across the counter for the offending coffee and bobbled it. Since the woman hadn't put the cap back on completely, scalded milk splashed over the back of Brandy's hand and onto the counter. *Sonofabitch! That hurt.*

"You idiot! You splashed that on my purse." The woman began furiously blotting the leather bag with a handful of napkins.

Brandy bit her tongue against the pain of the burn and the insistent pressure of the sarcastic response desperate to break free. She glanced up at the clock, praying for Clare to hurry up and get there already. She didn't mind covering for her perpetually late friend, but this morning she needed help and she needed it now. Throwing the perfectly good coffee in the wash sink, Brandy assessed the damage. She ran her hand briefly under the cold water, praying it wouldn't blister. The normally tawny skin on her hand was turning an angry red. Damn. She didn't have time for a serious burn.

"Hello? I don't have all day!"

Not trusting herself to speak, Brandy silently and efficiently made another supra, non-fat, sugar-free, no-whip, eggnog latte, exactly as she had the last one. She may have wanted to put this loud, inconsiderate, rude woman in her place, but Brandy couldn't afford to lose this job and the tips it brought in. Not this close to Christmas. Her family was depending on her this year, and she wasn't going to let them down.

"Here you go, ma'am. Have a nice day."

"Next time, get it right the first time."

The worst part of working the early morning shift at the coffee shop was trying to get people their caffeine before they'd had any caffeine. Not ideal. She turned to the next person in line. Miranda, brevis Americano, extra shot, room for cream. She was already filling the order before she ducked back to the register to ring it up. Back in her rhythm, she took orders, counted change, and crafted the overpriced coffee and tea creations that seemed to power Silicon Valley. It wasn't a great job, but it was a means to an end. God, she couldn't wait for the end.

Tinkling bells pulled her from her trance. She looked up to see Clare with her straight inky black hair peeking out from beneath a ridiculous jingling red elf hat hustling behind the counter. The college girl looked like a member of a K-Pop girl band who'd gotten a make-over from Santa.

"Where have you been?" Brandy whispered with another glance up at the clock. She sprayed whipped cream to cover her words. "You're forty minutes late." Her hands never stopped flying.

"Bad traffic on 101."

A likely story. Even more likely, her new boyfriend had woken up horny. Brandy would never begrudge her friend a morning quickie, but she could sure as hell be jealous. It had been months since she'd had time for a date, let alone a third and all that entailed.

"Cover the front for a minute. I need to put some burn cream on my hand." She ducked into the back and rummaged in her pack for her first aid kit. Old habits died hard. As a former army medic, she never left home without her pack. She ran her hand under cold water as she popped an ibuprofen. She briskly cleaned and dried the wound site, applied a lidocaine cream, and loosely wrapped gauze around it. With any luck, she'd avoid a blister.

"There you are. Why is Clare working the front all by herself during the morning rush? Get your butt in gear, Brandy."

Perfect. Anna. Late and making assumptions without asking questions, as usual. Once again, Brandy bit back the words she longed to set free. Arguing with her boss would get her nowhere fast. She stowed her kit, tucked her rambunctious curls back under her cap, and dove back into the morning fray. If anything, the army had taught her that she could do hard things if she just put her head down and tackled the job head on. She could do anything if it brought her closer to her goal.

When she'd left the army two years ago, she'd immediately applied to nursing school only to find out there was a long wait-list. But nothing was going to keep her from her dream. She'd taken all the pre-reqs she could. Now, it was a waiting game to see when they would let her in. In the meantime, she'd keep earning her checks, helping her mom keep a roof over her half-siblings' heads, taking care of her step-father, and doing anything else that needed doing.

The incessant jingling of silver bells pulled her from her thoughts as Clare bobbed her head along to the piped in Christmas music while she worked the register.

"For God's sake, Clare. What possessed you to get the one with bells?"

"'Every time a bell rings, an angel gets his wings.' It gives me hope."

"It's giving me a migraine." Brandy grinned at her friend as she began making the medio Mexican mocha just ordered. "There are going to be a lot of new angels before Christmas if you keep that up."

"Christmas spirit brings in the tips, Brandy." Anna commented from behind the other register. She shook the tip jar meaningfully. "You'd do well to remember that. Just look how much Clare brought in this morning while you were dawdling in the back."

"Yes, ma'am." She bit her tongue against her own defense, knowing she'd regret the lack of Christmas presents for the kids, no matter how good it would feel to spew the truth burning in her throat.

～

"Watch your step!"

Seth yanked his thoughts from ruminating on his disturbing dream just in time to avoid taking a two-by-four to the face. His hard hat wouldn't have protected him from a broken nose. His boss, Antonio Valenti, gripped his arm and pulled him back, as if he was still a young child.

"Pay attention, son. If I have to file a workman's comp claim on you, I'm gonna make you do the paperwork. Actually, maybe I should knock you out. It might be the only way I get you to actually sit down in the office and learn the ropes. When you're running things, you will need to have a finger on every pulse. It's not all demo days."

Why did every word of criticism make him feel ten years old? Maybe because the same man was delivering them then and now, a pitfall of working for Dad. Seth didn't belong on the construction site. He knew it. The crew knew it. The only one refusing to acknowledge it was Dad. For two years, he'd been putting Seth on crews, giving him busy work, trying to convince him that he had a place in Valenti Brothers Construction. His plan was backfiring. While Seth appreciated the paycheck and the chance to do a little demolition every now and then, he didn't love the repetition of construction. What he would love doing was anyone's guess, so for now he would break down walls and haul supplies for his dad. He could help out his family while he figured out the rest.

The addition of an outdoor kitchen space on the back of a

309

mid-century modern ranch was a two week job that his dad could do in his sleep. Though he could lay bricks or mud drywall with the best of them, Seth had no passion for it and zero patience for dealing with sub-contractors.

When he'd left the army two years ago, he had one unrelenting goal. *Just get home.* Beyond that, he had no idea what he wanted to do with his life. The job helping his dad was the least he could do, literally. His heart just wasn't in it, but he wasn't ready to risk his heart on anything important yet, so here he was on another job site, taking orders from his dad. But there was only so much of that he could take, especially on a day when demons from his past were chasing him.

He turned and headed for the front of the house.

"Where are you going?"

"Coffee run. I'll be back in fifteen."

SOMEONE SPECIAL EXCERPT

∼

Want to go back to where it all began? Someone Special was my very first romance novel. Meet Nick Gantry and Dani Carmichael as they fight their demons to find true love. Free on all platforms.

∼

"This is better than cable!" remarked Mrs. Grady, from her habitual perch by the window. Dani looked up from the stove. Something good must be happening two stories below on their normally quiet street. Dani briefly turned her attention back to the bubbling pots on the stove. Confident that her three meals were coming along nicely, she tucked unruly curls behind her ear and turned from the kitchen to join her neighbor at the window.

Below, two very muscular men with shirts removed, in deference to the fierce sun and brutal heat weltering up from the pavement, were wrestling an ugly sofa in through the double front doors of the building. Their lean muscles and trim waists twisted and flexed with effort. Dani's face flushed with heat, a welcome change from her recent numbness.

"They can move my furniture anytime! Then again, I'm not sure my blood pressure could handle it!" Mrs. Grady cackled. Dani continued to observe the scene below. While the slick and straining bodies held her gaze, the implications flooded her thoughts.

"I bet they're moving in the new tenant across the hall from us." An empty ache spread through her chest as Dani was hit by the grief that she managed to keep just below the surface. "Well, across from me. It will be strange having someone else living there in my old place." Her throat tightened at the reminder that she was living alone in Helen's apartment now.

She returned to the kitchen, grasping for calm, trying to avoid sinking into her grief. She drained the pasta, mixed in the home-made marinara sauce along with some freshly grated Parmesan, and reduced the chicken soup to a simmer. At least managing to create three large meals at once required her attention. She spun too quickly and knocked a wooden spoon to the floor. With a huff of frustration, she threw the offending utensil into the sink.

"Are you OK, Sunny?"

"Yeah, sometimes it just hits me that she's gone. That she won't sit at your Wednesday night dinner again. That she won't ever tell another crazy story about her service or her travels. That no one will be there when I open the door. It's just hard." Dani's voice cracked and her shoulders drooped under the weight of her sadness.

"I know, sweetheart. I miss her too. She was my best friend." Dani let herself be bundled into a hug, even though it was a poor substitute for the hug she missed.

"Mine, too. Now that she's gone, I feel lost."

"That's normal, dear. After all, you practically gave up your life to take care of her these last six months."

"What did I give up? A lackluster career in accounting and a dead end social life down in Houston? You know as well as I do, I didn't belong there." Dani shook her head. "No. I gained so much more, moving up here to help out. I met all of you, and got to spend more time with Aunt Helen. And with how quickly her health failed…well, I wouldn't have wanted to be anywhere else."

The pancreatic cancer had snuck in under the radar, and when they found it, it was too late. It hit vicious and fast. She'd been home for Christmas when Aunt Helen broke the news. Now, it was June and she was alone again.

"I know she loved having you with her. You were the grandchild of her heart."

Her grandfather's sister, Aunt Helen, had never married. She had no children of her own, and had spoiled Dani and her sister like crazy as a result. Summer trips wherever Aunt Helen happened to be living that year, fantastic surprises from abroad, and boxes of massive navel oranges every New Year's were her trademarks. And her stories! Dani had vivid memories of curling up at the foot of her chair and listening to her tell stories of her time in the Navy in her irreverent and slightly salty way. Dani let the fond memories roll through her mind.

"Remember how pissed she was when Dad brought up the idea of a nursing home?"

"Oh my goodness! I thought she'd have a stroke then and there, and save us another trip back to the hospital. She was not a woman to tolerate limits on her independence."

That independent spirit was her trademark, and Dani hadn't been able to stomach the idea of Helen losing that. When she had refused chemo and radiation, and begun to look at hospice care, Dani had offered to move into the vacant apartment across the hall and help take care of her. The move set her family at ease, and Dani felt blessed that she could help her surrogate grandmother wring every last drop of joy from her remaining days. They had visited favorite haunts and dear friends until leaving the apartment had become too difficult. Hospice nurses had come to handle Aunt Helen's medical needs, and given Dani a few much-needed breaks. Just handling her personal care had become around the clock job near the end. So Dani had given up her month-to-month lease on the apartment across the hall and moved to Helen's couch. Given the moving crew downstairs, she assumed her old apartment wouldn't be empty anymore.

Aunt Helen was gone, and Dani was as lost as ever. Everything she owned was in boxes and shoved into corners. She was surrounded by the remnants of her aunt's life, and it was difficult to see how hers could share the space.

She'd always had trouble figuring out where she fit in. She'd been raised to believe she could be whatever she wanted. But what if she couldn't figure out what that was? She'd bumped along okay until now, but she hadn't really pursued anything with passion. After going to college in Houston, she'd accepted a job working as an accountant at a multi-national energy firm. It had been lucrative, but it hadn't been satisfying, and her asshole ex-boyfriend even less so. She'd been sprinting on the hamster wheel and going nowhere. She had zero desire to hop back on. Coming home hadn't been a hardship, but what now?

"Moving in was the best thing for both of us. She kept her freedom, and I gained my own. But now I have too much freedom. I have no job, no friends, and no idea what to do about any of it. And I've got all of her estate to handle…I keep losing hours at a time just holding an afghan she knit or rearranging the framed postcards from her travels." The tears she'd been fighting to hold back ran silently down her cheeks.

"It's a big job. Don't rush it. You've got a lot to deal with. Losing Helen was hard on us all. Just keep putting one foot in front of the other. Come to our dinners. Talk to your friends. Bake her favorite desserts. Share stories of her that make you laugh instead of cry. It will get easier with time."

The timer ding pulled Dani from her maudlin thoughts, and she bent to remove the shepherd's pie from the oven. She set it aside to cool and quickly packed everything else into the fridge. At least her neighbors would benefit from her lack of a plan.

Dani turned back from the fridge, wiping the tears of frustration and grief from her cheeks. She had to shake things up and move on with her life. It's what Aunt Helen had wanted, and she knew she had to live up to her end of the bargain. When Helen had agreed to let her come help, it was always with the understanding that when she was gone, Dani would take up the reins to her life and do something spectacular. *Now if I could just figure out what that is...*

"Well, Mrs. Grady, you're all set. You've got the shepherd's pie for Monday night, the spaghetti and meatballs for Wednesday, and chicken soup for Thursday. Make sure you nuke a vegetable to go with. I stocked your freezer today, so you should have plenty to choose from. Also, let Joe know that I left the fennel out of the soup this time, just for him. Tell everyone I said hi." She gathered her things and moved toward the door.

"Are you sure you won't join us, Sunny? I worry about you eating alone so much."

The use of her aunt's favorite nickname for her sparked a brief smile, but Dani shook her head. "I just...can't yet. Maybe next week." To be honest, she couldn't stand to see the sadness in her heart reflected back in the eyes of her aunt's friends. It was bad enough to feel it herself. "I'm going to go bake some cookies to welcome our new neighbor to the building. I'll extend an invite to your dinner party on Wednesday, if you'd like."

"The more, the merrier, I always say. And if he turns out to be a bachelor, send him over on Tuesday!" Still chuckling, Mrs. Grady closed the door behind her, and Dani waited to hear the bolt snick in the lock. She'd fallen into the habit of checking up on her neighbors when Aunt Helen had gotten too weak to do it herself. Making meals, listening for locks, dropping off mail, it didn't take long and helped a lot. Sometimes it felt like those were the only things she accomplished in a day.

"I really need to change that," she muttered.

Dani walked down the hallway, skirting past a pile of boxes left outside the door across the hall from hers. One of the moving men came out of the apartment for another load, and sent her an appreciative glance and smile. Dani ducked her head with a blush and quickly headed inside. Why hadn't she said hi? Why on Earth had she blushed? She had to get out more, preferably with a male of the species. Shaking her head over her reaction and the dismal prospect of that happening any time soon, she pushed aside her worries in the kitchen, baking her famous dark chocolate chunk cookies for her mystery neighbor.

ACKNOWLEDGMENTS

This book is a community effort. I would not have finished without the support of many dear friends and fellow writers.

To the OSRBC Writers/NanoLA groups/BICC crew, thanks for the sprints and the laughs. OSRBC, thank you for reminding me of the best part of this genre, our amazing readers! To the Legends, your continued encouragement warms my heart. My RT Lovies, you know who you are, and you make me smile every damn day. Everyone over at Friends For Eva, thank you for coming to play with me when I need a break. Makeup tutorials with you were crucial research! To the Expanded Sassy Bitches, learning from you all about this crazy business has been enlightening. To the LeBou Crew for letting me crash once in a blue moon. The rest of my SVRWA sisters, you are my tribe and you keep me sharp.

To Jen and Julia, this book would not be worth reading without your eagle eyes and thoughtful suggestions. Lucy, thank you for your persistence in making my cover gorgeous and for our long-distance friendship. Many thanks to the author friends who tended to my mental health, both on the page and through Facebook messenger, during the making of this book. Sarah, Sophie, Sonali, Lenora, Joanna, Alyssa, Alisha, Cherry, Kate and

Kerrigan, thank you for creating characters and friendships that inspire me.

To Cass, for having open ears and understanding that I don't need to hear the answers. I need to speak until I find them. To Jasmine, my long lost sister, for understanding how powerful it is to hear that what we've written isn't crap alongside the well-placed questions. Also, for giving my baby a new "best friend." To all of my mom friends who get what I'm trying to do and step in to help along the way. Darcie, there aren't words to describe how grateful I am for the relationship that we have. The day all of our girls became best friends was such a blessing.

To everyone who came and visited and wasn't offended when I left my children with you and went to work, you are always welcome! To Mom & Dad, thank you for coming every time I've called for help. I love you to the moon and back. To my three darling girls, thank you for sending me off to work at bedtime with hugs and kisses instead of tears. And to my husband, you remind me day in and day out that love is in the details and that ambition is worth chasing. Thank you for your unwavering support.

And to you, dear reader, for your continued interest in my stories. You have no idea how much that means to me.

ABOUT THE AUTHOR

Eva Moore began reading fuchsia books when she was 12. Now she writes sexy contemporary romances in between soccer practices and glasses of rosé. Eva lives in Silicon Valley, after moving around the world and back, with her college sweetheart, her three gorgeous girls, and a Shih Tzu who thinks he is a cat. She can be found most nights hiding in her closet-office, scribbling away, and loves to hear from the outside world. Please visit her at www.4evamoore.com.

If you'd like to know about future releases and giveaways, you can join her newsletter here: http://bit.ly/evamoorenews

Join her fan page for rosé tastings, makeup tutorials, and other sparkly shenanigans at Friends For Eva Moore.